Everyone is talking about Kari Lynn Dell's Texas Rodeo

"When it comes to sexy rodeo cowboys, look no further than talented author Kari Lynn Dell."
—**B.J. Daniels**, *New York Times* bestselling author

"An extraordinarily gifted writer."
—**Karen Templeton**, three-time RITA Award–winning author, for *Reckless in Texas*

"Real ranchers. Real rodeo. Real romance."
—**Laura Drake**, RITA Award–winning author, for *Reckless in Texas*

"Look out, world! There's a new cowboy in town."
—**Carolyn Brown**, *New York Times* bestselling author, for *Tangled in Texas*

"A standout in Western romance."
—*Publishers Weekly* for *Reckless in Texas*

"This well-written tale includes strong characters and a detailed view of the world of bullfighting... Readers can look forward to getting a cowboy's education and a bird's-eye view on the rodeo circuit."
—*RT Book Reviews* for *Reckless in Texas*

"Dell's ability to immerse her readers in the world of rodeo, coupled with her stellar writing, makes this a contemporary Western not to miss."
—*Kirkus Reviews* for *Tangled in Texas*

Also by Kari Lynn Dell

TEXAS RODEO

Reckless in Texas

Tangled in Texas

Tougher in Texas

Fearless in Texas

MISTLETOE *in* TEXAS

KARI LYNN DELL

sourcebooks
casablanca

Published by Sourcebooks Casablanca, an imprint of Sourcebooks, Inc.
P.O. Box 4410, Naperville, Illinois 60567-4410
(630) 961-3900
Fax: (630) 961-2168
sourcebooks.com

Printed and bound in the United States of America.
OPM 10 9 8 7 6 5 4 3 2 1

This book is dedicated to my fabulous editor, Mary Altman, who kept picking through the shambles I sent her and pulling out the good stuff. Without her and the amazing Rachel Gilmer, there would have been no ending, happy or otherwise. And also to my brother, the ranch boy who hates cows.

Prologue

THE INSTANT GRACE MCKENNA STEPPED INTO THE barbecue joint, she was attacked from behind. She squealed in surprise as strong male arms hoisted her off her feet and swung her in a full circle.

"Grace!" Hank Brookman dropped her onto her feet and spun her around, and as always, her heart stumbled at the sight of his laughing face. "You're back! I was starting to think you were gonna spend the whole Christmas break at school."

"I had to work until yesterday." One of three part-time jobs that were putting her through college.

Hank thrust her out to arm's length, his brown eyes dancing as they took her in, head to toe. "What's up with the dress? I thought you were throwing them all out when you turned eighteen."

"I have a luncheon with my mom at the church." She really didn't want Hank to see her in this dull-gray dress and sensible shoes, but when she'd spotted his pickup outside the Smoke Shack, she'd reluctantly decided it was better to see him like this than not at all. "I'm changing into jeans the minute we get home."

"Aw. I sorta miss my little red-haired girl."

"My hair isn't red," she pointed out yet again. And now that she wasn't living in her parents' house, she no longer had to follow their dress code, except when she got roped into some kind of church function.

He tweaked one of her rusty-brown curls. "Close enough. And you've still got those cute freckles."

Cute! *Gah.*

But then he grinned at her again and all was forgiven, as it had been from the first time he'd flashed that smile at her in the fourth grade. Behind the mischief, Hank had a good heart and a sweetness that had saved him time and again from the consequences of his failure to think first.

"Order's ready, Hank!" the blond boy behind the counter called out. Then Hank's best friend spotted her. "Hi, Grace. How's it going?"

"Hey, Korby." Unlike some, he'd been friendly to the weird, nerdy girl whose family had moved into Earnest when they were all ten years old, and nowadays when their paths crossed on campus, he always said hello. Then again, Korby was the human equivalent of a golden Labrador puppy—he knew no strangers. "Do you have time for a Coke?" Grace asked, turning back to Hank.

"Not right now." Hank grabbed the large, fragrant bag with a combination grimace and eye roll. "Dad's got his shorts all in a twist because the vet's coming to Bangs vaccinate our heifers and Mom decided she didn't feel like cooking—or helping out at the corral. Melanie's working this weekend, so it's just me and the old man." He slapped his butt with his free hand. "Get a good look at this ass now, because it'll be chewed off by the end of the day."

Grace never knew what to say to his not-quite-joking comments about his family. *Sorry your parents suck, but at least your sister is cool?* Though never around since Melanie had graduated from college and gotten a job in Amarillo.

"Forget that." Hank's eyes lit up again. "I'm so glad

I saw you. Can you sneak away tomorrow afternoon and come to the Holiday Bull Bash in Goodwell? Jacobs Livestock is the contractor, and I am one of the bull-fighters!" He practically vibrated in place. "It's gonna be my first event with pro cowboys and the A-string bulls. I could use some moral support."

"The money goes to support their rodeo team," Korby added. "They have a pig roast and live music afterward, and all the alumni will be there signing autographs."

Whoa. That was a fistful of world champions, including the legendary Etbauer brothers. No wonder Hank was excited.

He grabbed one of her hands. "See? You've gotta come and watch."

Grace's pulse did a crazy jitterbug. For nine years she'd sat next to Hank in class and across from him at lunch, forbidden to date anyone, let alone that wild Brookman boy. Now finally, *finally*, she was out from under her father's thumb, and not only could Hank invite her to a rodeo, but she could say yes!

"I'll be there," she said.

Even if she had to steal her mother's car.

—∿∿—

In the end, Grace worked up the nerve to ask for the keys—after her father had left to help build props for the church nativity play. Her mother fussed about Grace going alone, but relented when she pointed out that it was an afternoon event and Goodwell was only an hour away.

She'd call later with an excuse to stay for the party— and deal with her father when she got home. *After* she'd had the time of her life.

As she walked into the indoor arena, Grace smoothed nervous hands over her hips, sure everyone in the place was staring at the rhinestones on the back pockets of the jeans she'd changed into at a convenience store along the way. The bling on her butt would have been too much for her mother.

She'd topped them with an emerald-colored *Cowgirl Tuff* hoodie that brought out the green in her hazel eyes, and had layered on more makeup after leaving the house. With the low-heeled roper boots she'd acquired along with her second job—cleaning stalls and exercising horses for a trainer outside of Canyon—she felt almost like a real cowgirl.

But when she spotted a cluster of her former classmates in the bleachers, she didn't have the guts to join them. They were the coolest of the cool in tiny Earnest, Texas, the rodeo kids who'd been competing since they were old enough to ride alone on a horse.

Girls who grew into women like Violet Jacobs, who sat horseback in the arena in full pickup rider gear, next to her cousin Cole. Jacobs Livestock had been putting on rodeos since the nineteen fifties, and the Panhandle-bred threesome of Violet Jacobs, Melanie Brookman, and Shawnee Pickett had won a national intercollegiate rodeo team championship. Since Melanie and Violet were the definition of BFFs and usually had Hank tagging along behind, he'd all but grown up on the Jacobs ranch.

They were as rodeo as it got, and Grace would need a lot more than flashy jeans and a pair of boots to be part of *that* crowd—unless she was with Hank. The thought bubbled like champagne on her tongue, making her want to giggle.

Searching the bleachers, she located an empty space next to a gray-haired couple. "Is this seat taken?"

The woman welcomed her to sit down, while her husband gave a stiff nod. "Don't tell me a pretty young thing like you is here all alone?" the wife asked.

"I came to watch a friend," Grace said with a twinge of pride.

"Oh?" The woman glanced at her program. "Which one?"

"The bullfighter. Hank Brookman."

"Then you must know my grandson Korby. He's riding tonight."

Of course he would be. For a guy who took laid-back to a whole new level, Korby was a surprisingly tough bull rider.

"Oh, look! There's Hank." Korby's grandmother waved as Hank came through a pass gate beside the chutes. Grace's heart gave another little flip. *Wow.* She'd never seen him in full rodeo gear—soccer-style jersey and shorts, cleats, and cowboy hat, plus a Kevlar vest and knee and elbow pads. He looked so official. Not just the kid she'd gone to school with, but a real pro.

The wave caught his attention and he trotted over, grinning. "Grace! You made it!"

Before she could answer, Cole Jacobs barked his name. "Gotta go," Hank said. "But come find me when we're done, okay?"

Then he was off to work his way along the front of the chutes, helping riders set their ropes. Like when he'd stepped onto the football field or basketball court, he radiated an infectious energy. Watching him, Grace could barely sit still.

They stood for the singing of the national anthem, and then Hank took his position, jogging in place a dozen yards out into the arena and off to one side of chute number one. His partner, an older man named Red, stood stocky and resolute on the opposite side.

The cowboy nodded and the first bull burst out of the gate. Grace didn't even have time to suck in a breath before the rider flew in the air and the bull jogged away without a second glance. Hank picked up the rope that had been dragged free by the weight of the cowbell and handed it to the cowboy, who let it trail dejectedly in the dirt as he limped out of the arena.

Well, that was anticlimactic.

Grace eased off the edge of her seat as one cowboy after another bit the dirt without giving the bulls much of a run for their money. Then her seatmate clutched her arm. "Here's Korby."

There was a subtle shift in the energy in the arena, spectators craning forward in their seats, the cowboys on the back of the chutes jockeying for a good viewpoint.

"This should be a great matchup," the announcer declared. "Dirt Eater is a young bull from Jacobs Livestock that had an impressive rookie year, and he's getting stronger all the time. This cowboy is going to have his hands full."

Hank paced in a circle, and Grace could practically see his nerves vibrating from clear up in the stands as Korby scooted his hips up onto his rope and nodded.

The silver-and-black bull took two long, high jumps, then cranked into a spin with Korby squarely in the middle of his back. The roar of the crowd swelled, second by endless second. Then Dirt Eater gathered to heave himself straight into the air, his body nearly vertical as he came down, front hooves driving into the ground. Korby reared back to avoid being flung onto the bull's blunt, curved horns, and Dirt Eater took advantage, his hind-quarters whipping left to sling the cowboy off the side.

Korby fought to recover his balance, but slid farther down with the next powerful lunge. One more jump yanked his hand from the rope and dropped him right under the bull's belly. The crowd gasped as a massive hoof slammed down a mere inch from Korby's helmeted face.

In a flash, Hank was at Dirt Eater's head, swatting at his nose and yelling to draw him away as Korby scrambled for the fence on hands and knees. For an instant it looked as if Korby was toast, then Hank yelled again and the bull charged him, practically blowing snot up the back of Hank's jersey as he sprinted toward the exit gate. Just inside the alley, Hank leapt onto the fence. Dirt Eater hooked a horn under his leg and tossed him like a rag doll into a crowd of cowboys on the other side before sauntering off to the catch pen.

Grace stood along with everyone else, holding her breath as she strained to see. Had that horn or the fall done serious damage?

Hank popped up, vaulted over the fence, and trotted out to the appreciative roar of the crowd, meeting Korby in the middle of the arena for a chest-bumping, backslapping hug.

The grandfather spoke for the first time. "That Hank might be even better than Korby's been telling us."

Grace couldn't help puffing up a little. That was her friend. And he'd invited her to be here for one of the biggest moments of his life—so far.

By the time the last bull bucked, Grace was as exhausted as if she'd been out there fighting them herself. Hank had had several more good saves and close calls, and as the arena cleared, cowboys paused to pump his hand and pound him on the shoulder in congratulations.

Grace hung back, saying goodbye to her new friends and waiting until most of the crowd had shuffled out before making her way to where Hank was packing his gear. He'd stripped off his jersey and was ripping loose the Velcro that held his vest in place, leaving a damp T-shirt beneath.

When he saw Grace, he dropped the vest on top of his bag to give her a sweaty hug. "That was such a blast!"

"You were great." She couldn't have forced the smile off her face. "Everyone was really impressed."

"God! I could have kept going all day." He laughed from sheer joy, then grabbed her hand and twirled her in an impromptu dance. "Hot damn! Look at you, all cowgirled up. Nice jeans."

"Thanks," she said, breathless from his proximity and approval.

"Hey, Hank! You about ready to go?" Korby called from a few yards away, where he lounged against the fence with his arm draped over the shoulders of a girl with blond hair that hung in sleek waves to her shoulders. Another equally pretty dark-haired girl stood beside them, eyes narrowed at Grace.

"I've just gotta swing by the locker room to change." Hank grabbed a manila envelope propped against his bag. "The photographer is printing out and selling pictures from tonight, and he gave me this one." He held it up for her inspection—a classic shot of Hank eye to eye with Dirt Eater, his outstretched hand brushing the bull's nose as Korby scrambled safely away. "Got a pen?"

"Uh, sure." She dug into her bag and found a black Sharpie she'd used to make poster boards for one of her class projects.

"Perfect." Hank propped his foot on the bottom fence rail and scribbled on the photo, then held it and the pen out to her with a wide grin. "Merry Christmas, Grace."

"Thank you." Her stomach jittered with pleasure as she squinted to decipher his scribbles.

To my little red-haired girl, from a future
National Finals bullfighter. Love, Hank.

Her heart tumbled, and it was all she could do not to clutch the picture to her not-so-impressive bosom. "This is great. My first autograph."

"Mine too." For an instant his smile dropped away, replaced by steely determination. "It's not gonna be the last."

"I'd better take really good care of this one. It'll be worth a fortune someday."

His eyes softened and he reached out to tug one of her curls. "Thanks, Grace. It means a lot, you being here. You've always been my good luck charm."

"Hank!" Korby called again. "We're gonna die of old age here."

Hank shoved his vest into the bag before slinging it over his shoulder. She'd taken a full step to follow him when he said, "Drive safe on the way home, Grace. See you at the Smoke Shack tomorrow?"

Grace lurched to a stop, unable at first to comprehend what was happening. But he'd said…he'd asked…

Oh.

He'd asked for nothing except for her to show up and cheer him on. As a friend. He hadn't said, "Be my date, Grace." Hell, he'd obviously already had a date. And he hadn't even mentioned the party. That had been Korby. But Grace had been so pathetically eager, she'd led herself on.

So she had no one but herself to blame for the fistful of hurt and humiliation that slammed into her gut.

Hank was still looking at her, friendly and expectant.

"I…have church in the morning," she stammered.

"So we'll make it later. Two o'clock, okay? I can't wait to hear all about the wild college life." And with that, he was gone, looping an arm around the brunette's shoulders as he walked away.

Grace sat carefully on the bottom row of the bleachers as tremors rolled through her. She was such a fool. As if all she had to do was change clothes and put on some makeup for Hank to notice she was more than good old Grace. When would she ever learn?

Not anytime soon, apparently. Once she'd choked down the rush of tears, she tucked the photo carefully back into the envelope instead of tossing it into the nearest trash can. And despite her current humiliation, at two o'clock the next afternoon, she would be walking up the worn wooden steps to the Smoke Shack.

Pathetic as it might be, she couldn't stop settling for whatever tiny pieces of himself Hank wanted to give her. But as she gazed out over the empty arena, a new resolve stiffened her spine. Having the freedom to do what she pleased wasn't enough. Real cowgirls—real *women*—like Violet Jacobs, Shawnee Pickett, and Melanie Brookman didn't wait for championships to fall in their laps. They grabbed life, gave it a shake, and told it exactly what they wanted.

From this point forward, Grace was going to be that kind of woman. And if she ever got a real shot at Hank, there would be no doubt in his mind that she was interested in more than his autograph.

Chapter 1

Blackfeet Nation, Northern Montana—Seven years later

CONSIDERING HOW MANY TIMES THE OLD BAT HAD threatened to shoot him, Hank was surprised to find a lump in his throat as he cradled Norma's cheap ceramic urn. It had been only a week since she'd come knocking on his door in the wee hours, woken by a blinding headache, her words so slurred that at first he'd assumed she was drunk.

At least the stroke had taken her fast. Norma had only had two wishes—the primary being to live out her days in a decrepit camp trailer beside the St. Mary River. And the second...

A bitter fall wind whipped straight, dark hair into Hank's eyes as he pried the lid off and held the urn aloft, tipping it so ashes swirled into the bright, hard blue of the Montana sky.

He was a long way from Texas. An eternity from the thoughtless boy he'd been for far too long. A string of increasingly bad choices had plummeted him from the highest of highs to unspeakable lows, until he'd bottomed out here, in a squatter's camp on the northern edge of the Blackfeet Nation, with a murderous old hermit for company.

And of course Bing—part-time rodeo secretary, full-time licensed counselor, and guardian angel of lost cowboys—hovering over him, guiding him toward the light. When he'd woken up in a hospital in Yakima with no money, no insurance, and no future to speak of, Bing had been there to scrape up the pieces, bring them here, and help him patch the wreckage into something resembling a man.

She leaned in to his side now, hunching deeper into her puffy coat, and tilted her head to watch the ashes disappear. "The way it's blowing today, she'll be scattered from here to the Sweetgrass Hills."

Hank tucked the urn under one arm and Bing under the other. "As long as some of her lands on Brantley's place. Figures Norma would want to trespass on his pasture for eternity."

"My kind of woman." With his spare frame braced against the elements, Gil Sanchez could have been rooted in this landscape, hundreds of miles north of his Navajo mother's homeland. He was the sole point of contact with Hank's former life. Cynical, sarcastic, borderline antisocial: Gil was the last member of the tight-knit, Earnest, Texas, rodeo community that anyone would have expected to show up in the wilds of Montana and declare himself Hank's sponsor.

"I'm not an addict," Hank had pointed out. Unlike Gil, who no longer made a secret of his struggles with prescription pain meds. "And you don't even like me."

Gil had just shrugged. "I know worse people. And one of the founding principles of Fucked-Up Anonymous is that after someone helps pry your head out of your ass, you're supposed to pay it forward. I figure you're a prime candidate. Brownie points for me with the friends and family back home, and you're too far away to stagger in and puke on my floor when you backslide."

"I'm not a drunk either."

"But you're still fucked up."

There had been no arguing with that. A year and a half later, here they were, on the high point of a ridge that ran parallel to and only a mile from the jagged east face of the Rockies—*Where the mountains meet the plains*, according to the local tourism slogan, and only a few miles from where the United States met Canada.

They observed the traditional moment of silence, just the three of them to witness this final step in a mostly uphill ninety-two-year journey—from birth to death, ashes to dust.

Then Bing slapped her gloved hands together. "Well, that's that. Let's go. I guarantee Norma wouldn't have froze her ass off for me."

They scrambled down a cow path, through the brush and stunted aspens to the gravel road where Bing had left her pickup. As Gil climbed into the back seat, a gust slammed against the door, nearly mashing his leg before he could yank it out of the way.

He swore with the eloquence of a man who practiced regularly. "I'll never bitch about the West Texas wind again."

That'd be the day. For Gil, cursing verged on a recreational activity.

Silence reigned as they wound down off the ridge. Bing stopped at the bottom of the hill to wait for a pickup and trailer to pull out onto the main road, hauling away the last of Norma's mangy bunch of cows. The proceeds of their sale would be used to offset the cost of her cremation. As the rig rolled away, her old piebald gelding gazed mournfully out through the back gate.

That damn lump swelled in Hank's throat again. Stupid, lazy nag. Hank should be glad to see the last of him. And those wild-ass cows. And the impenetrable tangle of brush where they'd liked to hide, making Hank long for his dad's good cowdog, Mabel.

He'd never been homesick, exactly. In the bone-chilling cold of the endless Montana nights, there'd been only a handful of things he'd craved with a pure, physical ache. The silk of Mabel's coat between his fingers. The sweltering southern heat. A bellyful of Smoke Shack barbecue.

And Grace.

The list was by no means in order of importance, but Mabel got priority because Hank knew if he reached out to her, *she* wouldn't rip his hand off. But Grace…

She'd been foolish enough to let herself get tangled up in his fall. Of all the things he regretted—and there were many—hurting Grace, betraying their friendship, ranked pretty damn high.

Bing followed the pair of ruts down to Norma's clearing, her pickup sloshing through puddles fed by water oozing from snowbanks that clung along the lip of the hill, remnants of an October blizzard. When the pickup finally rocked to a stop, Hank purposely avoided soaking up the view. Fall had stripped the squatter's camp down to its ugly bones—revealing every scrap of discarded metal in the flattened brown grass, turning the trees to tortured skeletons deformed by wind and snow.

He wanted to remember it rippling and green, with sunlight flickering through the aspen leaves and wildflowers bobbing in the ever-present breeze. His beautiful self-imposed prison—and now he was being paroled before his rehabilitation was complete.

When Norma had parked her ancient travel trailer on this scrap of land, most everyone had shrugged. It was tribal property, she was an enrolled member, and if they chased her out, they'd just have to put her somewhere else. With the old woman gone, the council had let Hank know he was expected to vacate the premises.

"You need help grabbing your stuff?" Bing asked, even though she knew better.

"No. I've got it." It had taken all of ten minutes to pack: three pairs of ragged jeans, a couple of sets of thermal underwear, a handful of socks and briefs, and his motley collection of secondhand T-shirts and sweatshirts. His entire wardrobe didn't fill one of the two duffels he'd had with him when he arrived.

The other had never been unpacked. It held a boatload of painful memories along with the body armor, knee and ankle braces, athletic shoes, and soccer cleats that had been tools of his trade as a bullfighter. He'd had no use for any of it since the day Bing had hauled him out of that hospital with a plate and pins holding together the worst of his physical injuries. No surgeon could fix what was broken in his head.

He should've hawked the gear months ago, but like too many other things from his past, he couldn't quite seem to let go, especially of the parts that hurt the most.

He grabbed both bags from the bare, stained mattress and dragged in one last lungful of mold and mouse shit that no amount of cleaning could banish. Then he walked out, tossed the bags in the back of the pickup, and climbed into the cab. "Let's go."

"How long are you staying at Bing's place?" Gil asked.

"Until I see what I can find for a job."

He wasn't optimistic. Intent on avoiding as much of humanity as possible, he'd scraped by on the meat Norma had shared in exchange for tending to her cows, picking up a little cash doing minor repairs on old beater cars for the locals, and this past summer, breaking colts for a couple of nearby ranches. Altogether, it kept him mostly fed and not quite frozen. It would not put a real roof over his head.

In the summer, when tourists flooded Glacier National Park, work was easier to come by. With the historic hotels and all the surrounding restaurants, gas stations, and gift shops shuttered for the winter, unemployment on the reservation climbed to epidemic levels. He might be able to pick up a few hours as a convenience-store clerk down the road in Cut Bank or Shelby, but it would be a stretch to put together enough money to cover rent and food.

"You could jump in with me," Gil said.

Hank twisted around in his seat. "To Texas?"

"To work. Your commercial driver's license is still valid, and I happen to run a trucking company."

"You want to hire *me*?"

Gil shot him an impatient glare. "Didn't I just say so?"

"But…" Geezus. Working for Gil?

He might have put up with Hank as a restoration project, but when it came to Sanchez Trucking, Gil's lack of tolerance was legendary. He ran the dispatcher's office the same way he'd ridden bucking horses—balls to the wall, no excuses, and nothing less than maximum effort from everyone around him.

"I've never done any real trucking," he said.

Gil dismissed that with a flick of his fingers. "Cole Jacobs trusted you to haul his stock. That's all the résumé I need. And the apartment above the shop is vacant, so I'll even toss in housing."

Hank cast a pleading glance in Bing's direction. She didn't look surprised. Obviously, Gil had already run this by her, but how could Hank leave her alone only ten days before Thanksgiving? "Let me look around here first. There might be something…"

"Nothing that will compare salary-wise. Or with benefits." Bing closed a warm hand over his chilled one, her jaw set. "It's time, Hank."

A lousy time. The worst part of the year for Bing. "You'll be alone for the holidays."

Her face tightened, but she didn't relent. "I'll manage. And who knows. Maybe I'll take some of that vacation time they're threatening to steal from me at the end of the year and come ride along with you. I can be your truckin' mama."

If only she'd been his actual mother. "Bing…"

She shook her head. "You've gotta move on, Hank."

"Fine! But I don't have to start by going backward." To face his mistakes, lovingly preserved in the minds and hearts of Earnest, Texas, as permanent as the initials five-year-old Hank had scrawled in the wet concrete in front of the Kwicky Mart.

"Yeah, you do." Bing cast him a sly smile. "And people are always in a more forgiving mood with Christmas coming on."

Hank gazed at her striking face, the expressive dark eyes that so often sparkled with laughter despite the grief lingering underneath. He had begun as one of her endless parade of lost souls, but they were infinitely more to each other now. Bing loved him by choice, not obligation, even though she'd seen the worst he had to offer.

He loved her back with a ferocity that stunned him... and now he was paying the price.

She believed in him, and Hank couldn't bear to let her down. For Bing, he was compelled to salvage something from the wreck he'd made of his life—even if it meant having to pick through Texas rubble.

And wouldn't you know, he'd land in good old Earnest three years to the day from the last time he'd tried to go home. He hadn't even made it to the ranch. One quick and dirty shouting match with his dad in the middle of the Corral Café, and Hank had stormed right back out of town.

It had been the blackest of Black Fridays, licking his wounds in Korby's college apartment, beating himself in game after game of pool at the pizza joint down the street—until Grace walked in.

Even as he'd trailed along to her dorm room, Hank had cursed himself for taking advantage of her. Sweet, innocent Grace, who had never even been to a homecoming dance.

Then his little red-haired girl had proceeded to rock his world...and in typical immature asshole style, he'd repaid the favor by running for the hills.

"Well?" Gil demanded. "I can't dither all day. I'm scheduled to drop my load in Sheridan at eight o'clock tomorrow morning."

Hank looked at Bing. She nodded. He closed his eyes. Shit. This was really happening.

Bing let go of his hand and put the pickup in gear. They rattled back to the main gravel road and over the ever-present washboards. A left turn at the stop sign, a few short miles down Highway 89 to Babb, and all too soon they were standing in the parking lot of a log-framed restaurant closed for the season.

Gil grabbed Hank's luggage and hauled it over to the waiting eighteen-wheeler—his transportation of choice, arranging loads that made his trips to Montana a paying proposition. Bing watched, arms folded tight around her body as the wind plucked at the glossy black spikes of her short-cropped hair.

Hank didn't bother to hide the tears that welled in his eyes as he gave her a hug. "I *will* be back."

"To visit. This isn't where you belong."

What is?

He'd shredded the umbilical cord that had tethered him to the Panhandle. Cut loose, he'd rampaged, then scrabbled, and finally drifted aimlessly, leaving a trail of smoking bridges behind him. Even if he wanted to, was there anything left worth rebuilding, or anyone willing to let him try?

He thought of Grace…and nearly laughed. It was too bad she hadn't stayed in Oregon, where she'd run after Hank had humiliated her in front of the entire town on that shitty New Year's Eve, thirty-seven days after the weekend that had turned him upside down and inside out. But last year she'd come back to the Panhandle for a job as a teacher and athletic trainer just down the road in Bluegrass. Hopefully being on the sidelines for every game of every sport would keep her too busy for their paths to cross—for her sake and his.

Hank gave Bing another squeeze. "I'll call you."

"I'll drive down there and kick your rear if you don't." She pushed him away and made a shooing motion. "Like the song says, I can't miss you if you're not gone."

"Thank you," Gil said. And to Hank's shock—and Bing's, judging by her expression—he kissed her on the cheek. Then he turned and tossed Hank a set of keys. "You are now officially on the clock."

As Hank opened the truck door, sunlight glinted off the gold lettering. *Sanchez Trucking, Earnest, Texas*. At least he would roll back into town in style. And as usual, he had to admit that Bing was right, on one point anyway. What better time than the holidays to face down everyone he had wronged? At least they would all be conveniently gathered in one place.

Hank climbed behind the wheel, fired up the big engine, and pointed the rig south.

Ready or not, here I come.

Chapter 2

GRACE PRIDED HERSELF ON KEEPING HER COOL — A vital skill in a profession where she might have to deal with anything from a ripped fingernail to cardiac arrest. But all the athletic tape in the world couldn't fix stupid.

"Everybody gets shin splints," the junior varsity basketball coach raged. "You are letting Andie milk this to get out of conditioning."

And you need to be smacked upside the head with your own clipboard. Bad enough that they'd called a Saturday morning practice, screwing up Grace's plans. Now she had to deal with an idiot who wouldn't be satisfied until she saw visible damage on a bone scan. It was Grace's job to be sure Andie's condition didn't progress to that point, and with the power vested in her by the school district, the athletic trainer's word was final.

But whenever possible she preferred to rule by reason, not force. "Andie's pain is caused by her horrible foot alignment. I am going to continue to restrict her activity until she has been fitted for orthotics and then eases back into practice."

"You're talking weeks! The basketball season will practically be over."

Grace made a suitably grave face. "You're right. I can't guarantee she'll be able to make a significant contribution to the team this year."

But she would be healthy enough to have a shot at

repeating her top-ten finish at the previous spring's state track meet in the eight hundred meters, along with anchoring a bronze-medal-winning two-mile relay team.

"What am I supposed to do?" The coach slapped her clipboard down on the nearest padded treatment table, temptingly close to Grace's reach. "She'll be dead weight, but her parents will raise hell if I cut her."

No doubt. Her mother had been an all-conference forward at West Texas A&M and was convinced her baby should follow in her hoop-shooting footsteps even though Andie had barely made the junior varsity squad.

Grace heaved an exaggerated sigh. "I could try to talk to them."

"Would you?" The coach leapt at the bait like a nylon-clad sucker. "They'll take it a lot better coming from you."

Grace made a show of sighing again, careful not to overplay it. "I'll do what I can."

"Thank you!" The coach snatched up the clipboard and charged out before Grace changed her mind.

The door had barely swung shut when it was pushed open again and a head poked inside. "Is everyone gone?" Andie whispered.

Grace leaned back in her chair and smiled. "The coast is clear."

"Did it work?"

"Like a charm."

"Thank God!" Andie hobbled across the room and threw herself onto a treatment table with a level of drama only a fifteen-year-old could muster. "And thank you, Miz Mac. I know I'm being a total wuss, but I just can't look Coach in the eye and tell her I don't want to take any chance that playing basketball will mess up my track season."

Ditto for her parents, but in cases like this, Grace didn't mind running interference. As the middle child of seven, Grace had played the fall guy for her younger brothers often enough that she had it down to an art.

"Tell your parents to call me this evening." She waved a shooing hand. "And get out of here so I can, too."

She paused to swap her nylon sweats, polo, and running shoes for jeans, a long-sleeved T-shirt, a sweatshirt, and boots, checking the time as she hustled across the empty gym and out the back door to the teachers' parking lot. Only nine fifteen, with the rest of a rare Saturday off to spend however she wished—which meant she would be roping.

First, though, she headed toward Earnest, the southeast point of a rough triangle that was around twenty miles on each side and ten miles across the bottom, with Bluegrass at the apex and Dumas on the southwest corner. The Jacobs ranch was ten miles on south of Earnest, so they'd probably be done working bulls by the time she got there. Grace had promised to help, not that she was good for much beyond filling vaccine syringes. She'd made herself a roper, but she was still no ranch girl.

What Earnest lacked in size, it was determined to make up for in holiday cheer. A few years back the Chamber of Commerce had designated their little town the Cowboy Capital of the Panhandle, then had set about proving it. As a result, grinning scarecrow cowboys twirled ropes, hefted branding irons, and galloped straw horses through clusters of pumpkins and cornstalks on every street corner and in every store window. Overhead, multiple strands of Christmas lights already crisscrossed Main Street, with a big, twinkling sheriff's star at the center of each swag and four-foot-tall elves brandishing six-shooters and tipping cowboy hats at the top of every streetlight.

As she rolled through town, Grace caught herself searching for a battered maroon-and-white Chevy pickup—slouched in front of the Smoke Shack or pulled up to the pump at the Kwicky Mart. Silly, to get anxious as Thanksgiving crept closer. Hank was far, far away, and given the state of affairs in the Brookman family, he wouldn't come waltzing home expecting turkey with all the fixin's. Last time he'd barely made it past the billboard at the edge of town. She glanced at it in her rearview mirror, though she knew the lettering by heart.

WELCOME TO EARNEST

**Home of
Delon Sanchez, 2x World
Champion Bareback Rider
Gil Sanchez, ProRodeo Rookie of the Year
Melanie Brookman, National Intercollegiate
Champion Breakaway Roper
Jacobs Livestock, Texas Circuit
Stock Contractor of the Year**

If Hank had continued as he'd started, his name would be next on the list. *Hank Brookman, National Finals Bullfighter*. Or the ultimate honor—*ProRodeo Bullfighter of the Year*.

But without the discipline or maturity to match his talent, she supposed his meltdown had been inevitable. And Grace had gotten caught in the fallout…the worst and the best thing that had ever happened to her.

When she'd scuttled out of Texas, there hadn't been a single person outside her family who'd missed her. Even within their church she hadn't had any real friends, and her lunches with Hank were the only contact she'd had with the cowboys and cowgirls she'd admired from afar. Now she knew everyone on that billboard personally— thanks, inadvertently, to Hank.

Raindrops spattered her windshield as she accelerated onto the rural road. Normally she would have been cursing the lousy weather, but now that she got to rope in Tori Sanchez's indoor arena over in Dumas, it was just an annoyance. That arena, along with the barn and pasture where Grace boarded her horse, was the reason she'd rented an apartment in Dumas. Living close to her horse was well worth the short commute to work.

All in all, life had been treating her pretty damn good since she'd moved back to the Panhandle.

She was turning into Cole and Shawnee's driveway when her phone chirped, so she stopped to check the text message. Alarm zinged up her spine at the sender's name, before she even read the words.

He's ba-ack.

Grace closed her eyes and swore. So much for assumptions. It seemed Hank had decided to come home and spread some holiday cheer after all.

Chapter 3

HANK WOULD RATHER HAVE HAULED A LOAD OF dynamite through Los Angeles during rush hour than drive out to the Jacobs ranch on Saturday morning, but the muffled sound of Gil's curses already wafted up through the floor vents from the dispatcher's office. Obviously things had not gone to his exact specifications while he was gone, and with Gil in that kind of mood, the Jacobs clan was definitely the lesser evil.

Hank rinsed his coffee cup and set it on the draining rack, then had to walk all the way into the bedroom for a sweatshirt. Compared to his mouse-infested camper, this was the penthouse suite. When Gil's younger brother had lived here, the walls had been covered with photos of Delon's winning rides, National Finals Rodeo back numbers, and shelves full of championship belt buckles. It was stripped bare now that Delon had married Tori and moved to her place in Dumas.

Were Hank's high school athletic trophies and all his photos and memorabilia gathering dust out at the ranch, or had his father dumped the works in the trash?

Still there, he decided as he shrugged into the canvas *Sanchez Trucking* jacket Gil had given him. His dad wouldn't waste the time it took to clean out his room. More likely, he'd left the old pictures on the walls so he could nurse his resentment along with the occasional beer. It sure as hell wouldn't be because he was proud of anything his son had accomplished.

Shut up, Bing's voice told that insistent, mocking whisper inside his head. *If you've got nothing good to say, go screw yourself*. He imagined her meeting his father…and grinned. Now *that* would be a sight.

The cold wind slapped at him when he stepped onto the exterior second-floor landing, and the glowering skies spit a few fat drops of rain on his head as he clattered down the metal stairs. The keys to one of the Sanchez pickups were in his pocket, and Gil had given him specific orders. He *would* make an appearance at the Jacobs ranch before he was seen anywhere else in town. With all they'd done for Hank—right up until he'd forced Cole to fire him—they deserved that consideration.

With that in mind, he skirted the edge of Earnest, the better to be unseen. As he headed south, his heart twinged at the sight of dusty-brown plains stretching to the horizon, broken only by the barely visible corrugated ridges of the Canadian River breaks.

Home. The recognition vibrated in his bones like a divining rod. Hank ignored it.

Ahead, brake lights flared as a snazzy short-box Ford slowed to turn into the driveway of what had been Cole Jacobs's childhood home. The house was set well back off the road, surrounded by trees. It had been used as a rental after Cole's parents and brother died in a car wreck and he'd moved in with his aunt and uncle. Now Cole lived there with his wife—the human wrecking ball named Shawnee Pickett.

Watching them hook up that last summer with Jacobs Livestock had been nearly impossible for Hank to wrap his head around, but silent, tense Cole and loud, outrageous Shawnee...*married*?

The Ford stopped just down the driveway, the driver either lost or fiddling with his phone. Hank drove on to the next turn and immediately noticed the upgrades at the main Jacobs homestead. A classy-looking manufactured home had taken the place of Violet's single-wide trailer, and down by the barn a shiny aluminum cattle truck gleamed beside the battered white bull hauler with JACOBS LIVESTOCK painted on the side in plain block letters.

But the parking area in front of the big, white frame house was empty.

Hank frowned. If they weren't gone to a rodeo, Steve and Cole Jacobs could always be found here after the morning chores were finished, making plans and catching up on the gossip over coffee and whatever Miz Iris had baked. Hank had spent his childhood loitering in Miz Iris's kitchen or trailing along behind Cole and Steve until Melanie, ten years older and already driving when he hit kindergarten, came to fetch him after her basketball practices.

Today, the place that had been more *home* to him than his own family's house was dark and vaguely forbidding, despite the pumpkins lining the porch and a scarecrow cowboy spurring a hay-bale-bucking horse.

They weren't home. Disappointment warred with relief in Hank's churning gut. He'd counted on getting this over with, the whole bunch of them at once. Now the day stretched in front of him, empty as his pockets. He supposed he should call Korby, but his former best friend would want to grab a beer, and the advance Gil had given Hank had been barely enough to buy a decent pair of jeans and stock up on cold cuts, bread, cereal, and milk at the last Walmart along the road.

His stomach rumbled, annoyed that it wouldn't be partaking of the anticipated banana bread or cookies. He could go skulk around his empty apartment, maybe fix himself a sandwich while he worked up the nerve to drive the dozen miles north of Earnest to the Brookman ranch and fetch some of his things…assuming his dad would let him in the house.

As he pondered his options, the door to the separate office building in the backyard opened and a woman poked her head out. Miz Iris? He had to squint to be sure. She looked…odd. His fingers were clumsy as he turned off the pickup and fumbled for the door handle. When he stepped out, her hand paused midwave, hung for a moment, then fell—along with her smile.

She swung the door wide, and it was Hank's turn to do a double take, trying to fit the round, well-padded version of Miz Iris he'd always known into this slender body. His heart skittered in fear. Was something wrong with her? Why was she so skinny?

"Hank." She said his name as if she was repeating a foreign word and wasn't quite sure what it meant.

He walked toward her, stopping a few yards short. He should smile, but his face couldn't recall how. "Yes, ma'am."

The corners of her mouth drew in as she studied him. He returned the favor, trying not to stare. The change was more than her weight. She looked different in a way that was hard to put his finger on. Something about the way she held herself that made her seem less like everyone's mother and more...*sophisticated* wasn't quite the word, but close.

He didn't like it.

"I expected Gil when I saw the Sanchez pickup." Her eyebrows pinched together—confusion, or annoyance?

"He's catching up at the office. We got in late." Now he should say something about how she looked or...damned if he knew what. He hadn't rehearsed this part, assuming by now she would be scolding him, then pelting him with questions as she bustled him into a chair and shoved something to eat or drink into his hands. Instead, she regarded him silently, her expression very...*undecided*.

Miz Iris wasn't sure she was happy to see him. The familiar dark threads wound around his heart and squeezed as her gaze landed on the *Sanchez Trucking* logo on his jacket and her brown eyes sharpened. "You're not just visiting?"

"No, ma'am. I'm back for..." However long it took to prove to Gil and to Bing there was nothing here for him. "A while."

"Have you told your sister?"

"No, ma'am." What difference did it make? It wasn't like he could pop by Melanie's place for dinner since she'd moved to Oregon to marry that condescending bastard, Wyatt. One more piece of his former life that hadn't waited around for him. He wrung the bitterness from his tone, leaving it tight and dry. "I expect I'll see her at Thanksgiving."

"They're not coming. She just let Violet know this morning."

"Oh." Was he relieved? Disappointed? He'd have to

decide later, when he wasn't putting all his effort into navigating this conversation.

An awkward silence fell, during which they were both intensely aware that in a former life, Miz Iris would have insisted he have the holiday dinner with them and he would have jumped at the offer. He worked his fists in his pockets. She folded her arms tight over her chest.

The office phone rang, to their mutual relief, but she didn't turn away immediately. "Joe and Violet and the kids are in Mexico with his mother. Delon and Tori went, too. Everyone else is over at Cole's place."

"Okay. Thanks."

She continued to regard him for another nerve-jangling *brrrinnnggg* of the old-fashioned black phone. "I suppose we'll be seeing you."

In Earnest? They could hardly help it. "Yes, ma'am."

She nodded, then turned and hurried into the office. As Hank strode to his pickup, he wondered if *We'll be seeing you* meant *Come on back another day* or *Get off my lawn*.

He could hope for the first, but he'd earned the second.

Back out on the highway, Hank barely got up to speed before slowing to make the turn to the other Jacobs homesite. His palms were damp on the steering wheel as he rolled up to the house. Hank pulled in beside that short-box Ford he'd seen earlier—exactly like he'd always promised he'd buy himself when he started working the big rodeos on a regular basis.

Hank's only memory of visiting Cole's family was from when he was around three, when he'd spun himself in the tire swing until he threw up—sort of like how he felt now. He did know the kitchen was around the back of the low stucco house, so he followed a redbrick walk to the rear patio. The yard was immaculate, the late-fall flowers warm bursts of orange and deep maroon in the flat light. There was no need to knock—the people inside could see him coming through the sliding glass doors.

The first three he'd expected, but it was the sight of the fourth that punched clear through him.

Grace. *Shit*.

He might have turned himself right around and made tracks if Shawnee hadn't yanked the door open and stood, hand braced on the frame, to give him a long, insolent once-over. She had not changed a whit—still built on the generous side and more than comfortable in her skin, with the wicked gleam in her eyes that said she wouldn't hesitate to bust his balls. Even her hair was the same, a waist-length snarl fighting the confines of the baseball cap she'd jammed over it.

"I'll be damned," she drawled. "It lives."

Chapter 4

HELL, DAMN, AND SON OF A BITCH.

Grace had expected to have more than fifteen minutes to recover from the news of Hank's return before they came face-to-face. Now it was all she could do not to gawk at the person Shawnee dragged through the door and shoved into the chair opposite her.

His sister had tried to warn her, but the transformation from grinning, carefree Hank to *this* had to be seen to be comprehended. It was partly the hair, falling to his collar around a face that had been stripped of all softness. If she squinted, she could see the bones were still the same. Everything else—the easy smiles, the spark of mischief in his eyes, any sign of warmth—was gone.

No wonder Miz Iris had been so flustered when she'd called to say Hank was headed their direction. He barely seemed housebroken, nostrils flaring like a skittish wolf that had wandered out of the Montana wilderness and didn't care for the smell of humans. He met her gaze—he could hardly avoid it from where he sat—and for an instant there was a flicker almost like regret. Then, without blinking or breaking eye contact, he retreated to a place she couldn't follow.

And didn't want to, if the shadows she saw were any indication of what she'd find there.

Cole, of all people, broke the silence. "You hired on with Sanchez Trucking?"

"Yep."

The old Hank would have rambled on about how and why and his next scheduled trip. Now he just stared them down with that half-wary, half-defiant tilt to his chin.

"They've built up a hell of a business," Steve Jacobs said in his deep, elder statesman voice. "Drivers say they're the best in four states to haul for."

"So Gil tells me."

Even his voice was different, the Southern drawl clipped and roughed up around the edges. They sat in an increasingly taut silence, Cole staring into his coffee cup, Steve's thick fingers drumming on the table, and Grace trying to disappear between them.

"Damn," Shawnee finally said. "I thought you were annoying when you wouldn't shut up. What do you want, Hank? A cinnamon roll? A pat on the head? A kick in the ass? I can dish 'em all up."

Hank blinked. Grace could've sworn she saw the corner of his mouth twitch as if he wanted to smile, but his voice was still flat. "Just checking in. Gil thought y'all deserved fair warning."

"Yeah?" Shawnee folded her arms. "Do you have plans?"

"For what?"

"Revenge. Redemption. The rest of the day?"

"I…no." For the first time, his composure slipped. He shot a sideways glance at the door, like he was fixing to bolt.

Shawnee clapped her hands together. "Excellent. Grace and I could use some chute help."

What? Grace's jaw came unhinged. *Oh no*. Please *no*.

Her sentiment was echoed on Hank's face. "I have to—"

"You just said you didn't have plans," Shawnee cut in. "Don't try to lie to me now."

The air in the kitchen seemed to contract, pulled tight by invisible lines of tension. Cole gave Shawnee a *what the hell* look. Everyone else stared at Hank.

He made a sound somewhere between a growl and a laugh. "Why not? I've tripped enough chute gates I could do it in my sleep."

He pushed his chair back, got up, and walked out. The door thumped shut behind him, and the kitchen was quiet until they heard the sound of his pickup starting.

"I guess that means he's gonna meet us there," Shawnee said, and reached for her sweatshirt.

Cole narrowed his eyes at her. "What are you doing?"

"Just breaking the ice." She gave him a smacking kiss on the cheek. "Don't worry. Me and Grace got this handled."

Speak for yourself. Lord knew Grace was beyond words.

"You *can* handle it, right?" Shawnee's eyebrows peaked, offering both challenge and support. *I've got your back…so suck it up, cupcake.*

What could Grace say? As far as anyone at this table knew, all Hank had to be sorry for was getting drunk and informing Grace—and everyone else at the Lone Steer Saloon's annual New Year's Eve bash—that, yes, the sex had been great, but, no, he wasn't interested in doing it again. After almost three years, any woman with a spine would be over it.

Grace stiffened hers and forced some conviction into her voice. "Sure."

But as they pulled on coats and boots, she allowed

herself the tiniest of sighs. This was the trouble with secrets. The people who had your best interests at heart could unknowingly force you to spend the afternoon with a man who was a whole lot more than an old embarrassment.

He was the father of a child that even he didn't know she'd had.

———ᨎᨎ———

As Grace hauled her saddle out of the tack room in Tori's barn, Shawnee gave her horse's mane one last swipe, then tossed the brush into the grooming caddy. "Are you pissed at me? I can't tell whenever you go all Yoda about things."

Considering this *thing* was one year, two months, and twelve days old, and Grace had just come face-to-face with its father for the first time since right after she'd discovered she was pregnant, she was nowhere near calm. Her family and her career had just taught her to fake it really well.

"It's a middle-child survival tactic. Mama calls it armadillo mode." Grace dodged the hoof that her mare, Betsy, aimed at her toes as she tightened the cinch. "And no, I'm not mad."

Stunned. Shaken. Guilt-stricken. And always, even now, irresistibly drawn to Hank. What was going on behind those impenetrable eyes when he looked at her?

Plus there was the fear, an oily film that tainted every other emotion. Grace couldn't leave her child to grow up with no knowledge of where she came from, even though an open adoption meant sentencing herself to exile when her family learned the truth, and possibly ruining these new friendships she treasured. But her secret wasn't built to stay hidden forever—and Hank's return could bring it to light a whole lot sooner than she'd planned.

Shawnee tossed a saddle blanket onto the bay and smoothed it into place. "I'm not just being an asshole. Your roping has improved a thousand percent, but your mental game is still shaky. I know you'd love to show Hank that little Gracie has got herself some serious skills...and how you don't give a crap if he notices. Now *that's* a pressure situation."

"So this is all for my benefit?" Grace asked dryly.

"You got it." Shawnee clicked a finger pistol at her, then shrugged. "And I'm not done with Hank. There's more to that story than Melanie has been telling."

Thank God. And thank the stars that when Melanie had stumbled onto the truth, she hadn't gone with her first instinct and run straight to Hank. But that wasn't the story Shawnee wanted to hear. She knew nothing about little Maddie—the spitting image of her daddy and her aunt, except with Grace's curls, and probably the cursed freckles when she was old enough.

Shawnee wanted to know what had turned happy-go-lucky Hank into a hard-edged, hostile man who Melanie had ultimately agreed was in no state of mind to be told that he could add *Congratulations, it's a girl!* to the mountain of regrets that had buried him alive.

Shawnee and Cole had witnessed the opening chapter of that long and sad tale. Three summers ago, Hank's infatuation with their rodeo announcer's daughter had exploded into an ugly scene that could have landed him in prison. It *had* left him unemployed. And worse, estranged from everyone involved with Jacobs Livestock—the support system that had stood in for his, at best, dysfunctional family. Was it any wonder he'd crashed?

Grace knew most of how Hank's downward spiral had carried him from Texas to Florida, along a meandering course to Washington State, and finally to that hovel in Montana. She had been just one of many stops along the way. For a wild, lovely, incredibly foolish weekend, she'd let herself think she could help him put on the brakes. He'd jammed the accelerator to the floor instead, leaving Grace in the dust—with a pink line on a plastic stick to show for finally getting his attention.

And now here she was, once again screwing up her courage to try to dazzle Hank.

Fate was a weird thing. If she hadn't taken a stupid gamble with her birth control, Wyatt Darrington wouldn't have gotten suckered into hauling a panicked Grace off to Oregon on the pretense of a great job opportunity. If Wyatt and Melanie hadn't fallen in love, Hank's sister wouldn't have found out about the baby, and she and Grace would never have become friends, and Grace would still be fumbling along on her own instead of being mentored by some of the best women ropers in the country. All because of Hank.

As Shawnee might say, *"Tell me how you really feel about him, Grace."*

In the months before and immediately after Maddie's birth, when she'd been stitched together with threads spun from self-righteous fury, she would have had no problem answering. Now, when her dream of being a real threat in the rodeo arena was tantalizingly close to coming true? The best she could come up with was *It's complicated*.

And fixin' to get more so.

Chapter 5

THERE WERE TOO MANY GRACES TO FIT INSIDE Hank's head. There would forever be his lunch buddy in her prim little dresses, rolling her eyes at his foolishness across a cafeteria table. College Grace, who was hot and naked and more than willing to educate him in all the things he'd only thought he knew about sex. And today's Grace, staring at him with zero expression in those big green-brown eyes.

At least she hadn't flung her coffee cup at his head, but Hank suspected that had more to do with good manners than forgiveness. He'd find out when it was just the three of them in Tori's arena. And since when were Grace and Shawnee roping buddies?

He still hadn't gotten anything to eat, so when he reached Dumas, he parked and went inside the fast-food joint that had once been a regular haunt. As he dug into his slim supply of cash and handed it over in exchange for the value menu burger and fries, he gazed longingly at the Coke machine.

"You want a drink with that?" the reluctantly perky twentysomething asked.

Hank shook his head. Much as he craved the cold, bubbly jolt, he couldn't justify paying almost three bucks for what he could grab at the Kwicky Mart for a dollar twenty-five.

He grabbed his tray and turned toward his usual booth,

but a new bunch of noisy, self-important teenage bone-heads had taken possession of the prime seats, where you could see everyone who passed on the main drag. As Hank stood, undecided, one of them lobbed a french fry at a girl who sat alone in the otherwise empty section. She flinched when it bounced off her shoulder, but only hunched deeper into her chair, burying her face in a paperback.

"Aw, come on, Polly," one of them taunted. "You know you want it. Open your mouth, and I'll give you a real treat."

Assholes. Hank couldn't claim he'd never teased a girl or made an inappropriate remark, but he hadn't intentionally made anyone miserable. Or taken such joy in it. Another of the boys lofted part of a chicken nugget. It hit Hank's chest and dropped onto his tray as he stepped between the tables. He picked up the scrap, examined it, then flicked it back at the kid.

"You dropped something," he said with his best dead-eyed stare.

All three boys shrank into the booth, not expecting a challenge, especially from some long-haired degenerate. Hank could see them imagining his prison tattoos. Good. They outweighed him by at least forty pounds apiece, and his fighting experience was mostly limited to hand-to-horn combat with males of the bovine variety.

And they were in a restaurant, not a back alley. He doubted any of them were packing a knife, or high on something that would inspire them to rip off his face—assumptions you couldn't always make where he'd been living. Most of the folks around Babb were good people, but Hank had encountered enough of the others to develop an edge that these pissant bullies didn't dare test.

Before they worked up the bravado, he broke eye contact and plopped his tray on the table, taking the seat opposite the startled girl. "Hey, Polly. Haven't seen you in a while."

Like, never.

"I…you…" She clutched the book to her chest like a shield.

"Hank Brookman." She was wearing a sweatshirt from a summer Bible camp, so he added, "I've been away for a couple of years. You probably don't remember me from church."

She blinked, wasting brain cells trying to place him. He angled his chair and leaned back against the wall to keep an eye on the boys, simultaneously moving as far out of her space as possible. He was trying to help, not scare the shit out of her. Her gaze flicked toward the booth, then back to him. He saw the moment she understood what he was doing, and her shoulders relaxed slightly.

See? He had been paying attention when his sister rambled on about body language.

He glanced at the cover of her book. "Victoria Schwab. That one's seriously dark."

Her eyes widened. Obviously, she didn't think he looked like an avid reader. Until he'd landed in that camper, she would have been right, but long, cold nights and lack of other entertainment had sent him diving into the e-reader Bing had lent him—a much better space to occupy than his own head.

Polly relaxed a few more degrees. "Have you read the Shades of Magic series?"

"Only the first one. I should get the rest on audio and listen while I'm driving."

If the library had them on electronic loan, and assuming his cheap cell could download the files. When they'd arrived in Earnest, Gil had tossed the clunker at Hank. "That's your company phone."

It felt weird being wired again, as if he was under surveillance. Considering the Sanchez drivers referred to Gil and his GPS-tracking dispatch system as Big Brother Trucker, Hank wasn't sure it was paranoia on his part.

Polly cleared her throat, nodding toward his coat. "So, um, you're working for Sanchez Trucking now?"

"Just started." And the name had serious clout in the Panhandle these days. Hank let his gaze wander over and sit heavily on the boys, raising his voice. "I'll be around if you need a hand with anything."

They waited until he looked away, then got up and sauntered out, leaving the table piled with their trash.

The instant the door shut behind them, Polly exploded. "God, they are such jerks!" Then her glare faded and she flashed Hank a grateful smile. "Thanks. Most people just pretend they don't see that crap."

The girl was tall, thin, and slouchy, with straight, muddy-blond hair that hung in her eyes—about as different from Grace as he could imagine. Still, "You remind me of an old friend who used to let me sit with her at lunch."

Starting with the first day of fourth grade, when he'd spotted her trying to become one with the school's brick wall during morning recess. She was so tiny, and so cute with her plaid skirt, shiny shoes, and crazy, almost-red curls, that he'd walked over and asked, "What's your name?"

She'd eyed him as if she suspected he had a snake hidden behind his back. "Grace McKenna."

"You're new."

"Duh."

He'd laughed, fascinated by the scatter of freckles over her miniature nose, and stuck out his hand. "Hello, Grace. I'm Hank. I like new girls."

Especially the one who'd cautiously slid her hand into his, then given it a firm shake. Making friends with Grace was one of his few good impulses—and like everything else, he'd screwed it up.

But maybe he could earn back a few karma points with random acts of *don't-be-an-asshole*. He smiled at Polly. She smiled back. And while he polished off his lunch, Hank pretended he'd rewound the clock to a time when he was sitting with the Grace who would've smiled at him, too.

———

Twenty minutes later, he stepped out of his pickup in Tori's yard—they all still called it Tori's, even though she and Delon had been married for, geezus, five years already?—and was greeted by a low, butt-puckering yowl. The mottled-gray beast of a cat eyed him balefully from the barn door and stalked him around the side to the indoor arena. Hank lengthened his stride. Muella had a well-known taste for blood.

The wind whipped needle-sharp raindrops into his eyes, and he shivered. It was too chilly for just his sweatshirt, but he hadn't wanted to get his new jacket dirty. He opened the walk-through door into the arena and nearly jumped out of his skin as the cat shot past his legs and disappeared into the shadows.

The building was about the same width as a hockey

arena and half again as long, with an interior fence set twenty feet off the wall at the closest end to make space for the roping chute and boxes on the right side. The remainder was all groomed dirt, with a gate out the far end and a narrow return lane along the right wall to bring the stock back to the chute.

Hank's dad would've killed for a place like this, back in the day.

Two horses were tied inside. Grace was strapping a skid boot on the rear leg of the nearest, but when Hank threw the latch on the interior gate, the roan yanked its foot out of her grasp to angle around and give him a once-over. Grace muttered a curse—presumably at the horse.

Shawnee eyed him across the back of a bay horse. "I was beginnin' to wonder if you got lost."

Yeah. About three years ago. But he only shrugged and started for the chute, then stopped when he saw the calves lined up, ready to go. "I thought you were roping steers."

"Not today." Shawnee swung aboard the bay. "We're getting Grace tuned up for the start of next season, and I'm training this gelding for a high school girl from Canyon."

But...that meant they didn't need him. He'd assumed they'd be team roping—one catching the horns, the other the back feet. If they were roping calves, they could take turns working the chute. So why had Shawnee dragged him—

Just then, Grace's horse whipped around, slamming her hip into Hank's chest and knocking him flat on his back. Instinct had him logrolling out of reach of her hooves before scrambling to his feet, wheezing, "What...the..."

Grace snorted. Shawnee burst out laughing. The horse

practically smirked at him from under her jet-black forelock, her eyes bright with familiar malice. *Betsy*. Like the cat, she was an equal-opportunity hater. The mare was barely bigger than a good-sized pony, with enough attitude for a herd of Clydesdales. She had to be in her mid-twenties, but she didn't look a day older than when Shawnee had roped on her in college. She'd hated Hank then, too.

He slapped at his dirt-caked clothes and bent at the waist to shake the dirt out of his hair, scraping the tangled mess off his face as he straightened to glare at the little bitch. "Why aren't you dead yet?"

"Betsy is too mean to die." And too talented to kick loose in the river breaks to fend for herself. Shawnee cocked her head. "Looks like you've still got the moves."

Muscles contracted one by one, the tension crawling up from his toes to his scalp. Yeah, his body functioned just fine. It was his brain that couldn't be trusted. He braced himself for the questions. *What's wrong with you? Why aren't you fighting bulls anymore?*

Instead, Shawnee waved to Grace. "You're up, short stuff."

Giving Betsy a wide berth as Grace mounted up, Hank strode over to the roping chute, yanked open the rear gate, pushed the first calf into position and turned. "Ready when you are."

Grace adjusted her rope and took a few warm-up swings, then tucked her loop under her arm and backed the mare into the corner of the roping box to face the chute…and Hank. Pinning her gaze firmly to her target, she nodded her head. Hank tripped the latch and the chute gate banged open. Grace took one, two swings and threw. As the loop curled around the calf's neck, Betsy slammed on the brakes. The hard plastic breakaway hondo popped free of the animal's neck with a *snap!* and the loose end flew back—right at Hank's head.

It whistled past his ear, clanging off the chute as he dropped to his belly. Grace whipped around in her saddle. "Are you okay?"

"Other than damn near losing an eye?" He scrambled to his feet, once more slapping dirt out of his clothes. Geezus. He'd be safer fighting bulls. Or possibly not.

"You've had breakaways coming back at you before," Shawnee drawled. "Your sister snaps 'em right in front of the chute on a regular basis."

"Well, yeah, but I wasn't expecting—"

"*Me* to catch so fast?" Grace finally smiled at him… with frost-coated triumph. "Stay on your toes. That wasn't a fluke."

He scowled back at her for two long beats. Then one corner of his mouth twitched as pride swelled, warm and bright in his chest. She'd finally done it—made a real cowgirl out of herself. Instead of offering her a high five, he slammed the front gate, opened the rear, and ran another calf in. "Okay. Let's see what you've got."

For an instant their gazes met, and a spark kindled in her eyes. The memory of their bodies, skin to skin, all but shimmered in the air between them, like heat waves rising off sunbaked pavement. He could tell by the way her lips shaped into an *O* that he wasn't the only one who'd just had a hot flash. Then she deliberately reined Betsy away so he was staring at two butts—one human, one horse—both excellent examples of their species.

And speaking of inappropriate…

Hank glued his wandering gaze to the white patch on the Hereford calf's shoulders, trying real hard not to dwell on how he already had seen *everything* she had. And how, regardless of time, distance, and his own stupidity, he had never stopped wanting to do it again.

Chapter 6

By the end of the practice session, Grace was exhausted from holding the *Hank who?* pose. But by damn, she had done it—not only roped well, but her very best. The burst of satisfaction gave her enough energy to haul her saddle into the tack room and heft it onto the rack that Tori had designated as hers.

How about that? Grace had her own saddle rack in a barn owned by a world-champion cowboy and a daughter of the Patterson family: the legendary Panhandle cattle barons whose reach extended around the world and deep into Washington, DC. And since Grace returned the favor by ranch-sitting whenever they were traveling—like now—she could just crawl the twenty yards to the living quarters of Tori's trailer and go face-down on the couch, while variations of the same refrain played over and over in her head.

Hank was back. *Hank* was back. Lord save her, Hank was *back*.

Other than when her breakaway had nearly cold-cocked him, the two of them hadn't exchanged a word. That *look*, though. Just the thought made awareness ripple through her. For that moment, at least, she'd had absolutely no doubt what Hank was thinking.

As the practice wore on, Shawnee had gone quiet too, but her eyes were sharp—on both Hank and Grace.

When they'd finished, Shawnee had said nothing but "That's it for today."

Hank had hesitated as if he couldn't believe he was getting off that easy. "So I'll just, uh, head out?"

"Yep. But thanks for stopping by," Shawnee said with a polite smile.

That's when Grace realized she was furious. Shawnee strode out of the arena without another word and was waiting, arms folded and face tight, when Grace emerged from the tack room.

Oh, shit.

"So...that went pretty well," Grace said brightly, edging toward the door.

Shawnee pinned her to the ground with a hard stare. "Don't even try it. Somebody is gonna tell me what the *hell* has been going on. That boy has not just been taking a *time-out*."

Whoo-boy. She was some kind of mad. But underneath the anger, there was hurt. It was obvious that Melanie had been seriously downplaying Hank's situation...and that she'd chosen not to confide in her closest friends.

Shawnee braced her feet. Fighting stance. "We were all shocked about senseless when we saw him today, but I got the feeling you expected the worst. Why is that?"

"I, um...was there, in Oregon, when Melanie and Wyatt flew out to Montana to see him."

"So she talked to *you*." Shawnee's tone verged on insulting. "Not Violet. Not me. You."

And from where Shawnee stood, that was a major betrayal.

"No." Which wasn't a complete lie. Melanie hadn't

said a word until she realized that Grace had a vested interest in her brother's mental state. Everything else Grace had pried out of Wyatt…and other sources. "Do you remember Philip? Wyatt's student?"

Shawnee frowned. "The one with the braid?"

"Yeah. He's Blackfeet, from the same general area as where Hank has been. And he knew"—she waved a vague hand toward where they'd last seen Hank—"about that."

Shawnee didn't look entirely convinced. "How did Melanie persuade Gil Sanchez to hire him?"

This, at least, Grace could answer honestly. "She didn't."

Shawnee's brows pinched, skeptical. "Right. Hank just walked in, and Gil, being the soul of human kindness, handed him a set of keys."

"I don't know about that, but Melanie has no idea Hank is here. Otherwise she would have told y'all to expect him." And she definitely would have told Grace.

Shawnee's eyes took on a gleam disturbingly similar to the cat's, which hunched at the edge of the hayloft sneering down at them. "So Mel is in for a shock of her own."

And her good buddy was going to enjoy delivering it, as a small measure of payback for being kept in the dark.

Grace moved toward the hayloft ladder. "I'll take care of the chores."

"Go ahead." Shawnee already had her phone in her hand. "Same time tomorrow?"

"Sounds good." Grace climbed into the loft, made sure she was out of sight, then snatched her own phone out of her pocket and punched up Melanie's number.

Brace yourself, she texted, thumbs flying. **Hank showed up today, and Shawnee is not thrilled that you've been keeping secrets.**

She hit Send and held her breath, praying Melanie would get the message before Shawnee's call. As Grace started to slide her phone back into her pocket, it buzzed. The reply was a single four-letter word.

Grace didn't bother to answer. Melanie had summed it up nicely.

It was only four o'clock when Hank rolled into downtown Earnest but dusk was already falling, setting the Christmas lights ablaze against the sulky, low-hanging clouds. He slowed to turn into the Kwicky Mart for that well-earned Coke…and was hit by the heavenly scent of mesquite-smoked meat. Hank's stomach gurgled happily in recognition.

As if pulled in by a tractor beam, he drove on to the next street, made a left, and found himself at the Smoke Shack. He was in dire need of a friendly face, and Korby was the only person he knew who was incapable of holding a grudge.

Other than the icicle lights dripping from the eaves and a fall wreath stuck on the weathered front door, they hadn't done a thing to spruce the place up. It was, literally, a wooden shack, barely big enough to house a kitchen in back and a tiny dining area out front. It must've been an actual color at some time, but the paint had faded in the relentless sun and wind. The wooden steps were still unpainted planks worn round on the edges, and the screen door creaked the same as it always had.

One more place he'd be leaving with an empty belly, because a brisket dinner would clean out his wallet. In that respect, at least, he had finally accomplished something his father wanted. Hank now knew what every penny that passed through his hands was worth.

It was too much to hope that Korby might be putting in a Saturday shift. His mother was there instead...par for this not-so-welcome home tour. She glanced up from her Sudoku puzzle book with a customer-friendly smile, which flat-lined as he stepped to the counter. "Hank Brookman...is that you?"

"Yes, ma'am." He fought the urge to push his hair back, wishing once again he'd had a chance to get it cut.

When he'd mentioned it to Bing during a call from a rest stop south of Billings, Montana, she'd told him to leave it be. "It's better if people can see right up front that you're not the person they used to know."

But where Bing came from, it was normal for men to wear their hair long, a sign of respect for tribal traditions. Folks in Earnest, Texas, drew a whole different set of conclusions. Korby's mother looked to be painting a 3-D portrait, but to be truthful, the stink eye she was giving him now was only a slightly magnified version of her usual expression. Every time they got in trouble, Korby's punishment had started with an order to stay away from Hank. As she'd been fond of saying, "The two you together have about half as much common sense as either one of you alone...and that ain't sayin' much."

She hadn't been wrong, which made it even harder to believe that Korby was a teacher, walking the same halls they'd once terrorized. Geezus. Talk about the blind leading the hormonally challenged.

"Is Korby around?" Hank asked before she could demand to know why he was darkening her door. "I lost his cell phone number."

"I guess that explains why he hasn't heard from you," she replied tartly.

Hank bit his tongue. *Just be quiet and respectful*, Bing had told him. *That'll really mess with their heads*. "Yes, ma'am," he said again.

"Well…he's chaperoning the FFA kids at a leadership conference in Abilene. He won't be home until late tonight."

Hank blinked at her.

"What?" she demanded.

"I'm having trouble making those words fit together. Korby? Leadership? Chaperone?"

Her mouth twitched, but she ironed out any hint of a smile. Her eyes were a sharper blue than her son's and her hair bleached a few shades blonder, but it was easy to see where he'd gotten his long, narrow face and knobby elbows. She gave Hank another critical head-to-toe inspection. "You're even scrawnier than when you hightailed it out of here," she said finally. "You want a full platter?"

Didn't he wish. A mountain of pulled pork, brisket, sausage, and two sides, plus a roll was three days' worth of dinners by his current standards. He fleetingly wished he hadn't spent so much of the money Gil had advanced him on new jeans—which now had to be washed, thanks to Grace and that devil horse—but damned if he'd let the church ladies crow about *that poor boy, did you see his clothes?*

"No thank you, I just ate." That crappy burger, hours ago.

"You can take it to go, save it for later."

The back of Hank's neck went hot. "I didn't bring my wallet," he lied.

She snorted. "That's never stopped you before."

"I'm not on my daddy's tab now," he shot back before he could stop himself.

"That is a fact." She jerked her head toward the logo on his jacket. "Does that coat mean you're workin' for Sanchez?"

"Yes, ma'am."

She pursed her lips, then gave a nod. "Then I know how to hunt you down if you don't stop back by and settle up."

Before he could formulate another excuse, she had bustled off into the kitchen. Hell. He didn't want to be a charity case. Then his appetite kicked his pride to the curb. He would pay the tab when he could, and he had literally been dreaming of this meal since he'd left Texas.

She plunked a to-go bag on the counter and set a large Coke beside it—forty-four ounces of sugary, carbonated bliss. She also slapped down the ticket. "I wrote Korby's number on the back." She paused, scowled, then added, "He'll be happy to see you."

That'd make one person. Hank pushed his mouth into something like a smile. "Thanks. I sure do appreciate it."

"You're welcome."

He noticed she didn't add how it was good to have him back in town. With an awkward nod, he hefted the bag and turned to leave just as the door opened…and Johnny Brookman stepped inside. They both came up short, face-to-face. Hank knew he should say something, but what? The only word that jumped onto his tongue had gotten his butt paddled when he was ten, and wasn't likely to get a better reaction now.

His father seemed to be having similar problems, his jaw working as if he couldn't quite build a sentence. Like the Smoke Shack, he hadn't changed a bit. Same dark, short hair under an Earnest Feed and Seed cap. Same broad, straight shoulders and powerful build that had made him a Texas Circuit tie-down roping champion and always made Hank feel…yeah, scrawny was about right. When the much-hoped-for pounds didn't pile on, no matter how much Hank ate and lifted weights, he'd concluded it was just more proof that he'd been born to disappoint his father.

"Hank," Johnny said.

"Yessir." He forced his eyes to remain level, his voice flat. At least he didn't have to worry about what to do with his hands, full as they were of food and drink.

His father waited, then blinked when Hank left it at that. He would have to remember to thank Bing for the advice when he checked in tonight. Silence was the last thing his old man expected. Hank let it stretch as far as was remotely polite before stepping aside with a *come on in* tilt of his head.

His father hesitated, then jerked a nod and walked on past. Hank caught the door with his foot, shouldered outside, and strolled down the steps and over to his pickup as if he didn't have a care in the whole damn world. He set his Coke in the cup holder—Gil would have his head if he spilled it in the cab—fumbled the keys into the ignition, and was halfway to Sanchez Trucking before he realized he was clutching the bag of hot food to his chest like a teddy bear…and shivering. It seemed like he was always cold these days, a chill that started in his bones and oozed out.

The last time he remembered being truly warm, he'd been in Grace's bed. And now he was cuddling up to a barbecue dinner instead. But hey, at least Korby's mom had thrown in a tub of macaroni salad, and at this point, Hank would take any hospitality he could get.

Chapter 7

THE HOUSE WAS COLD AND DARK WHEN JOHNNY Brookman walked in and tossed the two-pound bag of sliced brisket on the kitchen table. He really ought to invest in a timer to turn on the lights and heat in the evening, since his occasional, feeble attempts at a love life weren't likely to produce a wife. Hard to imagine, but he was even worse at dating than he'd been as a husband—and a father.

A man was supposed to be past this crap by his midfifties, settled into a boring routine of falling asleep with the television on except for a couple nights a month when he or his wife didn't doze off before they got around to having sex. Sharing his house with someone who could hold up their end of the conversation, unlike the dogs—one almost entirely white, one black—who gazed at him expectantly from the traditional black border collie masks, hoping for a belly rub and some of whatever smelled so good.

"Dream on," he said as much to himself as them.

Dreams. He'd had those once, before the wildfire that had wiped out the whole ranch and his rodeo career in one big *whoosh* of flames. Over two decades later, he could still taste the ashes.

By now he was supposed to be one of those former champs the camera picked out of the crowd every night at the National Finals, distinguished and proud alongside his lovely wife as he watched horses he'd trained carry the latest generation of elite ropers to championships of their own. Top cowboys would pop in when they were passing through from one rodeo to the next, eager for a dose of his expertise. *I've been hanging out at Johnny Brookman's place*, they'd say, dropping his name as proof they'd been admitted to rodeo's inner circle.

He glanced around the barren kitchen. Yeah, this was an exclusive club, all right. A circle of one, unless you counted the dogs. The ghost of a thousand regrets jabbed icy fingers into Johnny's gut, wearing his son's barely recognizable face.

Where's he been? Is he planning to stick around? How come he's not fighting bulls anymore?

A father should know the answers to those questions.

A quiet beep caught his attention. The light was flashing on the answering machine attached to his landline. He jabbed the button, and his daughter's voice echoed from the tinny speaker.

"Hey, Daddy. I tried your cell, but you must've forgot to charge it again."

Johnny pulled the phone out of his pocket. Yep. Dead as a doornail. He plugged it into the charger while she went on.

"I just wanted to let you know I heard Hank is in town. He might come by to pick up some of the stuff he left at the ranch." Melanie paused, adjusting her tone to somewhere between a plea and an order, with a hint of resignation. *"Try not to fight with him. He's not… Well, it's a long story, but go easy on him, okay? And call me when you get this."*

He pressed fingertips against his eyelids as the

recording clicked off. Hell. It was a moot point. Considering his reaction the last time Hank had shown up, why would the boy come anywhere near him?

Johnny was the first to admit he'd never been good with kids. Too impatient. Too cranky. With Melanie it hadn't mattered. Even as a toddler, she'd had a way of making up for what he'd lacked. Little wonder she was an ace at marketing.

Nothing had been easy with Hank. He'd been a fussy, colicky baby who'd been shuffled from babysitter to day care to trailing along after his sister while his parents were too busy bickering to raise him themselves. Johnny couldn't take any credit for what Melanie had made of herself...but he deserved at least half of the blame for whatever Hank had become.

And he didn't have time to mope about it now.

He shucked his town coat and pulled on a heavier chore coat, gloves, and a grimy wool cap with earflaps and laces above the brim before heading outside. This bitter wind was no good for riding a colt—it put a hump in their backs and white in their eyes—but he'd left the mare he called Ruby saddled while he ran into town. He'd intended to ride out through the cows this evening, but there were never enough hours of daylight, especially this time of year. If he worked her in the round corral tonight, though, she'd be ready to get some work done in the morning...and it was better than sitting alone in this damn house.

Ruby quivered, nostrils flaring, as he untied the halter rope. Damn weather—it made every four-legged creature on the ranch stupid. The colt spooked and nearly jumped on top of him when the white dog bounded out of the stall behind her. Spider was almost a year old and still not good for much but interfering with Mabel, proving his old man's assertion that two dogs were worse than none at all.

"You go lay down," he ordered the dogs.

Their heads drooped, and they cowered as if he'd kicked them.

"Go!" he repeated, pointing at the tack room.

Mabel gave him one last pleading glance before slinking away. Spider followed, but Mabel growled and snapped at the pup when she plopped down too close. Johnny just shook his head and slid a bridle onto his horse.

At the gate to the round pen, he flipped a switch to turn on the single mercury-vapor light overhead, then grabbed the long lunge line from where it hung on a post. He attached it to the near side ring on Ruby's snaffle bit, stepped back, and gave a cluck of his tongue and a flick of the line. She danced a few steps sideways. He clucked and flicked again, and she began to circle the forty-foot diameter pen, her strides longer and smoother as she went, her breath coming in puffs of silvery steam.

No more colts, he'd promised Melanie when she'd pitched a fit about the last one. It was too dangerous, she insisted, out here all alone. He'd argued that he could as easily get in a wreck on one of the older horses, but listing all the things that could go wrong out in the pasture hadn't exactly made her feel better, so he'd just promised to be careful.

When he judged that Ruby had worked the kinks out, he unclipped the lunge line and checked the cinches again before climbing aboard. At his gentle kick, she moved right out, and he consciously relaxed into the saddle, drawing a deep breath. The air was dense from the earlier rain, concentrating the scent of cow manure, horse sweat, and hay from the nearby shed.

Johnny lapsed into autopilot as he recalled Hank's gaunt face. He'd always seemed young for his age. Now he looked every one of his...geezus, what was it? Twenty-four, twenty-five years? Another of those things a father should know, along with whatever had sucked the sparkle out of Hank's eyes and left him looking so—

Something white flashed in Johnny's peripheral vision. He barely registered that it was Spider, popping up from under the fence, before the mare spooked, whirled, and came undone. The first leap jacked his butt out of the saddle and slammed him into the swells. He clutched at the reins, trying to yank her head up, but the second lunge blew his right foot out of the stirrup. Then she whirled again, slinging him off the side and into the fence.

There was a sickening crunch as Johnny's head and shoulder slammed into the heavy boards. Then everything went dark.

—⁓⁓—

A loud banging woke Hank from a dead sleep. He sat bolt upright, clutching the blanket to his chest to ward off the cold, then remembered he was in an actual bedroom, not that ratty old camper.

The banging sounded again, followed by someone yelling his name. He squinted at the digital alarm clock he hadn't bothered to set since he had nowhere to be at—for Christ's sake, seven fifteen?—on a Sunday. With a groan, he swung his feet to the floor and fumbled for his jeans, then a light switch.

"What the f—" He dodged a fist that nearly connected with his face instead of the door he'd yanked open.

"Oops." His visitor flashed a wide grin that sent Hank spiraling back to playing in mud puddles out behind the Smoke Shack—and getting their butts paddled for tracking the mess inside. "I should punch you, asshole. Take off and disappear without even a damn text now and then?" Korby looked him up and down, taking in Hank's tangled hair, bare feet and chest. "Geezus. No wonder my mother acted like she'd seen Wolf Boy."

"I went native for a while." Hank folded his arms over nipples that were puckering from the draft. Outside, the security lights cast long shadows in the predawn gloom.

"I guess you've got it in you. What is it, Osage blood on your Mom's side?" Korby didn't wait for an answer, rubbing a hand over his own formerly shaggy head. "I had to clean up my act."

"Tryin' to be a role model for the kiddies?"

"And keep Principal Dornbacher off my ass…still." He slapped Hank on the chest as he shouldered into the apartment. "It's good to see you, even if you did get even uglier."

Hank pushed the door shut and leaned his forehead against it, unable to process this much cheerfulness. "Is there some reason you're here before the butt crack of dawn?"

"Oh, right." Korby's grin faded. "Ma sent me to tell you—your old man is in the hospital."

Hank's gut dropped straight through the floor.

—◦◦◦—

Concussion. Fractured clavicle. Pins and a plate.

Between himself, his fellow bullfighters, and the bull riders, Hank had seen enough injuries to know basic medical terminology. Johnny had smacked his head and broken his collarbone bad enough to need surgery to put it back together. Hank's pulse bumped again at the idea of his father laid out cold in the dirt with not a soul around. Thank God he'd come to and been able to crawl to the house and call for help.

"It was damn near dark when I saw him at the Smoke Shack," he called to Korby from the bathroom. "What was he doing out there?"

"According to the neighbor, he asked himself the same thing all the way to the emergency room." Korby lounged on the couch, sipping coffee and flipping through one of Hank's stash of used paperbacks, no doubt looking for the "good" parts. He tossed the book aside as Hank walked out of the bedroom. "Are we going to the hospital?"

Hank stopped in the middle of pulling on a boot. Hell. What *was* he gonna do? His reflex had been to rush somewhere, but it wasn't like Johnny was on death's door, and Hank's presence wasn't likely to be a comfort.

He started at a series of booming thuds. Hank opened the door again and looked up—*way* up—at Cole Jacobs, filling the entire landing in a bulky chore coat and wool cap.

He gave Korby a glance, then looked back at Hank. "I guess you heard about your dad already. Shawnee said I should grab you and go on out to the ranch to see what needs to be done."

Hank blinked. "How would I know?"

"You've only been off the place for three years. Can't have changed much."

The ranch? Or Hank?

Korby unfolded from the couch. "I'll come along and—"

"No," Cole said.

"But—"

Cole gave him a withering stare. "No."

Hank stifled a grin. Looked like married life hadn't changed Cole much either.

Hank reached for his coat. "I'll catch up with you later, Korb."

He was climbing into Cole's pickup before it occurred to him that he also could have said no—but that wasn't how it worked in ranch country, or on the rodeo circuit. If someone got knocked down, people stepped in and gave them a hand up. It wasn't about friendship, or loyalty, or family. Or at least not *just* those things.

At the base of what people liked to call the cowboy code, it was about survival. No one could go it alone, and anyone who chose this life knew their day would come.

As they rolled out of town and onto the highway that stretched east, straight and flat as the landscape, Cole gave him an update. Johnny's concussion was mild, the break in his collarbone was clean, and he was going into surgery any minute. Steve and Iris Jacobs were with him, and if all went well, he would be released to go home with them that evening.

"What about Melanie?" Hank asked, trying to sound like he didn't care whether his sister was rushing home.

Cole shook his head. "They're in the middle of tryin' to get approved as foster parents. It came up kinda sudden.

Some guy who works for Wyatt has a younger brother and sister who just got taken away from their mother."

So Melanie was getting an instant family. She wouldn't even notice she was missing a brother. Hank turned his face away to look out the window, aware that it was stupid to feel slighted. How could he slap his sister away, over and over, then piss and moan when she finally went?

Or maybe he was jealous because she'd *chosen* these kids. She hadn't got stuck with them like she had Hank. He was the one everybody got stuck with: his parents, his sister, the whole Jacobs clan. Only Bing had picked him.

And before her…Grace.

Cole glanced over, taking in Hank's lightweight jacket and bare head. "You gonna be warm enough?"

"I've got stuff at the house." On the sunny May morning that wasn't supposed to be his last on the ranch, Hank had only packed what he'd needed for the summer. Now he could load up the rest without having to get past his dad.

"Where's Shawnee?" he asked.

"Picking up groceries. She's not expecting to find much food in the house."

Hank frowned. "How long do you figure we're gonna be out there?"

"Dunno. The chores shouldn't take long, but your dad was plannin' to go looking for some strays this morning, out in the breaks."

Great. That could mean anything from a couple of hours to days of searching every ravine and patch of brush along the Canadian River.

They drove in silence for a few more miles before

Cole said, "This is weird. You're supposed to do all the talking, and I'm supposed to just sit here."

"I thought you'd like the change."

"Me too." Cole's forehead knitted as if it pained him to admit, "I sorta miss the babbling. Takes the pressure off me."

"Sorry."

There was a weighty pause, then Cole said again, "Me too."

Well, shit. They weren't just talking about the lack of conversation anymore. But Hank had come home to make amends, so he might as well get on with it. "You had no choice. I broke the law. And I forced the whole crew to lie to the cops to cover my ass."

Cole frowned. "We had a meeting, and everyone agreed being fired was punishment enough under the circumstances. Even Tyrell."

After he'd broken Hank's jaw for messing with his daughter.

Mariah Swift—gorgeous, smart, irresistible—and at *almost* seventeen, two months shy of legal no matter how old she looked or acted. Hank had been toast the first time she smiled at him, and with his standard lack of judgment and self-control, he'd decided it didn't count if all he did was kiss her.

The law didn't see it that way. Neither did her father. If it hadn't been for Cole and Shawnee and the others persuading the cops that it was nothing but a little family squabble among the Jacobs crew, Hank could have served a mandatory two-year sentence. Been required to register as a sexual offender everywhere he went for the rest of his life. The Texas statute made no exceptions for idiots who thought they were in love.

But his friends had. Hank hadn't realized they'd all sat down, discussed the matter, and unanimously voted to protect him. He wasn't quite sure what to do with that knowledge.

"That should have been the end of it," Cole said.

It would have been, if Hank had kept his mouth shut. But no. He'd gone tearing off to Florida to spend the fall proving—all by himself, screw you very much—that he deserved to fight bulls at the best rodeos in the Southeastern Circuit. And he'd had the next year's contracts nailed down when he'd seen, via goddamn Facebook, that Mariah had celebrated her all-important birthday with a new beau. She hadn't been waiting for Hank, as he'd imagined. She'd *never* seen him as anything more than a summer fling.

He'd reacted badly—go figure pouring his woes into an ear that wasn't sympathetic or discreet. By the time the story circled back, it had been embellished to the point that his prospective employer had declared he wouldn't let some pervert anywhere near his fourteen-year-old granddaughter and offered to *escort* Hank out of the state.

That's when it had sunk in. It wasn't the law, or Tyrell, or Cole, or even Mariah who was out of line. It was Hank. Reality had finally bitch-slapped him hard enough to get his attention...and send him reeling.

Too far the other direction, Bing insisted. Yes, he'd screwed up, but he wasn't nearly as bad as he made himself out to be. Hank wasn't so sure. He had, however, promised he wouldn't waste time brooding, so he summed it all up by saying, "It was my own fault."

Cole jerked a nod, staring straight ahead. Hank let out a long, silent breath. Lord love pickups, where two men could have a serious conversation with no risk of eye contact. Cole jabbed a button on the radio and filled the cab with the sound of the morning Texas ag report — cattle and grain markets, weather conditions, the usual feed-and-seed commercials.

Hank's throat tightened. He'd hated this station when he was stuck riding along with his dad, fingers twitching to dial in some indie rock from Amarillo. The same reporters had been going through the same routine for so long, Hank would know those voices if he heard them on a crowded street in New York City.

This morning, they sounded like home.

Chapter 8

GRACE HAD JUST FINISHED FEEDING THE HORSES and roping cattle when Shawnee came roaring down the gravel road, hours before their scheduled practice session. Grace hurried to meet her as the pickup lurched to a stop.

"What's wrong?" she demanded when Shawnee rolled down her window.

"Johnny Brookman got bucked off last night and broke his shoulder."

"Hank's dad?" Grace's brain shifted into athletic trainer mode. Did broken shoulder mean scapula, humerus, clavicle... "How serious?"

"Just his collarbone. He's in surgery." Shawnee gestured toward the passenger seat. "Get in."

Grace blinked. "Where are we going?"

"Out to his ranch. Someone's gotta do the chores and stuff."

"But..."

"Get a move on, sweet cheeks. Cole left an hour ago, and I told him I'd be on my way as soon as I grabbed you and some groceries."

Grace did as ordered, but as she fastened her seat belt, she said, "I don't know anything about cattle."

"Fine. You can cook. It seems like that's all I do, trying to keep Cole fed, especially since he can't go next door and mooch cookies." Shawnee scowled ferociously. "The world is *not* a better place since Miz Iris went low carb."

———∿∿∿———

Hank could feel the years slipping backward as they made the twelve-mile drive from Earnest. The flat plain above the river valley was a patchwork of farm fields with towering center-pivot irrigation systems, many brilliant green with winter cover crops and dotted with cattle. The Dennerts had put up a new hay shed, he noticed, and Brandy Gilman must've had a baby a while back, judging by the toys scattered on the lawn of her single-wide trailer.

But a faded wood sign bolted to an iron wagon wheel still marked the driveway of the Brookman ranch. Looking around the yard, Hank felt like he was stepping out of a time machine instead of Cole's pickup. There was his old half-ton Chevy, parked in its usual spot. And over by the corral, the same four-door dually pickup and battered stock trailer were backed up to the chute, as if still waiting to load the steers he and his dad had gathered that last morning. And Hank's boots had barely hit the ground before a dog came streaking around the back of the barn.

"Mabel!" He crouched and threw his arms around her wriggling body as she tried to lick his face. At least someone here had missed him. Then a second body slammed into him in a flurry of thrashing legs and rooting head. Mabel growled and snapped, barely missing Hank's nose.

The white dog dodged out of Mabel's reach, and Cole managed to snag her collar. He rubbed her ears and she keeled over, exposing her belly. "After last night, Spider might be looking for a new home. She's a half-sister to Mabel, but your dad says she doesn't seem to have any cowdog in her."

Or his dad didn't have a clue how much work had gone into making Mabel a cowdog. Johnny hadn't witnessed the sessions at the Jacobs arena with a few calves, a very young Mabel on a long leash, and Hank running his ass off while Cole showed him how to teach the dog to respond to basic commands: *come by, away to me, walk up*, and most important, *down*. Cole said as long as a dog had a decent set of brakes, you could stop 'em before they really made a mess of things.

Hank would bet his dad had turned Spider loose and expected her to learn by following Mabel—who snapped the pup's head off every time she took a wrong step. He gave the white dog a sympathetic rub. *I know how you feel, kid*.

Meanwhile, the horses had come up to the fence to see who might be bringing them grain. Hank recognized the brown gelding, Ranger, and the older black mare they'd dubbed Tick because she swelled up like her namesake at the sight of good feed.

He nodded toward a pretty sorrel mare. "She's the one that bucked him off?"

"Yep. He calls her Ruby." Cole walked over and plucked a halter from a fence post beside the gate. "You go grab some warmer clothes. I'll feed these guys."

Hank hesitated, then turned and strode toward the house, the dogs racing circles around him, but paused when he opened the door. The house smelled wrong. Dust and dog and stagnant air, as if his dad had been gone for a month. And when Hank opened the closet in the mudroom, his old chore coat was on its usual hook, with his wool winter cap hung over the top and his insulated leather gloves in the bin above, as if he'd tossed them there yesterday.

Everything as he'd left it, but not waiting for him specifically. Just…stalled. As if the whole place had dropped into some weird limbo. Spider and the young mare, Ruby, were the only signs that time hadn't ground to a complete halt—and Johnny Brookman along with it.

Or Hank was reading way too much into the fact that his dad hadn't cleaned out a damn closet. He pushed his hair out of his face, tugged the standard rancher's wool cap down low over his ears, and went out to find Cole tossing hay into mangers in the barn. The trip hopper feeder mounted on the flatbed of the chore pickup was already full to the brim with cake—the large pellets of compressed grain with vitamin and mineral supplements that were the cow equivalent of PowerBars.

Cole checked the settings on the control panel. "Five pounds."

"What's he got out on the wheat field?"

"Two hundred stocker calves, he said, and three pounds apiece."

Hank did the math in his head. Six hundred total pounds of feed, dumped out five pounds at a time. "A hundred and twenty clicks."

Cole nodded and headed around the back of the pickup. "You drive."

Hank blinked at him, stunned. Between rodeos and bouncing around the Jacobs ranch, he and Cole must've traveled ten thousand miles together, with Cole *always* in the driver's seat. But now he planted himself on the passenger's side.

Well. Okay then.

When Hank opened his door, both dogs piled in, a ball of hair, legs, snarls, and yips. Mabel's tail swatted Hank in the face as he tried to squeeze onto the seat. Cole got an arm around Spider and pinned her to his side. Mabel plunked down next to Hank with an expression that clearly said, *Hah!*

The last three years had not been kind to the chore pickup. The clutch slipped as he started out, and the front U-joints were clanking. Bouncing over mounded bunches of big bluestem and slamming into badger holes hidden in the switchgrass took a toll, and it wouldn't be like Johnny to fix anything until it completely gave up the ghost.

Half a mile down the highway, Hank turned onto an approach that led to an irrigated field of winter wheat, planted in late summer to provide grazing for stocker calves: four- to five-hundred-pound weanlings purchased in the fall, then sold in the spring at twice the size. They were a fairly reliable way to increase a ranch's income unless the market went bottoms up, or feed prices skyrocketed, or the weather went nuts, or whatever.

There always seemed to be a *whatever* when it came to cows.

These were the juvenile delinquents of the bovine world, mobbing the gate at the sight of the feed truck, pushing, shoving, calling one another stupid mothersuckers, and ripe for any excuse to go tearing around trashing stuff.

Hank dropped one forearm over his crotch and rolled down the window. "Push 'em back, Mabel."

The dog used his lap for a launch pad—hence the protective measures—as she vaulted out and hit the ground running. The calves scattered when she flew under the gate, nipping noses and toes to clear enough space to get the pickup inside.

Spider practically turned upside down, but Cole maintained his grip. "Your dad said whatever we do, don't let her out with the calves. Last time he ended up with cattle running through the fence and down the highway."

Hank closed the window, then grabbed Spider and hauled her over to his side of the pickup while Cole got out to open the gate. Cole. Riding shotgun. Opening gates while Hank drove. If the dog hadn't been all but clawing holes in his leg, he might think he was still dreaming.

"Down!" he commanded.

Spider licked his face. Sighing, Hank shoved her off so he could drive through the gate. Cole shut it behind them, ambled over to switch on the feeder's electric motor, and waved a hand to indicate that Hank should go ahead. The conveyor in the bottom of the feeder's tank began to rattle cubes of cake into the hopper box. Hank put the pickup in low gear and started off at a steady pace as the metal trapdoor opened to dump a five-pound pile of feed, then slapped shut.

One click.

He began to count automatically. Hank had done this so many times he'd sometimes caught himself counting the taps of a windblown branch against the side of that old camper in Montana. Some people preferred to use the electronic counter mounted on the dashboard, but it had stopped working before he was big enough to see over the steering wheel.

As the mass of jostling bodies rocked the pickup, he kept an eye out for animals that hung back or had a droop to their ears, the earliest signs of illness. Meanwhile, Cole strolled through the herd, examining them close up for a limp that might mean hoofrot, or a tear-streaked face that might be pink eye.

One hundred and eleven, one hundred and twelve, one hundred and thirteen...

At a hundred and twenty, Hank stopped the pickup and started to jump out. Spider slammed into him, and he barely grabbed a leg before she escaped.

"Down!" Hank barked, shoving her to her belly with a hand on the middle of her back before he scooped her up and stuffed her into the pickup. Meanwhile, the feeder had continued clacking away. He hit the off switch, but a mound of cake had accumulated while he wrestled the dog. Crap. Hank squatted to scoop up the excess.

"Leave it," Cole said. "An extra ten pounds won't hurt anything."

Was he kidding? Hank eyed Cole as if he'd sprouted a second head. "Since when? I swear, you used to make me count out the kernels of grain when I was feeding your bucking stock."

"That's different. They're athletes." Cole made a sheepish face. "And I've learned to pick my battles since Shawnee came along."

Hank laughed. "I'll bet."

Cole's grin was downright devious. "Sometimes I still do it just 'cuz it's fun to watch her get wound up."

An odd pain twisted through Hank at the easy humor and affection in Cole's voice. He was...happy. Not just with his life, but with himself. All it took was a woman who could love him for exactly who he was—and thirty-three years to find her. Measured by that stick, Hank had eight years to go, assuming he had smartened up enough to recognize what was right under his nose.

If dating Grace had been a possibility, would he have looked at her differently back in school? She hadn't been allowed to go to movies or dances, and sneaking around was not an option with Mr. McKenna stalking the halls that he kept polished to a high sheen. God save the fool he'd caught scribbling curse words on the bathroom wall, let alone anyone who touched his daughter. Some days it took all of Hank's nerve just to sit across a cafeteria table from her. Their friendship had played out under surveillance and within ironclad boundaries that hadn't left room for so much as a wayward thought. Would he have had them, given the space?

Luckily, he'd never had a chance to find out, or he might have lost Grace sooner.

Hank dropped the cake pellets and stood, then paused with his hand on the pickup door. "Why am I driving?"

"It's your ranch." Cole paced off toward the gate, leaving Hank to laugh in disbelief.

His? Yeah, right. Maybe marriage was making Cole soft in the head after all.

Hank wasn't a bit surprised to find his saddle on the same old rack in the barn, but he got another stab in the gut when he saw the empty spaces where Melanie's stuff should have been. It was yet more proof that she was really, truly gone.

Cole threw one of the other saddles on Ruby.

"Are you sure that's a good idea?" Hank asked.

"Johnny said she's never bucked before. She should be fine as long as that dog doesn't get underfoot again."

Hank led Ranger into the back corral. The air was damp and laced with scents of grass and brush and earth that were indefinably different than the Montana range. They triggered a rush of memories…and longing. He loved this land. The endless stretches of sky, and riding out on a good horse with his dog loping alongside. He would have been happy to make this his home base forever, if he could have found a way to coexist with his father.

He might've even learned to tolerate the stupid cows.

Chapter 9

THE BROOKMAN RANCH WAS NOTHING LIKE GRACE had imagined.

She had woven elaborate fantasies where she was a real cowgirl and rode the range with Hank, checking fences, trailing cows, pausing beside the river to share the canteen and a stolen kiss. Hokey, yes, but everything she knew about cattle, she'd learned from old movies in the library's DVD collection.

Her father did not believe in television. Or the Internet. Or anything that might cause his children to consider viewpoints other than his own.

Even Grace had heard about the Brookmans, though. They were local legends, generations of the best ropers and horse trainers in Texas going back to Hank's great-grandfather, who'd traveled all the way to Madison Square Garden to compete in the earliest version of the National Finals Rodeo. It was natural to assume their ranch would be steeped in that history, a place of towering oaks, weathered wood, rocking chairs on shady porches, and horses dozing at a hitching rail.

In reality, the place couldn't have had less personality if it had been designed by an architect who specialized in tract housing.

There was a midsized manufactured home with no landscaping beyond a few sad-looking bushes, and a steel-sided pole barn built from a trucked-in kit. Even the corrals were ugly—heavy pipe posts with oilfield sucker rod for rails. Beyond the iron wheel that served as a signpost, there was nothing rustic in sight. Everything original had been consumed by the fire and replaced by whatever was quickest and easiest, but someone should've cared enough to spruce the place up a little in the thirty years since.

The saddest sight, though, was the arena. Weeds had grown up in the fence lines and roping boxes, and cattle munched at round bale feeders evenly spaced down the middle of what had once been the plowed surface.

Shawnee followed her gaze and shook her head. "It's a damn waste. Johnny Brookman is a genius when it comes to rope horses."

"Hard to do alone, I guess."

Shawnee made a sound that was equal parts irritation and agreement and headed for the back door of the house. Grace was uncomfortable invading someone else's personal space, but Shawnee barged through the mudroom and into the kitchen with the assurance of someone who'd visited often. The scarred wooden table was covered in junk mail, feed-store flyers, crumpled receipts, and at least three months' worth of *The Cattleman* magazine.

Shawnee dumped her trio of reusable grocery bags on the narrow island separating living room from kitchen. One end of the couch was heaped with unfolded laundry, and beside the recliner, a coffee mug and an open carton of Oreos sat next to the television remote.

"Geezus," Shawnee muttered. "You might as well put a sign up that says *pathetic divorced male*."

"It's not as bad as I expected." Grace shuddered at

the memory of drinking glasses in her brother's apartment that had been left so long that whatever was inside looked—and smelled—like gray sewage. These countertops appeared to have been wiped recently, and a cereal bowl and a few plates were stacked on the drainboard.

"He pays the neighbor lady to come over and clean every couple of weeks." Shawnee peered at a collection of photos on the closest wall. "Look at those baby faces."

Grace looked, and was confronted with a picture of Melanie that could have been Maddie's beaming face. Her daughter had definitely inherited the Brookman genes. Grace turned away to dump her bags on the island and peek inside drawers and cupboards in search of pots, pans, and cooking utensils.

Shawnee wandered through the living room and down the hall, opening a door on the right. "The bathroom is safe."

The refrigerator was too, stocked with only canned pork and beans, a partly used package of hamburger, the remnants of a take-and-bake lasagna, and a Smoke Shack takeout bag. *Mmm. Brisket.*

Shawnee's phone chimed. She glanced at the message and headed for the door. "Cole wants me to bring the side-by-side and fencing tools down to the pasture. We probably won't be back until around one o'clock."

She thumped out the door, leaving Grace almost two hours to manufacture enough food for four, including Cole. Shawnee hadn't said who he'd wrangled to bring with him—probably one or two of the Jacobs hands—but having grown up in a family of nine, Grace could throw together a large meal in short order. Once she'd gathered the necessary tools, she sautéed vegetables in a Dutch oven, added cubed, cooked chicken, then poured in stock and a bag of frozen southern-style hash browns, one of her mother's favorite time-savers.

Now for dessert. She dumped canned peaches in a large pie pan, sprinkled them with cinnamon and brown sugar, tossed in a few dabs of butter, and whipped up a simple batter of flour, sugar, cinnamon, and milk to pour over the top. While the stew simmered and the cobbler filled the house with the mouthwatering aroma of cinnamon and peaches, she threw together a pasta salad and stirred up a batch of biscuits, ready to slide into the oven while her diners washed up.

There. That would do. She gave the stew another stir before tackling the mess on the kitchen table. Receipts went in one careful pile on the island, magazines and newspapers in another, and mail in a third. Everything else went in a fourth pile, including a used plastic syringe, a couple of yellow ear tags, and half a roll of elastic veterinary bandage. After she'd wiped away dust, smears of barbecue sauce, and a sprinkling of hay, she found silverware and plates to lay the table.

Satisfied, she headed for the bathroom. Three other doors led off the hallway, the one at the end left open to reveal a master bedroom. The others would belong to Melanie…and Hank.

Temptation nudged Grace with sticky fingers. She could just take a peek…

She marched herself straight to the bathroom, then right on back to the living room. Once there, though, it was impossible to ignore the photos. There was Melanie, propped in front of her daddy in a shiny new trophy saddle at the famous Pendleton Roundup with her hair pulled up into sassy ponytails tied with pink ribbons to match her boots, and that smile so much like Maddie's.

And talk about smiles—back in the day, Johnny Brookman had had one that could make a girl's heart flutter. Grace had only seen him being large, dark, and grim at school events, but here his eyes brimmed with laughter and a hint of the mischief that used to constantly dance in Hank's.

Damn life for taking the joy out of them, turning all that potential to pain. And damn them for letting it. People shook their heads at Hank, the way he'd squandered the opportunities handed to him, but how was that any worse than his father? Johnny had had three decades to recover from the devastation of the fire, but it didn't look as if he'd even tried to revive his rodeo career. Grace had worked so hard to become a roper she couldn't fathom being that good and just walking away.

She'd barely known the sport existed until the McKenna clan had moved to the Panhandle after her daddy had been hired as head custodian by the Earnest school district. From day one, she'd been awed by the girls who climbed out of beat-up pickups to saunter past with long, loose-hipped strides. *Bring it on*, their body language shouted. *I can rope it or ride it better and faster than you.*

Grace had immediately decided that somehow, some way, she was going to be a cowgirl.

She'd had to wait until college to begin turning that vow into reality. Had had to beg a horse trainer on the outskirts of Canyon to hire a clueless town girl, first to muck stalls, then to groom horses, and finally to be his exercise rider. Though rodeo wasn't his specialty, he had taught her to swing and throw a rope, using a hay bale as a dummy calf. And he'd located Betsy for her, lounging around a pasture after the teenager who'd gotten her from Shawnee had lost interest in roping.

She'd had to scrape up money for feed, beg for opportunities to rope, and pay by the run, but she'd stuck with it. It made her vaguely sick to see all the signs of a Brookman rodeo legacy being allowed to wither and die. How did someone go from that proud champion, showing off his new saddle and his precious daughter, to an arena overrun by ragweed and thistles?

And how did Hank go from a laughing kid in an Earnest Badgers football uniform—seventh grade, and so skinny Grace had been sure he'd get snapped right in two on every tackle—to a flinty-eyed man who seemed like he'd forgotten how to smile?

At the rattle of the door, voices, and the scuff of boots in the mudroom, she spun around and hustled toward the kitchen.

"It smells great," a familiar deep voice said, but the man Grace crashed into as she rounded the island was not Cole.

Hank grabbed her arms as her nose practically mashed into his chest. Recognition blasted through her at the scent of Irish Spring and warm male skin that had forever defined Hank. Like bees catching a whiff of clover on the breeze, her hormones buzzed to life. She jerked away. "What are *you* doing here?"

His mouth twisted. "You know what they say about bad pennies."

She did. And damn her fluttering pulse, because Hank seemed determined to keep turning up when she least expected him.

Chapter 10

IT WAS THE BEST MEAL HANK HAD EVER EATEN AT his family's kitchen table.

Partly because he'd never been this kind of hungry when he'd lived here—working a full morning with nothing in his stomach but a bowl of generic raisin bran—but mostly because he'd been raised on dry pot roast, rubbery potatoes, and warmed-over hamburger casseroles, with ketchup accounting for ninety percent of their vegetables in an effort to make the rest edible.

His dad had been close to helpless in the kitchen, but Hank could swear his mother did it on purpose, revenge for her forced indenture as a ranch wife. Until he had started making his own breakfast, he hadn't realized it took effort to stir together water with mix from a box and somehow create leathery pancakes. Their lot had improved some when Melanie took over the cooking, but she'd never served biscuits that melted in your mouth like these.

He helped himself to a third, using half to mop up every drop of gravy from the chicken stew as Grace dished up whatever made the kitchen smell like sugary cinnamon heaven. When she set the plate in front of him, Hank nearly swooned. Peach cobbler with a scoop of Blue Bell butter pecan ice cream. He moaned a little when he took the first bite.

Shawnee grinned. "That good, huh?"

Hank could only nod.

A smile tipped the corners of Grace's mouth as she gathered the empty dinner plates to rinse and stack in the dishwasher. Springy curls had escaped from her ponytail to frame her face, which was flushed and glowing from the heat of the kitchen.

A lot like she'd looked as they'd tumbled into her bed that Thanksgiving weekend, three years ago.

Grace was small, but not delicate except for her pixie face. She reminded Hank of the Quarter Horses his dad had preferred when he was roping, not too tall or flashy, but put together in a way a man might not appreciate until he looked real close and ran his hands over the firm, compact curves to feel the quiver of response. He'd been fascinated by her skin, so fine-grained that his palms felt like sandpaper against it. He couldn't stop stroking her arm, her shoulder, her hip as they lounged against a pile of pillows, wrapped together in nothing but a comforter with a Texas A&M football game on the dinky television in her college apartment.

While Grace had alternately cursed, cheered, and groaned at the players, Hank had tried to count the freckles on her nose. She kept swatting his finger away, declaring that she hated the damn things. And he'd made the mistake of telling her they were cute. Among the many, *many* things Hank hadn't grasped back then was the fact that, in the mind of a woman, *cute* was the opposite of sexy, or sophisticated, or unforgettable.

He hadn't forgotten anything about Grace. Hadn't even tried. Those hours with her had been too precious and real to erase. He remembered in painful detail how neatly she'd fit in his arms. How her smile had made him feel ten feet tall at a time when he was lower than the proverbial snake's belly.

If he'd stayed, would she have lifted him up? Or would he have dragged her down? It had been too soon after the disaster with Mariah to take a chance. What if he couldn't get his career back on track? Worse, what if the ugly black mark next to his name rubbed off on Grace?

So he'd forced himself to walk away and leave no promises behind. In the cold, lonely weeks that followed, he'd somehow resisted the urge to send a text begging to see her when he came back at Christmas. He'd given her no reason to suspect that he craved the sound of her voice, her quick laugh, and the sense she gave him that everything might be okay.

But she'd still tracked him down at the Lone Steer Saloon.

All he remembered clearly about that New Year's Eve was making the decision to drink until he was incapable of obsessing about Grace. And how his heart had leapt at the sight of her. And then his anger. He'd fought so hard to stay away—for her own good, dammit—and now there she was, standing right in front of him. Where was her pride, not to mention her common sense? Grace was supposed to be so smart. Couldn't she see that he was a nonstop wreck looking for a place to happen?

Well, he'd showed her—and everyone else.

His fork scraped the plate, and he realized he'd polished off the rest of his cobbler without even tasting it. One more good thing he'd failed to appreciate until it was gone.

"…while you and Grace find those last two strays," Cole said.

Hank jerked to attention. "What?"

Grace was staring at Cole, her eyes wide and water dripping from her hands onto the floor.

"Pay attention, buckwheat," Shawnee said. "There's half a dozen cull cows in the arena that are supposed to go to Hereford for tomorrow's sale. We've got some, too, so we're gonna go load our truck, then swing by here and pick up yours on the way."

And leave Grace here? Alone with him? Before he could point out the many reasons that was a terrible idea, Grace said, "I don't know anything about cows."

Shawnee frowned impatiently. "You can ride, you can rope, and you help gather the steers out of Tori's pasture. This is the same thing in a bigger field."

"But—"

Hank cut in. "I can manage."

"Maybe, but it'll be a lot easier with help," Cole said.

"Not to mention safer than beating that brush alone," Shawnee added.

Hank glared at her. "My dad does it all the time."

"And he's lucky we didn't find his dead body out there in the round pen." Cole shoved away from the table. "Put her on Tick. That ol' mare could damn near go out and gather up a cow by herself."

As far as Cole and Shawnee were concerned, that was that. They thanked Grace for dinner, grabbed their coats, and left. Hank and Grace stood frozen in mutual consternation as Cole's pickup rumbled out of the driveway, leaving Shawnee's behind so Grace could head home whenever she was ready.

The clock above the kitchen sink *tick-tick-ticked* in the protracted silence. Grace turned back to the sink and grabbed a scouring pad to attack the stew pot.

"I don't need you to come with me," Hank said.

Her soft mouth went stubborn. "Like Shawnee said, I'm not totally useless."

"I didn't say—" Hank stopped, took a breath, and blew it out. There was no tactful way to say, *Listen Grace, I appreciate the offer, but I don't trust myself not to make a complete jackass of myself in some way or another.*

And besides, Cole was right—as usual. The two cows still missing were the cagiest of the bunch, and more likely to fight than run if he sicced Mabel on them. They'd run a single horse and rider in circles around whatever willow thicket they were hiding in. If all Grace did was block one escape route, she'd be a huge help.

"There's extra hats and gloves in the closet." He waved a hand toward the mudroom. "Grab whatever you need."

She waved the scouring pad at the stack of dishes. "I should finish clearing up."

And he should offer to help, but the quarters in the narrow, cramped kitchen were way too damn close. "Go ahead. I'll catch Tick and find a saddle that'll fit you."

She made a face. "It'll have to be whatever Melanie rode in grade school. That's the last time she was this short."

No comment. But as Hank shrugged into his coat and yanked on his wool cap, he couldn't help but recall that Grace's legs had fit around him just fine.

Chapter 11

GRACE WAS WELL AWARE THAT SHE WAS NO RANCH hand, but she'd assumed she could get out of the barn with her dignity intact.

And then Hank handed her a pair of chaps. "You'll need these if we have to go through any brush."

They were actually chinks, meant to stop just below the knee, but they nearly reached Grace's ankles. She eyed them with consternation, never having had a reason to wear the things. Watching Hank from the corner of her eye as he donned his with thoughtless ease, she figured out which end was up and got the waist buckled, but the legs were a different matter. While he went to tie Spider up, she reached down and behind as she'd seen him do, fumbling blindly for straps and buckles that did not seem to match up. Mabel observed with interest and what looked suspiciously like amusement, but didn't offer any suggestions.

Grace was bent double trying to look at the back of her own thigh when Hank cleared his throat. "Problem?" he asked.

She glanced upside down under her arm to see if he was laughing at her too, but nothing showed on his impassive face. "I can't find the buckle that goes with this," she admitted, flicking the bottom strap.

"You missed the one at the top, so they're all wonky."

"Oh, I—" The words died in her throat when Hank

strode over to crouch behind her. His fingers brushed the inside of her thigh, shooting electricity straight up her leg. "You don't have to…" she choked out.

She tried to step away. He held her in place, hobbled by the chaps, as he unfastened what she'd done wrong and tugged the leather flap into the correct position, millimeters below her crotch. "These things haven't been used in a while," he said. "The straps are stiff and shrunk up so the tongues will hardly fit in the holes."

Oh God. Tongues. Fitting into…eep! His knuckles pressed into the bottom curve of her butt cheek as he wrestled with the uncooperative buckle.

"I…uh…see." She tried closing her eyes, but that only made her more intensely aware of every brush of his hands, mere inches below a part of her body that, judging by its response, didn't know the difference between old Hank and new Hank, or why it shouldn't be getting excited about either of them—especially when he didn't seem to be the least bit bothered, damn him.

She bit her lip as his fingers slid underneath and along the strap for one final adjustment. "I didn't expect you to rush out to help your dad."

"You either."

She stifled a gasp when he transferred his attention to the top of her other leg. "A person doesn't say no to Shawnee."

"Or Cole." Hank tugged the last strap into place and stood. "There you go."

"Thanks."

He turned to yank his horse's bridle rein from the

tie rail, then curse when the free end flipped around the pipe like a whiplash and whacked the brim of his cap.

"Careful there," she warned. "Wouldn't want to put an eye out."

He muttered something that sounded profane and strode out, the bay trailing behind. Grace stuck out her tongue at his retreating back, then waddled over to untie her own horse and follow wherever he led.

~~~

Hank barreled out into the corral, hoping the chilly wind would cool his jets, but he couldn't stop feeling his hand sliding between Grace's legs, and seeing her firm, round butt—perfectly framed by those chaps—so close to his face he could've taken a bite.

He kicked a dried horse turd across the corral. Then another. Then scattered a whole pile. Shit, shit, *shit*.

Tick's hooves clopped on the hard-packed dirt, and the fringes of the leather chinks slapped against Grace's legs as she walked out behind him. Before turning, Hank tugged the brim of his cap low over his eyes, in case any part of what was simmering in his blood showed. The whole point of this pilgrimage was to make amends, not repeat the same mistakes.

He had yet to get over hurting her the first time. How the hell would he live with himself if he did it again?

~~~

Grace was so busy trying to read Hank's thoughts from the stiff set of his shoulders that she didn't realize they'd reached the bluff until he reined up at the edge. She sucked in a breath. "Wow."

"Yeah." He folded gloved hands on his saddle horn and gazed out over the landscape spread at their feet, his face softening.

Below them, the silver thread of the Canadian River wound through a wide, flat valley framed by the breaks—row upon row of jagged hills and steep ravines carved into the bluffs. The recent frosts had cracked open Mother Nature's paint box, splashing color across the landscape. Pastel pinks and grays glowed in the exposed earth, and the rippling grass was every shade from burnished gold to crimson to near purple, set off by the brilliant yellow of a scattering of trees that had dressed up for fall, and patches of shamrock green where grazing cattle had clipped the bottomland as smooth as a lawn.

"Where are the cows?" she asked.

"Cole and I pushed them up around the bend this morning, away from where the fence was down, and gave 'em a little extra feed to keep them out of the way."

Grace took an appreciative lungful of the wind-whipped air, unsullied by undertones of asphalt, exhaust, and humanity. It would be heavenly to get on a horse and ride through all of this whenever she wanted.

Hank pointed toward a cluster of smallish trees that choked the mouth of a narrow ravine on the opposite side of the river. "We'll start there and work our way down the river."

"What do you want me to do?"

"See that ravine to the right?" Hank indicated one that was wider and less clogged with scrub. "You ride up that one, then down the other and block the trail above the willows. Then I'll come in from the bottom and flush the cows out...if they're there. Most places you can't tell without beating the brush for them. If they're not in that patch, you ride across the top to the next ravine, I ride across the bottom, and we keep going until we find them."

Whoa. There were dozens of ravines and brush patches that could be potential hiding places. How long was this going to take? She'd figured on stumbling through an hour or so in Hank's company, not the rest of the day. But if she was on the top of the bluff and he was on the bottom, she wouldn't have to worry about making small talk, so no big deal, right?

Right.

So why, as Hank led the way down the trail, was she so sure this wasn't going to be as easy as he made it sound?

Chapter 12

DOWN BELOW, THE TRAIL CURVED THROUGH A stretch of stirrup-high, pale-gold sideoats, seeds dangling from the graceful downward curve of the heads. Grace let out an embarrassing squeak when a flock of quail blasted out of the grass practically under her horse's nose. Tick barely blinked. After a short burst of furious flight, the birds glided another fifty yards and disappeared again into the cover of the grass.

The dog started to bound after them, but Hank said, "No, Mabel."

She stopped, tail waving as she stared longingly after the quail, then heaved a doggy sigh and turned back to fall in behind Hank's horse. She perked up again a few minutes later and raced onto the expanse of hard-packed red sand that flanked the Canadian River, diminished to a sluggish stream by the dry summer months. As they splashed across, Grace couldn't help grinning. Now *this* was more like those movies of hers.

Hank waved her to the right. "That's your trail."

He veered left, and at a cluck of Hank's tongue, Ranger broke into an easy lope. Grace did the same, and Tick settled into a smooth, rocking pace. In no time at all, they topped the bluff and trotted across to the next ravine. This trail was narrower and steeper, the sage crowding in on either side to scratch at her boots as the mare picked her way down. Grace peered into the maze of scrubby willows, but as Hank had predicted, it was too thick to make out any cow-shaped shadows.

He was slouched in his saddle below the trees, waiting for Grace to reach the spot where the branches of the willows closed over the trail, creating a low tunnel. The base of the ravine had narrowed to a cut, the sides near vertical. For the last few yards, the passage was barely wide enough for a horse to turn around, and water had oozed from some unseen spring to paint a slick layer of mud over the packed earth.

"Away to me, Mabel!" Branches rustled and snapped as Hank began to push through, searching for the wayward cows.

Grace tightened her hold on the reins, her breath shortening. She didn't like the confined space or the questionable footing. Was she supposed to stand her ground no matter what? Hank would have warned her if these cows were dangerous, wouldn't he? And Cole had said this mare was foolproof. Still, Grace's nerves coiled tighter as Hank and Ranger crashed around inside the willow patch. She hated not being able to see him or whatever might be coming at her—possibly at a high rate of speed—and she startled at Mabel's sudden frenzied barking.

Then there was an ear-splitting shriek, and a monster barreled out of the brush.

Grace caught a horrifying glimpse of rough hair and yellow tusks as the beast careened toward them. Tick squealed and tried to spin away, but her hooves skidded on the mud and she pitched sideways.

No room, no room…

Grace instinctively kicked her feet out of the stirrups and threw herself clear of the falling horse, straight into a clump of sagebrush. She flung her arms over her face to ward off branches that snapped and jabbed but also cushioned her fall. Rolling onto the ground, she lay facedown, stunned, as Tick scrabbled to her feet and stampeded up the trail.

And down in the willows, another large body crashed toward her. *Oh God. There's more!* Grace began clawing blindly up the side of the ravine, but the chinks twisted around her legs and her gloves couldn't get a grip on the steep, crumbling bank, and it was like one of those slow-motion *I'm trying to run but I can't move* nightmares. Her breath came in sobs as the creature bore down on her, and she fought even more desperately to haul herself out of its reach.

Go! Go! Go!

"Grace!" The adrenaline pounding through her blood kept her body moving even after her brain had registered that it was Ranger who'd burst out of the trees. Hank vaulted off the horse and caught Grace by the ankle. She kicked him.

"Ouch! Shit!" Hank jerked his hand back, but the contact had popped the bubble of terror that had consumed all reason.

Slowly Grace's arms stopped churning, her palms and her cheek pressing into the earth as her heart banged against her ribs. She slid down until her boots hit bottom, and only the fact that she was hugging the bank kept her knees from buckling.

"Grace?" In the foggy periphery of her vision she saw Hank reach out, but he didn't touch. "Are you okay?"

She kept her face turned away as she tried to take stock. Thanks to the sagebrush, she had no major bruises that she could feel, and her chaps and heavy coat had protected her from being shredded by sharp branches. Her cheek stung, though, and when she pressed the back of her hand against it, her glove came away smeared with blood.

"Only a scratch," she said, mortified when her voice came out all trembly and weak.

"Let me see," Hank said.

"No."

His hand hovered for a moment, then settled on her shoulder with a gentle tug. "Come on, Grace."

"*No!*" She plastered herself against the bank. "Go away."

"I can't leave you here." The hand on her shoulder tightened impatiently. "What is wrong with you?"

Nothing. Not one damn thing, except her nerves were jangling like fire bells and her breath was trying to hitch and Hank had seen her flailing like a scared hamster trying to climb a glass cage.

And dammit, she did *not* panic.

Hank tried softening his voice. "Grace, would you please—"

"I'm *fine!*" She spun around so fast her elbow connected with his gut, knocking an *Oof!* out of him as he stumbled back.

"Geezus, woman! I'm trying to help."

Unaccountably, that made her want to punch him on purpose. She clenched her fists so tight her knuckles creaked. "You could have started by warning me about that...that...*thing!*"

"I would have if I'd ever run across one here before!" He swiped an arm across his eyes as if he couldn't believe what they'd seen. "Christ. When I realized you'd fallen off right in front of—"

"I did *not* fall off. I jumped."

Hank glared at her. "Do you have any idea how dangerous a feral hog is?"

"I was supposed to let that fat horse squash me instead?"

Her monster was a damn *pig*? Somehow that was ten times worse, even though she'd seen those tusks and… her heart clutched. *Oh God. The horse.*

Grace's anger abruptly fizzled. "You have to go find Tick. If she got hooked…"

"You have to come too. There could be more of them." Hank gestured toward the thicket, which Ranger continued to eye with flared nostrils as Mabel crouched beside him, their ears swiveling in search of any suspicious sound. Grace considered the narrow ravine, the steep trail, and her short legs. It was a well-known fact that feral hogs would eat anything, including small, slow humans.

Hank flipped his reins over Ranger's head and stepped aboard, then kicked his foot out of the left stirrup and held a hand out to Grace. "Get on."

"What?"

Hank gave his hand an impatient shake. "Get on behind me."

"I…don't know how."

"You've never ridden double?"

"Hey! Not all of us grew up on horseback." Grace scowled at Ranger. Why did he have to be so tall? And climbing the horse would require her to practically climb Hank too, since she didn't see anything else to grab on to. "You ride on the back. I'll drive."

"Fine." Hank kept hold of the reins, but hitched himself back to sit behind the cantle.

Okay. Good. But Grace still had to contend with the unfamiliar bulk of the chaps and bones that wanted to collapse into a shuddering pile. And she couldn't see any way to swing her leg over the saddle without waving her butt under Hank's nose. Again.

Ranger, bless his heart, stood stock-still as she grabbed the saddle horn, got her foot hoisted up and into the stirrup, and took a deep breath. So much for fantasies. Not one of her daydreams about Hank and this ranch had included a damn pig.

Chapter 13

HE COULD HAVE GOTTEN HER KILLED.

The tiny part of Hank's brain still capable of logic argued that there was no way he could have known about the hog—when had those bastards moved this far north, and why hadn't Cole told him?—but it was drowned by the echoes of that unearthly shriek.

A sound far too reminiscent of the screams of a distant crowd that leaked in from his nightmares, dragging along the vision of a massive hoof slamming down, square in the middle of a fallen cowboy's back as Hank lunged for the bull's head. Too far away. Too late. Always, forever too late.

Dakota Red Elk had clawed at the ground too, that night in Toppenish, his eyes wild with terror. *My legs. I can't move my legs.*

He would never move them again.

When Hank had seen Grace trying to drag herself up that bank...God, his heart had just disintegrated. Nothing had ever hurt so good as when he'd reached out and she'd kicked him. He'd gotten lucky this time. More precisely, the person who'd been counting on him had gotten lucky.

Distracted, he didn't lean out of the way when Grace heaved herself into the saddle, and the leg she'd intended to swing over the horse landed a roundhouse kick square to his rib cage.

"Shit!" He clamped his heels to keep from being knocked clean off, digging them into Ranger's flanks. Startled, the bay gave a single, high kick that threw Grace up onto his neck. Hank caught a fistful of her coat with one hand and the reins with the other before Ranger could bolt. The gelding danced in a circle as they teetered, a tangle of arms, legs, and curses.

"I…can't…breathe," Grace gasped.

No wonder. The saddle horn was digging into her belly, and Hank had her pinned in place. He started to slide off, but Grace squeaked when she was dragged with him.

Hank stopped. *Damn*. The toe of her boot was hooked in the pocket of his coat. He hitched his hips back to the center of Ranger's rump and took stock. He had a fingernail grip on the reins, his cheek was mashed up against Grace's butt, and even Ranger wasn't going to tolerate this much longer.

She had a double-fisted, white-knuckled grip on Ranger's mane, so Hank let go of her coat and reached down to grab her ankle, prying it out of his pocket and letting it drop so she had a leg on either side of the horse. Better. Now if he could just get himself straightened out…

"'Scuse me," he said as he planted his palm on her left butt cheek and pushed himself upright. She stiffened but didn't try to kick him. "Scoot back," he said.

She wiggled. Grunted. Wiggled some more. Hank got hold of the back strap of her chaps and pulled. She didn't budge.

Her words came in short puffs. "I'm…stuck. Front of my…chaps. Over…the horn."

Oh. Shit. That was not good. Hung up like that, if Ranger did bolt, her head would end up between his front feet. Hank slid off the side, thankfully keeping his feet under him. Ranger shied a step, his eyes rolling toward the woman who was draped over his neck, clinging like a monkey. Her coat was rucked up to her armpits, and the brim of her hat had been shoved around so the earflap covered her eyes and tufts of curly hair stuck out every which way.

A wild bubble of laughter swelled in Hank's throat. He swallowed hard. There was no time for hysterics. He eased the rein over the horse's head and unclipped one end, then put a calming hand on Ranger's shoulder while he tried to figure out how to get Grace loose.

Damn. No matter what angle he studied it from, there appeared to be only one option. "I have to lift you up and over the horn, then catch you before you hit the ground."

"Okay."

"I'm going to have to grab you by the crotch."

"Oh." Her hips twitched, as if in protest, but she said, "Well, uh, male cheerleaders do that all the time, right? No big deal."

Yeah. That sounded convincing. He shucked his gloves, wrapped the end of the rein around his hand, and stepped so close that her face was buried in the curve of his neck. "Hang on to my shoulders."

She untangled her fingers from Ranger's mane and latched on to Hank. Her breath was hot against his skin, and he both felt and heard her soft *eek!* as he slid his hand, palm up, between her thigh and the saddle.

"Ready?" he asked.

Her chin dug into his shoulder as she nodded. Before either of them had time to think about exactly what he was grabbing, he slid his hand to the center, hoisted her hips up, and then pulled forward.

She dropped like a rock, her weight slamming into his chest. He went down hard on his butt, then his back, Grace sprawled on top of him. Ranger shied, but Hank kept his grip on the rein. The horse stopped, snorting and wide-eyed as he stared down at them.

Hank let his head flop back and his arms splay, spread-eagled in the dirt, limp with relief. He'd done it. She was safe.

Then Grace started to shake, tremors that rocked her body as she made a choked, hiccupping sound. Oh shit. She was crying. Was she hurt? Scared half to death? Fixing to slam a knee into the same part of his anatomy as he'd just—

Her laughter burst out, ringing in his ears and echoing off the sides of the ravine. "Oh…my…God!" she gasped. "That was so *ridiculous*. If anyone had seen—"

She broke off, quaking against him, and the vibration broke something loose inside him.

This wasn't funny, dammit. Except it was, especially when he lifted his head to see her blindfolded by her cock-eyed hat, hair sticking out every which way and giggling her fool head off.

A deep, uncontrollable belly laugh rocked him. And the harder he laughed, the harder Grace laughed, and then Mabel started jumping and yipping around them, eager to join the fun, and they laughed even harder, helpless to fend her off when her tongue swiped at their faces. The horse stared down at them as if they'd lost their ever-loving minds. Maybe Hank had. Exhilaration burned through him—sudden, irrational—and sent his heart soaring for no reason at all.

Sweet Jesus, it had been a long time since he'd laughed this way—bone-shaking, uncontrollable laughter that left him as drained and limp as mind-blowing sex. The last time Grace had been sprawled across his chest, there had been nothing between them but sweat-damp skin and two hearts hammering against each other as they floated back down to earth.

Slowly, the laughter trailed away and reality, that cold-hearted bitch, elbowed aside the all-too-fleeting sense of joy. Grace lifted her head, and Hank tugged her cap straight, then skimmed his fingers across her forehead to push aside the hair that straggled in her eyes. Her nose was red and her face was smeared with mud... and blood.

He had imagined a thousand ways, a million words to explain what he'd done, why he'd done it, but in the end there were only three that mattered. "I'm sorry, Grace."

She went still as a rabbit frozen in a spotlight, and her throat moved as she swallowed.

"Not just for this." His fingertip rested lightly below the thin, red scratch on her cheek. "I shouldn't have—"

"Don't." She clamped a gloved hand over his mouth. "Hearing you say how much you wish you'd never seen me naked will *not* make me feel better."

He pushed her hand off his face. "That's not what—"

"Just stop." She climbed to her feet, yanking her coat down to her hips. "That ol' horse was dead on arrival. I do not want to beat it, or perform an autopsy, thank you very much. Like you said before, we should get out of here."

Mabel stuck a concerned nose in his face. He shoved

it away and sat up. She was right. This wasn't the place to dawdle. He should concentrate on getting Grace home safe. She held out a hand, her expression…well, damned if he could tell what she was feeling.

"Unless you want to lie there until that hog comes back to have you for dinner," she said, waggling her fingers.

He grabbed hold and let her help him up.

She immediately stepped away. "Show me how to get on the back."

"Are you sure? I can walk."

"That would be stupid. Just don't bounce me off on my head or blab about this to Cole. I do not need to be the butt of Shawnee's jokes for the rest of my life."

"She'll find out," Hank predicted gloomily. "There are no secrets around here."

Grace's smile was sharper than he would have thought possible from a mouth that soft. "You'd be surprised what people don't know."

"Especially me?"

An unidentified emotion flickered in her eyes before she tucked her chin to stare down at the ground. "You can't hog all the blame." Her mouth twisted into a lopsided smile. "Hah. Hog. I'm such a comedian. Anyway…" Her gaze came up to meet his, clear and steady. "Let's be honest, okay? We both know I had a crush on you for years. And I knew you were on the rebound when you showed up in Canyon that night, but I finally had a chance to get my hands on you, so I took it. I was selfish. And you were hurting in ways that I didn't bother to figure out. What were the odds that it was going to end well?"

"At that point in my life? Less than zero."

"Exactly. But I chose to ignore all the warning signs

and grab what I wanted." She stuck out a gloved hand. "Let's just call it a draw, okay?"

He hesitated, then accepted the handshake. "So... friends?"

"Friends." She pumped his hand once, then let it drop. "*Now* can we go find my horse?"

When they were safely aboard Ranger, with Grace hanging onto the sides of his jacket and her boots bumping his legs every few strides, Hank blew out a long, silent breath.

Friends.

That was good. Better than he'd dreamed possible. So why couldn't he shake the notion that Grace's forgiveness had come too easily? Everything she'd said made perfect sense, but it still felt like he'd been given a free pass. Once upon a time he would have grabbed it and run without a second thought. Not anymore.

He had learned the hard and very painful way that anything he hadn't earned wouldn't last.

Chapter 14

BUMPING ALONG ON THE BACK OF THE HORSE, Grace had to resist the urge to throw her arms around Hank's waist and try to squeeze out another laugh. She barely needed to hang on at all, since he took care to make the ride as smooth as possible.

Looking out for her…just like he used to.

Her heart gave a treacherous little skip. The boy she'd adored had been like a puppy: sweet and funny and so clueless sometimes she'd wanted to swat him with a newspaper. This man had gotten lost in the wilderness and been adopted by wolves—honed down, watchful, and likely to bite if cornered. But also gentle and protective. Some of the best of Hank was still there, peeking out around the edges to see if it was safe to show himself.

Even before Maddie, he had been permanently woven into the fabric of her life. To be close to him, Grace had volunteered to be the student manager for first the football team, then the basketball team, persuading her father the experience would look impressive on scholarship applications. She'd handed Hank water bottles at practice, taped his ankles before games, bandaged his scrapes, and strapped ice packs onto his bruises and sprains. Somewhere along the line, sports medicine had turned into her passion and was now her vocation.

Every time she joined the sideline celebration of a

touchdown pass, she remembered how Hank would catch her up in his sweaty embrace and swing her off the ground. When her Bluegrass boys took a time-out with the game on the line, she recalled bumping fists for luck before Hank trotted back out onto the court.

Friends.

Did she dare get that close to him? Anger was so much safer than the slippery slope of forgiveness, then friendship, then…well she knew what. But for Maddie's sake, she had to at least be civil—assuming Hank would want anything to do with his daughter. Or with Grace, when he found out what she'd done and asked the one question she couldn't answer.

Why, Grace?

"There she is," he said.

Grace started, then realized he was pointing at Tick, who grazed under a towering cottonwood on the river flat, brought up short by the temptation of green grass. When they found no sign of trauma to the horse, Grace climbed on, surprised when Hank pointed Ranger toward home. "Aren't we going after the cows?"

He shook his head. "It's getting late, and I've had enough thrills for one day."

As they rode up to the barn, a semi rumbled into the driveway, Jacobs Livestock in block letters on the front of the shiny aluminum cattle trailer. Hank stepped off his horse and opened a wooden gate leading into an alley that ran toward the arena.

"Go ahead and unsaddle. Mabel and I can bring the cull cows up to the loading chute."

"I'll help…" Grace began, then huffed out a sigh.

"Never mind. At the rate I'm going, it'll be easier without me."

"You weren't so bad."

"Sure. I just threw in a little trick riding for the fun of it."

"It was pretty damn entertaining." Hank's eyes took on a hint of that once-familiar teasing gleam. "Can't say I've ever seen anyone hang upside down from the saddle horn. Look, Ma! No hands!"

She made a sour face. "Gee, I feel so much better now."

"I thought you felt fine before." The smile he lobbed at her was so unexpected, she had no chance to duck. "And since we're being honest...I am really *not* sorry I let you show me the best time I've ever had, and I was lying my ass off when I said I didn't want to do it again."

Grace could only stare as he vaulted onto his horse and trotted away without a backward glance. All the times she'd imagined Hank saying those exact words, and now she had no idea what to do with them.

———

Well, that was brilliant. They'd just agreed to be friends, and he was already trying to screw it up by dragging sex into the mix. But he couldn't let her go on believing whatever drunken bullshit he'd spewed that night at the Lone Steer, and even though it was pathetically little and years too late, he'd had to try to undo the damage. Grace deserved that much from him, no matter what she said about bygones.

Ten minutes later, he pushed the last few cows onto the truck Cole had backed up to the chute and rolled the segmented door down with a clatter.

"Good to go?" Cole asked.

"Yep."

Cole double-checked that the door was fastened securely—a habit so ingrained Hank couldn't take offense—then said, "Shawnee's gonna ride along with me. Grace'll take her pickup home, so she can drop you off on the way."

Hank's pulse jumped. He smacked it back down again. *Uh-uh, buddy.* There had already been enough alone time with Grace for one day.

"I'll take Dad's chore pickup instead. That front end is gonna fall apart if it doesn't get some new U-joints." He walked down the slanted loading chute, meeting Cole at the bottom. Mabel flopped on the ground, job done. Spider bounced off his thigh with both front feet, narrowly missing his crotch.

"Down!" he commanded for the fiftieth time that day.

She sat for about two seconds, then commenced her Tigger the Tiger routine. He'd gotten her to pause though, so that might count as progress. Shawnee came out of the house, Grace trailing along behind carrying the empty grocery bags. She'd washed her face and squashed her hair back into the ponytail. With the mud and smear of blood washed away, the scratch on her cheek was barely noticeable.

Cole zeroed right in on it, though. "What happened?"

"Wild hog spooked her horse," Hank said.

Cole let loose an unaccustomed profanity. "They've been fightin' 'em over in Oklahoma for a while. I suppose it was only a matter of time before the bastards worked their way on up the river. I'll call Parks and Wildlife and spread the word so everybody can be on the lookout." He turned to leave with a wave at Hank. "See you in the morning."

Hank started to argue, but Cole and Shawnee were already climbing into their truck. Oh well. One more day wouldn't kill him, then that was the end of it. Gil had him scheduled to leave Tuesday with a reefer full of frozen beef bound for Gulfport and come back to Amarillo on Friday loaded with fish. If Hank got turkey and stuffing on Thanksgiving, it would be the special of the day at whatever truck stop he was camped at—and that was just fine with him.

"I've got a few things to do before I go," he said, not quite looking at Grace.

"I'll take care of the horses," she offered.

"Thanks. Hay's in the lean-to. Toss a whole bale in the feeder."

Hank went around closing up the arena and alley. The wood-plank gate that led to the loading chute still sagged on its hinges, so heavy that even now he had to put his shoulder into it. As a kid, it had been impossible, which had invariably drawn a curse from his father when he had to drop what he was doing to stride over and yank the gate out of his son's puny hands, muttering, "When I was your age…"

You were six inches taller and thirty pounds heavier. Instead of pointing out what he'd assumed was obvious, Hank had generally waited for the first opportunity to make himself scarce. Why hang around when the whole damn ranch was a series of tests that were rigged against him?

He rested his hands on the top of the gate, recalling in vivid detail the first time he'd opened it all by himself. He'd been so proud. Finally—

"Don't just stand there," his dad had barked. "Help me push these cows up."

Hank kicked the gate. Stupid memories. And stupid him, still pouting over them. It wasn't like his dad had purposely set him up. Johnny just never got around to fixing anything that could be half-assed to work for now.

The trouble was, his temporary fixes tended to become permanent. Melanie used to joke that if they ran out of baling twine and duct tape, they'd have to sell the place. There hadn't been a single piece of equipment that didn't have some glitch. Fuel gauges perpetually read *Full*, so if a distracted teenager forgot to top off the tank before heading out with the tractor, he might get to walk home, every step dogged by the certainty of the ass-chewing he was about to receive.

Door handles were broken, so getting out required rolling down the window and reaching around to the outside—assuming the window crank didn't fall off in your hand. Windshield wipers scratched and streaked if they worked at all. And if that rattle in the front end was any indication, the chore pickup wasn't going to limp along much farther.

As Hank chained the last gate, Grace came out of the barn. "I found the dog food and filled their bowls. They have beds in the tack room, so I assumed they stay in the barn?"

"Yeah, unless it gets real cold." They stood awkwardly, each petting a dog to avoid making eye contact. "I'd better get going if I'm gonna get that pickup fixed tonight."

She nodded. "I told Cole I'd follow you, in case it breaks down on the way."

"I have to go to Dumas for parts."

"No problem. That's where I live. I've got an apartment in that complex by the junior high."

Hank knew the place. Nothing fancy, but a big step up from a couple of bare rooms above a shop. Or a shitty old camper. He wondered what kind of pictures she'd hung on her walls. If she still had that same fleecy blue blanket on her couch for snuggling on cold nights, or if she'd burned it to kill the Hank cooties.

He spun away toward the chore pickup and said, "No, Mabel" as the dog made to follow. She wilted, then slunk back to the barn. Hank ignored the twinge of guilt. The dogs would be fine. Mabel was too territorial to stray from her designated turf, and Spider wouldn't leave without her.

"Hank?" When he turned back, Grace hesitated, teeth pulling at her bottom lip. "In case nobody else bothers to say so, it's good of you to pitch in. Most people wouldn't under the circumstances."

Heat rose in his face. "I didn't have much choice."

"Yeah, you did." And she smiled at him.

Warmth trickled into his chest and pooled behind his sternum. He didn't trust what he might say, so he settled for a jerky nod.

As promised, Grace stuck with him all the way to Dumas, even though the pickup felt like it would come apart if he tried to go over fifty miles an hour. When he turned right on the main drag, she went left with a beep of her horn and a wave.

He had to fight not to flip a U-turn and follow her.

Chapter 15

WHEN JOHNNY SURFACED POST-SURGERY, HIS ex-wife was sitting beside his bed and...*smiling* at him? He blinked again and saw that of course he was hallucinating. It was Iris Jacobs perched in the beige vinyl hospital chair, looking slender and unfamiliar.

After a lifetime of a seeing a person a certain way, it was damned unnerving when they up and changed.

"How are you feeling?" she asked.

Numb. Disoriented. The sudden nothingness of anesthesia freaked him out—waking up with hours of his life lost, no sense of the time passing, and the slim but ever-present possibility that he might have zonked out and never come back.

The niggling suspicion that no one would really miss him.

And that was just morbid. Iris and Steve had dropped everything to be here with him. He and Melanie had talked on the phone while he'd been waiting to go into surgery. There'd been a flurry of calls from folks in Earnest, checking up on him. What more could a man expect?

Nothing...at least from his son. No call. No visit. No mention of Hank by Iris or Steve, who had to know he was back.

Johnny hadn't rushed to the hospital when Hank broke his arm. Wouldn't have even if he'd known about it at the time, instead of finding out months later by way of Melanie. Oily guilt churned in his otherwise empty stomach at the thought of his son waking up like this— broken, vulnerable, a little scared, and half a country away from the people who were supposed to look out for him. But when a man chose that kind of career, he couldn't expect his daddy to come running every time he lost a fight with a bull.

Besides, who would feed the damn cows?

"The chores…" It came out as a croak.

"Done." Iris held a plastic cup of ice water so he could sip from the straw. "And Cole got those cows loaded and off to the sale."

"Thanks." From the bottom of his checkbook, which could always use a boost. Throw in the cost of this surgery, and…no, he wasn't going to think about that when his head was muddled and throbbing.

He closed his eyes and settled back into the pillow, but he couldn't switch off the slow trickle of worry that leaked into his brain. Where would he find a hand he could trust on short notice? Melanie was tied up in the red tape of becoming a foster parent, so she couldn't fly home to take charge at the ranch, and in less than a week the Jacobs crew would load up their stock and head for the National Finals.

He must have dozed, because he had to shake himself awake when a nurse bustled in to poke and prod and tap notes into one of those tablet gizmos. Iris was still there, and now Steve was with her. When they made as if to leave, the nurse gestured for them to remain seated.

"The doctor is on his way, and he'll want at least one clear head in the room." She tapped Johnny's knee through the sheet. "There's no saying how much this one will remember."

The surgeon ambled into the room, still wearing scrubs and the blue shower-cap thing. "How are you feeling?"

"A lot better than when I came in."

"That's the pain meds talking." The doc turned to Iris and Steve. "The discharge nurse will give you his prescriptions and go over the signs and symptoms of infection or a blood clot. The biggest concern is falls, so for the next week, you'll need to keep a close eye on him…"

A week? The rest of the doctor's spiel was drowned by a wave of shock. "I can't sit on my ass for a week," Johnny blurted.

"I agree," the doctor said. "You need to sit on your ass for at least a month. Possibly more, depending on how well the bone is healing."

"But I…the ranch…" Johnny started to lift his arm in an ill-advised attempt to show it wasn't that bad. Pain speared through the haze of morphine, stealing his breath and crossing his eyes.

The doctor clucked his tongue. "If you can refrain from being stupid, you should be good as new before calving. If not…well, it's up to you how much of my kid's college tuition you end up paying." He left the threat hanging in the air as he turned to Iris. "As soon as he's had something to eat and held it down, he's all yours."

She smiled. "We've got it handled."

Johnny scowled at her. He did not want to be *handled*. He wanted to go home. He wanted…dammit, why wasn't anyone asking him what he wanted?

Iris's smile widened. "If I had a nickel for every time I saw that look on Melanie's face. Or Hank's."

She'd have a lot more nickels than Johnny, since

she'd seen a helluva lot more of Hank than he had. His son had made no bones about preferring the Jacobs ranch and their bucking stock over the Brookman place with its roping arena and beef cattle.

"Listen to the doctor." Steve's voice was like the low rumble of thunder, impossible to ignore. "If you don't give it time to heal up proper, it could turn into a long-term problem."

And Johnny could afford that even less. "I don't suppose you've got a hired hand you can spare?"

"Cole has someone in mind."

Probably some broke rodeo cowboy looking to build a bankroll before the new season started. And who might, *please, God*, have a clue about ranching. Exhaustion rolled over Johnny, flattening him into the pillows.

"If you trust Cole's judgment, we'll tell him to go ahead and take care of it. Can you manage seven hundred dollars a week?" Steve asked.

He'd have to. "My wallet is in that bag with my street clothes."

"We'll start with a week's wages and see how it goes." Iris had the checkbook out and was shoving a pen into his hand before he could pry his eyes open.

Thank God he'd at least had the sense to screw up his left shoulder. He scrawled the amount, then paused, his brain stalling at the *Pay to* line.

"Leave it blank, just in case," Iris said.

Right. He scribbled his name and shoved the checkbook toward her. "I need to talk to whoever he hires, get them lined out."

A glance passed between Iris and Steve, quick and almost…sneaky? But then she was smiling again and patting his uninjured arm. "You rest until that anesthesia wears off, then we'll get you out of here."

Johnny closed his eyes and let himself drift. The nurse was right. He must be wonky in the head. What could his good friends have to hide?

———

Hank got the necessary parts—after showing a picture ID to convince the woman at the service counter that yes, he was Johnny's son, and she could charge the stuff to his dad's account—and rattled back to Earnest, parking in front of one of the service-bay doors at Sanchez Trucking. Inside, guitar music wafted down the hall from the dispatcher's office, a soft, complicated tune that put him in mind of rustling grass along the river bottom.

Gil looked up from the strings, his gaze measuring Hank from head to toe. "Lookin' pretty ranchy there."

"Cole enlisted me." And he would lose all faith in the Earnest grapevine if Gil didn't know every detail of his father's injury, including how Hank had spent the day. "Mind if I pull the chore pickup in and replace the U-joints?"

"Why?"

Hank blinked. "Excuse me?"

"Why are you fixin' your dad's pickup?"

"I don't have anything better to do tonight, and the way it's clattering, we might not make it through feeding tomorrow."

"You're going back?"

Heat crawled up under Hank's collar. "Just tomorrow. Then I'll be on the road."

"About that." Gil set the guitar aside, leaned back,

and laced his fingers over his stomach. "Manny was supposed to do a swing through Illinois and Ohio, but everything's screwed up from that big ice storm. I have to give him your loads."

Dismay stabbed at him. "But I'm all set."

"Manny's got seniority and a truck payment to make. In fact, with the shuffling I've had to do, it'll be at least a couple of weeks before I get you another load."

Hank stared at him, his stomach knotting into a queasy ball. "What am I supposed to do in the meantime?"

Gil smiled. *Shit*. This wasn't about seniority or the availability of loads. Gil reached a lazy hand over and picked up a check that was propped on his computer keyboard. Hank assumed it was his pay for their trip from Montana until he saw the name stamped in the upper-left corner.

JOHN L. BROOKMAN.

"You've probably heard there's an opening for a ranch hand," Gil said.

Hank resisted the urge to tear the check in half. Gil would just laugh at him. "You can't make me accept this."

"Nope. But like the sign says…" He pointed toward one that read HE WHO DISPATCHES, RULES. "I can make sure you don't have anything better to do."

Hank's fingers quivered with the urge to ball up and take a swing. At Gil. The wall. Something. He drew a deep, *deep* breath, staring down at the check. *Seven hundred dollars*. More than he'd had in his possession at one time since his last bullfighting job.

At least they hadn't had the gall to write in his name.

"That's per week," Gil said. "And you can stay here if you want."

"Gee, thanks," Hank said, his voice as dry as his throat.

"You're welcome."

Then the other implication of the blank check hit him. "Does he know who you hired?"

"No. They figured it'd be better to get him locked up in Iris's house first."

Well, shit. Hank had to swallow a laugh. Was the joke on him, or his dad? "Is this a test, or do you just enjoy torturing me?"

"Both." Gil smirked, enjoying himself way too much. "And I like to shock the crap out of the sanctimonious pricks in this town. What's the last thing they'll expect from you?"

Responsibility. Maturity. Respect for his family. *In case no else bothered to say so, it's good of you to pitch in.* The old cronies down at the café could kiss his ass, but if it would mean something to Grace…

He carefully folded the check and tucked it in his pocket. "Only until he can come home. I'll work for him. I won't work with him."

"Fair enough." Gil eyed him suspiciously. "I expected more of a fight."

"Would it do me any good?"

"No."

"Then there's no sense wasting my breath. And we both know I can use the money." He patted his pocket… and grinned. "Besides, I survived Norma. You might want to explain that to my old man, in case he gets a hankering to rush out and bust my ass."

Gil watched him for another beat, then reached for his phone.

"Change your mind?" Hank asked.

"Nah. I'm just gonna share the good news." Gil flashed a lethal smile. "And tell Cole to lock up the shotguns."

Chapter 16

When Monday's final bell rang at Bluegrass High School, Grace's training room became instant chaos.

Her empire was a long, narrow space between the boys' and girls' locker rooms. A countertop ran the length of one wall, with cabinets above and below. On the other side, her desk was tucked into a corner with four padded treatment tables lined up in the middle section. The far end was the rehab area, with a stationary bike, whirlpool, and a collection of what the kids called her implements of torture.

She spiraled prewrap around an ankle, a routine so practiced she could simultaneously direct traffic. "Hop on the bike and do a ten-minute warm-up, Kevin, then I'll have a look at your range of motion. Cooper!" she barked, and a wrestler leaning against the counter dropped the rolls of tape he was juggling. "Are you here for a reason?"

"Just waitin' for Kevin."

"This isn't a lounge. Wait somewhere else." As Grace ripped off the last piece of tape and smoothed it into place, a basketball thumped on the concrete floor.

She fired a glare at the culprit, who immediately stuffed the ball under her arm with an apologetic grimace. "Sorry, Miz Mac. I forgot."

Again…but Grace could understand why. The basketball had been an extension of Jennifer's body since she was big enough to wrap her pudgy toddler hands around one. She'd won a national free-throw competition at age eleven, beating out thousands of competitors, boys and girls. Nobody had to push this girl onto the basketball court or into the weight room. If anything, her parents worried about their daughter's single-minded obsession with the game.

Grace patted the treatment table. "Jump up here, and let's take a look at that foot."

Jennifer did, hugging the ball as if it were a trophy she'd just been handed. "Did you hear? *They called!*"

"Really? Baylor?" Grace looked up from the blister on the ball of Jennifer's foot to meet her shining gaze. "That's awesome."

"They offered a verbal commitment, and we accepted." She clutched the ball between her hands, momentarily overwhelmed. "Holy crap, Miz Mac. I'm going to *Baylor*. Do you realize that they're the third-ranked team in the entire country right now?"

Grace had not, but she did know they were a basketball powerhouse and Jennifer's dream school, and that it had been a decade since any athlete at Bluegrass High School had been recruited by a program of that caliber. She held up a fist for Jennifer to bump. "Congratulations. When y'all knock off UConn for the national title, I'll be able to tell everyone I used to touch your sweaty feet."

With the blister padded and taped, Jennifer danced off. Grace finished the rest of the taping, then guided Kevin through a set of strain-counterstrain exercises before applying Kinesio Tape to his sore hamstring and sending him off to the wrestling room. When she hustled the last athlete out the door, she grabbed her tablet, and made her way to the gym to keep an eye on the varsity girls' basketball practice while she entered treatment notes and injury reports.

Before she could settle into her folding chair, her phone rang. She checked the number, then retreated into the corner before accepting the call.

"Can you talk?" Melanie asked.

"Until someone comes up lame. Or just whining. I've never seen a bunch of ninth graders with more creative ways to get out of morning weights."

Melanie laughed. "I always hated 'em myself."

But Grace doubted she'd missed a single session— rain, shine, in sickness or in pain. There was a reason Melanie could've played basketball in college if she hadn't chosen the rodeo team instead.

"Speaking of goofballs, I heard Korby is coaching the sixth-grade boys in Earnest. Is it a total disaster?"

"Oddly enough, no. My youngest brother, Matthew, is on the team, and they're doing pretty well. One thing about Korby: he never gets mad, and he never seems to run out of patience."

"Well, he should have learned something in high school. Hank spent hours and hours with him, going over plays."

Grace thought back to all the times she'd seen Hank with Korby and a friend or two on the playground courts or the practice field, before school or during summer vacation. "Huh. I always thought Hank was just avoiding your dad."

"That too, but you know how he was. Give him two days, and he'd have the entire football playbook memorized—offense and defense—and I don't care what people say about dumb jocks, that shit is *complicated*. If he'd ever cracked a book, he could've breezed through his classes."

Grace rolled her eyes. "Why bother when he could spend fifteen minutes reading my notes at lunch and go ace the quiz?"

"You should've been the one named MVP," Melanie declared. "Did you ever tell Hank the coaches gave you extra credit in their classes for keeping him eligible to play?"

"*Hell* no. He might've stopped bringing me Butterfingers."

Melanie laughed again. Then her voice dropped to a more serious note. "Shawnee called this morning. She told me you helped out at the ranch yesterday. That must have been awkward."

"You have no idea," Grace said, picturing herself dangling from Ranger's saddle.

"Damn. I should be there, taking care of Daddy and everything. This couldn't have happened at a worse time."

Grace fingered the scratch on her cheek, retracing Hank's featherlight touch. The tangle of his body with hers. What he'd said...

Uh-uh. Don't be going there, Gracie. She pushed the conversation in a safer direction. "Shawnee didn't try to pump me for any more information. What did you tell her?"

"Everything except Maddie. And I asked her to keep Hank's stuff amongst ourselves." Meaning the combined Jacobs-Sanchez clan, Grace assumed. "I was hoping if she knew, she'd cut him some slack."

"It worked. She backed way down."

"That's good. He needs the space. Or so I assume."
Bitterness leaked into Melanie's voice. "Now that I've
crossed over to the dark side, I don't get firsthand information. But he must've come a long way since the last
time I saw him, or he would've slammed the door when
Cole came knocking." She hesitated again, then asked,
"How is he, Grace?"

She'd known this question was coming, and she'd
spent a good part of the previous evening pondering the
answer. "Different, but not entirely in a bad way. And
we talked. I think we're okay…for now."

Until she had to tell him the next monster truth.

She moved closer to the basketball court as a mob
of wrestlers came out to jostle for a drink at the nearby
water fountain. The girls were at the far end, standing
with hands on hips as the coach made broad gestures to
indicate where each player should go during the next play.

Grace lowered her voice. "Wyatt's theory might be
right. After watching Hank yesterday, I think being
oblivious was his way of surviving your parents. You
tuned in to your parents, read their moods, and tried to
head off the worst. But Hank tuned out."

"Shutting down your radar is one way to deflect
constant negative input," Melanie agreed, sounding so
much like Wyatt it must have been a direct quote.

But tuning out meant blocking signals of all kinds, the
equivalent of wandering through life wearing emotional
blinders—and constantly stepping on toes. It would be
a helluva shock when those blinders were ripped off.
Hank had responded by retreating as far from the human
race as he could get—with the exception of the woman
named Bing.

And oddly, after all the hours they'd spent discussing Hank, it suddenly felt as if they were invading his privacy. Grace changed the subject. "Will you have the kids by Christmas?"

"I wish, but the wheels don't turn that fast. Plus we'll be gone for two weeks to the National Finals, and we want Scotty to live with us too, so on top of everything else, we're buying a house. One of those big Victorians on the North Hill, only three blocks from downtown. We should close this week."

"Even with Thanksgiving?"

Melanie snorted. "Have you met my husband? It's amazing how fast Realtors and bankers can move when you know which arms to twist. Once we move in, we can schedule the home inspection with social services and hopefully get the kids early in January."

And Scotty—the youngest of Wyatt's baby bullfighters—could finally stop worrying about what fresh hell his mother or one of her boyfriends were inflicting on his brother and sister. "How old are they now?"

"Eleven and fourteen."

Wow. Almost the same ages as her youngest brothers—Matthew and Lucas. Grace shuddered at the thought of having full responsibility for two adolescents. "Are you scared?"

"Terrified. What do either of us know about being parents?"

"There's a whole herd of young bullfighters who owe their careers to Wyatt." And in some cases, possibly their lives. *Disadvantaged* didn't begin to describe the students Wyatt chose to take on. "Plus you practically raised Hank."

Melanie made a derisive noise. "And now he doesn't speak to me."

"But he *is* taking care of the ranch."

"Under duress."

"True, but he seems okay with it as long as he doesn't have to deal with your dad."

Melanie sighed. "Can't say I blame him. I sure hope Steve and Iris can keep a leash on Daddy when he finds out."

The basketball coach blew his whistle and tossed the ball toward the hoop. As the center grabbed the rebound, a group of players raced down the court in a fast-break drill, and Grace locked her gaze on the action. Murphy's Law of athletic training guaranteed that the instant she looked away, someone would go down.

As always, Jennifer was flying down the court. The pass hit her in stride as she broke toward the basket and a defender stepped out, hands high. Jennifer planted her foot to make one of her deathly quick cuts around the block. Her left knee buckled and she cried out, tumbling to the floor.

Grace's stomach lurched. *Oh no. Not Jennifer. Not now, dammit.*

"I've gotta go." Grace dropped her phone and tablet on the bottom row of the bleachers and jogged onto the court to crouch beside the injured girl, who was clutching her knee and moaning, tears already streaming down her face.

Grace put a steadying hand on her shoulder. "Hey, Jen. What happened?"

"It's my ACL," the girl sobbed. "I felt it pop."

"I heard it," the coach added grimly, hunkered on her other side.

From what Grace had seen, they were probably right.

It had all the trademarks of a noncontact anterior cruci- ate tear—rapid deceleration, change of direction, and the audible pop.

"Let's get her in the training room." Grace caught the assistant coach's eye. "You can give me a hand while Coach calls her parents."

They carried her between them, fireman-style, with Jennifer's arms clutching their shoulders and Grace sup- porting the injured knee. When they had her settled on a treatment table, Grace handed her a towel to muffle her sobs and gently maneuvered the leg into a slightly bent position, one hand on Jennifer's thigh while she pulled forward on her calf.

Jennifer gasped as the tibia slid forward with sicken- ing ease, no longer moored to the femur. *Damn, damn, double damn.* Grace eased a pillow under the knee, her own throat going tight. "I'll get some ice."

"It's torn, isn't it?" There was a note of pleading in the girl's voice, as if she still held out a tiny hope that Grace might say no.

Grace nodded. The nightmare that disproportionately stalked female athletes had come true, and they all knew exactly what it meant. Jennifer's senior season was done, and the offer from Baylor that she'd barely had time to celebrate would most likely be withdrawn. All because of one wrong step.

It was part of the game. Part of life. And it sucked.

Eventually, they would talk about what it would take to get it all back. Reconstruction. Months of therapy. Pain and sweat, pushing through mental and physical barriers until she could prove to college scouts that she was one hundred percent.

All of that would start when the orthopedic surgeon verified the diagnosis. For now, Grace wrapped her arms around Jennifer's quaking shoulders and let the girl cry out her broken dreams.

Chapter 17

AT SEVEN O'CLOCK ON MONDAY NIGHT, HANK WAS back at the auto parts store in Dumas, this time for new bearings before the wheels fell right off the chore pickup. The woman at the service counter recognized him on sight and automatically pulled up Johnny Brookman's account. At the rate Hank was buying parts, he would be at the top of their Christmas card list by the end of the week.

He'd fired up his old Chevy for this trip. The body was rusted out around the fenders and the maroon paint was flaking off the hood, but it ran well enough. Once Hank aired up a couple of low tires, it was good to go.

As he headed down the main drag, he spotted the sign for the sports bar ahead on the left. His stomach grumbled, reminding him that he'd put in a lot of hours since he and Cole had polished off the leftovers from Grace's Sunday dinner. And since he'd dropped that seven-hundred-dollar check into the night deposit at the bank, his checkbook and debit card weren't just souvenirs.

He hadn't been surprised when he'd called in and the teller had said yes, his account was in good standing, with a balance of thirty-three dollars and nineteen cents. It would be like Melanie to make sure there was enough to cover the monthly service charges. He'd have to get the deposit records and figure up how much he owed her. That was one debt he would not leave outstanding.

In the meantime, he might as well enjoy this paycheck. His hospital bill from Toppenish had been turned over to collections, and he assumed the agency had his account flagged. At the first scent of money, they would come after whatever they could get. With interest and penalties, he'd probably get them paid off about the time he qualified for social security.

He had to park in the far back corner of the bar's lot. Sure was busy for…oh, right. Monday night. Sports bar. He hadn't even thought about football—and him a Texan. This was what he got for falling off the grid.

As he stepped inside, he was hit by a wall of noise and mouthwatering aromas. The place was packed, but the only one who paid him any mind was the frazzled hostess, who blew a loose strand of hair out of her face as she hurried over to dump an armload of menus into the rack, then pull one out again along with a welcoming smile. "Eating or just drinking?"

"Food, please."

She ran a practiced gaze around the restaurant. "It'll be a few minutes until I can seat you."

"What about that one?" Hank pointed to a table tucked in behind the hostess stand.

"You can't see the game from there."

He checked the nearest screen, where the Jacksonville Jaguars were lining up on offense against the…what? "When did the Chargers move to LA?"

The hostess laughed and handed him the menu. "Table zero it is. I'll send a waitress right over."

"No rush."

The only date he had was with an empty apartment and the last few chapters of his book. He preferred the company of a couple hundred strangers, and what the hell, one cold brew wouldn't hurt him. When the waitress swung by, he ordered a tap beer and settled in to read the entire menu, even though he already knew what he wanted. He was pondering his choice of sides when a familiar voice made his head jerk up.

"…taco pizza to go," Grace was telling the hostess.

"I'll go check on that for you." She hurried off.

Hank's first instinct was to hide behind his menu. He had no idea where they stood after his confession of undying lust. Then he heard himself say, "If you want a taco, why don't you just order a taco?"

Grace froze, her head bent over her wallet. For a moment, he thought she didn't remember that he'd used the same opening line at that pizza joint in Canyon. Or that she was going to pretend she hadn't heard him over the din. Then a boisterous group of twentysomethings crowded through the door, forcing her to turn toward Hank to let them pass, and he caught a glimpse of puffy, red-rimmed eyes.

He jumped to his feet. "Grace? Are you okay?"

She ducked her head again, rubbing at smudged mascara with the side of her finger. "Yeah. Just a rough night. Our leading scorer blew out a knee at practice, not even a whole day after giving her verbal commitment to play at Baylor. She was crying, her teammates were crying, her mom was crying…"

"You were crying."

She scrunched up her face. "Not until they were all gone."

"I'm sorry," the hostess interrupted with an apologetic smile. "The kitchen is slammed, so it's going to be another ten or fifteen minutes for the pizza. If you want to have a seat, I'll have someone bring you a Coke on the house while you wait."

"Sure. Dr Pepper would be great." Grace glanced over at the bench opposite the hostess station, then at Hank, clearly undecided.

He pulled out the other chair at his table and steered her into it. Lord, she looked wrung out, her hair straggling out of an off-center barrette, freckles and the thin, red scratch standing out against pale skin.

"Wow. Baylor. That's huge."

"It was." She blew out a weary sigh. "Until tonight our team had a legitimate shot at going to the state tournament. And Jennifer will probably lose that scholarship."

"No wonder her mom was crying."

Grace half smiled at his lame attempt at humor, then gave herself a visible shake. "She's tough. She'll come back and play somewhere once she's through rehab. It just might not be a top-ten Division I school." She paused as the waitress set down their drinks, and her gaze caught on Hank's beer for an instant before she picked up her straw and peeled off the wrapper.

He ordered his chicken-fried steak and the waitress left. "It's hard not to let it get to you."

"Yeah, but I have to keep my perspective." She took a long and obviously much-needed drink of her Dr Pepper. "If I get too invested in the competition and all, it affects my ability to make the safest decision for the athlete. And torn ligaments aren't the end of the world. It's not like…" She trailed off, her face stricken.

"She won't walk again?" Hank asked, going with sarcasm because he hadn't practiced anything else.

Grace's cheeks flamed. She braced an elbow on the table and pressed her forehead into her palm, closing her eyes. "We don't have to talk about it."

Yes, they did. Hank preferred to know how far the story had spread—and more important, if it was still anywhere close to reality. "Who told you?"

"Not your sister," she said flatly. "I heard it from Philip Makes Thunder."

Oh. Him. Hank had only met Philip a couple of times, but he was another of Bing's lost boys—and Wyatt's chosen ones. "What did he tell you?"

Grace's brows pinched with aggravation. "You really want to get into this right now?"

"Yes."

"Fine." She leaned back, folded her arms, and began to recite the story in a monotone that would have done Cole proud. "You were working the Indian rodeo at Toppenish when a guy named Dakota Red Elk got bucked off. The bull stepped on his lower back, causing a fracture-dislocation of two lumbar vertebrae and an incomplete spinal cord injury, and leaving him with almost no use of his lower body. On the video, it appears that you were out of position when the ride started and slow to react. However, since Dakota fell directly under the bull, there is considerable doubt whether you could have prevented the injury anyway."

Hank could only stare at her, everything blurring around the edges the way it had been that day, even before the injury.

Grace kept going, a recording with no pause button. "You were so upset that several people asked if you were okay to go on. You refused to answer, and when the next bull came out of the chute, you stood there and let it run you down. You had three cracked ribs and required surgery for reduction and internal fixation of a displaced distal fracture of your radius and ulna."

Jesus Christ. She sounded like she'd read his medical records. And she'd obviously taken a good look at the video from that night.

"Is that all?" Hank choked out.

She tilted her head. "You wanted the facts. Everything else is speculation."

He made a motion with his hand. *Bring it on.*

Grace picked up her Dr Pepper and took a swig, then set it down again, her gaze locked on him the whole time. "Mariah Swift competed in the barrel racing on Saturday night. As far as anyone knows, that's the first time you'd seen her since she got you fired. No one saw you drinking afterward, but the assumption is that's why you were off your game on Sunday." She let the words lie on the table between them for a long moment, then added, "Some people are convinced you wanted that bull to hurt you. Or worse."

Bing's question echoed in his head, blunt but not unkind. *"Were you trying to kill yourself, Hank?"*

No. Yes. He didn't know. Didn't remember wanting or knowing anything. The inside of his head had been a giant roar and crackle, like he imagined the wildfire had sounded as it swept up from the breaks and devoured their ranch. He recalled faces that had floated past, voices that didn't add up to words. Overwhelmed, he'd pushed them away and retreated to the one place where he could be alone—the middle of the arena.

He'd understood they were going to buck that next bull. Hadn't he? He wasn't surprised when the chute gate opened. Or when the huge brindle burst out. It was happening, but at the same time it wasn't. Like a dream. No, a nightmare. The worst kind, where his feet stuck to the ground, and he could do nothing to save himself as a ton of muscle, bone, hooves, and horns bore down on him. Then the pain had exploded through his body, and the nightmare had become excruciatingly real.

Hank pressed both palms into the edge of the table, fighting the urge to jump up and run out the door. He'd already tried to escape. Mile after mile along the river, over the hills, into the mountains on bear-infested trails that didn't show on any tourist map. And deep, deep into himself, curled under a blanket in the camper for so long even Norma had started to worry. No matter where he'd gone, the darkness went with him, locked inside his head.

"Take a breath, Hank." Again Bing's voice was there, penetrating the toxic fog. *"Count to ten. No rush. Another breath now."*

Slowly, the present filtered in—shouts and groans from fantasy football fanatics at the bar, the clink and clatter of dishes, the ebb and flow of normal, happy voices. Light, shining from the lamp over his head, reflecting off the mirror behind the bar, pulling him free of shadows that clutched at his legs.

And there was Grace, sitting across yet another table from him, staring into her glass as she poked at ice cubes with her straw. "I'm sorry. I shouldn't have said that."

He was surprised when he opened his mouth and words came out. "I asked for it."

"I know, but that was harsh." She glanced up with a ghost of a smile. "I've gotta be careful about channeling Tori and Shawnee. It's some powerful stuff."

"Combined? It's terrifying."

Her smile grew. "I guess that's why they win so much roping together. Pure intimidation."

The conversation had turned ridiculous, but it did the trick. Hank's muscles unclenched, and he didn't feel as if a two-ton truck was parked on his chest. He took a tiny sip of his beer, then another when that one went down okay. They sat for several minutes, retreating into one of the silences that had been another of the hallmarks of their friendship.

With three younger brothers underfoot in their too-small house, Grace had craved any space or moment of peace she could get when she was in school. For Hank, it had been the relief of not having to *be* anything. Not Johnny's son or Melanie's brother, the latest Brookman who would, naturally, carry the team to Friday night glory. With Grace he didn't have to be the cool guy, forever ready with a grin and a joke. He didn't have to wonder if, like the Jacobs family, she might only be putting up with him because his own parents weren't interested. And in exchange, he shielded the geeky girl with her wild curls and schoolmarm dresses against anyone who might have been tempted to harass her.

He'd missed the comfort of their shared silences.

Finally, though, he had to break this one. "Mariah didn't know she wasn't legal in Texas. Where she's from it's only fifteen, not seventeen."

"She knew her daddy was gonna come unglued if he found out," Grace said, a simmer of anger beneath the words. "Once that shit hit the fan, there was no way Cole could keep both of you on his crew. And yes, I've heard how she felt just terrible about what happened…while she sashayed on about her life and left you to pay the price."

Hank took in the bright spots of color on Grace's cheeks. She was furious. Not at him, but *for* him. He shook his head, baffled. "Why are you sticking up for me? It seems like you'd enjoy seeing me get kicked in the gut."

She gave a short, brittle laugh and slouched into her chair. "It's hard to explain."

"Try me." Because he really, *really* wanted to know.

She wove the paper straw wrapper between her fingers as she considered her words. "Driving home tonight, I was thinking about Jennifer and how fast your life can change. One wrong step and *boom!* You're in a totally different place. But sometimes what seems like a disaster can lead to good things…once you get through the hard stuff."

He didn't really follow, but, "O-kay."

"What you said to me that night at the Lone Steer… it really hurt."

He winced. "I know."

"But because of it, I went to Oregon. I got to know your sister, and through her Shawnee and Tori, and you've seen what that's done for my roping. None of it would have happened if you hadn't been a jerk, so cursing your name seems…I don't know. 'Hypocritical' isn't the right word, but something like that."

Hank had no idea how to respond. She had just called him both a jerk and, indirectly, her personal disaster, but somehow her life had turned out better for knowing him. So that was a good thing?

The hostess appeared with Grace's pizza. "Here you go! Thanks for your patience."

Grace jumped up and snatched the box, clearly done with a conversation that seemed determined to drag them toward places that were far too sensitive to the touch.

Hank stood too. "Do you have games tomorrow night?"

"No." She eased back a step, wary. "My teams play in Thanksgiving tournaments, so they leave this Tuesday open."

"Are you roping?"

She shook her head. "Shawnee has one of her check-ups in Dallas."

Cancer screenings, she meant. Between a bout with lymphoma in her teens and her family history, Shawnee's risk was high, and Tori had dragged her into the best long-term study she could find involving new methods of early detection.

"I could come over and run the chute for you," he offered and, before she could say no, added, "If you don't mind me bringing Spider and working her on the roping calves. In the indoor arena, I don't have to worry about her running them through a fence."

Grace hesitated, her reservations clear.

"I've been eating your food for two days. I owe you a dozen nights of roping practice for the peach cobbler alone." He tested a casual smile. "Besides, what are friends for?"

She still looked uncertain, but finally she nodded. "Okay. Around six?"

Hank exhaled. "Great. Thanks."

"You're welcome." She drummed her fingers on the

pizza box as if debating her next words. Then she gave a slight, *what the hell* shrug. "I don't either."

"Excuse me?"

"Despite how it turned out, I don't regret dragging you home." She smiled, enjoying knocking him for a loop. "Have a good night, Hank."

He watched until the door swung shut behind her. Then he sank into his chair, nodding blankly when the waitress set his plate in front of him and asked if he had everything he needed. It was like being thrown ass over heels by a bull. After everything Grace had hit him with, it was gonna take him a while to figure out which way was up. But he couldn't help smiling as he cut off the first bite of steak and swirled it in gravy.

By damn, it *was* a good night.

Chapter 18

"I WANT TO GO HOME," JOHNNY SAID ON TUESDAY afternoon, after he'd eaten his lunch and had his nap like a good little boy. "I need to have a look around and make a list of chores for when Cole hires me some help."

Steve and Iris exchanged a glance, then Steve clasped his big hands around his mug. "About that...we already hired someone. He started Sunday."

"Sunday? But you said—"

"With Cole's supervision," Iris rushed to add. "He stepped right in like he'd never left."

Johnny's mug banged down, sloshing coffee onto the table. "*Hank?*"

Iris leapt from her chair and grabbed a dishcloth. "He's here, Gil was willing to give him the time off, and he knows the place almost as well as you do."

Johnny snatched the rag. He'd clean up his own mess, thank you. "And he ran off every time I turned my back for more than a minute. You think he's gonna stick around with no one riding herd on him?"

Steve fixed him with a flinty gaze. "We could always count on him."

Then why did you fire him? But Johnny knew the answer. Another stellar example of his son's lack of common sense.

He shoved his chair back and stood. "Take me home."

Iris opened her mouth to argue, then pressed her lips

into a tight line at a gesture from Steve, who drained the last of his coffee before getting to his feet. As he rose, up, up, and up some more, Johnny was reminded that this man was more than his match on a good day.

Iris made a clucking sound but said, "Don't stay too long, or you'll be late for dinner."

They didn't offer to help with his coat, but Steve did stay close going down the steps, in case Johnny decided to do a face-plant. At the pickup, Steve climbed behind the wheel and waited while Johnny figured out how to hoist himself into the four-wheel drive without using his left arm. He bumped his elbow twice, jarring his shoulder hard enough that his eyes watered. Steve put the pickup in gear and turned up the radio so they could listen to analysts guess at the reasons the cattle market was down again.

"How did Hank persuade Sanchez to hire him?" Johnny finally asked.

"He's a good driver, and it sounds like he's making a real effort to set things right. Gil decided to give him a chance." Steve tossed him a pointed look. "Maybe you should think about doing the same."

What could he say? *No thanks, I prefer to be the world's lousiest father?* But it was too late to fix anything between him and Hank. The nearly unrecognizable man who'd looked straight through him at the Smoke Shack didn't need—or want—his daddy.

Half an hour later, they turned into Johnny's driveway. At first glance, everything seemed fine. A warm front had pushed in overnight and the horses dozed in the sunshine, their feeder full of hay. Hank was nowhere in sight, though, and neither were the dogs.

"Where do you suppose he ran off to?" Johnny grumbled.

"Sanchez Trucking. He mentioned to Cole yesterday that he'd reserved a repair bay this afternoon to swap out the wheel bearings on your pickup."

Johnny glared at him. "You knew he'd be gone."

"Hell yeah. Did you figure I'd toss the two of you together after what happened last time?"

Johnny cringed. Almost exactly three years ago, Hank had strolled into the Corral Café as casual as if he'd only been gone a day, not six months. And Johnny had been so shocked that the first words out of his mouth were "What the hell do you want?"

To say the conversation had gone downhill from there would be a massive understatement.

"If you're so sure it's gonna be a wreck, why did you hire him?"

Steve sighed. "You had to hire someone. And we were hoping this might be the shove you both needed to work things out."

Was that why Hank had accepted? Did he *want* to come home? Johnny couldn't imagine why, but he was rapidly losing the ability to think at all. The ache in his shoulder had grown teeth, and he was wiped out from a stroll around the yard. He sure as hell wasn't up to butting heads with his son.

"I want to grab a few things from the house," he said stiffly.

But when Steve opened the door, Johnny smelled food, and the mouthwatering scent of roasting beef was coming from *his* oven. As he stepped out of the mudroom, the figure at the stove turned…and his jaw dropped.

There was a woman in his house. A beautiful, copper-skinned, black-haired woman in faded jeans and a bright-pink shirt that matched her toenails. And if he wasn't mistaken, she had been dancing to the music playing on the radio.

Barefoot. In his kitchen. And cooking actual food.

She smiled, amused by his goggling. "You aren't the Brookman I was expecting."

But she must have seen them drive in and watched them walk around. And had plenty of time to prepare herself—unlike Johnny. Now that his eyes had adjusted, he realized she was older than he'd first thought. Closer to fifty than forty. But who...

"I'm Bing," she announced. "A friend of Hank's."

Johnny's eyebrows shot up. First a teenager, and now...this?

Her red-painted lip curled. "Not that kind of friend, but I'll take it as a compliment."

Steve stepped around Johnny and extended a hand that swallowed hers, even though she was taller than average and what you might call strong-boned if you were trying not to notice her curves. "I'm Steve Jacobs. Sorry for barging in. We didn't see a car outside."

Wait. Was Steve apologizing because Johnny had walked into his own home without knocking?

"Hank has told me all about you." Bing clasped her other hand over Steve's with a smile so dazzling it was like a flashbulb going off. "And I don't have a car. Gil picked me up from the airport and brought me out."

Now that he'd regained a few of his faculties, Johnny realized this had to be the woman Melanie had told him about. The one who'd fetched Hank from the hospital in Yakima and all but adopted him.

"Ah. You must be from Montana?" Steve guessed, in the absence of any attempt at conversation from Johnny.

"Yes."

"What are you doing here?" Johnny blurted, then winced. *Real smooth, Brookman.*

Head cocked, arms folded, she inspected him from head to toe. She didn't look particularly impressed. "It took me nineteen months to undo a fraction of what you did to that boy. I don't intend to let you fuck him up again."

Steve made a choking noise that might've been laughter. Nice that someone was getting a kick out of this. "Did you find a place to stay?" he asked, deploying his southern manners to fill the charged silence. "There are football playoff games in Dumas and Canadian this weekend, so it might be hard to find a motel with a vacancy."

Sunlight from the window caught in the inky-black spikes of her short hair as she glanced around, then back at them. "Melanie said I could use her room."

Here? She intended to plant herself in Johnny's house? With Hank, and with Melanie's blessing. Damn it all, they were ganging up on him.

"You and Hank are welcome to join us for Thanksgiving dinner," Steve said, another dash of salt in the wound.

Something flickered in her eyes, dimming their sparkle. "I appreciate the invitation, but I don't celebrate that particular holiday."

"Oh. I, uh…" Steve's face reddened. "I didn't think… I can see why you wouldn't. Native Americans, I mean. Not exactly a landmark moment in history for y'all."

Amusement played across her striking face. "Most of us like our turkey and stuffing as much as the next white guy. It's a personal thing with me."

"Oh. Well…"

"How long are you staying?" Johnny choked out.

"Until you're back on your feet." That dark gaze pinned him to the wall, and she all but bared her fangs. "Or you say one word to Hank that doesn't sit right with me."

Johnny was set back on his heels by her outright hostility. Not much question whose side she was on. He fought the bizarre urge to laugh. Wouldn't you just know it? There was finally a woman his own age in this house again, and she hated his guts.

And this one wasn't even married to him.

"We should be going," Steve said.

"I'll let Hank know you stopped by," she said.

As if this was their place, and Johnny was the intruder. *The hell with that.* "I'm staying."

He had the satisfaction of seeing her eyes go wide.

"You can't—" Steve began.

"It's my house," Johnny said. "And now I won't be alone in it…so I'm staying."

Steve swore under his breath.

Bing just raised those perfectly sculpted eyebrows. "Go ahead, make yourself at home."

"I will." And before his knees failed him completely, he strode across the living room, down the hall, and slammed his bedroom door behind him. He waited inside for a few beats, but Steve didn't come after him.

But what now? Johnny couldn't make her leave, and he couldn't share a house with that woman. She'd probably poison his coffee. But he'd have to figure it out later, because right now he had to get horizontal before he fell on his face. He lowered himself onto the bed and stretched out flat with a huge sigh. His bed. His pillow. Lord, he'd missed them. And as long as he was gonna act like an overtired brat, he might as well take a damn nap.

When he woke, his room was dark. He levered himself out of bed and staggered to the attached bathroom. Even taking a piss was a major operation without the use of his left arm.

The house was dead quiet. Maybe that woman—what kind of name was Bing, anyway?—had left with Steve. But when Johnny cracked the door to Melanie's room, he saw a suitcase on the bed, clothes spilling out along with a scent that made him think of exotic flowers and tropical nights.

He shuffled into the living room, lit by the lamp beside his recliner. Over on the bar he spotted a covered dish. He peeled back the foil and breathed a curse. She had unearthed Hank's childhood Sesame Street plate from somewhere in the cupboards. One compartment held potatoes and gravy, the second carrots, and the third pot roast—all cut into toddler-sized pieces.

As he slid the plate into the microwave, he could see her laughing at him. But he wasn't gonna waste good pot roast.

Chapter 19

TUESDAY EVENING, GRACE LET HERSELF INTO THE living quarters of Tori's trailer, tossed her school bag on the couch, and rushed to change clothes before Hank came knocking.

And no, she would not grab the jeans that made her butt look the best. This wasn't a date. She and Hank had never had a date. Just a baby, and Grace couldn't let herself forget either of those things, even for a second.

She yanked on an already dusty long-sleeved thermal and sweatshirt, traded her khakis for her least attractive jeans and pulled on her boots. There. She was dressed. And feeling ridiculous because *Seriously, Grace?* Did she think he was gonna come charging in here to ravage her?

Nope, nope, *huge* nope. Just because they'd stumbled over a few embers glowing under the pile of ashes didn't mean they should go poking at them.

Grace plucked a banana from the bunch on the counter, a Dr Pepper from the fridge and headed for the barn. She'd turned the horses out into the pasture on Sunday, since they hadn't planned to rope for a few days. The other two—Fudge and Shawnee's bay—were standing at the fence, waiting for their grain. Betsy was clear out in the far corner.

Aw, crap. It was gonna be one of those nights.

Grace let the geldings into their runs on the off chance that seeing them go inside might inspire Betsy to come running. Horses were supposed to be herd animals. The mare remained stubbornly planted in the pasture. Grace leaned against a post and sighed, considering her options. She could take a bucket of grain and halter out there as bait, or she could chase the mare into the open gate of her run. Or she could say the hell with roping because it would be long past her bedtime before Betsy fell for either of those—which was why Grace didn't turn her out on the days she intended to practice.

Peering down from the hayloft, Muella made a noise that sounded suspiciously like *Hah!*

A vehicle rumbled into the yard. Hank, right on schedule. Grace folded her arms and waited. Sure enough, he came in the barn looking for her, Spider attempting to hog-tie him with her leash and Mabel trotting behind. At the sight of them, the cat gave an unearthly yowl, followed by a stream of spitting and hissing that could only be interpreted as feline profanity.

Hank and the dogs scrambled backward. From a safe distance outside the door he called, "Are you almost ready?"

"No."

A pause, then he asked, "Is there a problem?"

"Just Betsy."

His footsteps crunched in the gravel, and he appeared alongside the first run. It only took one look for him to see the problem. "Now what?"

"Normally? Shawnee gets on a horse, goes out, and ropes her, but I'm not quite that handy."

"You want me to do it?"

"Can you?"

He all but rolled his eyes. "I've roped a few broncs,

Grace. When you hang around the Jacobs ranch, you learn these things."

"Oh. Well, if you want to give it a shot…" It would be fun to watch him try, if nothing else.

He locked the dogs in his pickup while she caught Tori's horse, Fudge, and within a few minutes he was riding out, building the extra-large loop required for horse-roping. Between Tori's security lights and spillover from the two houses just across the fence, the small pasture was lit well enough for safety.

The mare knew the routine. When she saw Hank coming, she revved for takeoff, head swiveling in search of the best escape route. Hank approached at an angle that left her a slightly larger gap on his right. As he began to swing the rope, Fudge chomped at the bit, also primed and ready for the game. Betsy made the first move, throwing up chunks of sod as she blasted down the fence. Hank's loop sailed through the air, wide and flat as a fisherman's net, and dropped over her head. He ripped out the slack, and it came snug deep around her chest and shoulders.

Hank didn't try to stop her, just kept pressure on the rope and let Fudge track the mare as she made one more circle before slowing to a trot, then a walk, ears pinned in irritation.

Grace did a slow clap as she walked over to take the rope. "Very impressive."

"Thank you." He bowed from the waist, then patted Fudge on the neck. "This is a super-nice horse."

Grace reeled Betsy in and, once she had the mare on a short leash, started for the barn. "Tori's family raises some of the best Quarter Horses in the country. Why would she own some old plug?"

"Good point." He rode ahead of her, giving Grace ample opportunity to admire the lean, supple lines of his body under his heavy flannel shirt. He already seemed less gaunt—and some of that was from her cooking. It was dangerously appealing to think that food she'd created had become a part of him, settling into his muscles and bones, making him happy and—

"Ouch! Would you get off of me?" She drove her fist into Betsy's side as the mare smashed her into the fence, then danced away to snort and squeal with Shawnee's bay.

"And that"—Hank jabbed a finger at Betsy—"is the opposite of nice."

But it was worth it to see the laughter in his eyes… and know she'd help put that inside him, too.

———

When Grace had finished roping, Hank jogged down the arena, his muscles twitching at the feel of plowed dirt beneath his feet, and his system revving in anticipation of the pop of adrenaline he only got from taking on a ton of bull. He wiped that thought from his mind and concentrated on his dogs. Instead of chasing the calves up the return lane to the chute, he opened the gate into the catch pen wide and sent Mabel to bring them out into the arena. When Spider tried to follow, he gave the rope leash a sharp tug. "Down!"

She dropped to her belly, trembling with the effort of being still. He'd kept her on a leash everywhere they'd gone for the past two days, practicing the *Down!* constantly. During his latest stop at the auto parts store—the woman at the counter had given him a smile *and* a couple of mini Hershey's—he'd bought fifty feet of light nylon rope for tonight's session.

Hank scratched Spider's ears, then stood. "Come on."

Spider shot toward the calves, but was brought up several feet short when she hit the end of the rope. She strained at the leash, feet scrabbling in the loose dirt.

"Down!" Hank commanded. She stopped, eyeing him as if to see if he really meant it. He gave her a fierce stare. "Down," he repeated.

Her ears drooped...but she sank to her belly.

"Good dog!" Grace said, pausing to watch as she coiled her rope.

Hank smiled like a proud papa. "We're making progress."

He'd expected to feel awkward tonight, but the sense of well-being from last night's dinner had carried over into today, boosted when he'd finally located those two strays and managed to get them home. He hadn't seen any more hogs, and only one area of the torn-up grass that was a prime reason they were considered a scourge. They destroyed acres of prairie that would likely never recover, taken over by weeds and shrubs instead of native sod. But that was a problem for the Parks and Wildlife folks. Hank wouldn't be hanging around long enough to deal with what promised to be a huge headache.

Grace hung her rope on one of a row of hooks on the fence. "I'm going to unsaddle Betsy and finish the chores."

"I'll put the calves up when I'm done."

She stood for a moment, shifting uncomfortably. Now that the roping was done, it was all too obvious that they were alone in the quiet arena, and all the reasons they couldn't fall back into their old, comfortable ways came rushing in to fill the void.

"I saw the lights were on in Tori's trailer," Hank said to break the stiff silence. "Are you staying here while they're in Mexico?"

"Yeah. With all the animals, it's good to have someone here at night." Grace darted a look at the door. "I'll just, um, go then."

He gave her an awkward half wave, half salute. *Geezus*. What was *that*? And asking her about staying in the trailer…Christ, did it sound like he was angling for an invitation to join her? Not that he'd mind the company, but knowing who'd rocked that trailer in the past, it was damn near the only place he couldn't imagine getting Grace naked.

Spider yanked on the leash, her patience at an end.

"Yeah, yeah," he said. "Okay, girls. Come by!"

They all took off at a sprint, Mabel leading the way and Spider dragging Hank along as they circled around the calves to the left and pushed them to the end of the arena. Then Hank called, "Away to me!" and they all raced around the right side of the bunch. He worked the dogs back and forth, throwing in an occasional "Down!" After three passes up and down the arena, Spider was getting a clue and Hank had to stop, hands on knees, doubled over and sucking air. Geezus, he was out of shape. If Joe Cassidy could see him now, he'd never let him hear the end of it.

Fast isn't enough. It's a long damn season, and you've gotta have stamina if you're gonna survive.

Hank actually missed the pain. The aches and bruises from shots he'd taken for a cowboy or to protect one of his partners, each one a badge of honor. He squatted to give Spider a congratulatory rub, burying his face in her neck to obliterate the images of all that he couldn't let himself have. Mabel rooted at his other arm, and he gave her chest a scratch. There was nothing like a dog to make you like yourself a little better.

When the calves were penned, Hank headed for his pickup but hesitated when he saw the barn door was open and the light on. Was it rude to leave without saying good night, or would he be making a pest of himself? But his feet had already steered him that direction. Inside, the horses were all munching hay, but there was no sign of Grace until the scuff of a footstep sent hay dust showering from between the boards of the loft, and her legs appeared on the ladder.

Hank cleared his throat, intending to warn her of his presence, but at the sound, a pile of hissing fury launched itself from beneath one of the mangers. Spider yelped as the cat raked claws across her nose, then streaked up the ladder…right across Grace's hand.

Startled, she lost her grip and her foot slipped. Hank leapt forward, and stars burst in his head as her flailing elbow cracked him square in the eyebrow. Somehow he managed to hold on to her, stumbling backward until he slammed up against the front of the nearest stall and slid down, plopping onto his butt with Grace in his lap—again.

Hooves clattered as the horses stampeded out into their runs. Grace clutched his shoulders, her breathing ragged and her hair tickling his chin and smelling of hay and arena dirt and something like sugar cookies. His arms tightened in reflex.

"Are you okay?" he asked, his voice wobbling as a nightmare vision flashed behind his eyes of Grace falling, her head cracking against the floor, her neck…

God. She could have literally broken her neck, and it would have been his fault, bringing his dogs into what he knew was that hellcat's territory.

"I'm fine. Just a little…you know." She pushed out another breath that played warm across his cheek, then pulled back to brush aside his hair and gingerly touch his throbbing eyebrow.

"Ouch."

She scrunched up her freckled nose. "That might leave a mark."

"Not the first one." His gaze drifted down to her soft mouth. Would she taste like a sugar cookie, too? There was a reason he shouldn't try to find out—several, he was sure—but he was having trouble remembering what they were with his head spinning and Grace all warm and soft against him.

His fingers came up to trace the faint remnant of the scratch on her cheek. There was one. "Every time you get close to me, I end up hurting you."

"You never mean to."

He gave a soft, bitter laugh. "And that makes it better?"

She hesitated for few painful thuds of his agitated heart, then her mouth curved ever so slightly. "Yeah. It does."

He flattened his palm against her cheek, intending only to touch. God, her skin was so soft. She tensed but didn't pull away. He should stop. She should stop him. But she didn't—just stared at him with those wide hazel eyes as he lowered his head to press his mouth to hers.

For a moment, he thought it would be just that. A gentle press of lips on lips before she pushed him away. Instead, her fingers laced behind his neck as she opened up and let him in.

Oh yeah. Definitely delicious, but not like a cookie at all. More like sliding into a pool of warm honey, the intense sweetness of the kiss flowing over and through him as her tongue stroked his. Slow. Easy. He tilted her head for a deeper taste.

"Well, this is awkward."

Hank broke the kiss so fast, the back of his skull smacked against the stall gate. He blinked. Stared. Blinked again. The woman who'd spoken was still there.

"*Bing?*"

"In the flesh." Her eyebrows arched as her dark, inscrutable gaze took in the scene. "And here I thought *you* were gonna get a surprise."

Chapter 20

HANK NEARLY DUMPED GRACE ON HER BUTT AS he shot to his feet, only remembering at the last second to haul her up with him. She sagged against the stall, her system in chaos from the suddenness of the kiss and its even more abrupt end, while Hank threw his arms around the woman in the doorway.

"Bing." His face shone with such joy that Grace's heart clutched. "What are you doing here?"

She laughed up at him, so much younger and prettier than Grace had expected, despite what Melanie had told her. "I was gonna ask you the same thing. It's too late for style points, but you could try to show some manners."

"Wha…oh!" Hank's expression was almost comical when he realized that he'd practically shoved Grace aside in his haste. "Shit. Grace. I'm sorry."

"Still keeping it classy, I see," Gil Sanchez said from over Bing's shoulder, but his eyes were fixed on Grace, his gaze drilling a hole straight through her.

With as much dignity as she could muster, she offered Bing a smile. "Hi. I'm Grace. Obviously not short for graceful."

Bing laughed, a big, unfettered sound that loosened a few of the knots in Grace's stomach. "I see why you like her."

Hank's face went a dusky red, and his gaze bounced from Grace to Bing to the horses that poked tentative noses into their stalls, too curious to stay outside. He finally settled on capturing Spider, who'd come bounding back and was winding her leash around Bing's legs. The cat gave a hair-raising yowl from up in the hayloft, fangs bared and ears flat.

Grace brushed at the hay clinging to her jeans. "We should get out of here before she attacks again."

"Oh, so we're blaming it on the cat." Gil's tone was caustic.

Bing smacked his arm. He ignored her.

"What are you doing here?" Hank asked Bing as they filed into the yard.

"I told you I had vacation time to burn." She hitched a shoulder. "After you told me you'd gone to work for your dad, I decided I'd better put it to good use. Turns out I'm just in time. He decided to come home today."

Hank skidded to a stop and glared at Gil. "You said he was staying at Miz Iris's for at least a week."

"I was wrong." There was nothing apologetic in his voice, but then he added, "But I said you could leave when he came home, so if you want out, I'll schedule you a trip as soon as I can."

Hank hesitated, looking to Bing for guidance.

"It's up to you, but you've already been paid for the first week, and I'll make sure he doesn't give you any grief." The set of her jaw suggested that she might enjoy dishing out some of her own.

After another moment, Hank shrugged. "I'll stick it out, unless he tells me to leave."

Grace paused just outside the barn door, fisting her hands inside the front pocket of her sweatshirt as she tried not to stare at Hank, his face hidden by the unexpectedly soft hair that had slid, cool and slick, through her fingers. Her mind struggled to absorb the insane reality of that kiss, even though she could still taste him and her body was still throbbing at every point where it had been pressed up against the hard angles of his. And Gil, damn him, could see right through her.

Under the security light, his midnight-blue Charger gleamed like a phantom menace. He circled the car and braced his forearms on the roof, his face carved into harsh lines as he waited for Hank to wrangle his dogs into the pickup.

She avoided his eyes and gave Bing another awkward smile. "It was, um, nice to meet you."

"Do you want to have supper with us?" Bing asked. "We're going to the roadhouse downtown."

"Thanks, but I need to get caught up on my lesson plans."

Bing gave Grace a blatantly speculative look before turning to the men. "Who am I riding with?"

"Me, if you don't mind a little dog hair," Hank said. "Or dog breath."

"I'll let you two catch up. I've got another stop to make." Gil fixed Grace with one more of those dark, penetrating stares, then climbed in the Charger and slammed the door.

As he turned to Grace, Hank tucked his fingers in the front pockets of his jeans, shoulders hunched against night air that had cooled significantly since he'd arrived. "So, um…"

Ignoring the protests of her body, Grace drew herself up and set her mouth in a determined line. She had to stop this now, before Hank got it into his head that the friendship they'd agreed to had any possibility of benefits.

"I can be your friend." Up to a point, and after tonight, she would have to seriously reconsider what that point would be. That slope she was teetering on had turned out to be a whole lot more slippery than she'd expected. She tilted her head toward the barn, a raw ache blooming in her chest. "I can't be that."

Hank's face went stiff. "My mistake."

"Mine too." She reached for a breezy, *no big deal* tone. "I'll try to stop falling on you."

He didn't smile, just gave her one more abrupt nod, got in the pickup, and drove away.

Grace blew out a long, gusty sigh and trudged around the barn to her temporary home in Tori's trailer. The living quarters had a ten-foot slide-out on one side that held a dangerously comfortable leather couch, leaving plenty of floor space between it and the banquette table. A small bar curved around a kitchen area equipped with a gas cooktop, stove, and double sinks.

Home sweet rodeo home.

Grace kicked off her boots and started toward the bathroom at the rear, pulling her sweatshirt over her head as she went. She had both arms stuck up over her head when a fist banged on the door so hard she stumbled and plowed into the wall. Wrestling the sweatshirt off, she tossed it on the couch and smoothed down her hair with unsteady hands. She didn't have to guess who'd come calling.

She'd barely touched the latch when the door was jerked out of her grasp and Gil snarled up at her, "What the hell are you trying to do to him, Grace?"

She hung her head, unable to hold his furious gaze.

"That was an accident. We can't seem to avoid each other, so I thought…I was hoping it would be better if we could be friends again."

"Or you could make it worse if he starts counting on you." He plowed a hand through his black hair, raising spikes that made him look even more like an angry demon. "There are already too many people who matter keeping secrets from him. It's gonna be ugly enough when he realizes Melanie and Wyatt are in on it."

"You too," Grace whispered miserably.

He hissed a stream of air between clenched teeth. "Yeah. Me too."

Of the handful of people who knew about Grace's pregnancy, Gil Sanchez had been the first, purely by accident. The morning after that disastrous New Year's Eve, he'd found Grace sobbing over the filing she did one Sunday a month at Sanchez Trucking to help their secretary keep up. He had made the mistake of asking what was wrong, and she'd blurted it out. And then he'd pawned her off on Wyatt because, Gil said caustically, he was a lot better candidate as white knights went.

But Gil had been totally unaware that Wyatt was in love with Hank's sister. And now the three of them were stuck in this hellish limbo, forced to lie to Hank for Grace's sake. And in the case of Maddie's parents, forced to live with the worst kind of uncertainty. They had agreed because they understood exactly what she would lose when her family found out, but the longer she put off the inevitable, the more they all suffered. Grace could justify her selfishness when Hank was fifteen hundred miles away and mired in what Bing had told Melanie was best described as a major depressive episode.

But he was better now, or Bing wouldn't have let him come back to the Panhandle…and Gil wouldn't have brought him.

Grace shoved her hands into the pocket of her sweatshirt, where Gil couldn't see the white of her knuckles as she knotted her fingers together and said what he wouldn't. "It's time to tell him."

The breath he released was equal parts resignation and relief, leaking through a rare crack in his armor. "It would be best to do it while Bing's here."

"How long will that be?"

"Maybe until New Year's." Gil shrugged. "It depends on how long Hank sticks around."

Something like dismay clutched at her heart. "He's not staying?"

"Why would he?"

Not a single reason she could think of, and a dozen why he'd want to be anywhere but here.

Grace was about to make that a dozen and one.

"Let me know when you're planning to talk to him," Gil said. "At least I can be there to stop him from doing anything stupid."

"He's not going to be happy with you."

Gil's smile was a grim slash. "That's okay. I'm used to it."

After he left, Grace went to sit alone on the couch, grappling with the in-your-face reality of a moment that had, for so long, been a storm on a distant horizon. She had to tell Hank. Soon. Tonight's kiss had proven that beyond a doubt.

But she also had to find some way to accept that this could be her last Thanksgiving at Mama's table.

Chapter 21

ON WEDNESDAY MORNING, HANK GRABBED A TANKER-sized travel mug of coffee from the shop's break room on his way out the door. Even after reading until well past midnight, he'd struggled to sleep, and he had to be alert if he was gonna face his dad.

But Bing would be there, so it couldn't get too ugly. If his dad told him to leave, he'd leave. He'd barely touched the seven hundred dollars, so paying back what he hadn't earned wasn't a problem. And since he expected absolutely nothing from Johnny Brookman, he wouldn't be disappointed.

He would miss Mabel, though. And Spider. She sorta grew on a guy.

But before he left for the ranch, he had orders to stop by the dispatcher's office. Gil hadn't said why. Hank stepped through the office door and stopped dead at the sight of the woman leaning over the reception desk, her unnaturally bright-red hair held back by a wide head-band that matched her blue polka-dot dress.

She glanced up and gave him a wide scarlet smile. "Look what the cat dragged in."

Hank goggled at the *I Love Lucy* clone. She was wear-ing pearls, for God's sake. And one of those little sweat-ers. He squinted, not sure he trusted his eyes. "Analise?"

"Who else?"

"I...wow. What happened to..." He waved a hand

in a circle around his face to indicate the goth hair and multiple piercings she'd sported when she'd been the rodeo secretary for Jacobs Livestock.

"I like to change things up." She did a saucy twirl that made her skirt flare out. "You like?"

"It's really…disturbing."

"Thank you!" She beamed at him, then rolled her eyes toward the low rumble of curses filtering through the door to the dispatcher's office. "You might want to turn back. I don't know *what* happened last night, but he's in a filthy mood even by Gil's standards."

"In that case, maybe you could let him know I stopped by—"

The door was yanked open, and Gil glared at him. "No, she cannot. Get your ass in here."

Analise wrinkled her nose in sympathy as Hank shuffled reluctantly into Gil's cramped space.

"Is there a problem?" he asked warily.

Gil flung himself into his chair and bared his teeth. "What do you think?"

"Uh…yes?" But he wasn't sure why. He'd spent every minute either at the ranch or the shop, except… "Is this about Grace?"

"*Ding! Ding! Ding!* Give the boy a prize!" Gil punched the air for emphasis. "Apparently the last time wasn't enough of a disaster. You had to go back for more."

If it was anyone else, Hank would have let loose his spurt of temper, but after endlessly listening to him whine about his poor choices, Gil had earned the right to his opinion. "It won't happen again."

Gil's eyes narrowed. "Are you sure?"

Yes, because Grace had said so. *I can't be that*. Hank

still felt the words like individual slaps in the face. "She made it very clear."

Some of the angry tension bled from Gil's shoulders as he studied Hank from under heavy lids. His expression softened, as close to sympathy as Hank had ever seen from him.

"It's a shame. Under other circumstances..." He summed up Hank's countless mistakes with a shrug. "The two of you have always had something special. You might have been good for each other."

The finality in his voice was like a heavy steel door slamming down between Hank and any hope of rewinding to the moment when he'd crawled out of Grace's bed—but this time having the guts to say that he wanted more. Not just sex. The connection, the *knowing* that he felt with her. But what had he expected? Grace wasn't dumb enough to stick her hand in the same trap twice.

Gil stood, plucking another check from his desk and holding it out. "That's your pay for the trip from Montana. Let me know how it goes with your dad today. I can find you another load by the end of the week if I have to."

"Thanks." He started to leave, but Gil's hand came down on his shoulder, stopping him.

"I'm sorry. Believe it or not, I was trying to help." Then he stepped back and closed the door with a gentle click.

Hank met Analise's wide eyes. "Did he just apologize?"

"I know," she said. "Now *that* is disturbing."

It took Hank most of the drive to the ranch to recover his equilibrium, but he couldn't shake a weird sense of dread. He could handle Gil ripping into him. But being nice? It made him feel like a condemned prisoner.

And the sidewalk to his dad's house felt a lot like walking the plank.

Hank paused at the door to take a steadying breath, then turned the knob and walked into the kitchen to find Johnny hunched over a plate of pancakes, looking like regurgitated hell with two-day stubble, bloodshot eyes, and half his hair standing on end.

Bing leaned against the counter, spatula in hand. "Breakfast?"

Hank looked at Johnny again, waiting for some kind of reaction. There was none.

"Just coffee." Hank held up the mug he'd drained on the drive out, and she sauntered over to take it. Damn. He hadn't expected his dad to be quite this…broken.

"Have you checked the cake bin?" Johnny asked, without looking up.

"It's almost empty," Hank said. "The feed store is delivering a load this morning."

His dad grunted. "Dennert called last night. He shot what they figure was that pig you ran across."

Of course Cole would have told him. "That's good. Hopefully it didn't bring friends."

Johnny grunted again.

"There's a cow down in the river pasture with porcupine quills in her nose," Hank went on. "When I'm done with the chores, I'm gonna saddle up and bring her in. Want to come along?" he asked Bing.

"Sure. I'd like to see more of the place." She'd been with a rancher for several years and was a decent hand on a horse. The guy was also a roper, the reason she'd started working as a secretary at the Indian rodeos. She'd kept the job a lot longer than the man.

"I'll saddle Tick for you. When we're done, I'll give you a tour of the big city of Earnest."

"Sounds good."

He accepted the coffee mug from her and waited to see if his dad would speak. Finally, Hank asked, "Anything else?"

Johnny shook his head. Hank shot Bing a questioning look.

She tapped her shoulder. "His pain meds are back at Miz Iris's. He spent most of the night not sleeping in the recliner."

And Bing would know. This close to Thanksgiving, he doubted she'd slept at all, but his dad must have provided enough of a distraction to keep her from calling Hank. He felt a reluctant twinge of sympathy for his dad. Then again, if the dumb-ass hadn't been so hardheaded, he'd be resting comfortably at Miz Iris's house.

Hank cleared his throat. "I'll get to work, then."

No one objected, so he went out to start the chores.

———⁓———

When Hank was gone, Bing walked over to the coffee maker, poured a mug, and set it in front of Johnny. "There. Was that so hard?"

He took a greedy, scalding gulp before answering. "Is this how you treat your patients?"

"By withholding caffeine until they do what I want?" She cocked her head, annoyingly pleased with herself. "It's worth a shot if it works this well."

"They probably aren't at your mercy," he muttered.

"Hey, you're the one who wanted to stay. One phone call and you can be outta here."

Not damn likely. He wouldn't go crawling back to Miz Iris's with his tail tucked between his legs.

"I'll take that as a no," she said. "That smoked brisket is still good, so I'll make up sandwiches for lunch. Do you prefer macaroni or potato salad?"

He squinted at her suspiciously. "Why? So you can make the opposite?"

She laughed at him. And dammit, a woman that mean shouldn't have such a great laugh. "Consider it part of our deal."

"What deal?"

"The one we're about to make. You refrain from being an asshole to your son, and I will keep you fed and watered." She held out a hand, her fingernails the same vibrant pink as her toes. "Agreed?"

It wasn't like he had a choice, so he took what was offered. Her hand was cool and soft, her grip firm, and she held on for a few beats as their gazes locked. His pulse gave a funny little skip.

She smiled and let go. "Excellent. And now that we understand each other…macaroni or potato?"

Chapter 22

GRACE REFUSED TO HANG OUT IN THE WRESTLING room, even if they were the last team to finish practice on Wednesday morning. It was like breathing condensed sweat, and no matter how many times they scrubbed the mats with bleach solution, the place still reeked.

She set her folding chair just outside and cracked the door a few inches instead, close enough to hear if anyone called for her. Then she fired up her tablet and proceeded to accomplish almost nothing. Her mind refused to focus on treatment notes when it could spin in useless circles, from Hank's kiss to Gil's warning, from Hank's laughter to Maddie's cheeky grin.

Her phone chirped. She checked the message and smiled at Shawnee's standard post-checkup text, sent out to everyone waiting to hear the results. OK.

"Hey, Grace. Good news?"

Grace looked up to see one of the custodians pushing a wide dust mop down the sideline of the basketball court. "Hi, Loretta. And yeah. Something to be thankful for."

"On top of an entire Thursday without seeing the inside of this place?"

Grace laughed. "That too. Got big plans for tomorrow?"

"Dinner with Mama's side of the family." She rolled her eyes, looking like one of the students in her jeans and plaid shirt, with her wispy blond hair pulled into a ponytail. "Want to make a bet on how many of them will ask if I've found myself a man yet? As if dealing with Tatum's daddy isn't enough of a pain."

"Is he giving you a hard time?"

"Just the usual." Loretta folded both hands over the end of the broom handle. "He's been insistin' since August that he was taking her to visit his family in San Antone for the holiday, and they were gonna ride the boats along the Riverwalk and spend a whole day at Six Flags. She's been so excited. Then he calls me last night and says *Hey, darlin', I had a change of plans*. And he didn't even have the balls to tell her himself."

"Ouch."

"Yeah." She made a rude gesture with the broom handle. "I told him he could *Hey darlin'* this if he ever does it to her again."

Grace twiddled her thumb over the edge of her phone. "I don't know how you do it all."

"I don't." Loretta swept an arm in a wide circle. "I do this, and I try to be a decent mother, and occasionally I sleep. I swear, if I'd had any idea it was going to be this hard…" She bit her lip, as if it wanted to tremble.

Would you have made a different choice? Grace wondered. *Did you ever look at an ultrasound image and instead of getting a rush of warm fuzzies think, "Oh, hell no. I am not raising a kid."* Obviously not. Unlike Grace, she had a smidgeon of maternal instincts.

Loretta sighed, then squared her shoulders. "I'm sorry. Here you were thinking happy thoughts, and I had to come along and dump my sad story on you."

"It's fine." Other than Shawnee's news, Grace's thoughts hadn't been all that happy.

"I imagine you're used to it." Loretta swiped the broom

under the end of the bleachers. "You're a real comforting person, Grace, and I never feel like you're judging me... unlike most folks. And I do love my baby. No matter how tough it gets, I'd never give her up, you know?"

No, Grace did not. How would Loretta judge her if she knew that not only had Grace given up her daughter, but that it didn't haunt her the way it seemed like it should. She didn't ache from the loss every time she saw a tiny pink bundle, or suffer pangs of anything but guilt when a toddler batted its eyes at her.

Mostly, she was relieved that she didn't have to take it home with her.

And no matter how many times the therapist in Oregon had insisted that motherhood wasn't an imperative and that, if anything, her feelings validated her decision to give Maddie up—it was a hard line to sell to the daughter of a woman who'd had seven children with four miscarriages in the spaces between.

"Aw, now I've got you moping," Loretta said.

Grace manufactured a smile. "You just got me thinking about family and how I'll manage to sneak out early tomorrow without my tattletale sister ratting me out."

"Oh, honey, I hear you." Loretta winked at her. "If all else fails, go with the menstrual cramps. It freaks out the men and the women can feel your pain, so nobody argues."

"Thanks. I'll keep that in mind."

As the door to the wrestling room burst open and a herd of boys thundered past, Grace stood and folded her chair. "That's my cue. Enjoy your day off."

Tori had texted that they were home, so when the wrestlers finally cleared out, Grace locked up and drove to her apartment. There was three days' worth of mail in her box. She stuffed it under her arm, unlocked the door, and wrinkled her nose at the stench of a garbage can she'd obviously forgotten to empty. Dumping the mail on the kitchen counter, she began sorting through the pile. Her hands went still when she came across a heavy, cream-colored envelope. Not an off-the-rack Christmas card, and the handwriting was as lovely as its owner. There was no return address—a concession to their privacy agreement. A friend or family member wouldn't stumble across it and ask Grace who was sending her greetings from Portland, Oregon.

Her heart thudded painfully as she pulled out a table knife, slit the envelope, and pulled out the photo. Her breath stalled in her throat. Lord, Maddie was adorable in a red velvet and lace dress with a matching beret. The outfit probably cost more than Grace's mama had spent on her wedding dress. The woman who held her was even more exquisite, a miracle of shimmering blond hair and porcelain skin. The second woman, standing with a possessive, protective hand on the blond's shoulder, was equally stunning, her hair jet black and her skin a deep brown, her features drawn in bolder lines.

Everything Grace didn't feel shone in their faces. The pride. The joy. The fierce, unqualified love. Their smiles were so brilliant that Grace had to close her eyes. In all the months since she'd realized she was pregnant, those smiles were the best answer she had to the first question Hank was bound to ask.

Why, Grace?

It was almost midnight on Wednesday when Hank parked his pickup in front of his dad's house, after Tex-Mex and a movie in Amarillo with Bing. The lamp was on in the living room, but he could see through the window that the television was off. His dad hadn't waited up for them.

And it was damned annoying that Hank had felt a little guilty about getting back so late. They hadn't abandoned Johnny. Steve and Miz Iris had come after lunch to bring his medication and whatever else he'd left at their house, and the neighbors who'd hauled him to the hospital had called to say they were bringing over an apple pie that evening to welcome him home.

"Are you sure you don't want me to stay?" Hank asked Bing.

She squeezed his hand. "Just keep your phone close, and come for breakfast first thing. There will be caramel rolls."

"Count me in." He turned his hand over and returned the squeeze. "I don't have so much as an aspirin in my apartment, and there's no place in Earnest to buy booze at this time of the night."

She sketched a thin smile. "I'm not worried."

"Yes, you are. And like you keep telling me, it doesn't have to be rational to be real."

She huffed out a breath of a laugh. They sat for a few moments, the wind whistling around the cab. He had planned to take her into Amarillo tomorrow, then on down to Palo Duro Canyon, but as distractions went, he thought he could do better.

"I want to go to dinner tomorrow," he said abruptly.

She blinked. "At Miz Iris's?"

"Yeah. I…miss it." Lame, but if he made her think it was important to him, she'd be more likely to go along. "And you can entertain yourself by calling out anybody who even looks at me sideways."

Her teeth gleamed in the moonlight. "I can do that."

"I know." He leaned across the cab to give her a hug. "It's one of the things I love best about you."

Chapter 23

JOHNNY HADN'T SLEPT FOR CRAP SINCE HIS SURGERY, so he didn't realize at first that the pain hadn't woken him this time. Then he saw the glowing white figure leaning over him...and he screamed.

His visitor yelped, stumbling backward into the dresser and knocking over his collection of ancient Father's Day cologne bottles, then cursing as she scrabbled to set them right.

Johnny rolled onto his right side to squint at Bing in the moonlight shining through the window, his heart kicking into his ribs. "What are you doing?"

"Nothing! I just..." She fumbled one bottle upright and cursed again as she knocked over another in the process. What Johnny's sleep-logged brain had registered as a ghost was a baggy white T-shirt worn over gray sweatpants. She gave up on the cologne bottles and pressed her palms onto the top of the dresser. "I'm sorry. I didn't mean to scare you. I was just checking."

"For what?"

She made an odd, gulping sound. "To see if you were still breathing."

He pushed himself upright and swung his legs over the side of the bed, wearing only his sling and thigh-length basketball shorts. "Were you plannin' on making me stop?"

"What?" She jerked around, leaning back against the dresser to steady herself.

Was she drunk? Johnny inhaled, but didn't smell booze. Stoned, maybe? "Were you gonna smother me with my own pillow?"

"Oh! No." Her laugh was as shaky as the hands she raised, pressing all ten fingers along her hairline. She took a couple of deep breaths, and her voice was almost normal when she spoke again. "As charming as you've been, I'm not feeling homicidal...yet." She wrapped her arms around herself, as if chilled. "I'll let you get back—"

"Could we have some hot chocolate?" he blurted.

"Now?"

"You're already up, and I'm not gonna be able to go back to sleep."

Her eyebrows rose. "Even if the crazy lady promises not to suffocate you as soon as you doze off?"

"Are you?"

"Crazy?" She turned her face away as she meticulously set one of the cologne bottles upright. "The politically correct term would be compulsive, and mostly only for a couple of weeks out of the year."

And this appeared to be one of them. He stood, then realized his mistake when it put his almost-bare body firmly inside her personal space. Her startled gaze flew up to his face, then drifted down to his chest.

"I'll just go..." She sidled along the dresser, turned, and hustled out the open door.

By the time he'd wrestled on a zippered hoodie and a pair of sweatpants, she was on the couch, sipping hot chocolate. She'd set another steaming cup on the end table beside his recliner. As he got himself situated, a cell phone chirped. She fished it out of the pocket of the sweatshirt she'd pulled on, checked the message, typed in a couple of letters, and hit Send.

When she caught Johnny's curious gaze, she said, "Hank's just checking in."

"At two thirty in the morning?"

"He knew I'd be awake."

"And you'd be wondering if he's still breathing too?" Johnny guessed.

"Yeah." She gripped her mug between both hands. "I suppose I owe you an explanation."

He could have been polite and said no, but it *was* two thirty in the morning, she *had* scared the crap out him… and he wanted to know, even if a little voice was warning him this wasn't going to be a happy bedtime story.

"My grandson died of an overdose two years ago," she said. "In my house. I found him on Thanksgiving morning."

Jesus. Christ. Johnny stared at her bowed head for much too long, and when he did find words, he could only ask, "Was it…"

"Accidental. He and some friends scored some fentanyl, after they'd already been drinking most of the day." Her voice was mechanical, a little scratchy, like a recording she'd played too many times. "I was at a friend's and didn't get home until almost ten. I peeked in his door and saw he was already in bed, but I didn't check…"

To see if he was breathing. Sweet fucking hell.

She kept talking, every word like a drop of blood squeezed from her heart. "I tried everything to make him stop. Got him into treatment once, but he was using again a week after he checked out. I yelled. I begged. I tried to reason with him. Nothing worked."

As she spoke, she huddled deeper into herself. To

ward off the pain? Or contain it, so she didn't howl out the agony written in every line of her body? If Johnny had had two good arms, he might not have been able to stop himself from gathering her into them.

But another part of his mind was struggling to put the pieces together. Drugs, all-day drinking binges—had he heard her wrong? He could've sworn she said *grandson*, but that would've made him… "How old?"

"Twenty." At Johnny's shocked silence, she lifted her head, her mouth twisting. "Yes. I had a grandson almost the same age as Hank."

"I didn't mean…" But of course he had. "What about his, um—"

"Mother. She's in North Dakota with a Chippewa. From what I hear, he treats her okay. She and I have always had our problems. Not exactly a stable family dynamic, you know? And of course now she blames me, so…" She gave a shrug that encapsulated too much to put into words.

Another realization hit Johnny. "That's why you rescued Hank."

"It's a habit of mine. I didn't expect him to rescue me back." Tears gathered in her eyes. "He doesn't even try to fix anything. He just listens and makes sure I know he's there if I need him."

Was she really talking about his son? The boy who could disappear in the blink of an eye? Johnny would have said that Hank had a gift for *not* being where he was needed, but Steve and Cole Jacobs didn't have any qualms about trusting him with their stock. Gil Sanchez was willing to put him behind the wheel of a quarter-million-dollar rig and send him off across the country.

And now Bing was saying he was the guy she counted on, no matter what.

Which begged the question—if Johnny was the only one who had a problem with Hank, what were the odds that Hank had never been the problem?

Johnny took a sip of his hot chocolate. It had gone lukewarm. He sighed, rested the mug on the armrest, and lay back, closing his eyes. "I don't recall waking up one morning and thinking, 'You know what I wanna be when I grow up? A real son of a bitch.'"

That surprised a short laugh out of Bing. "And yet, here you are."

"Some people might try to make me feel better," he said sourly.

"In my line of work, we call that enabling."

He cracked an eyelid to see that at least he'd headed off the tears. "Yeah? Do you also have a twelve-step program for grouchy bastards?"

"Would you sign up?"

He had a vision of standing up in front of a roomful of crotchety old men and announcing, *"Hi, I'm Johnny, and I'm an asshole. I chased my entire family clear out of the state of Texas."* But it might be worth it if he could get through the day without wanting to beat on an inanimate object with a fence post.

"I wouldn't even know where to start," he said.

She cocked her brows at him. "That seems fairly obvious."

"With Hank?" His fist closed around the mug. "Why would he even want to try? According to his sister, he can trace about ninety percent of his problems straight back to his lousy relationship with his father."

"You're giving yourself too much credit. Don't forget his mother."

"I should be so lucky." Then Johnny huffed out another sigh. "And that's not fair. We were pretty good together at the beginning, but this isn't what she signed up for."

"The son of a bitch, or the ranch?"

"Both. Neither." Johnny had never talked to anyone about the slow-motion disaster his marriage had become, but considering the chunk of her soul that Bing had bared, his problems seemed fairly trivial. "She lived for the rush and the spotlight, and she made the mistake of thinking I could give it to her. Instead of finishing her degree in broadcast media, she married me and became my road manager." He shook his head in reluctant admiration. "Geezus, that woman could drive. She'd pull the all-nighters from one rodeo to the next and let me sleep so I could rope better." He gave a half smile. "I guess that's where Hank gets his trucking gene."

"But she wasn't so good at staying in one place," Bing guessed.

"Not this place anyway. She busted her hump helping me rebuild, figuring after a year or so we'd be back on the road, but my dad had the beginnings of COPD before the fire and never recovered from the smoke inhalation." His chest ached with the old despair of watching a strong man reduced to a wheezing shell. "My sisters were both gone, married with families, so it was up to me to take over the ranch."

Which he'd planned to do eventually, after he'd had his fun and made his name. He sure as hell hadn't planned on having to start at what looked like ground zero—nothing but smoke and ashes—when he was twenty-seven years old and halfway through the best season of his life.

Resentment rose like bile in his throat, no less bitter with age. He swallowed it one more time. "She went back to college—Melanie was in school by then—and worked as an intern at a crappy little AM station in Amarillo. We barely saw her. She was a semester shy of graduation and pretty much had her bags packed and ready to move to a bigger market when she got pregnant with Hank."

"That was inconvenient." Bing almost managed to keep her voice neutral. "But she could have gone anyway."

"And what? Leave her baby? Try to be a single mother working anything from four a.m. to midnight? She didn't have much of a choice. But she got on at one of the talk-radio stations in Amarillo, doing the ag updates." He twisted off a smile at the irony. "They wanted someone with local ranch connections, so she played it to the hilt."

"And tied herself to this place in the process."

"Yep. She got her own show, and it got picked up by a regional network, but she had branded herself as the true-blue ranch wife, so she had to keep playing the part...at least when other people were looking."

And had made no bones about how much she despised the role when they weren't. So the two of them just kept stumbling along, handcuffed together by circumstances—with their kids caught in the middle.

Johnny set the now-frigid hot chocolate aside. "The Hank you know is a stranger to me. I don't have any idea how to reconnect."

"*Re*connect implies that you had a bond to start with."

"I meant to." He bowed his head, ashamed. "When

he was four and started T-ball, I was gonna catch and hit with him, and when he was five, I was gonna teach him to swim down at the river like I learned, and I was gonna build a doghouse with him for a 4-H project. I had all kinds of plans I never got around to because there was always something with the ranch that seemed more important. When I finally looked up, his sister had taught him how to field ground balls, his mother had signed him up for swimming lessons in Dumas, and he'd quit 4-H altogether."

Bing's voice was more sympathetic than he expected. "My uncle says you don't own cows, they own you."

"Them and the bank." Johnny shook his head. "Hank was in day care until he started kindergarten. Then he took the bus to Miz Iris's after school and stayed until Melanie brought him home. Hell, Melanie took him everywhere. It wasn't fair to either of them."

"And it didn't give the two of you much common ground."

"No." Johnny grimaced. "It sounds stupid, but even when he was little, it seemed like he went out of his way to hate everything that was important to me."

"Could be." When he blinked at her, she shrugged. "His mother sounds like a high priestess of passive aggression, and from what he's told me, she encouraged him to piss you off every chance he got."

He knew that. In retrospect, he'd seen how many times she'd fueled the fire with a casual comment about how Hank sure didn't seem to take much to ranching. Or roping. Or his father.

"He's my son," he repeated. "I'm supposed to love him despite all that."

Bing held up a hand to stop him right there. "Forget that bullshit. What Hank needs is conditional love."

"What?"

"He needs to earn respect. Be wanted for what *he* has accomplished." She pulled her bare feet up to sit cross-legged. "Have you ever heard of imposter syndrome?"

"Like in a kidnapping?"

"That's Stockholm. I'm talking about people who, no matter how successful they are, feel like a fraud. They're convinced it's luck, or a fluke, and any minute someone is going to realize they've been faking it. Most eventually crumble under the pressure of keeping up what they see as an act. Drugs, drinking, self-sabotage… There's no predicting how, but they will crash."

Johnny considered, then rejected her diagnosis. "Hank was fighting bulls at pro rodeos when he was *nineteen*."

"Working for Jacobs Livestock, who let him hang around because Steve Jacobs would do anything for his daughter's best friend, including giving her pain-in-the-ass brother a job."

She had to be kidding. Didn't she? "He was invited to work the Fort Worth Stock Show with the two best bullfighters in the country."

"One of whom was engaged to said best friend. The other had the hots for his sister. Excellent motivation to be nice to Hank."

She made it sound so reasonable that Johnny couldn't immediately pinpoint the faulty logic. "That is just… *wrong*."

"Of course it is. But you take a kid who feels unwanted by his father and has been used over and over by his mother for whatever cheap thrill she got from hurting you, then give him opportunities based on who his family knows…it's not hard for him to imagine he doesn't deserve his success."

Johnny didn't want to believe her, but the stab in his gut said she was right. His own dad had told him never to be intimidated by the cocky ropers who were always running off at the mouth. They were just hiding their lack of confidence. And Johnny was a huge part of why his son's extreme insecurity had sent him into free fall.

He slid down in his chair with a groan. "How the hell do I fix this?"

"You can't. You have to start from scratch." Bing leaned forward to be sure she had his full attention. "Get to know the man, not *your son*, and treat him like anyone else you would have hired. Don't give him anything. Let him work for it."

"I haven't given him much reason to try."

"But he's here anyway." Her smile was so unexpected and so warm, it dazzled him all over again. "He's a pretty awesome guy, all things considered."

Johnny fiddled with his sling, adjusting the strap where it dug into his neck. "If I go stumbling in blind, sure as hell I'll trip over my own dick. I should at least know what really happened out there in Washington."

Melanie damn sure wasn't telling him everything. As many times as she'd covered for her brother, Johnny knew a half-truth when he heard it.

Bing gave it a long moment's thought. Then she nodded. "You're right. You need to understand what he's been through."

And she told him a story that broke even his crusty heart.

Chapter 24

ON THANKSGIVING MORNING, MUFFLED GIGGLES WOKE Grace. She raised her head to squint at her alarm clock, then let it fall back onto her pillow with a groan. When the giggles came again, she rolled out of bed and staggered across her room.

Fourteen-year-old Lucas was sprawled on the love seat and twelve-year-old Matthew on the air mattress they'd slept on, pushed out of their own beds by the invasion of older McKenna siblings and their broods. With TV banned at home it was natural for the boys to want to squeeze in as much viewing pleasure as possible, but seriously?

"It's barely five a.m.," Grace said.

Her brothers exchanged a guilty look. "Sorry," Lucas said.

"We turned the volume way down," Matthew added.

Grace had intended to order them to keep it down and crawl back in bed, but the sight of them clutched at her heart. Finances had forced their mother to take a job in Dumas when Matthew was only three, so oversight of these two and Jeremiah—now in his first year of college—had fallen to Grace. They were her boys and her partners in crime, the four of them delighting in finding ways to circumvent their father's strict rules, especially regarding music, electronics, and junk food. Jeremiah, Lucas, and Matthew were the biggest of the reasons Grace had moved back to Texas. There were times she'd been nearly sick with missing them.

And yet, she'd been able to hand her own baby to strangers and walk away almost without a backward glance.

Grace closed her eyes against the familiar twist of guilt and dread. Telling Hank about their daughter was the equivalent of turning the secret loose to run where it would. One word to Korby, and they might as well put a birth announcement in the *Earnest Herald*. Grace would have to confess all to her family before that happened—and that would be the end of sleepovers with her brothers.

She grabbed a fuzzy throw from the rocking chair, nudged herself a space beside Lucas, and was enveloped in the scent of stinky boy feet.

God, she was going to miss them.

Thanksgiving had always been Hank's favorite holiday. For whatever reason, it was the single day of the year his parents had seemed to declare a cease-fire. Christmas was a minefield of unmet expectations and the inevitable explosions that followed. Birthdays were worse. Easter was during calving and generally slipped past without fanfare. But even they couldn't screw up Thanksgiving.

While Melanie made pancakes and their dad fried bacon, Hank and his mother would sit at the kitchen table shelling pecans for pralines—her only culinary specialty. They'd all eat breakfast in the living room to watch the Macy's parade, and then, while his mom made the pralines, the rest of them would hurry through the chores and get cleaned up for dinner at the Jacobs ranch.

Hank could practically taste the brown sugar melting

on his tongue as he and Melanie huddled in the back seat of the pickup, sneaking warm candy from a paper bag while their parents pretended not to notice.

There would be dozens of people crammed into Miz Iris's house. Thundering herds of kids and dogs overflowing onto the back lawn and enough food to founder on, with bundles of leftovers shoved into their hands as they left for home, just like every other dinner at the Jacobs ranch.

But Thanksgiving morning was special—the few hours of every year Hank had been able to count on feeling like he was part of his own family. Now they didn't even have that.

The stars had barely faded when he arrived at the ranch. He shushed the dogs as they raced from the barn to greet him, suffering the curse of sad puppy eyes when he refused to let them follow him into a house lit only by a dim glow from the kitchen. He expected to find Bing tiptoeing around to avoid waking Johnny while she made her famous caramel rolls. Instead, it was his dad who turned from the coffee maker to hold up a warning finger. Hank raised questioning eyebrows. Johnny tilted his head toward the living room. Easing forward, Hank peered over the bar to see Bing curled under a blanket, sound asleep on the couch.

His dad had gone back to staring at the dripping coffee as if he might stick a straw into the carafe rather than wait until it filled. He still looked terrible, but he appeared to be functioning better.

Hank toed off his boots and moved silently into the kitchen, close enough to his father to whisper, "Was she up all night?"

"Pretty much. She finally dozed off at four."

Hank narrowed his eyes in surprise. "You stayed up with her?"

"My shoulder was aching. Feels better sitting in the recliner." The coffee maker beeped, and Johnny snatched the pot. He grabbed a mug from the wooden rack on the counter, poured it full and pushed it toward Hank. "I don't imagine you got any sleep either with all the texts."

Damn. His dad had seen… "Did she tell you why?"

"Yeah." Johnny poured a second mug, held the too-hot coffee under his nose and inhaled as if he could snort the caffeine. "She told me a lot of stuff."

Shock flashed over Hank, first cold, then hot. How could Bing give him up like that? He waited for…what? Sympathy? Disgust? But his dad's face remained carefully blank as he took a first cautious sip.

Okay, then. They weren't going to talk about it. Fine with Hank. He angled past his dad and checked in the fridge. The promised pan of unbaked caramel rolls was on the bottom shelf. He pulled off the plastic wrap and set them on the counter to rise. Then he stirred a couple spoonfuls of sugar into his coffee and took it to the kitchen table. Johnny stayed where he was, leaning on the counter. With Bing sleeping, they had a perfect excuse to drink in silence.

Johnny finished first, draining his mug and setting it by the sink. "Mind if I come and feed the calves with you? I'd like to get a good look at them."

"Uh, sure." Hank slugged the last of his coffee and rose. "I'll feed the horses while you get dressed."

Before he left, he unearthed a stubby pencil from the pile of odds and ends on the bar and scratched a note on the back of a feed store flyer.

Doing chores. Text if you need me.

It was still half an hour before sunrise when they pulled onto the highway, the edges and colors of the landscape muted. As they accelerated, Johnny cocked his head. "The front end isn't vibrating anymore."

"I hope not. I've replaced damn near the whole thing."

Johnny frowned. "How'd you get to be such a good mechanic? You sure as hell didn't learn it from me."

"Cole," Hank said.

"Ah. I guess that's why you were constantly trying to organize my tools."

"Yep." *Try* being the operative word.

As usual, the calves were mobbed at the gate. The dogs bailed off the flatbed and flew at the herd.

"You'd better not let—" Johnny began.

Hank cut him off with a shrill whistle. Both dogs dropped to their bellies.

"Well, I'll be a son of a bitch," Johnny said.

Hank refrained from taking the open shot, but it was not easy. He hustled out to unchain the gate from the new latch before he changed his mind.

"When did you put that on?" his dad demanded when he got back in the pickup.

"Yesterday. It's gonna be a while before that arm of yours is good for much, so I've been making the place more user-friendly."

"Oh." Johnny paused, then added, "Thanks."

Hank did a double take. "Uh…you're welcome."

He pulled the pickup through and went back to shut the gate behind them, flip on the feeder motor, then jump back into the cab as the hopper started doling out piles of cake while Hank drove in a slow, wide circle.

Johnny leaned forward to squint at the dashboard counter in disbelief. "You got that thing working?"

"It just needed rewiring."

"Huh."

When they were done feeding, Johnny hopped out and got the gate one-handed, looking amazed at how well it worked. Hank couldn't decide whether to be annoyed or proud, so he turned on the radio. No market reports on the holiday, so the station played classic country instead—the real old twangers. They drove on down to the pasture to feed the mother cows—another gate Hank had rerigged so Johnny could manage it—and were back at the house as the sun crawled above the horizon, setting the countryside aglow.

Before Hank could escape, Johnny said, "Wait."

Hank paused, one foot out the door.

"You were only hired through Saturday." Johnny braced his palm on his knee, obviously working up to something. "I'd like you to stay on."

Whoa. Hank wasn't expecting that. "For how long?"

"We can take it a week at a time, see how it goes."

A week. An hour. A minute. Hank had gotten used to tackling life in small increments. But living and working in close proximity with his dad? That could get interesting. Then again, Hank didn't have a whole lot to lose. With a standing offer at Sanchez Trucking, he could walk away from the ranch any time he felt the need. "Okay."

"Okay." Johnny shoved the door open and slid out, detouring to fetch something from his pickup while

Hank walked inside. The glorious smell of baking bread filled the air. Bing was freshly showered and dressed in jeans and a blouse the color of the sky outside the window, her eyes brighter than he'd dared hope.

"Chores all done?" she asked.

He nodded. "What did you two talk about last night?"

"Oh, this and that. Why?"

"He offered me a job."

Johnny came inside, too slow with the door to keep the dogs from pushing past his legs.

Bing squatted to rub both of their heads, then lifted her eyebrows at Johnny. "Sounds like it's been an interesting morning."

"Yep." He hefted a paper bag that clattered when he set it on the table. "Miz Iris gave me these a couple weeks ago. They're off her trees."

Hank peeled open the crumpled top, and his gut did a funny little twist as he scooped up a handful of pecans. "Have you ever made pralines?" he asked Bing.

"No, but I'm willing to try if you've got a recipe."

"In here." Johnny moved to reach into the cupboard beside her. Hank got a weird pang, seeing them standing so close, looking so domestic. Almost like…

Johnny handed her the ancient cookbook and stepped away. "It was my mother's. And it must be pretty simple."

"If Mom couldn't ruin them?" Hank concluded.

His dad grinned at him. Actually *grinned*, the two them sharing an inside joke.

So many things weren't the same. His mother had moved to California with her new husband. Melanie was off in Oregon with that asshole, Wyatt. But Bing had given Hank a real smile on Thanksgiving morning, and he'd spent a whole hour alone with his dad and come away better for it instead of worse.

Who knew? Thanksgiving might still be that magical day they couldn't screw up.

Hank shucked his coat and went to turn on the television so they didn't miss any of the parade. If they were gonna do this, they might as well do it up right.

Chapter 25

IT WAS ONLY QUARTER AFTER ONE WHEN GRACE slipped out the back door—a personal record. Of course, she had to give props to their minister, who had *suggested* that his flock forgo both dinner the night before and breakfast that morning in order to be more thankful for their bounty. Her mother had set the turkey on the table at precisely twelve o'clock, and the five McKenna boys had demolished it plus all the sides and two kinds of pie in less than half an hour. If speed was any measure, they were the most grateful family in Earnest.

And then—on this day of celebrating the original immigrants—her father had jumped right into a speech about how refugees were going to be the ruin of the country.

Grace had excused herself from the table before she pointed out the blatant contradiction with the occasion they were celebrating. There was no argument she could present that would change any of the adult minds at that table, but she might still have felt guilty at not trying if she hadn't caught Matthew and Lucas exchanging a stealthy eye roll.

Her work here was done. And since it was the day for it, she sent up a small *thank you* that the hordes would be leaving tomorrow.

Despite her haste, she found Jeremiah already sitting on the back steps, elbows on his knees and a pensive expression on a face that had changed in some fundamental way over the past months, from boy to man.

Grace sat down beside him, tucking her skirt snugly around her legs to ward off the breeze, and he looped an arm around her shoulders to share his warmth.

"Is he getting worse, or was I just that oblivious?" Jeremiah pitched his voice low to avoid being overheard.

"Both, I think. I definitely noticed it a lot more after I started college, but since I came back from Oregon..." She smoothed a pleat in her skirt, searching for the right words. "It's like he crystallized. Everything is sharper. Harder. And the big three just sit there and nod and smile."

The big three being Grace's oldest two brothers and her sister. They had all followed in their father's regimented footsteps without question. And then came Grace, who questioned *everything* and taught her younger brothers to do the same.

"So what happened to you?" Jeremiah asked.

"I used to think I got it from Mama. Sometimes she gets a look in her eyes..." Then Grace sighed. "But she'll never stand up to him."

Her voice tried to catch, and Jeremiah angled her a questioning glance. Of all her siblings, he was the most tuned into her wavelength.

"What's up, Gracie?" His normally teasing gray-green eyes were sober. She started to shake her head, but he caught her ponytail. "Don't say nothing. You can't lie to me."

But could she tell him the truth? She was ninety-nine percent sure he would understand. Even so, her heart raced and her lungs constricted. And if it was this scary with Jeremiah, how would she ever face their father?

One step at a time. She slanted a meaningful gaze toward the kitchen window above their heads. "Not here."

"I'll walk you to your pickup." He jumped up and flashed a grin that instantly made him fifteen again. "I see you parked for a quick getaway. I'm writing this down for when I can afford a car."

"Note that I also left my coat in the pickup so no one could tell I was leaving. Get back here with that arm."

He did, hugging her close as they eased along the side of the house, through a gap in the hedge, and onto the sidewalk. When they were safely out of sight, Jeremiah gave her a squeeze. "Confession time. Things have been weird with you for a long time…like the way you up and left six months before you started that job at Pendleton High School."

"There wasn't much to keep me here after I graduated."

"You could've got a job in Amarillo. You didn't have to abandon us completely."

And he couldn't hide his hurt, especially from Grace. She'd missed half of his sophomore and all of his junior year, when being excluded from the social order was increasingly painful, and Grace hadn't been there to persuade their parents that the Devil would not snatch him directly off the floor at a high school dance.

"I'm sorry." She pressed her cheek into the scratchy knit of his wool sweater. "I did come back in time to get you to the senior prom."

He made a face. "With Papa driving us."

"Hey, at least you got to go." None of the boys had bothered to ask Grace, although she could have taken Hank up on his offer to find her a date…with someone else. And he couldn't fathom why she'd been insulted.

"I did manage to sneak off long enough to kiss her." Jeremiah smiled dreamily. "She was my first."

"Glad I could contribute to your moral decay," Grace quipped.

He laughed. "Speaking of which…we're supposed to be discussing your guilty secret. What did you do out there in the Wild West? Join a pot-smoking motorcycle gang? Or worse, the ACLU, Lord save your soul. Mama and Daddy would probably be less scandalized if they found out you'd run off to have Hank's love child."

Grace tripped over a nonexistent crack in the sidewalk.

Jeremiah's grin faded, his eyes going wide as he pulled her around to face him. "That was a joke, Grace."

She ducked her chin. As signs went, this one was a freaking neon billboard. *Tell Him Now*.

"Grace? You're messing with me, right?"

She lifted her head and met his gaze. "No."

"Jesus Christ, Grace! You had a—"

She slapped a hand over his mouth. "Shh! Someone's gonna hear you."

He peeled her hand away, his voice dropping to a furious whisper. "Does that bastard know?"

She shook her head.

"And the baby? Where is…um…"

Grace tugged on his arm, resuming their stroll so it wasn't obvious to any random observer that this wasn't a casual conversation. "*She* lives in Portland."

Jeremiah shot her another incredulous look. "You know the parents?"

"They're friends of Wyatt's. I didn't want Maddie to have to wonder where she came from." But would she ever be able to explain why?

"Maddie," her brother repeated. "You had a baby, and she has a name, and…wow."

They had reached Grace's pickup. She trailed her fingertip along the edge of the box. "I also found out after the fact that they had paid off my student loans," she said abruptly.

Or more precisely had arranged to have them "forgiven." There were now people in Maddie's life who could make that sort of thing happen, and route it through so many convoluted channels that no one could be accused of violating the laws that limited compensation to the mother's expenses during pregnancy.

"Is that bad?"

"It's not precisely legal. And it makes me feel…" *Like I sold my baby.* She screwed up her face against the pang of guilt. "And then when Maddie was six months old, I got a letter informing me that a trust had been set up in my name. Anonymous benefactor. Her parents swear it wasn't them, and Wyatt had someone try to trace it to be sure I couldn't get into trouble. They're all sure it was one of the grandparents, but no one can prove it. The money was just there, and I didn't have a choice whether to say no."

"How much?"

She swallowed. "Twenty thousand dollars."

"Whoa. They must have some serious cash. Is that how you can afford this thing?" He rapped his knuckles on the side of the pickup.

"Sort of." She'd financed the pickup and left the money safely invested. It wouldn't put her brothers through college, but it would buy textbooks and a lifetime supply of ramen noodles.

"Well…shit." Jeremiah stared at a plastic Santa Claus waving merrily from a lawn across the street. The Moores were always the first on the block to drag out the Christmas decorations. "You have officially blown my mind."

"I'm sorry," she whispered.

"You should be." He scowled at her. "You could have trusted me, instead of going through all that by yourself."

Relief washed through her. This was the reaction she'd hoped for, but there had always been that nagging one percent uncertainty. "You were fifteen. What were you going to do?"

He scowled harder, but let it drop. "Do you have a picture of her?"

"Not with me." She couldn't take the chance that Shawnee or any of the Jacobs family might see it with Maddie being a dead ringer for Hank's sister at that age. "You can sneak a peek at their Christmas card when you bring the boys over tonight."

"I promised to take them to a movie first. They claim they're the only kids in Earnest who haven't seen the latest *Star Wars*." He managed something close to his usual mischievous wink. "If anyone asks, we were at your place the whole time."

"Count on it, my fellow bad influence." Grace held up a fist, and Jeremiah bumped his against it. Then she sighed. "This could be my last weekend with them. Once I tell Daddy and Mama—"

"Don't."

If only that were an option. "I have to."

"Why?" Jeremiah put his hands on her shoulders and gave her a little shake. "Think of the children. Matthew and Lucas need you."

"It's going to come out eventually," Grace insisted.

"What happens when Maddie is sixteen and wants to meet the rest of her birth family?"

"They'll freak. But no more than if they find out tomorrow, so why rush it?"

Why indeed? To clear her own conscience? At the expense of her brothers, and with no immediate benefit to Maddie. But... "I can't let them hear it from someone else."

"Why would they, unless..." Jeremiah's gaze sharpened. "You're going to tell Hank."

She nodded.

"Why? You've kept him in the dark this long."

"You have no idea. Hank has been in an extremely dark place. But now he's not, and I promised myself that I would tell him when I was sure he could handle it." For the sake of everyone else she was holding hostage.

"Then do whatever is necessary to keep him quiet. Beg, cry, tell him I'll hunt him down the way I should have three years ago."

She threw her arms around him. "You're the best, no matter what I used to tell you."

"I know." He gave her a quick hug, then pushed her away. "Now get out of here before someone realizes you're gone. I'm gonna walk around until I don't feel like I've been gut-punched."

Jeremiah stood on the sidewalk, hands in pockets, as she beeped open the locks and got in her pickup. He smiled and gave her a dorky thumbs-up, and the rush of love was so intense that Grace had to close her eyes for a moment.

The time wasn't going to get any better. If she dropped the bomb now, Hank would have Bing to talk him through the aftermath, and Grace would have Jeremiah to mop up her tears.

And if she was gonna ruin a holiday, at least it wouldn't be Christmas.

Chapter 26

HANK HAD BARELY SET FOOT ON MIZ IRIS'S BACK steps when the door flew open.

"You're back!" Beni Sanchez all but tackled him, sending Hank staggering.

Holy crap. The kid could damn near look him in the eye. "When did you turn into a beanpole?"

"It's the Jacobs coming out in me." Beni gave him the patented Sanchez grin. "Grandma says I must be eating my Wheaties."

"Along with everything else in sight," Joe Cassidy added.

Hank's breath stalled as he looked up to see his former mentor leaning in the door, arms folded. This was the man who'd shown a raw, undisciplined kid what it meant to be a pro, whether Hank wanted to listen or not. Joe's eyes narrowed, and Hank braced himself for another version of *What the hell are you doing here?*

"Geezus," Joe said. "Cole wasn't kidding when he said you're looking even scruffier than me."

The tension in Hank's muscles snapped like a million tiny wires, leaving him dangerously close to wobbly. So that's how they were going to play this. Hank had apologized to Cole and he had spread it around, to be applied across the board.

God bless them every one. Maybe the Christmas

spirit *was* on Hank's side. He rubbed a hand over his clean-shaven jaw. "What's this?"

"It's the latest thing...and you know how I like to be stylish." Joe fingered the beard that, along with his shaggy, sun-streaked hair, made him look more like a misplaced hippie surfer than usual. He looked past Hank to nod a greeting at Johnny and Bing. "Come on in. These days Miz Iris only cuts loose in the kitchen on special occasions, so there could be a riot when she puts out the homemade rolls."

Inside, Cole hoisted a beer in welcome from where he was already planted at the table, taking no chances. Shawnee paused to wave before resuming whatever story she was telling Violet and Tori—something about roping, judging by the swinging arm that had everyone giving her a wide berth.

Beni grabbed their coats and scrambled through the crowd to rejoin Delon, Gil, and a vaguely familiar teenager in the video war raging in the den. "Come on, Hank. You can help me kick ass."

"Language!" His mother cuffed him on the shoulder as he passed, then said, "Hey, Hank."

"Hi, Violet." He paused, but there was no meaningful eye contact, or indication that she was avoiding it. Anyone watching would think she'd seen him yesterday.

As they stepped into the living room, Gil jerked a nod in greeting. *Holy double crap*. Was that man-child his son? But then Quint would be...what? Thirteen? Maybe even fourteen. Damn. Suddenly Hank felt ancient.

And just as suddenly, Miz Iris appeared in front of them. She did smile this time, but the way she would smile at a guest, not a boy who'd once had a designated booster seat at her table. Hank's gut tightened. So, the forgiveness wasn't universal.

"Johnny, Hank—glad you could make it. And you must be Bing."

Bing offered an equally throttled-down smile as she and Iris measured each other. "And you're Miz Iris."

"Just Iris to you. You've met my husband, Steve." She waved a hand toward where he held court in the living room. "Les, make room on the couch so Johnny can sit down."

The two men on the couch—twins collectively known as the Leses—both rose, flashing Hank identical grins. "You been practicin' your poker face?"

As a matter of fact, Hank had whiled away many a cold, dark night playing cards with Norma—but never for money. He'd seen right off that he wouldn't be walking away with a penny in his pocket once that old bird was done plucking him.

Hank took Bing's arm. "Come on. I'll try to sort out this crew for you."

They worked their way around the room, with Hank describing each person based on either relation or job description, starting with the Leses, truckers who'd been hauling Jacobs stock since Hank was in diapers. Almost half of the crowd answered to the name of Sanchez—the dad, Merle, plus Gil and Quint, Tori and Delon, and of course Beni. He belonged to Delon and Violet, the result of an inebriated one-night lapse in judgment between friends that they'd never repeated.

Almost the direct opposite of Hank and Grace. He'd been dead sober when he tumbled into bed with Grace, and his only regret when he woke up next to her was that he couldn't stay indefinitely.

Gil jerked a nod from the den and introduced Quint—another of what Beni called the Sanchez surprises. Quint's mother came from big Oklahoma money and, according to Hank's mother, thought she was too good for everyone, including Gil.

"Hey, Mutt Face. Glad you could make it." Shawnee hooked an arm around Hank's neck and ground her knuckles into the top of his head as if he was still Beni's age.

Being back in the house, surrounded by these people, made Hank feel like he was being sucked backward through the looking glass, except that Bing was here and Melanie wasn't, and Miz Iris could barely stand to look at him.

"Hank!" Another hug, this one from the older sister, Lily. There was a lot more of her than he remembered.

He peeled her off to get a look at her swollen belly. "You're pregnant!"

"Ya think?" Lily gleefully rubbed the massive bump.

"That's awesome," he said, a little choked up by her radiant smile. Fate was such a bitch. While Violet got knocked up on a one-night stand, Lily—who'd wanted babies since she'd gotten married at nineteen—had never been able to conceive. "I'm real happy for you, Lil."

"Me too."

A toddler wandered out of the forest of legs and planted herself in front of Hank to demand, "What's your name?"

"I'm Hank."

And this had to be Rosie. She stared up at him with eyes as green and nearly as cynical as Joe's. Otherwise, she favored Violet, which was probably for the best in a girl.

After a thorough inspection she said, "Okay," and ambled off.

"I guess that means you can stay," Tori drawled.

"Whew!" Hank swiped a hand across his brow, only half joking.

Through it all, Bing stayed mostly quiet, and Hank kept a careful eye on her. Was this big family scene dredging up painful memories? But those fine lines weren't drawn tight around her mouth. She was just drinking it all in, her mind busy measuring how each person interacted with Hank, and with each other.

He relaxed another few degrees. He'd been right to bring her here. By the time he and Bing had made the rounds, dinner was on the table. Joe hadn't been kidding about the rolls. Cole took three and nearly started a brawl. Miz Iris had been diagnosed with pre-diabetes, Violet explained, and Steve's cholesterol wasn't great. And hard as they might try, none of the others could quite replicate Miz Iris's homemade rolls.

Well, at least Hank wasn't the only one who'd been turned away empty-handed. He snatched the last roll out of Beni's fingers.

"Hey! No fair!" Beni whined.

"If you wanna eat at the big-dog table…" Hank said, and settled in to fill his belly to bursting.

On his left, Steve, Cole, and Delon argued whether Tiger Warrior or Killer Bee was the rankest bucking horse on the planet, while Joe and Merle wondered who, if anyone, could break Sage Kimzey's stranglehold on the bull-riding world championship. Gil bitched about the Vegas traffic and crowds, and how the upcoming National Finals was a magnet for every idiot from Backwoods, Idaho, who couldn't hold his booze.

On Hank's right, his dad and Shawnee were making bets on which team ropers would come out on top, and a tag team of Violet and Lily failed to keep Rosie from slapping both hands down, squealing with joy as she splashed gravy on everything in a six foot radius.

"She's such a brat," Beni muttered.

Tori did an exaggerated eye roll. "Seriously? From you?"

Hank had shoveled in the first bite of pie before he realized the one thing no one had mentioned: his sister's name. Or Wyatt. Or the fact that a week from now, Wyatt and Joe would walk into the arena together at the Finals, once again chosen as the best bullfighters in the country by the riders themselves.

Today, Wyatt and Melanie were ghosts in the corner, present but not acknowledged. Hank struggled to swallow the mouthful of pumpkin and whipped cream that had turned to paste in his mouth. He glanced up, and Miz Iris pinned him with a level gaze…and then her eyebrows rose as if she'd been reading his mind. He had no trouble deciphering her silent question.

So? How long do you intend to keep this up?

Hank attacked his pie, mashing it into a blob. Everyone else at this table liked Wyatt just fine. Why couldn't Hank make peace with Melanie's choice of a husband, instead of the rage that welled up every time he thought of them together?

It wasn't rational, it wasn't healthy, and it sure as hell wasn't doing Hank any favors. But like that old fable about the monkey trapped with its hand in a jar, he couldn't seem to unclench his fist long enough to set himself free.

Chapter 27

DURING THE POST-MEAL SHUFFLE, HANK PULLED BING aside. "Have you had enough?"

"Yeah. And your dad's about done." Then she yawned.

"Looks like he's not the only one."

"Three hours of sleep." She yawned again, wider, before lifting an eyebrow. "Are you going to see Grace?"

The thought had crossed his mind. He didn't like how he'd left things, kissing her and running off. Again. But he didn't have her number or address, and she likely wasn't home anyway.

"She's got family in town," he said, and disengaged to go wash dishes. Men in the Jacobs house knew the rules—she who cooked did not clean up. Even Johnny grabbed a casserole dish and carried it to the sink before being shooed away.

Once all was put to rights, Hank grabbed his jacket. "I'm out. I've got chores to do."

He tossed out *thank you*s and *see you later*s without slowing down. Dinner had gone better than he had a right to expect…and once he'd left, they could all relax and stop watching their tongues.

Outside, clouds had gathered on the western horizon, ushering in an early dusk. The breeze had died and the cool, still air amplified every shuffle, snort, and low, rumbling bellow from the stock pens. The sounds drew Hank like a magnet, down to the pipe-railed corrals that held the bucking horses and bulls already sorted for the following day's activities.

While others elbowed their way through the malls, herds of cowboys would descend on the Jacobs arena for their annual Black Friday Buck Out, where up-and-coming riders could test their mettle against the new generation of bucking bulls and horses. It had been the first place Hank had been tested too, when he was fifteen, cocksure—and shaking in his cleats.

He folded his arms on a cold, iron rail and watched the bulls mill around the hay feeder, giving one another the occasional shove to maintain the pecking order. Even standing in a pen, they looked more badass than in the old days. Sleeker, more athletic, with an arrogance that was a testament to improved genetics.

A classic gray Brahma—high horns, silver-gray hide with black face and legs—caught sight of Hank and took three deliberate steps toward him, then paused to sling his head, eyes glittering. Hank's blood rose to meet the unspoken challenge.

I could take him.

Could. Past tense.

"Consorting with the enemy?"

Hank jerked his head around. Delon Sanchez strolled over to lean on the fence, studying the bulls with only mild curiosity. Now, if they'd been bucking horses…

"They're not the bad guys," Hank said. "They just do what comes natural."

Delon inclined his head. "I like the term 'dance partners.'" And he knew damn well the *Bull Dancer* was Wyatt's alias. "Do you have any idea how much I hated Joe when he first showed up here?" Delon asked, picking up the silent thread.

Hank had been too busy worshipping Joe at the time, but now it seemed obvious. "He was sorta moving in on your turf."

Delon turned to face him, bracing one muscular shoulder against the fence and tucking his hands in the pockets of his leather jacket, looking like he'd walked out of a television commercial promoting the best pro rodeo had to offer. "I considered Violet and Beni my family, so I wouldn't have liked anyone who waltzed in and took my place. But the fact that it was Joe made it ten times worse."

"He can be a little rough around the edges," Hank admitted. "But even Cole had to admit he was damn good help."

"Exactly. Great bullfighter. Great with the stock. A real ranch cowboy who knew rodeo production inside out." Delon tipped his head to indicate the bulls. "The things I'm not."

To Hank, the Sanchez brothers had never been anything but cowboys, but as tough as they were in the arena, their hearts had always been in the trucking business, not this one.

"Joe is like my brother. Gil was the star—all flash and fire—while I was Steady Eddy, just plugging along behind." Delon studied his riding hand as he clenched, then relaxed the fingers. "I used to figure people thought it was shame that Gil was the one who got hurt."

Hank gaped at him. Was he kidding? With last year's National Finals Rodeo contestant jacket hanging open and a gold world champion's buckle gleaming on his belt, it was impossible to imagine anyone thinking Delon didn't deserve the spotlight.

"What about now?" Hank asked.

A grin ghosted across Delon's face. "I got over it."

"Thanks to the love of a good woman?"

Delon laughed. "More like a kick in the ass. My insecurity screwed things up with Tori the first time around, and damn near the second. I didn't think I was enough for her. It was the same for Joe with Violet. And Cole and Shawnee…" He paused, then shook his head. "That one is beyond explanation."

Hank snorted, but his head was spinning. Here was someone he would hold up as a shining example of success, and Delon was saying he'd considered himself unworthy. And not only that…

"How'd you get over hating Joe?"

"Did I say I had?" When Hank's jaw dropped, Delon laughed. "Just kidding. Mostly." He shifted to press his back against the fence, feet braced as he gazed at the house. "Joe and I are never gonna be best buddies. Same for Tori and Violet. There's some history you can't completely erase. But if it's important enough, you find a way to deal with each other."

"Like me and Wyatt."

"Like that," Delon agreed. "Melanie was the only one in your family you could count on, and he took her. Now you've got to decide—do you care enough about her to tolerate Wyatt?"

As if Hank hadn't gotten around to asking himself that question. He scowled at Delon. "Did Miz Iris send you to talk some sense into me?"

"No. I needed a break from playing nice with the other boys and girls, and I saw you down here." Delon tilted his head back to gaze at the darkening sky. "You know what turned me around? The day Gil got pissed and told me I had too much talent to waste. I had to believe him. Gil doesn't say anything to be nice. And you can believe it when I say the same about you."

But… "You told me once that you weren't sure why no one had strangled me yet."

"You were an annoying little bastard. Maybe you still are, but I haven't had the urge to throttle you all afternoon, so that's an improvement. And nobody can say you aren't talented."

There were a dozen well-worn arguments lined up and ready to leap out of Hank's mouth, but they shrank in the face of Delon's casual certainty. This wasn't his sister, it wasn't Bing, and it wasn't Joe. It wasn't anyone who had a reason to prop Hank up, tell him what he needed to hear. Hell, Delon had admitted he wasn't sure he even liked Hank that much.

Hank stared at the bulls, who had stopped eating to wander over and eavesdrop, a dozen pairs of eyes all asking the same question.

"I'm not ready," Hank told them.

"Well, this is the place to come when you are." Delon straightened and clapped Hank on the shoulder. "But you're too damn good to be peeking through the fence."

Hank stood until Delon had disappeared inside the house, then gave the bulls another long look before walking to his pickup.

He was too restless to go back to his empty apartment and too edgy to trust himself in his dad's company. He should give Korby a call, but he wasn't in the mood for beer and a football game. And, well…shit. He might as well just admit it.

He wanted to see Grace.

Chapter 28

GRACE WAS IN TORI'S INDOOR ARENA, PRACTICE roping a calf dummy, when she heard a vehicle pull into the driveway. A minute later, Hank walked in. Her pulse jumped, but not in surprise. Apparently she had expected him to come looking for her, so she'd waited in the one place he was sure to find her.

And here he was.

He stopped just inside the arena gate and shoved his hands into the pockets of his jacket, looking as if he wasn't sure why he'd come, or if he was welcome. She took four swings and threw the loop she'd already built. The *whack!* of rope against plastic was like a gunshot in the silent arena.

She walked up, pulled the loop off the calf's neck, and turned to face Hank as she coiled the rope. Her heart fluttered at the sight of him, looking almost polished in the black Sanchez jacket and starched jeans, until you got to the hair, and those dark, wary eyes. She hooked the rope in the crook of her elbow and mimicked his stance, hands in the front pocket of her sweatshirt.

So. This was it. All the waiting, all the wondering how he would react ended tonight—and she wasn't quite ready to lose that little wisp of friendship they'd been nurturing. After tonight, he might never give her another of those special smiles. His eyes might never light up again just because she'd walked into a restaurant. He'd sure as hell never wish that she would drag him into her room and have her way with him.

She had a nearly irresistible urge to march straight up to him, latch her arms around his neck, and kiss him senseless. Feel his hands roaming over her and the hard length of his body pressed against hers, taste his dark, swirling heat and breathe in that unmistakable scent. Imprint all of it on her mind.

One last time.

"How was your day?" she asked, clenching the fingers that itched to slide through his hair.

He thought about it for a moment. "Weird…but good. You?"

"It had some moments." And it appeared there were going to be more.

His gaze wandered up into the rafters, where a pair of pigeons cooed softly. The cat must be taking a night off. Grace pulled out her phone and checked the time. The movie would be just starting. She only had two hours before Jeremiah and the boys showed up. No more time to waste.

"I'm done here, but if you want to come over to my place, it's apartment 5C. Give me half an hour, though—my brothers sort of trashed the place." And she had to give Gil time to make the drive over from Earnest. She hung her rope on the fence rack and waved toward the door. "Go ahead. I'll close up and turn out the lights."

He hesitated for a beat, then nodded. "I'll meet you there."

Grace released a long, shuddering breath. Then she punched up Gil's number and texted: Hank, my place, half an hour.

The reply came back immediately. On my way.

If this were the movies, the box Grace pulled out of her dresser would be silver, or carved from some precious wood, with a tiny padlock and a key that she wore on a gold chain. Or it wouldn't be a box at all. Every picture inside would have been lovingly pasted into a scrapbook that she could weep over on Mother's Day.

Grace took her shoebox into the living room and perched on the edge of the couch to sift through the photos. Not the Christmas card. Too much information. She needed a shot that told just enough of the story at a glance, like this one. Maddie at the animal farm, dressed in toddler-sized boots and jeans. In that outfit, no one could miss the resemblance.

Grace tucked the picture into the pocket of her sweatshirt. Then she dug to the bottom of the box and pulled out the eight-by-ten Hank had autographed for her that Christmas so many years ago. It had seemed logical to put it in here. Father and daughter neatly tucked away, out of sight but never out of mind. God, Hank was such a child himself in that shot. *Future National Finals bullfighter*. Had he been that sure of himself, or was it always an act?

She replaced the picture, put the lid on the box, and smoothed her hand over the top. Should she put it away? Or keep it handy in case Hank wanted to see the rest of the photos? She compromised and set the box on top of her dresser. No digging through her underwear, but not within easy reach if he decided to throw something at the wall.

Her heart slammed into her throat at the ding of the doorbell.

The carriage-style lamp beside her door should have revealed every detail of his face, but his eyes were even darker, bottomless pools that only reflected light. Grace stood back and wordlessly invited him in. As he passed, she surveyed the streets adjacent to her apartment complex. A block away, headlights came on and Gil's Charger slipped out of the shadows.

She closed the door.

Hank had walked to the center of the living room and stopped, his body drawn tight, as if he sensed that she'd invited him here for reasons he didn't understand...and wouldn't like. She considered offering him something to drink, then decided no. Worst-case scenario, this could go so horribly wrong that she packed up and moved again at the end of the school year, and Coke stains were impossible to get out of a light-colored carpet.

Nice time to be thinking about your security deposit, Grace.

Hank turned to face her. "I brought you something."

He reached into his pocket, pulled something out, and offered it to her. Oh God. A Butterfinger. How many times had he passed one across the cafeteria table to her with a crooked, sheepish smile? *Sorry I didn't get my part of our biology lab report finished.* Or *Please, Grace, can I just peek at your algebra homework?* And sometimes, with a triumphant grin, *Steve and Cole let me fight bulls at practice last night!*

Something perilously close to a sob caught in her throat as she took it from him. "Thanks."

"You're welcome. I just wanted you to understand..." He stopped to scrape a hand through his hair, letting it slide through his fingers. "I've missed you, Grace. I've missed *us*…and I don't even know what we are anymore. But I want to find out."

He was killing her, one word at a time. Now, when it was too late, he was saying all the things she'd waited so damn long to hear. She had to stop him before she came completely undone.

She pushed her hands into the pocket of her sweatshirt and exchanged the candy bar for the photo, cupping it in one palm. Her voice trembled when she said, "Do you remember how you used to call me your good luck charm?"

"My little red-haired girl," he said, almost teasing.

"I never really was. Your girl, I mean." She pulled the picture out and offered it up on the flat of her hand. "But *she* is."

—ᴧᴧᴧ—

Hank was confused.

Why was Grace giving him a picture of Melanie? Was that why she'd invited him here, as part of some master plan—first Delon, then Grace—one person after another badgering Hank until he made up with his sister? Where did they even find that picture? He didn't recognize it—and he would have remembered because he would have been dead jealous that she got to play with a miniature goat. Then the caption on the bottom caught his eye. *Happy Easter*.

He snatched the photo from Grace's hand to take a better look. No, he hadn't read it wrong. The date was *this year*. And that baby… Melanie had never had a hint of curls.

But Grace did.

In Hank's high school first-aid class, they'd talked about how shock was literally the blood draining from your head and pooling in your limbs. He could feel it now. A cold trickle down the back of his neck, into his arms, his chest, his legs—leaving his brain high and dry. Sentences tried to form but the words scattered, then spun, whirling around and down like water in a drain.

He snatched one that seemed important. "Yours?"

"Yes." Grace's eyes were steady on his face. Not brown or green. What did they call that, when they were mixed up? Like the woman's name. Hazel.

He looked at the picture again. The baby's eyes weren't hazel. They were plain old brown. The color of old leather. Or mud.

Brown like his eyes. He grabbed a couple more words as they swirled past. "And…mine?"

"Yes."

Oh. Shit. "I need to—"

Grace pushed him gently backward until his legs bumped a piece of furniture and his knees buckled, dumping him on the love seat. It was like the time he'd sliced the end of his finger almost clean off with a butcher knife. For a frozen second, he'd just watched the pulsing blood in disbelief, unable to process that it was his. If it was real, he should feel something other than a curl of nausea in his stomach.

And then he'd started screaming.

He could do that when he was five. When a man was twenty-five and staring at…at…

"How?" There. That was key. The reason this couldn't be right. "We used stuff."

Grace sank down on the very edge of the rocking chair, her fingers tightly knitted. "It was the end of my last semester of college. I was crazy busy, and I hadn't been seeing anyone for a while. I got sloppy about taking my pills. But I thought I was probably still safe, and you were using condoms..."

That had been rattling around in the bottom of his bag since the beginning of the summer. And that duffel had been hauled thousands of miles, baked inside the scorching cabs of pickups, kicked into corners, and used as a seat at a beer-cooler poker table.

The knifepoint of reality pressed into his skin. "It was an old box. I figured since you said you were on the pill..."

"We were both wrong."

And the result was smiling up at him from this damn picture. But...

He had a thousand other questions. *Where? Who?* He also had answers, though, bearing down on him with fists cocked.

"This is why you wanted to talk to me that night at the Lone Steer."

She nodded.

Wham! A shot in the ribs as he conjured up the hazy memory of her pale, stricken face. "Geezus, Grace. I was in no shape for...anything that night."

"I know."

And he'd humiliated her so badly that she'd given up on him and turned to—

Bam! The next blow snapped his head back. "Gil knows." The follow-up landed before his vision cleared. "Gil has *always* known."

Of course. Hank had never understood why Gil had

given a crap about him. Now the reason was staring him
in the face.

"It wasn't his fault—"

Hank jumped up, too late to dodge the truth that
slammed into his gut. *Fucking Wyatt.* "You went to
Oregon to have the baby. Wyatt knows about this."

Grace cringed, as if she saw the sledgehammer
coming straight at his chest. *Boom!* The pain of it was
blinding. "Melanie too," he choked out.

Her agonized expression was all the answer he
needed. The noise that came out of him was a raw,
primal thing. Somehow he was at the door, clawing at
the knob. Then he was outside, stumbling off the curb
toward his pickup.

And the Charger that was parked crossways behind
it, blocking him in. Gil slid from his seat on the hood
to stand, legs braced, face set. He had known from the
beginning. He and Wyatt and Melanie—but they hadn't
seen fit to tell Hank.

Hadn't considered Hank fit to be told.

"You son of a bitch." Hank broke into a run, lowering
his head to drive his shoulder straight into Gil's sternum.

Chapter 29

THE IMPACT JARRED HANK'S TEETH. GIL WAS A LOT more solid than he looked...and he'd been in way more fights. As they slammed onto the hood of the Charger, Gil rolled with their momentum and shoved, sending Hank flying off the other side to crash onto the pavement.

Fuck! He scrambled up, clutching his elbow over the tear in his jacket.

Gil was already standing on the other side of the car, his breath ragged. "I told you I wasn't your friend."

"That's your excuse?" Hank circled the front of the car, but Gil mirrored the movement, keeping the Charger between them. "It was okay to lie to me as long as you didn't pretend to like me?"

"I never lied."

Hank banged a fist on the roof of the car. "Screw that bullshit! Who else, Gil? Wyatt and Melanie for sure. Who else? Did everyone around that dinner table today know except poor stupid Hank?"

"Just me." He didn't add Melanie and Wyatt, but they hadn't been at dinner, and Gil was an ace at this game of not-quite truths.

"Why did you bother? If you'd left me alone, I wouldn't have come back here, and I wouldn't have had to know."

"Yet." Gil ran his fingers through the back of his hair and winced. Good. Hank hoped his skull had left a dent in his precious car. "Grace could've cut you out completely, claimed she didn't know who the father was, but she refused, so your name is on the birth certificate."

Hank froze. Christ. Did that mean…

"Until you sign the papers relinquishing your rights, the state of Oregon considers her a foster child," Gil said flatly. "Legally, you are still her daddy."

Daddy. The word was an icy fist plowing into his gut.

Gil's lip curled. "Yeah. Shit just got a little more real, didn't it? Imagine if I'd strolled into that dump in Montana and said, 'Hey, dude. Wanna meet your kid?'"

The anger roared back. "Or here's a thought—maybe someone could have told me *when they found out Grace was pregnant*."

"And then what?" When Hank blinked at him, Gil sneered. "After what you said to Grace, what were you gonna do? Turn around and say, '*Oops, my bad. Wanna get married, darlin'?*' Or you could've offered to support her on all the money you weren't raking in. Except neither of those things was gonna happen…and you know why?"

"You don't think I would've stepped up."

"Wrong again. When I caught Grace sobbing all over a pile of fuel receipts in our office, there was only one thing she knew for sure. She did *not* want to raise a kid. Not with you. Not without you. Not at *all*." Gil curled his fingers around the edge of the car roof. "So then what, Hank? Were you ready to be a single dad?"

The suggestion struck terror clear down into his bones, but he wasn't giving up that easily. "I never got the chance to decide. And you, of all people, took that away from me, after everything you did to keep your son."

"You think that was about fatherly devotion?" Gil's

voice was pure acid. "I was stupid in love. So fucking desperate I would've given Krista anything—a ring, cash for an abortion, *anything*—but she just wanted me to go away. So I decided if that bitch was gonna make me miserable, I'd do whatever it took to return the favor. It had nothing to do with the baby."

But…Quint. All the years of battling attorneys and driving to Oklahoma City. How could Gil claim…

"When Krista got pregnant, I was the reigning ProRodeo rookie of the year," Gil went on, relentless. "I had eighty grand in my pocket from the National Finals, and I was as close to being on top of the world as you could get without owning the gold buckle. *And* I had a family that was behind me a hundred percent. I still cracked. You…" He shook his head. "You were already a mess."

Hank couldn't listen anymore. His head was pounding and his chest felt like it was caving in, crushing his lungs. He yanked out his keys. "Move your car."

"No."

The keys dug into Hank's palm as he fisted his hands. "Move the damn car, or I'll drive over it."

"Go ahead and try."

Hank made a low, bellowing sound of frustration. "What the hell is *wrong* with you?"

"I have a hip that's stuck together with thumbtacks and superglue, which is the only reason I'm not beating the crap out of you." Gil rubbed a fist over the spot where Hank's shoulder had made contact. "Maybe if I'd had someone to body-slam, I wouldn't have slid my motorcycle off a curve doing seventy miles an hour. I might not have thrown away the one thing that mattered to me more than my life…and I damn near lost that, too. *That's* why I bothered."

Hank stared at him for a beat. "Fine. You win. Here's your prize."

He threw the keys at Gil's head as hard as he could and started off across the parking lot just as his dad's pickup came roaring down the street. It screeched to a stop in front of him, and Bing jumped out of the driver's side, pausing to point a finger at Johnny in the passenger's seat. "You *stay!*"

Then she whirled around, looking first at Hank, then Gil. "I came as quick as I could. What is going on?"

Hank stalked straight past her to the back door of the pickup. As he climbed in, Gil picked up the photo Hank had dropped.

"This is Hank's," he said, holding it out for Bing to take.

Then he continued on to where Grace was standing in front of her apartment, eyes wide and arms hugged tight over her chest, looking small and scared. Gil pushed her inside and shut the door.

Bing looked at the picture. Then she got in the pickup and passed it to Hank's dad.

Johnny studied it for a long moment before he said, "Well, shit."

—◦◦◦—

Gil slumped against the wall in Grace's entryway and pressed his palms to his face.

"Are you okay?" she asked.

He dragged his hands down to look at her with eyes that were drained beyond exhaustion. "I've been clean for almost thirteen years. I was stoned for two years before that. And I have never wanted a drink more than I do right now."

Grace would have said she was sorry, but every time she'd tried before, it had only made him mad. But he attended meetings nearly every week so… "Should you call someone?"

"I did. Delon's meeting me at the café down on Main."

Grace stiffened. "Are you going to tell him?"

"No."

"Won't he wonder why…"

One corner of Gil's mouth twisted. "I'm an addict. Some days being awake is reason enough."

But if he fell off the wagon tonight, it would be her fault. "Do you want me to drive you?"

"To be sure I make it past all the bars?"

"There are a lot of them."

"I noticed. But if I don't show up, Delon knows where to look."

Oh God. In that moment, Grace felt like a natural disaster, laying waste to everything within reach. She had only caught snatches of the angry words Gil and Hank had thrown at each other, but they had obviously left a mark.

And if it had done this to Gil, Lord only knew what shape Hank was in.

Gil sighed. "Relax, Grace. If I was seriously considering cracking, I would have snuck off and done it without telling you. I'm going to have a cup of coffee with my brother, and we'll bicker about which horse would be his best draw in the first round of the National Finals. Then I'm going home to show my kid that he still can't touch me in a game of *Guitar Giants* and remember why I got clean to begin with." He pushed away from the wall and looked down at her. "What about you?"

"I have to call Melanie. And Jeremiah will be here soon." Grace swallowed hard, fighting tears she refused to shed as she followed him to the door.

Gil dangled Hank's keys from one finger. "I'll take these with me. Somebody will come and get his pickup in the morning."

"Thank God he's not driving right now." If it had been anyone but Gil, she would have hugged him. "We're lucky you were here."

He snorted. "Tell that to Hank."

"I will…if he ever speaks to me again." And jumbled in with the guilt, there was a soul-deep sense of loss.

"He'll be back. He's gonna have a lot of questions before he decides whether to sign those papers, and you're the one with the answers." Gil flashed a cynical smile. "For now, it's all in the hands of the Lord…and Bing."

Hank slumped in the back seat and let the miles tick by without comment or explanation. Johnny and Bing were happy to let him.

His dad waited until they were turning into the driveway of the ranch to ask, "Where is the baby?"

"I don't know. Oregon, maybe."

"Oregon?" The clicks were nearly audible as Johnny made the connections. "So…Melanie?"

Hank nodded. His dad cursed softly. "How long has she known?"

Hank shrugged. He didn't know much, except that he had been evaluated by a jury of his closest peers and found unworthy. *Don't tell Hank. He can't handle the truth. After all he's done, he doesn't deserve to know.*

And Grace…

Every time he tried to think about Grace, his thoughts turned to static, too many signals from too many directions. He'd jumped her and dumped her. She'd lied to him. She'd tried to tell him. He'd chased her away. She could have written him a letter. Sent an email. He'd done nothing to earn even that much.

Her parents would come unglued if they found out.

That single thought rang clear. They couldn't know, or Grace wouldn't even *be* part of the family. And everyone else… Was it possible that Melanie hadn't even told Violet? Or Miz Iris? Or…

His heart stumbled. "They didn't tell you?" he asked Bing.

"No!" She yanked the keys from the ignition, bailing out to march around and stand by in case his dad needed help.

The dogs came flying from the barn, yipping and whining in welcome. As Spider barreled toward his dad, Hank snapped, "Down!"

She dropped like she'd been shot, tail thumping wildly and eyes imploring.

Bing leaned down to scratch her head and coo, "Good dog! See how smart you are?"

Well, that made one of them. How stupid was Hank, to not even suspect? It was so damn obvious now. Grace, so desperate to talk to him that she'd waded through a packed bar. Then Wyatt, whisking her off to Oregon for a job that he'd conveniently conjured up. Melanie, practically adopting Grace.

And Gil…

Hank could barely comprehend that Gil Sanchez had

gone so far out of his way for anyone. Thousands of miles, at least a dozen times. For Hank? That was so ridiculous he nearly laughed. Hell, maybe Gil had been telling the truth about his motives. If anyone had racked up some cosmic debt, it would be him.

And the bastard had torn his coat. Hank peeled off the Sanchez Trucking jacket, balled it up, and threw it into the bottom of the mudroom closet. Johnny and Bing filed in behind him. She hung her coat on one of the kitchen chairs, then sank down to prop both elbows on the table and plow her pink-tipped fingers into her hair.

He'd hurt her, implying that she might have been lying to him all this time. He walked over and rested his hand on her shoulder. "I shouldn't have asked. I know you wouldn't have done that to me."

She didn't answer. Didn't react at all for a few moments. Then, slowly, she lowered her palms to the table and raised her head, staring straight ahead. "Yes, I would have."

"What?" Hank dropped his hand.

When her gaze came up to meet his, it was both apologetic and resolute. "You'd barely gotten your feet under you when Melanie and Wyatt came, and just seeing them set you back for another two weeks. So yes, if they'd asked me what they should do…" She gave a helpless shrug. "I would have had to say they shouldn't tell you."

Even Bing had had no faith in him.

It was a trapdoor dropping from under his feet. The snap of a rope he'd thought would never let him fall. His stomach lurched at the sensation, and he did the one thing he had never imagined…or dared.

He turned his back and walked out on her.

Chapter 30

WHEN THE DOOR SLAMMED BEHIND HANK, THE starch went out of Bing. She slumped back in her chair and let her arms fall limply to her sides. Johnny stood halfway between her and the door, at a loss. Should he try to follow Hank? Stay here with Bing?

"I couldn't lie to him. Too many people have been lying to him." Her midnight-black eyes glittered with tears and anger. "I can't believe Gil did this to him. He was Hank's *sponsor*. The person who sees every square inch of your guts and soul. And he came there, put himself in that position, knowing this." She heaved to her feet and paced over to the window, cupping her hand against the glass to peer outside. "Hank didn't take the pickup. Where will he go?"

"I don't know." Then he thought again. Whenever Hank was in trouble or upset, he would disappear, sometimes for hours. Naturally, it was Melanie who'd discovered his hideout. Johnny calculated his own fatigue, the low throb in his shoulder, and added in the possibility that he was the last person Hank wanted to see. "I'll go talk to him."

Bing's expression did not convey overwhelming confidence.

"I won't criticize, and I will not try to *father* him. But for once in his life, I would like to at least show up. So…please?"

She gave it a painful amount of thought before bowing her head. "You can't do much worse than me."

"I wouldn't bet on it."

His attempt at a joke limped away unnoticed. Bing looked so drained—as if she'd had her emotions bottled up all day, and someone had pulled the stopper. Impulsively, he slid his arm around her and tucked her face into the curve of his good shoulder. Her hair tickled between the fingers that cupped the back of her head, and he was drenched in her tropical-night scent.

She was so warm. And so—

She pulled away, a flush rising in her cheeks. "Go. I'll make coffee or something."

And he had to concentrate on his son. Johnny grabbed a flashlight and tucked it in his coat pocket. If he was right about where Hank had gone—

As he stepped outside, a blur of white emerged from the lean-to alongside the barn that acted as a hay shed. Spider. *Bingo!* "Down," he said quietly.

She plopped onto her butt. Close enough. He rubbed her head in approval, then made his way to the hay shed with the dog dancing circles around him. Like most everything else, the design hadn't worked out quite like he'd planned. The roof was too low to stack bales with the tractor, so the work had to be done by hand, and the lean-to held more than he needed, so he never dragged the bales all the way to the back to begin the stack. Instead, he started flush against the inside wall and ended up with a gap along the outside—a narrow passage that led to what had been Hank's hideaway.

Johnny clicked on the light and turned sideways to ease alongside the stack. When he stepped into the arm's-width space at the rear, he found Hank sitting on a hay bale with Mabel curled beside him, her head in his lap. He didn't blink, or speak, or acknowledge Johnny's arrival in any way. Only the fingers that rubbed slow circles in the dog's ruff moved.

Setting the flashlight shiny end down, Johnny lowered himself onto another bale. The shadows and the scent of cured alfalfa wrapped around him—warm, safe, and a million miles removed from the outside world.

"I see why you come in here," he said.

"I didn't think you knew about it."

Whew. He'd expected to be met with stony silence. "Melanie told me when she left for college, in case I needed to find you." He hesitated, then said. "Your sister always was good at keeping your secrets."

Hank made a harsh noise. "Yeah, *from* me."

Spider nudged a cold nose into Johnny's palm, her eyes wide and earnest in her black mask. He scratched her ear, and her whole body waggled with delight. "Finding out about this baby…it's a helluva thing."

"You would know."

Johnny laughed, a low *huh*. "Lord. When your mother told me she was pregnant…well, I'm not proud of how I reacted. I was twenty years old and barely scraping together enough winnings to stay on the road. And then a baby?"

"Twenty?" Hank repeated. "But…that would've been Melanie."

"Yeah. All I could think was that a baby would ruin everything…gobble up energy and money, screw with my focus. But your mom swore she'd make it all okay." He combed his fingers over the dog's head, and they both sighed. "That's what she did back then. Make everything okay so all I had to do was rope."

Hay rustled as Hank shifted on his bale. "You didn't want *Melanie*?"

"I know. It sounds terrible." Johnny angled him a sheepish look. "I would, um, appreciate it if you didn't tell her."

"But she was your little buckaroo."

Johnny hitched his good shoulder. "She had to be. It was just the three of us in a pickup and trailer, pounding up and down the road. You had a swing set and a tricycle. Melanie had a rope and a dummy and got to ride around on my horse. It was just lucky she took to it, or we would've had to pawn her off on her grandparents."

"You would have *done* that?"

"In a heartbeat." Johnny ran his fingertip up the white strip between the two halves of Spider's black mask. Unable to really see or be seen, the words spilled out like he was in a confessional. "I was an addict. So was your mother. And there isn't a weekly meeting of Rodeo Anonymous, so when we had to go cold turkey, it got ugly in a hurry."

"And then I came along and made it even worse."

"*That* was impossible." Johnny rubbed behind Spider's downy soft ear. "Yes, I was shocked. I couldn't believe your mother had let it happen. But then…" He trailed off, reliving his foolishness. "I thought you might bring us back together."

"Wrong," Hank said flatly.

"Yeah. And oddly enough, having another baby didn't magically turn us into decent parents, either."

They sat and listened to the hiss of the breeze around the corner of the barn and the occasional snuffle or groan from one of the dogs as Spider and Mabel reveled in the unexpected attention.

"Melanie told me you'd found yourself another Miz Iris," Johnny said.

Hank gave a *pfft!* "If Miz Iris joined a motorcycle gang and got herself a set of brass knuckles."

"Bing is a tough lady." But also soft. And she smelled really good. And she couldn't be more off-limits. Johnny pushed his attention back to the person who needed it most. "She would do almost anything to protect you."

"Even lie?"

"If she thought it was best. But it would have damn near killed her." And thank God no one had forced her to make the choice. Johnny tried for a lighter tone. "I suppose she told you about scaring the spit out of me."

Hank smiled slightly. "I wouldn't have minded being a fly on the wall."

"I may have screamed," Johnny admitted.

There was a weighty pause. Then Hank said, "I'm glad she had the company."

They went quiet again, and Mabel sat up to stick a concerned nose in Hank's face. Rather than pushing her away, he wrapped both arms around her. In a blink he was a boy again, hiding out and telling his troubles to his dog. Even his voice sounded younger and a little scared when he said, "I have a daughter."

"Yep."

"I don't know how I'm supposed to feel about that."

Neither did Johnny, to be honest, and the baby wasn't even the half of it. The more he thought about it, the deeper the chill struck in his chest. Every one of them — Gil, Melanie, Wyatt, possibly even Grace — had known how much this would hurt, but they'd done it anyway, because they were convinced that Hank had to be protected…from himself.

And that scared the ever-loving shit out of Johnny, but he couldn't very well look at his son and say, *Please don't stop breathing*.

He braced a hand on his knee and carefully pushed to his feet. He was exhausted, and they had reached what the ag consultants called the point of diminishing returns. He'd contributed his two cents. Anything more would be a waste, at best.

"You've got time. Hell, it's waited this long." He fended off a face lick from Spider as he bent to pick up the flashlight. "Come on inside. We'll have coffee and caramel rolls and turn on a football game."

He'd worked his way nearly to the front of the hay shed when a quiet voice said, "Thanks, Dad."

—◁◈▷—

For obvious reasons Hank couldn't go back to the apartment, so he squared his shoulders and headed down the hall to his former room. Every day, he'd told himself he should go through his old stuff and see what was worth keeping, but he'd kept finding excuses to put it off.

Number one being that he'd rather not have a staring contest with his past.

He pushed the door open and switched on the light. It was exactly as he'd left it, right down to the dirty T-shirt he'd yanked off and hurled into the corner that last day. They'd just finished gathering the stocker calves to haul to the sale, the reason his mother had made an appearance. She always showed up when there was a check coming in, to make sure she got her cut.

As usual, everything had taken twice as long as it should, and Hank had had to beg off staying to load the trucks because he was working an evening performance down in Paducah.

Predictably, his dad had blown a fuse. "If you're gone to a rodeo every time I need help, you're no damn good to me!"

And his mom had yelled, "Fine, we just won't come back!"

"Good! I don't need any dead weight around here." Johnny had slammed out the back door.

She'd slammed into their bedroom to fling clothes into a suitcase.

And Hank had been left standing there wondering what the hell had just happened. He and his dad had been having some variation of this fight since the first time Hank went on the road with Jacobs Livestock. They'd always gotten past it before. Hank would work it out with Cole so he could be home for branding, and a few days here and there to catch up on other stuff. Despite the huffing and the muttering, Johnny would be damn glad for the extra hand.

Now he was dead weight?

And since when did his mother give a damn what he did, let alone speak for him? Eventually, he'd realized that she'd already had her mind made up to leave, but why take the blame when she could make his dad out to be the bad guy one last time?

Hank had let the angry words burrow under his skin and fester, though, using them as an excuse to stay away all summer and fall. Then he'd gotten the bright idea to come home for Thanksgiving, somehow thinking the holiday would make it all right.

Wrong. First came the shouting match with his dad at the café. Then he'd gone off to Canyon to lick his wounds at Korby's place. And then he'd run into Grace.

And now they had a baby. Somewhere. Christ.

He forced his gaze to circle walls that were plastered with memorabilia. Posters from the rodeos he'd intended to work someday—all the big Texas shows, plus the Cheyenne Frontier Days, Red Bluff Roundup, La Fiesta de los Vaqueros. Action shots of some of the baddest bulls ever, and autographed photos of legendary bullfighters like Miles Hare, Loyd Ketchum, and Rob Smets.

And there were pictures of Hank. He could still feel the nerves jumping in his gut that night at Goodwell—but it didn't show as he crouched eye to eye with Dirt Eater, a hand on the bull's nose as Korby scrambled safely away. Did Grace still have the autographed picture he'd given her?

Grace. Shit.

Everything inside him twisted. Half of him wanted to scream at her. The other kept seeing her as she'd stood there tonight—so scared, so vulnerable—and could barely stand to think how much worse it must have been. She'd had a *baby*. Alone.

Well, almost alone. Wyatt must have been there. Shit. Had that bastard held Grace's hand while she had Hank's baby?

He focused on the picture of Joe that had hung above his bed since Hank was thirteen. Right next to that was the only empty space, framed by yellowed tape marks, where a matching picture of Wyatt Darrington had once hung. Hank had torn it down the day after Joe Cassidy married his sister's best friend, after he—and everyone else at the wedding reception—had clearly seen that the airplane and the fast cars, the fame and the fancy clothes weren't enough for a super-cool super-stud like Wyatt. He had to have the best and the brightest, so of course he'd wanted Melanie.

It had taken five years, but he finally had her. And Hank had a room wallpapered with wasted dreams. He stared at that dusty, blank space and wished with all his heart that the picture was still there so he could tear it up again.

There was no way he could sleep in here.

He dragged the comforter and a pillow off the bed, then dug in a drawer for sweatpants and a T-shirt. Bing came out of the hall bathroom as he hauled everything out and shut the door. Her eyebrows rose a fraction, but she didn't ask questions. She hadn't asked anything since he came in the house, just walked into his arms and held on as he hugged her tight.

The door to his dad's room opened. He held out a prescription bottle. "Could one of you open this for me?"

Hank's arms were full, so Bing took the bottle. "How many?"

"One."

She tapped a single tablet onto her palm. He took the pill and set it on his dresser.

"In case I need it later." When Bing tried to hand him the bottle, he shook his head. "Tuck that under your pillow. Maybe it'll help you sleep."

After he shut the door, Bing curled her fingers around the bottle and clasped it to her chest. "He's not a complete loss."

Hank smiled wryly. "Like father, like son."

And for tonight, *not a complete loss* was the best any of them could claim.

Chapter 31

GRACE COULDN'T STOP SEEING THE LOOK ON HANK'S face. Not the stunned disbelief, but what came after. The realization that people who were supposed to care about him had not only kept the truth from him but considered him incapable of being trusted. Grace hadn't fully understood how devastating that would be until she'd watched the havoc it had wreaked.

That *she* had wreaked.

"Hey," Jeremiah said softly from the door of her bedroom. "Anything I can get you?"

"No. I'm…" Not fine. Bless his heart, her brother was trying, but what could he do besides let her drip all over his shoulder and shush Lucas and Matthew? He'd told them she was in bed with a migraine and needed the dark and the quiet, so they tiptoed and whispered and kept the TV turned down low, as if she could sleep, or even close her eyes.

As she stared up at the ceiling, she was gripped by an urgent need to know that Hank was safe.

Johnny Brookman was listed in the Earnest directory. Would Hank's dad even speak to her? She'd never spoken to him, had always thought he was slightly terrifying, and she misdialed twice while punching in his number.

There was a clatter as the receiver was snatched up before the end of the first ring. "Hello?"

Grace stiffened. Damn. *Damn*. Why hadn't it occurred

to her that Hank might pick up? She heard rustling, like blankets being pushed aside, and then he said, "Grace?"

She let out a breath. "How did you know?"

"Dumas cell phone number." His voice was muted, as if he didn't want anyone to hear. "And who else would panic when I answered?"

Excellent deduction. Her heart was hammering, and her palms had gone damp. "I didn't expect to talk to you."

"Then why did you call?"

"I just wondered…"

When she trailed off, he finished, "If I was still breathing?"

"Uh…I was going to say safe."

"Same thing."

After an interminable pause, she realized he wasn't going to continue. She should say *okay, great* and hang up, but now that she'd established this tiny thread of connection, she didn't want to break it. "Why are you whispering?"

"Dad and Bing are asleep." She heard another rustle and pictured him scooping the hair back off his face, a gesture that was already becoming familiar. "Why are *you* whispering?"

"Jeremiah and the boys are here."

He breathed, slow and even, in and then out. Meditative breaths, she realized. This Hank would do that kind of thing. "I was afraid you were alone."

The admission gave her a queer little pang. After all this, he could still worry about her? "Are you okay? I mean, after you and Gil…"

"A couple of scrapes. Nothing major."

"That's good." Grace pulled the comforter over her

head, closing herself in with the blue glow from the phone and the thump of her heart. The longer she stayed on the line, the more likely that he would ask the inevitable questions. *How could you? What's wrong with you?*

She had answers. A pat little list drilled into her by that counselor in Oregon. If she rattled them off, could she make Hank believe what she never quite had?

The silence went on so long that she started when he did speak. "Who was with you when the baby was born?"

Not the question she'd expected. "The couple she lives with now. In Portland. I moved there when I started to, um, show." She had actively suppressed the memories of her pregnancy and Maddie's birth, bundling them up and shoving them in the drawer along with that shoebox. Dragging them out now, she found the edges were still sharp enough to draw blood. "I left here in March and stayed in their guest house until it was time."

"I thought you were in Pendleton."

She hadn't been sure he'd even known she'd gone to Oregon. Had he cared enough to ask after her, or had Korby assumed he'd want to be updated? "I told my family I was in Pendleton, but I couldn't let everyone there see me pregnant, then show up for work at the high school in August with no baby."

"Right. Makes sense." Oddly, he seemed relieved. "So these people, they can afford a guest house."

"They can afford a *lot* of things." Including some that directly involved Hank, but she wasn't blurting that out now, over the phone.

"Huh. So that's good. For the baby, I mean."

"Yes." Better than Grace could ever have done, and not just in terms of money. Maddie was with people who desperately wanted a child. Surely that would be enough to offset Grace's lack of interest…and convince Hank that his daughter was in a very good place.

Another lengthy silence. Hank seemed to have run out of questions, or the ability to absorb anything more. When he'd had time to regroup, he would probably be furious with her all over again. He had the right. As Maddie's birth father, he had a lot of rights, should he choose to exercise them. The prospective parents had been willing to gamble that he wouldn't fight for custody—or had wagered that he didn't have the resources to win, especially given his recent history. Wyatt had never said so, but Grace knew he didn't believe Hank would have the heart to tear a child away from the only parents she knew.

And somehow, Grace had to make Hank understand that she'd left Wyatt and Melanie almost no choices. "Wyatt didn't ask for any of this, but once Gil had told him, it wasn't like either of them could un-know it. And I swore them to secrecy because I couldn't let my family find out." She gave a defeated sigh. "I'll have to tell them now."

"What the hell for?" His voice was so loud that it startled her. He instantly muted it again, but remained emphatic. "Your dad damn near strung me up just for wearing my cowboy boots on his gym floor."

Grace giggled, then clapped a hand over her mouth in horror. "I'm sorry. I may be a little hysterical."

"I know the feeling." He puffed out another long breath. "I've only been home for six days? And there's been my dad, and the ranch, the big dinner at Miz Iris's today—and now this. I'm tapped out. So if you could hold off so I don't have to deal with your parents, and everyone else in town…"

He sounded exhausted. But steady, she realized, and almost, well, dignified. Something in his voice made her think of the stately old cottonwood behind her parents' house. She had seen it battered by wind, stripped down to bare branches by hailstorms, but its roots were dug in so deep that nothing short of a lightning bolt could level it.

Somewhere in the process of recovery, Hank had set down emotional roots and gained the strength to weather all these squalls. By comparison, Grace felt like a tumbleweed that was barely hanging on.

And she was more than happy to steer around this particular storm. "As long as it stays between us, there's no reason I have to tell them anything."

"Who else knows?"

"Here? Only Gil, and now the three of you."

He went quiet for a few more endless moments. Then he sighed. "Why didn't Gil just leave me to rot in that hole I'd dug for myself?"

Grace had to take a moment to catch up. His questions were odd, as if he was grasping at random thoughts and blurting them out. "He said he understood better than anyone could, and he wasn't going to let another one of Miz Iris's boys crash and burn like he did. If he could use his experience to help you, then maybe it wasn't a total waste. And obviously he thought you were worth the effort."

Now the bond they'd forged was broken, because of Grace. "I'm sorry. I shouldn't have dragged him into this. If I'd just taken care of myself…" She would have been, and would possibly still be, alone. But she wouldn't have hurt Hank so much worse than necessary. Her throat tightened around a fresh ball of tears. "I have to go."

"Grace—"

"I'm sorry," she said again. She hung up and turned off her phone. Then she gathered in her second pillow and balled it up against her stomach, curling herself around it the way she'd cradled her growing stomach. Wave after wave of remembered emotions swept through her: fear, dread, the sheer uncertainty of what was to come.

And loneliness. Dear God, she'd been so lonely. She'd wanted her mother to hold her hand and tell her it would be okay, she could do this. Jeremiah to tease her about how she'd waddled like a penguin in those last few weeks. Matthew and Lucas to race circles around her on their bikes while she walked through incredibly green parks in Portland, with ivy and moss crawling everywhere.

But deep in the darkest hours of the night, it was Hank she'd missed the most, and how he'd spooned his body around hers when they slept, as if she was as precious as the baby she carried.

And it was Hank's arms she craved now.

Chapter 32

Sunlight spilled into the living room on Friday morning. No one else was stirring, so Hank reheated a cup of yesterday's coffee, doused it with extra sugar, and grabbed the last caramel roll to take with him. Outside, it was one of those intensely clear fall mornings, when the air was cool and sweet as spring water.

They couldn't ask for a better day for the Black Friday Buck Out at the Jacobs ranch.

Hank split the last quarter of his roll between the dogs, then set about his chores. Funny, how the routine made his situation seem less drastic. Last night, he'd felt like the earth was cracking down the middle. But the sun still came up, the horses still nickered for their morning grain, and the cattle still had to be fed. He let the dogs ride in the cab of the pickup, and they still squabbled like a pair of kids over who got the best seat—the way he and Melanie used to.

It would take a while to reframe his entire childhood based on the things his dad had said the night before, but he didn't have to do it alone. He had Bing. He had his dad—and how weird was that?

And he also had Grace, if that call last night meant what he hoped it did.

Any trace of anger toward her had dissolved in a quiet *whoosh* of relief at the sound of her voice. She cared enough to worry, and to try to set things right between him and Gil, even after all Hank had done. Not just the scene at the Lone Steer, but the six weeks of deliberate silence and avoidance that had forced her to hunt him down at the damn bar.

Could he blame her for saying the hell with him and doing whatever was best for herself…and the baby?

And when she'd finally come clean, he'd proved her right by running away again. He should have stayed— last night and all those other nights. If her brothers hadn't been with her, he would've gotten up and driven to her house after he'd heard her voice clog with tears.

Instead, he'd lain awake, sorting through his own emotions. When he pushed everything else aside and narrowed it down to only him and Grace…well, hell, he damn near broke out in a cold sweat just imagining her looking him in the eye and saying those words.

"Hank, I'm pregnant."

He would have flipped out, and no doubt would've done and said a bunch of stupid shit. Ten times worse than last night. And now…there was no gut-wrenching sense of loss. No urge to rush to Oregon and reclaim his child. If Grace had cornered him, told him the truth and suggested putting the baby up for adoption, he would have snatched the pen out of her hand and asked where to sign.

And yeah, the things his dad had said out in the hay shed made that a whole lot easier to admit.

Hank would like to think he'd have stuck with Grace through the whole ordeal, but chances are he would've made a mess of that too. It was pretty much all he'd done back then. As it was, she'd fought through it without him. He could never make that up to her, but he could at least respect the decision he'd left her to face. And he could let his daughter have what he would've given anything for—two parents who actually wanted her.

But he could choose when and how he dealt with the baby and her parents. Those papers had waited this long, and it would be years before Maddie could comprehend why she should give a flying shit about him, so Hank had decided to focus on the other people involved. Especially Grace.

When he finished the chores, Bing was making French toast and scrambled eggs. Johnny was at the table, once again looking like fresh hell. His dad had never been a morning person, and with bedhead and five days' stubble, he was like a big ol' bear growling into his coffee cup.

Hank strolled over to hook an arm over Bing's shoulders and peer into the frying pan. "Is any of that for me?"

"If Bigfoot over there doesn't polish off the rest of the bread. We're running low on groceries." She studied Hank closely. "You're awfully chipper this morning. Got plans for the day?"

He snagged a chunk of scrambled eggs and popped it in his mouth. "Can you drive me over to get my pickup?"

Her spatula paused. "Gil called."

Figured. "And?"

"I yelled at him. And he let me, so he must really feel like shit."

"Good. Anything else?"

"Your pickup is at Sanchez Trucking." She flipped a piece of toast and nudged at it. "Are you sure you want to go right away?"

When he was still fuming, she meant. Except…he wasn't, thanks to Grace. Plus, his mind kept skipping past last night's argument to that strange moment in Gil's office. The quiet, uncharacteristic apology.

Believe it or not, I was trying to help.

And he had. He'd spent hour after hour ruthlessly plucking at every festering sliver in Hank's psyche with an accuracy that only someone who knew his entire history could, until they'd flushed most of the poison from his system.

The doubt demons hissed in Hank's ear, trying to tell him that Gil didn't really give a shit about him. Gil had done it for Grace, they whispered, or for himself, or maybe even for the baby. But Grace said he'd literally gone the extra mile—thousands of miles—for Hank, and Bing believed Gil had been right to keep him in the dark.

If there was one thing Hank had learned, it was to listen to the voices that were trying to build him up, not the ones tearing him down. Especially if they were his own.

As Hank walked into the reception area at Sanchez Trucking, Analise popped out of the dispatcher's office. Today she was wearing super-skinny, bright-turquoise pants that stopped halfway to her ankles, a sweater set, and a long turquoise scarf tied around her head with the ends left loose.

"You actually make that look kinda hot," he said.

"It's a gift." She patted her hair, then snagged his keys from one of a series of hooks and tossed them to him. "If you want Gil, he's in the break room."

Hank cocked an ear. The music he heard wasn't coming from a radio, but that voice was too high and clear to be Gil's. Hank sidled down the short hallway and peeked around the doorframe. Quint Sanchez was bent over a guitar, his forehead puckered in concentration as he strummed and sang. Sitting in a chair facing him, Gil tapped his fingers on his own guitar to keep the tempo, a half smile on his face. Quint finished the chorus, hit the final chord with a flourish, and broke into a triumphant grin.

Gil nodded approvingly. "That was great. You've been putting in some serious practice time."

"I wrote a song," Quint declared with that combination of bravado and defensiveness only a boy of a certain age could muster. "It probably sucks."

"Probably," Gil agreed. "I did on my first dozen tries—still do sometimes—but you've gotta work through the bad stuff to get to the good."

Geezus. How many times had he said the exact same thing to Hank? And, more important, been a walking promise that there *was* still good stuff to get to.

"Come on," Gil said. "Let's hear it. As your father, I am honor bound not to make fun of you…much."

Quint rolled his eyes. Gil laughed.

Yeah, sure, it was all about revenge.

"You are such a lying piece of shit," Hank said.

Quint's eyes went wide, but Gil only slouched back in his chair. "I prefer to call it selective truth."

"Whatever." Hank strode in and threw the torn jacket in his lap. "You owe me a new coat."

Gil tossed the jacket back at him. "Tell Analise what size you want. Quint's got a couple more songs to play for me, then we're headed to the Buck Out."

"Great. I'll see you there."

Gil's eyebrows peaked. "You're going?"

"Yeah." Hank pushed a little bravado into his own voice. "They can always use chute help."

He'd been to rodeos since that night in Toppenish, earning a few extra bucks by pushing calves and turning out broncs at the arena just down the river from Norma's place. It would be hard to face all the curious eyes, but he reminded himself that Grace had moved halfway across the country to live with strangers, had gone through pregnancy and childbirth virtually alone, then picked herself up and gotten on with her life.

Hank could go to the damn Buck Out.

As he made for the door, he added, "By the way, I'm keeping your phone until I can afford a decent one."

After he'd showered and dressed, he transferred his wallet, change, and pocketknife to his clean jeans... but he left his gear bag in the closet. They would already have bullfighters lined up for the day, and Hank wouldn't take the chance of failing so publicly when he wasn't the only one who might suffer the consequences.

Chapter 33

"SORRY. BASKETBALL PRACTICE RAN LATE." GRACE flopped into a lawn chair beside the Jacobs arena, between an EMT and Tori. "Did I miss anything?"

"Nope. They're just starting the mutton busting." Tori was wearing jeans, scuffed boots, and a sweatshirt with a BAD MOTHER-TRUCKER logo, her caramel-brown hair pulled through the loop of a CLASSIC ROPES cap. She reached into a cooler beside her and pulled out a full plate. "Hungry?"

Grace accepted the offering gratefully, inhaling the heavenly aroma of smoked meat and baked beans. She waved a corncob toward the flawless blue sky. "Is this an amazing day or what?"

"So everyone is saying. And they're not just talking about the weather."

"What…?" And then her heart shot into her throat as she saw Hank leaning over the waist-high gate of the miniature bucking chute to show a little cowpoke how to get a proper grip on the wool.

Tori lifted her Dr Pepper can in a mock toast. "I gotta give Montana its due. We sent them a half-grown colt, and they gave us back a stud. I never realized Hank had such great…shoulders."

As she spoke, the chute gate opened and the sheep bolted straight toward where they sat, the boy clinging like a tick to its back. Hank loped easily alongside as the boy began to slide off the side of the sheep. Just before the kid's helmet hit the dirt, Hank caught hold of the protective vest and swung the boy up and into his arms, offering him a high five. The kid grinned ear to ear as they slapped palms.

Grace's heart wrung itself out like a sponge. She'd forgotten how wonderful Hank was with kids.

He set the boy on his feet and, glancing up, spotted Grace. His smile dropped and his nostrils flared, like a mustang scenting trouble and debating whether to attack or run. "Grace."

She squeaked an answering "Hank."

For a long, *long* moment his gaze held hers. Then he turned and jogged back to the mutton-busting chutes.

"Well now, *that* was interesting," Tori drawled. "Care to explain why I feel like I got caught in a nuclear blast?"

Grace took a huge bite of her corn on the cob and waved an apologetic hand in front of her face. *Sorry, can't answer, my mouth is full.*

Tori smirked. "Just be glad I'm *here*, and those two are out there."

Grace followed the tilt of Tori's Dr Pepper can to where Violet and Shawnee sat horseback, observing the mutton busting from a safe distance. They both wore the stiff, padded chaps designed to protect a pickup man — or in this case, woman — from the banging and kicking that was part of fetching cowboys off the backs of bucking horses at the end of the eight-second ride.

Grace swallowed and set her corn down. "I don't suppose you could forget to mention this to them."

"What?" Tori blinked wide, uncomprehending eyes at her. "I didn't see a thing."

Grace sighed in relief. Her gaze slipped back to

Hank, easy to pick out of the crowd in his red western shirt as he moved to the next chute. Oh shit. There was Gil, lowering a little girl onto the sheep. *Please God, nobody throw a punch in the middle of the arena.*

As they came face-to-face, Hank said something. And Gil laughed.

He *laughed.*

The steely fingers clenched around Grace's esophagus loosened their grip. It was okay. In fact, Gil looked almost cheerful...for Gil.

And Hank looked way too damn good for her peace of mind.

Hank caught Grace watching him again, her gaze jerking away the instant he looked her direction. He hadn't realized how often he'd been looking back until Korby nudged him.

"Dude. You've been staring at her all day. Are you thinking about giving that another shot?"

Yes. No. Hell, he didn't know. He did a half shrug in answer. That had been his intention when he'd gone to her apartment last night. But now? Complicated didn't begin to cover their situation. Or maybe it had gotten a whole lot simpler. Without that monster secret looming over her, Grace could kiss him if she wanted. And judging by the way she'd responded that night in Tori's barn, Grace *definitely* wanted.

But he had to tread carefully, or she'd decide his attraction to her was some weird reaction to finding out about the baby. Not likely. He'd felt this way before she'd handed him that picture. Hell, he'd been feeling this way for most of three years. So, no rush. He'd keep things in the friendship zone until the dust settled. But the baby gave him a perfect excuse to invite himself over to her place, if he could catch her after the—

Korby waved a hand in front of his face. "Hello. Staring again. Do I need to find someone else to help buck these bulls?"

Hank dragged his mind back to the job at hand. "I've got it."

"No kidding." Korby shook his head in mock disgust. "And it looks to me like you've got it *bad*."

Thankfully, the bulls came rattling and banging up the alley so Hank could pretend he hadn't heard. Behind the chutes, a chorus of cowbells rang out as riders gathered their ropes. The Black Friday Buck Out was a novice-only event, so the established cowboys were relegated to arena crew and coaching. Delon and Gil had done their part with the bareback riders. Now they were lounging on the grass in the shade, sipping Cokes.

The planks Hank and Korby were standing on shuddered as Cole vaulted up to give everyone their marching orders. "You know how touchy these young bulls can be. Korby, make sure the boys don't diddle around when they're gettin' on. And, Hank...you and Beni got the gates?"

"Yep." Hank climbed over the chute and dropped to the ground. Farther out in the arena, Joe was in full gear, pointing and gesturing as he instructed his partner for the day, a twenty-year-old from down in Stinnett. Word was that he was good but not great.

"Nothing like you," several of the cowboys had said, followed by a pause they expected Hank to fill. He refrained.

The first cowboy worked his glove in the handhold as Korby stood with both feet braced, pulling the rope tight.

Steve planted one big hand on the cowboy's chest to stop him from getting a face full of steel chute if the bull snorted and bucked inside the close confines. Out front, Hank leaned into the gate and released the metal catch, holding it shut with a soft rope, a process that eliminated the possibility of the latch jamming. Beni held the end of a longer rope used to swing the gate open while keeping the gateman safely clear. When the cowboy stuck out his chest, cocked his free arm, and nodded, Hank released his rope and Beni yanked the gate wide.

The bull hesitated, then crashed straight forward, ramming its shoulder into the corner post of the chute and forcing the cowboy to jerk his leg up. The next jump was a long forward lunge that tipped the kid onto his rear pockets and ripped the rope out of his hand. He shot straight out the back end, but instead of flying clear, his body was jerked to a stop midair.

Shit. His spur had caught in the flank strap, and now he flopped head down and helpless between the bull's kicking, stomping legs.

Joe was there instantly, grabbing the cowboy by the armpits to hoist him out of the danger zone and hopefully yank him loose. The other bullfighter threw himself on the bull's hips, fumbling to release the flank strap. The bull kicked high and hard, flinging him off like a horn fly and tearing the cowboy out of Joe's grasp.

Without consciously making the decision to move, Hank found himself in the midst of the fray, knife in hand. He dodged a flying hoof and, as the bull's rear feet began to descend, leapt for the loop of the flank strap where the spur was caught. With a quick, hard swipe, he cut the rope, then dropped the knife as the bull's hip crashed into his chest. Rolling with the force of the blow, he kicked his legs up and over in a backward somersault, landing on his knees and popping to his feet, ready to either dive back in for another try or run for the fence.

He didn't have to do either. The cowboy had come loose, and Shawnee had the bull roped around the horns. As she dragged it toward the catch-pen gate with Violet riding along behind to urge it on, Joe dropped to his knees beside the rider lying facedown in the dirt. Hank's body went numb, unable to move as his mind jumped back to another arena, another cowboy.

Then Grace came running, with the EMT and Tori flanking her. She leaned down to speak directly into the cowboy's ear while the EMT ran his hands over arms, hands, and legs. After what seemed like an eternity, the kid wiggled his feet.

Air blasted out of Hank's lungs. Geezus. *Geezus.* He bent at the waist, bracing his hands on rubbery knees as he gulped for oxygen.

A hand closed on his shoulder, too big to belong to anyone but a Jacobs. "You okay?" Cole asked.

"Yeah." Hank straightened, glad for Cole's steadying grip. "Did you see where my knife went?"

"Over there."

Joe had already picked it up. He inspected the blade Hank kept honed to a razor edge, then folded it and walked to where Hank and Cole stood.

Hank tucked the knife into his back pocket, where a clip held it within easy reach. "Thanks."

"I think that's our line." And as he'd done at the very first rodeo they'd worked together, Joe cuffed Hank on the back of the head. "Show-off."

Then he walked away to help collect ropes and nerves so they could go on to the next ride.

———∿∿∿———

They took the cowboy to the ambulance for a thorough evaluation, but thanks to a helmet, a Kevlar vest, and Hank, he hadn't suffered anything worse than a large scrape on one arm and a few bruises.

"Damn," Tori said as she settled back into her seat. "They made me spill my Dr Pepper."

Grace's laugh quivered with ebbing adrenaline. Her college mentor had said athletic training was hours of monotony broken by moments of sheer terror. The trick was staying alert during the monotony and calm while everyone else was panicking.

Hank hadn't panicked. His reaction had been as swift and sure as if he'd never stepped out of the arena. And when the dust settled, no one had looked more surprised than he did.

Luckily, nothing happened during the remainder of the rides that Joe and his partner couldn't handle with ease. As soon as the last score was announced, Grace stood. "I'm gonna head home."

Tori hitched an eyebrow. "You're not staying for the party?"

"It's been a long week. I need some alone time."

She was still scraped raw from the previous night, stupid tired from a mostly sleepless night. And she was suffering from overexposure—to Hank, not the sun.

Seeing him with Korby and the others made all the ways he had changed more obvious. Once, he'd bounced around in a whirl of banter, trash talk, and laughter. Grace had to admit, she liked this newfound reserve, broken by an occasional guarded smile. His shoulders did seem broader, and his body, though leaner, somehow carried more weight. And yes, fit very well into a pair of jeans.

She said her goodbyes and made her way to her pickup, but as she tossed her bag into the back seat, a shadow fell over her. When she spun around, Hank had one hand hitched over the top of the open door and the other braced on his hip, suddenly, disturbingly close. "Nice pickup."

She bristled, instantly defensive. "I'm paying for it myself."

"Why wouldn't you?"

Behind him, Korby strolled past with a gaggle of bull riders. He caught Grace's gaze, grinned, and waggled his eyebrows while the others stared. Panic clutched at Grace's throat. Had Hank said something to them? *Everyone* was looking at them. Could they tell? Or was it because Hank had made himself the center of attention?

"Grace?" He leaned in closer, lowering his voice. "Is something wrong?"

"You…I…" Had to get out of there. Away from the speculation and the whispers, and all those eyes. She searched frantically for something that would make him take a step back. "Go check your credit report, Hank."

"What?"

She took advantage of his confusion to duck under his arm, yank open the driver's door, and give the rear one a shove, forcing him to jerk his hand out of the way as it slammed. "I don't want to do this here."

As she backed out, he stepped into the space she'd vacated, staring after her with an expression that said, *What the hell was that?*

Chapter 34

HANK WAS WATCHING GRACE'S PICKUP EASE OUT OF the crowded driveway when Violet slung an arm around his neck. "Nice save. We owe you one, Buckwheat."

"Awesome. Got a computer I can use?"

The words had just popped out, half joking, but Violet shrugged. "I'm off the clock. What do you need?"

Five minutes later they were in the backyard office, with Hank leaning over her shoulder to squint at the website that would give him his credit report. Violet stood and gestured for him to take her seat. "Just follow the prompts. I hope you have your social security number memorized."

He nodded. "This will give me a list of all my out-standing loans and debts?"

"Yep. Plus a credit score, and whether it means you can replace that piece-of-crap pickup."

Which he had no intention of doing. An auto loan had been the only thing he could think of that required an emergency credit check. And why the hell would Grace tell him to check his credit? "Thanks."

"The least I can do." Someone outside called her name and she turned to go.

Since he'd never had a credit card or taken out a loan, when the results popped up the report consisted of one line item: *Yakima Valley Collections*. His hospital bill had been over sixteen thousand dollars for all the tests, the surgery on his arm, and an overnight stay, plus interest and late fees. And it had been paid in full around a week after Melanie and Wyatt had dropped by to see him at Norma's place.

His first furious thought was that Wyatt had taken it upon himself to wipe out the debt. But what had Grace said about the baby's new parents? *They can afford a lot of things.*

And they had accessed his account and shelled out thousands of dollars without his knowledge or consent. He sprang to his feet, banging the chair off the wall. Outside, the shady lawn was a sea of cowboy hats. Gil had set up his sound system and was doing a cover of a Reckless Kelly song, accompanied by a bass guitar and a guy tapping out the beat on what looked like a wooden box. A few people were already feeling happy enough to dance.

Over their heads, Joe gestured for Hank to join a cluster of cowboys gathered on the side porch. Hank returned the wave but veered off to where he'd spotted Bing, impossible to miss even in this mob. Her blouse was a brilliant yellow, and the contrast with her dark skin made her stand out like a black-eyed Susan in a field of white daisies.

She gave him a fierce hug. "I knew you still had it in you."

"It was just a reflex."

"Exactly. You can't fake those."

Hank shook his head, unwilling to assign too much importance to something that had happened so fast he hadn't had time to second-guess himself.

"We're leaving. It's time to get Grumpy Bear back to his den." She signaled to his dad, who was having his ear bent by one of the old codgers.

Johnny made his excuses and his escape. "Thank God. Do you have any idea how many times I've heard about how Vernon spurred one to win Houston but got hosed by the judges?" He offered a hand to Hank, who was so startled he accepted the quick, hard shake. "That was one slick move you made."

"Uh…thanks." Hank could practically hear the ripple of amazement as word spread that he and Johnny were having a civil conversation. "I'm gonna get out of here before Korby starts trying to pour beer down my throat."

"Where are you going?" Bing asked.

"To see Grace, if she'll let me." And after what he'd just learned, she *was* going to talk to him, one way or another.

"Good luck," his dad said, then stuttered, "Um, I mean…you know."

Hank didn't bristle like he would have before, recognizing that what he'd once pegged as sarcasm was more often Johnny's gift for sticking his foot in it. "I'm staying at the apartment, so don't wait up," he said, and made a run for it.

Back in Earnest, he stopped at the Kwicky Mart and got a large Coke. Weird to see a teenager he didn't recognize behind the counter. He sat down on a bench outside and drained half of the cup. *Ahh.* Nothing like that first icy-cold swallow when you were the kind of tired, dusty, and thirsty that only came from a long day at the rodeo.

And basking in the glow of a damn good save.

But his thoughts flipped over to Grace, the baby, that payment on his loan. It was as though his brain—hell, his whole life—had been split into two layers. On the surface, he kept rolling along like the cars that idled past on Main Street: headed home from work, to the café, to the bar, or just passing through with barely a glance at some guy sitting on a bench. Nothing special to see here.

Underneath, though, he was a sticky mess. He was a father. But not. And it hadn't struck him until he'd stood beside Korby, felt the new, invisible barrier between them, that there was a huge difference between the many things Hank didn't want to talk about and this one thing that he couldn't.

The sense of separation must be a thousand times worse for Grace. Pregnancy, childbirth... That was some major shit, the most profound experience of a woman's life according to most, and she had to pretend those months of her life had never happened. But not when she was with him. In a strange way, they were back to where they'd started—they could tell each other the things they would never confess to anyone else. And damn, he'd missed that too.

He polished off the Coke and tossed the cup in the trash. Time to roll up his sleeve. Yes, singular. He unbuttoned his cuff and pushed it up to see the number scrawled on his forearm in dense black. He'd copied it from his dad's caller ID with the only pen he could reach while he was talking to Grace.

He kept the text simple and to the point. We need to talk. Please?

When there was no immediate response, he got in the pickup and started driving. He was on the outskirts of Dumas when his phone chimed. He pulled over to read the dinky screen.

I'm at home. When?
Now.

He tossed the phone aside, hit the gas, and three minutes later he was standing at her door. It swung open and there she stood—her eyes huge and smudged with purple under her delicate skin. God, she was such a little bit of a thing to be so strong.

And it was time he started carrying his share of the load. "I shouldn't have run off last night," he said. "Or any of the times before. I swear, Grace, it won't happen again."

Tears pooled in her eyes. He opened his arms to gather her up and just stood there holding on as she made a small, choked sound and pressed her cheek against his heart.

—◆◆◆—

Grace had imagined a thousand versions of this conversation—what she'd say, what Hank would say. She'd been prepared for last night's rage and disbelief, but not this bewildered acceptance.

Or the way he had tucked her up close against him on the love seat.

She tilted her head to study his face for any sign that he was about to snap out of it. "You're awfully calm."

"I don't know what else to be." He absently rubbed her arm as he searched for an explanation. "It's like you breaking your arm when you were two years old, and saying it didn't count because you don't remember how it felt. I know I was involved, but I'm just not feeling it."

"Yet."

"True, but it doesn't feel like a freak-out waiting to happen." His brows pinched together. "I am a little annoyed that they swiped my credit information."

She sighed. "It's more like they *own* it. Or bought it

from the people who did. At least that's what they did with my student loans."

He recoiled. "Christ. That might be worse. Who are these people, the Mafia?"

"Close, but with fewer hit men." Well, not the kind that carried guns. These mobsters enforced their will with money, influence, and high-powered law firms, metaphorically burying anyone who got in their way. She extracted an envelope from her back pocket and handed it to him. "That's the PIN and debit card to access an account with a twenty-thousand-dollar balance, all in your name."

Hank stared dumbly at the letter. "And if I don't want their money?"

"It'll sit there and earn interest until you die. The Cowboy Crisis Fund is the beneficiary."

"Geezus." His dazed eyes came up to meet hers. "What did you get?"

She shifted uncomfortably. "They covered all my medical bills and living expenses for the pregnancy, which is standard. And then someone wrote off my student loans and set up the same kind of account for me, which is not. Gil was so pissed."

"Why?"

"Because Krista's parents tried to do the same thing to him. It's a bribe, to encourage you to relinquish your parental rights and ride off into the sunset. They figure if they give the rednecks some money, they'll just go make another baby if they want one instead of bothering with Maddie."

"*Bothering?* Christ." He scooped his hair back, then shook it into place. "And these are Maddie's parents?"

"Grandparents...not that anyone could ever prove it.

But her mom told them to knock it off." Grace hesitated, reluctant to stir things up, but she had to say, "That's what Wyatt was trying to escape when he left home, and he took Maddie's mother with him. She was one of his closest childhood friends…and his first ex-wife."

"*First?*" Hank's jaw dropped. "How many does he have?"

"Um, two. Not counting Melanie, but she's not his ex, so—"

"What about the baby's father?" Hank cut in. "Besides me, I mean."

"She doesn't have one." Again, Grace paused for a breath. "She has another mother."

Hank blinked, took a couple of breaths, then spoke slowly, pausing as he arranged the pieces. "So…Wyatt has an ex-wife no one has ever heard about…who is now married to another woman…and he helped them adopt our baby."

"Foster for now, but that about sums it up."

"Geezus." Hank splayed his free hand over his face. "My head is going to explode."

In that case, she might as well show him the Christmas picture. She fished it out and set it on his knee. "Those are her parents."

His hand dropped slowly to pick up the photo and angle it for a better view. Finally, he said, "Wyatt was married to the blond?"

"Yes."

"And the other one is…"

"Black?" Grace supplied.

He did a slow, dumbfounded headshake. "If your dad sees this, he's gonna lose his shit."

Yep. He might eventually have forgiven her for giving her baby to what he considered a *suitable* family. Someone like Violet's sister, Lily, as white as her name and with a husband who was a minister. A mixed-race couple would've stretched her father's tolerance to the absolute limit. But a married gay couple?

Grace touched a fingertip to one face, then the next. "The black woman is Julianne, and the other is Laura. They are lovely women who wanted a baby so much. How could I say *Sorry, but my papa wouldn't approve?*"

"So you basically gave him and his church a stiff middle finger instead?"

She had to smile at that, just a little. "You know how I've always wanted to. And I haven't exactly been his favorite since, um, you know."

"I dragged your name through every mudhole in the Panhandle?"

She winced at his self-disgust, but nodded. He lapsed into one of the silences she'd begun to expect from him. Those moments he took to step back, evaluate, and examine his reaction. The apartment was so quiet she could hear her own nerves crackling. As she tried to move away, Hank's arm tightened. She extricated herself long enough to set her phone in the dock of the stereo system and choose the playlist she called *Mellow*.

The haunting lilt of Brenn Hill's "With a Whisper" filled the room as Hank pulled her back into the hard curve of his body. It felt so good to be held this way that she barely choked back a hot rush of tears.

Hank nodded toward the shoebox. "Is that more pictures and stuff?"

"Yes."

Neither of them made a move to open the lid. The song ended and another started, "Diamonds and Gasoline" by the Turnpike Troubadours. Two verses played before Hank said, "Would it be weird if I said I don't want to see?"

"I…" Hadn't considered the possibility. "It's up to you."

His fingers drummed on his kneecap. "I'm not saying never. But it's not like she needs anything from me right away, other than my approval for the adoption, and I've got a lot of other crap to handle."

A part of her gut that had been knotted up for months and months relaxed so suddenly she was almost nauseous. He wasn't going to try to tear Maddie away from the parents Grace had chosen for her. "I understand."

"I don't." His gaze suddenly locked on hers. "Why did you even try to talk to me in a jam-packed bar when I was shit-faced?"

"I didn't have your phone number." And wow, that sounded lame when she said it out loud. "I'd heard you were back in town, but I didn't run into you anywhere else. By the time I realized how wasted you were, it was too late."

She had already attracted his attention, and he'd turned on her with droopy eyes and a cruelty she'd never seen in him. *Sorry, Gracie. You've already had the only piece of me you're gonna get.*

"And you didn't expect me to be a complete prick." Hank gathered her in, cradling her head against his chest as he heaved a broken sigh. "Dammit, Grace. I was supposed to take better care of you than this."

Her heart stumbled over the ragged edges of his voice. "I didn't expect you to."

"I know. And that really sucks."

Oh, Hank. This was what he'd hidden behind the laughter and the jokes. But Grace had seen how hard he was on himself. Worse than his dad could ever be.

She tilted her head back, giving in to the urge to brush the hair out of his eyes. "You thought you were doing me a favor by staying out of my life. I'd say that counts as looking out for me, even if it was stupid."

"Was it?" His gaze narrowed on her face. "If you hadn't been pregnant, if it was just us, do you really think you would have been better off with me around?"

"Yes." And if she'd given him a real chance, he would have done as right by her as he could, but pride had stopped her from trying again. She didn't want to be his obligation…and she didn't want to be obligated to raise his child.

"I made the decision to go it alone," she said. "I made all the decisions. And deep down, that's the way I wanted it. I got to choose my career and my freedom without having to take what you wanted into account."

His hand cupped the back of her head, holding her there, so close she could count the varying shades of brown in his eyes. "You make it sound so cold, and I know you better than that, Grace."

Do you? She shook her head. "I just did what was best for me."

"And for Maddie." He pressed a kiss to her forehead. "Take it from someone who's been there. She's a hundred percent better off than she would have been with a couple of people who were just making do."

"Oh, Hank." This time she sighed the words out loud. "You deserved so much more."

His thumb skimmed the side of her neck, making her shiver. "Maybe, but that's all history. What I want to know now is, do I deserve you?"

"I…what do you mean?"

He shifted, sliding his hand down to mold her against him. "I want you, Grace. And I need you. I've been imagining holding you like this since the day I walked out your door. I was planning to take it slow, but now I've got you here and I don't want to let you go." His thumb moved to her mouth, tracing her bottom lip. "What do I do about that?"

Heat surged in her at his words, his touch, the lean length of him against her, and hunger came roaring in behind it. She pressed her palms against his chest. She should push him away. But God, she wanted to pull him closer instead. Taste the salt she could smell on his skin. Explore every angle of this new, harder body. His heartbeat accelerated beneath her hand, a heavy thud that matched her own. She spread her fingers to absorb every degree of the heat pumping off his body. It was crazy to even think what she was thinking.

She was so damn tired of being sane, though, and she wanted his hands on her, his body at her mercy, to be known and cherished in a way only he had ever made her feel.

But she wouldn't sacrifice their friendship to flames.

"We can't let this come between us again." Her fingers drifted down across his stomach, perilously close to the obvious bulge in his jeans, and she felt him stiffen in response. "No matter what happens tonight, I still have to be able to sit at your lunch table tomorrow."

"Always." And he took her mouth, his kiss

super-heated with frustrated desire. Her own rose to meet it, a white-hot blast that fused them together and incinerated any remaining doubt. He hooked his hand behind her knee and pulled her across so she was straddling his thighs, then dragged his palms up her back, plastering her against him.

Grace strained and arched, shamelessly greedy for his taste, the rough silk of his tongue, the scent of rodeo dust in his hair and the grit on his skin. The kiss went on and on, two parched souls slaking a bone-deep thirst.

His hands came down to cup her butt and he tipped forward and stood in one fluid motion. She tightened her arms around his neck as he carried her into the unlit bedroom and lowered them both onto the bed so she was pinned by his delicious weight.

Finally he broke the kiss, his breath coming fast and hot. "I don't have any condoms."

"Top drawer." She made a vague gesture in the direction of her nightstand. "I'm sort of a stickler about providing my own now."

His smile flashed in the dim light. "That's my girl."

Chapter 35

It wasn't a dream this time. He was in Grace's bed, with Grace wrapped around him, her mouth as warm and intensely sweet as those precious Thanksgiving pralines. And as always, he was torn between gorging himself and slowing down to savor every nibble.

Her hands worked his shirt free and dragged it up, her fingernails scraping lightly across his skin. He groaned. The hell with slow. If he knew Grace—and he *knew* Grace—there would be a second helping. He levered onto his knees and let her unbutton his shirt so he could strip it off.

She grabbed his left arm. "What is *that*?"

"Your phone number. I couldn't find paper or a regular pen so I grabbed the one Dad uses for marking numbers on ear tags." He rubbed at it with his fingers. "There's a reason they call it indelible ink."

She traced one of the digits. "You're gonna have some explaining to do if you get naked with anyone else."

"I've got you." He caught her chin, tilting her gaze up to his. "Why would I want anyone else?"

"Uh…okay."

Okay? He might have demanded a better answer, but she yanked her own shirt off and unsnapped the front catch on her bra. He sucked in a breath of appreciation as it fell away. "Beautiful."

She made a *whatever* face. Grace always had underestimated her appeal in that department.

"Don't insult my friends." Hank stretched out beside her to set his palm on her stomach and let his eyes follow its path up and over the subtle curves, enjoying the catch of her breath. Her skin glowed like pearl dust, pale and nearly translucent. His fingers reacquainted themselves with the delicate lines of her rib cage, the tender pucker of her nipples.

"Beautiful," he whispered.

Her breath fluttered out in a sigh…and she smiled.

He peeled himself away from her and stood, drinking in the sight of her as he unbuttoned and unzipped her jeans, hooked his fingers in the sides, and stripped them and her underwear off in one move. Her smile deepened as he kicked off his boots and shucked his jeans. Before crawling back onto the bed, he reached into the night-stand for the condoms.

Jealousy dug razor-tipped claws into his gut when he found the box open. He couldn't think about anyone else seeing her in nothing but her satiny skin, with her not-really-red curls spilling around those wide, hungry eyes.

Then she sat up and pressed her hot mouth to his stomach, her tongue flicking, swirling, then trailing down the crease of hip and thigh. Her curls tickled like a thousand tiny fingers, and when her hand cupped his balls, he stopped thinking completely. He buried his fingers in the thick mass of her hair to steady himself as she tasted and teased, driving him to the point of exquisite pain. When he couldn't take any more, he hitched his hands under her arm-pits and tossed her into the middle of the bed, then grabbed the condom and followed her. He let her take the packet, groaning at the stroke of her hands as she rolled it on, and at the hot, slick heat he found when he touched her in return.

Her hips jerked as he slid a finger inside, and again when his thumb found even more sensitive flesh. She rocked into his hand, her breath coming faster, and her fingers digging into his shoulders. He remembered what she liked, and he'd had a long time to imagine doing exactly what he did now, using tongue and teeth to push her almost to breaking. Before he could take her over the edge, she pushed his hand aside and pulled him between her thighs, rising to meet him as she guided him into position.

It was a long, slow slide into heaven.

Buried inside her, he went still, the better to feel every pulse and clench of her body around him. *Sweet Jesus*. All those frozen nights in Montana, when he'd had to satisfy himself with the memory of her, he'd decided that she couldn't have really felt this incredible.

But holy freaking hell, it was even better. She started to move, a subtle tightening with a rock of her hips that electrified every inch of him. His body clenched with the urge to pound into her, but he endured the torture for as long as he could, burying his face in the curve of her neck and feasting on tender, vanilla-scented skin. Then she did that thing that drove him absolutely insane, sliding her hand between them to alternately caress him, then herself, winding them both tighter and tighter until she gave a low, throaty moan and arched against him, the power of her orgasm rocking them both. His control broke, and he drove hard and deep until he exploded in a blinding rush.

As the last shudder passed he collapsed, taking her with him as he rolled onto his back so he didn't crush her. They sprawled together, chests heaving, and he managed one coherent thought.

Now he was home.

—ᴍ—

Whatever else might have changed, Grace was happy to see that Hank was still the ultimate spooner. He had one arm cradling her head and the other looped around her waist, tucking her snug against his body for maximum skin-to-skin contact. And it wasn't just in bed. When they'd lounged in her dorm room watching football games, he'd held her in the cradle of his thighs, her back against his chest, his fingers playing with her curls or stroking long, bone-melting lines up and down her arms.

Even if this had been a really bad idea, she felt too damn good to care. Besides, they hadn't stumbled into it this time, eyes firmly closed. They'd had a reasonable, adult conversation about what they expected.

He nuzzled a kiss into the curve of her neck. "You have no idea how many times I have fantasized about this. Not the sex—well, okay, not *just* the sex—but holding you this way. Being so warm."

Grace smiled sleepily. "If warm was what you wanted, you shouldn't have picked Montana."

"It picked me. I'm not sure where I'd be right now if it hadn't." He spoke of it like a living thing, as if the land itself had chosen him. "You can't even imagine those mountains, Grace. Like a huge wall that shoves straight up out of the prairie. And there's one right above where I lived that's set out from the rest. Chief Mountain. I never pronounce the Blackfeet name right. It's one of their most powerful sacred places, a huge slab of vertical rock you can see for fifty miles. They say Thunder lives up there and uses his power to renew life."

There was a reverence in his voice as he went on. "I

used to hike to the top of the ridge below it and just sit. There's something so overpowering about that mountain, your mind can't comprehend it's real. But at the same time it's fragile because it's made of shale so it's constantly shedding rock. There's a big divot from a slide that happened when Bing was a kid."

"It sounds awesome," Grace said, because she couldn't think of a word that did his description justice.

He gave a soft, self-deprecating laugh. "Bing called it my vision quest—staring at that mountain and realizing you can stand tall even when you're falling apart around the edges."

The air balled up in Grace's throat, and she made an embarrassing little hiccupping sound. She'd been right about Hank finding his roots, but they were planted in the ancient stone of the Rockies, not the Texas soil. Would they drag him back the way the Panhandle had tugged at her?

He kissed her shoulder. "I want to take you there. We'll go visit Bing, maybe hike to the top of Chief Mountain. The view from up there is mind-boggling…if Thunder isn't throwing a party and you're not too worried about grizzlies."

Whoa now. How did they go from *I need to jump your bones* to planning future vacations? Slivers of alarm darted inside her chest like minnows, cold and slippery.

Hank laughed, misinterpreting her sudden tension. "Forget the hike. I'm not joking about the bears, and you are kinda bite-sized."

As if to demonstrate, his teeth grazed her shoulder where his lips had been. Grace shivered at the gentle scrape, but her mind was reeling off in a totally different direction. This was just Hank rambling on in postorgasmic bliss, right? He couldn't be thinking this was the beginning of…something.

"That would be awesome." Shit. There was that word again. "Too bad I've got school and sports straight through May."

"Mmm." He was working his way toward the nape of her neck, sending goose bumps across her skin. "It'd be better to wait until July, to be sure the Going-to-the-Sun Road is open. We don't want to drive all the way to Montana and miss the best scenery."

July? For an instant she was sucked into a vision of the two of them meandering across the country, stopping wherever and whenever they pleased, nothing but sunshine and laughter and giddy freedom. Then reality threw a grim shadow over her daydream. Sucked in was right. How many times had she let Hank's enthusiasm sweep her up, only to have him leave her flat when the next shiny thing caught his attention?

Yes, he had changed. But did she really know how much—or if he would eventually lapse into his old ways? And it wasn't just the two of them anymore. They had to think of Maddie.

He made a low sound of protest when she scooted out of his grasp and reached for the nightshirt hanging on her bedpost. She pulled it over her head and tugged it down to her thighs. "Montana sounds lovely, but let's just take this as it comes, okay?"

He pushed up onto his elbow. "How do you mean?"

"You said it yourself—you've only been home a week, and you've had a lot dumped on your plate. This was awesome…" Geezus. Was that the only adjective left in her vocabulary? "But I don't think it's a good time to be making long-term, um, plans."

She couldn't even say *commitment*, for crying out loud. And how could he think it, after three damn years of total silence? "Look, maybe I'm taking this wrong and you were just telling me about a place you obviously love."

Enough that once he'd wrapped up all the loose ends here in the Panhandle, he might head right back there to commune with his precious mountain. And why was she so annoyed? She shook off the irritation and deployed her Miz Mac, *everybody just stay calm* voice. "You were right about taking it slow. I don't regret tonight, but I don't know what more you expect from me under the circumstances."

"I want you, Grace." He reached out to caress her bare thigh, but she stepped back. He frowned up at her. "Are you saying that you don't trust me?"

"Duh." The word popped out before she could stop it, and he flinched. Crap. Snark was not helpful. She grasped the hem of her nightshirt, wishing desperately that she'd put on some underwear before starting this conversation.

He slowly sat up, bent his knees, and propped his elbows on them. The sheet slipped down to several inches below his navel, revealing the taut curves of his butt. Lord, he was nothing but muscle, sinew, and bone, a minimalist sculpture of the ideal male form. His shoulders lifted and she braced for his anger, but he blew out a sigh instead. "Okay. I earned that, but I want to prove I'm not that guy anymore. What do you need from me, Grace?"

Huh? She blinked, thrown for a loop by his quiet resolve. This was not going the way she'd expected, and she really, *really* hated feeling like she'd been prepping for months and none of the material she'd studied was on the test. "I need time. Me…you…this…" She swung a hand around, palm up, to indicate everything that had passed between them. "You can't even look at pictures of our daughter yet, but you want…"

Hell. What was he asking for?

"A chance?" His expression was dead solemn. "Yeah. I do. And I didn't say I *couldn't* look at the pictures. I just feel like there are more important things I need to focus on first…like you."

He said it so simply and so calmly that panic shot icy bolts through her gut.

"No." She shook her head once. Then again. "You don't get to waltz back in here and pick up like you walked down to the corner store for a Coke instead of disappearing into the freaking wilderness."

He slapped a hand on the bed. "Then what was this about?"

"I thought I made that clear!" She pulled down so hard on her nightshirt that the collar dug into the back of her neck. "I asked if we could still be friends. And you said *always*."

"I meant it. But is that really all you want? Lunch now and then and a roll in the hay when we're both in the mood?"

"Yes! Maybe. I don't know!" She stopped mangling her pajamas to throw up her hands. "A week ago I wasn't sure if I'd ever see you again, and you don't even know how long you intend to stay. Excuse the hell out of me if I'm not comfortable diving headfirst into…whatever."

He scowled, then let his head drop between his arms. "That's fair."

"Thank you." And she noticed he didn't insist he was home for good.

He flicked the comforter aside and stood in one fluid movement that left him gloriously, unceremoniously naked. He bent to pick up his clothes, giving her an eyeful, and pulled on first his black boxer briefs, then his jeans, every movement somehow choreographed to show his body to the best advantage. Or maybe he didn't have a bad angle. He shoved one arm, then the other into his shirt and turned to meet Grace's gaze as he made leisurely work of the buttons.

"What are you doing?" she asked.

"Taking my time. Giving you space." Then he made a liar of himself by stepping close and hitching his arms around her hips. "As long as I still get to see you. I suppose you're working tomorrow."

She had to fight the temptation to lean into him. "At three. I've got boys' basketball games. And in the morning I need to exercise my horse."

"How do you feel about Indian tacos?"

She blinked. "Um…why?"

"Cole's bringing his welder to help me fix a couple of broken gate hinges, so Bing's making fry bread and Indian tacos for dinner. Shawnee will be there too. Come and eat with us before you go to work."

She was shaking her head before he finished. "I thought we just agreed—"

"That we have no problem sitting down to lunch together." Damn him, turning her argument back on her. "Dad and Bing would like to get to know you."

She narrowed her eyes. "That's all?"

"Pinkie swear. I will pretend your old man is still

standing over in the corner looking like he'd run me through the paper shredder if it wouldn't make a mess of the carpet."

Grace snorted. Oh yeah. She remembered that look.

Hank leaned down, his gaze soft and pleading. "Pretty please?"

She should say no, but dammit, he was no easier to refuse now than he had been at ten, or sixteen, or twenty-two. Besides, she would have to face his dad eventually, and Bing, no doubt. A woman that protective of Hank wasn't going to leave without getting a good look at his baby mama.

Come to think of it, doing this meet and greet with Shawnee there as back up might not be a bad idea.

"Okay," she said reluctantly.

"Thank you." His kiss was slow and soft. A *see you later* kind of kiss that he confirmed by turning her loose and backing toward the door. "Come any time before noon, and bring your appetite. Bing makes killer Indian tacos."

Don't say it. Don't say it.

"Awesome," she said, and waited until he was out of sight before slapping her face into her palms. *Gah!* The man made her soft in the head.

And no matter how reasonable he made it sound, this sorta friends, sorta lovers, and—oh yeah!—sorta Maddie's parents thing was bound to blow up in their faces.

Chapter 36

HANK DID NOT SQUEAL HIS TIRES AS HE DROVE AWAY from Grace's apartment, and he didn't flip the bird at an SUV that cut him off as he pulled onto the main drag. Nope. He was a model freaking citizen, obeying every speed limit and stopping extra-long at every stop sign. He didn't even run the yellow light on Route 287 as he turned left toward home.

Just past the Dumas city limits, he pulled into an empty gravel lot and got out. Then he very calmly hiked his leg back and slammed his bootheel into the side of the pickup with a satisfying crunch. That was the nice thing about driving a junker. What was one more dent when you direly needed to kick something? He considered doing it again, but his foot might go right through the rusty side panel, so he slapped his palms onto the side of the box instead, hard enough to sting.

You stupid son of a bitch.

He'd had one chance—*one*, goddammit—to show Grace that he wasn't still rolling through life like a barrel of rocks, crashing and smashing and never looking or thinking ahead. Not three hours ago he'd told himself this would happen if he rushed her. Then the minute he got his hands on her, he'd gone brain dead and done exactly that. And just like he'd figured, she'd found a reason—and a damn good one—to doubt his intentions.

He ripped off a few of Gil's favorite curses as he

dropped his elbows onto the edge of the pickup box and buried his face in his hands. The deed was done. Exceptionally, mind-blowingly well done, but still. How was he gonna convince her this wasn't one more of his legendary wild hairs? Sure, he could say he'd thought of her every damn day for the last three years. Claim he'd known then that she was the best thing that could ever happen to him.

And she would believe him…why?

Maybe the Grace he'd known in high school would have fallen for that load of crap. Not that it *was* crap, but how would she know? He hadn't given her any reason to think otherwise. And this was no infatuated girl. He was dealing with a grown woman whose best friends and role models all belonged to the take-no-shit club.

He pushed himself upright and stared out over a dark prairie dotted with the lights of a few scattered houses and ranch buildings. What he needed was advice…and he knew a guy who'd managed, against all odds, to woo the most difficult woman of the bunch.

The trick would be making him talk.

───

Cole showed up at ten thirty on Saturday, minus Shawnee. "They're roping this morning," he said. "Then she's gonna catch a ride out here with Grace."

From anyone else, it might have been a leading comment. *Why is Grace coming to dinner?* Cole was just stating the facts.

Hank waited until Cole had finished reinforcing the heavy iron hinges for the loading chute gate—*Try to sag now, you two-ton piece of shit*—and they had hoisted the monster back into place. Then he said, "If I swear on a stack of Bibles never to do it again, can I ask you a question?"

"Is this about Grace?"

"Yeah."

Cole grunted. "You really have wised up."

"I'm trying, but how do I prove it to her?"

Cole propped an elbow on the gate, frowning. "Why are you asking me?"

"When I left Texas, Shawnee was swearing she would never get married, but here you are." Hank draped the coiled extension cord over a post to be put away later, not taking any chances on letting Cole escape. "How did you change her mind?"

Cole's eyes narrowed. "You want to marry Grace?"

The question was like a cattle prod to the base of Hank's spine, snapping him straight. *Marriage?* Hell, he was still trying to figure out how to get her to go steady. But they weren't kids anymore. If he was gonna start something with Grace, he owed it to both of them to know where he wanted it to end, so he took the time to poke around inside his heart and see what he found.

He'd always liked her. A lot. Respected her, even if he'd done a lousy job of showing it. He sorted through a jumble of feelings, identifying each one. Admiration. Pride. Guilt. Protectiveness, from day one. And let's not forget good old lust. Possessiveness, for sure. *His* little red-haired girl. When he laid them out, stepped back, and took in the whole picture, there was absolutely no doubt what he was looking at.

Love.

Whoa. But after an initial jitter, his heart settled

into a strong, steady rhythm, as if it had finally found its groove, and he marveled at the absolute sense of rightness.

He loved Grace. Probably always had. That would explain why no other relationship had ever stuck. No matter how pretty, how smart, how cowgirl perfect for him, there had always been something that didn't quite add up, because none of them had been Grace.

He gave himself another minute to enjoy how freaking *good* it felt to admit that, and wallow in the warm flush of emotion. Lord knew Cole wasn't in a hurry to get on with their chat.

Finally Hank said, "Yes. I do. But she's determined to shove me out the door."

"Then you keep ringing the doorbell." The stern lines of Cole's face softened as he remembered. "That's pretty much all I did. Just kept showing up and letting her know I was gonna be there no matter what. Between her cancer risk, her jackass dad, and not being able to have babies, Shawnee had a *lot* of whats."

Damn. Hank hadn't known that she couldn't have kids. "That must've been tough. You wanted a family."

"I have one," Cole said gruffly. "And there are other ways to be a parent. There's only one Shawnee."

Geezus. And he'd been worried he wouldn't be able to get Cole to open up. Hank choked down a massive lump that threatened to cut off his air supply.

"Are we done?" Cole asked.

Hank wasn't sure if he was talking about the heart-to-heart or the corral repairs, but he nodded yes to both. "I think I can handle the rest."

Cole nodded back, then to Hank's shock added, "I

like Grace. And you're not so bad, either. Let me know if there's anything else I can do."

He hefted the welder with one big hand and carried it over to his pickup like it was a lunch box. Hank grinned as hope, bright and hot, bloomed in his chest.

If Cole was an example of the kind of miracles love could work, anything was possible.

Chapter 37

JOHNNY'S DAD HAD ALWAYS TOLD HIM THAT perseverance was as important as talent. With so many unpredictable elements in rodeo—horse, calf, weather, arena conditions, pure bad luck—cowboys stayed sane by repeating the mantra, "All you can control is your effort." So Johnny had kept backing in the box, nodding his head, and giving it his best shot.

If he had applied any of that to raising his kids, his son might not have needed psychiatric care...and his daughter wouldn't be calling on a Saturday morning to see if Johnny had driven him back into treatment.

"How are *you* feeling?" Melanie asked.

"I'm sleeping more every night." Which Bing claimed was doing wonders for his disposition. "I offered Hank a job for as long as he wants to stay."

"Oh. Wow. That's great."

"So far." He wasn't feeling quite as optimistic today, with Hank barely speaking while they did chores and Johnny pretending he didn't notice that massive new dent in the side of the old Chevy. He'd assumed things hadn't gone well with Grace, but then Hank had announced that she was coming for dinner.

"I thought you'd want to get to know her," he'd told Bing.

She'd narrowed her eyes at him. "When her friends are here to stop me from getting too personal?"

"Yep. Do *not* scare her off." And the look Hank had given her made it clear he expected her to be on her best behavior.

She'd met it with one that expressed serious concerns about his motives, but finally shrugged. "It's your call."

Johnny turned his attention back to his own conversation as he fumbled a shirt one-handed off a hanger in the closet. "Did you hear what happened at the Buck Out yesterday?"

"A full play-by-play from both Joe and Violet. And she sent video."

Johnny shook his head, still in awe. "It was incredible."

"I'm glad you got to see it."

"It helps if you're looking."

"Yeah, it does. I'm glad things are going so well." Her tone shifted in a way that made him pause. "But it makes me think it would be best if we didn't come home for Christmas."

Johnny frowned. "You can't stay out there alone."

"We're not. I have my own version of Miz Iris, you know. Helen is cooking up a big ol' Christmas feast at the Bull Dancer for anyone who doesn't have someplace else to go, and Wyatt's footing the bill. We'll have a full house."

It was wonderful to open up their bar and their wallets that way, but she and Wyatt shouldn't have to skip Christmas with family and their closest friends. With Bing to mediate, Johnny and Hank had gotten closer in a handful of days than all the years before. Now all the secrets were out—sweet Jesus, what more could there be?—imagine what they could do with another month.

"Let's see how things go. You don't have to decide

now." Since Wyatt had his own plane, they didn't have to worry about getting tickets.

"And if we do come home and it goes really wrong?" Melanie asked.

"What do you mean?"

"Hank might never forgive Wyatt for helping Grace hide her pregnancy, or me for not telling him the truth as soon as I found out. In his place, I'm not sure *I* would get over it."

Johnny dropped the clean shirt on the bed. "I'm not going to choose between my kids."

"I already did it for you, Daddy." Resignation drained the color from her voice. "I picked Wyatt and Oregon instead of Hank. I haven't been there to take care of you or help on the ranch, but he is, and there's a chance he might stay. From where I'm sitting, that makes it a no-brainer."

The familiar knot began to tighten in his chest. He was so damn tired of having options snatched out of his hands. But Melanie *had* made her life halfway across the country. The most he could hope for were fleeting visits, these phone calls on Sunday mornings, and emailed photos that would be there and gone. Everything he could have with Hank stretched into the future. Someone to ride beside him across the pasture and in the pickup, a voice that didn't come out of a radio, a second set of shoulders to bear some of the load. If Hank did decide to try fighting bulls again, they'd make it work. And eventually there could be a daughter-in-law, grandkids…

Well, *more* grandkids, he corrected.

"You see what I mean?" Melanie asked softly.

The knot twisted, wringing acid out of his stomach. "We can work this out."

"I hope so. But you need to think about what's at

stake before we decide to gamble—or you could lose him all over again."

After they hung up, Johnny got both arms into his shirt, then just sat, scratching his jaw as he brooded. This goddamn beard was driving him nuts. That, at least, he could fix.

Or so he thought. The third time he cut himself, he threw the razor at the mirror. That felt so good, he grabbed the shaving cream and slammed it into the trash, knocking the metal can over with a satisfying crash. *Goddamn helpless bastard…*

The door to his bedroom flew open. "Johnny? Did you fall? What—" Bing stopped dead when she saw him standing at the sink, his face blotched with shaving cream, patches of missed whiskers, and drops of blood. Then she took in the trash can and the shaving cream that had rolled over to rest against the tub.

"I'm trying to shave," he said.

"And giving me heart failure. I was sure you'd passed out in the shower. Don't you own an electric shaver?"

"They give me a rash."

Her shoulders climbed toward her ears, then dropped as she huffed out an aggravated breath. "Just a minute. I have to set the bread dough to rise."

He barely had time to retrieve the razor and shaving cream and pick up the trash can before she was back, carrying one of the kitchen chairs. She thumped it down, facing the mirror. "Sit!"

He sat. She plucked the razor off the vanity and positioned herself behind him.

"Are you going to put me out of my misery?" he asked, a little unnerved by the glint in her eyes.

"I managed to shave my uncle after his stroke without cutting his ornery old throat." She grabbed his chin and jerked his head up. "I can see where Melanie gets her temper."

The fury had drained away as quickly as it had risen, and as usual, he felt stupid and ashamed. His gaze met Bing's in the mirror. "Hank *will* forgive her eventually, won't he?"

Her grip gentled, and her night-flower scent wrapped around him as she drew the razor carefully up his neck and over the corner of his jaw. "I think he wants to."

"But?"

"It's complicated. Hank can't help wondering if he was mostly just a mess she had to clean up after, and Melanie has to deal with the guilt of knowing she felt important to you and he didn't."

Christ. It always came back to Johnny. But on the other hand… "If Hank and I fix things, that should make it easier for the two of them."

"Theoretically…but there's still Wyatt. Baby aside, the man tags every one of Hank's insecurities. He's intellectual, driven, reeks of culture…and gorgeous on top of it."

Yeah, Johnny had noticed. Hank wasn't the only one who felt like a country bumpkin next to his brother-in-law. "His family is one step removed from the Rockefellers. Of course he's got class."

"But he turned his back on all that and made himself into one of the best bullfighters in history, with no rodeo connections or background—unlike Hank." She poked his cheek. "And quit making faces or I'll nick you again."

Johnny smoothed out his expression and tried to talk without moving his lips. "He had money, though. That makes everything easier."

"I know. But it's also one more example of how Wyatt has all the power, and Hank has none. His mentor is Wyatt's closest friend. His sister married the man. From Hank's perspective, Wyatt is holding all the cards except one—his approval. Withholding it is the only thing he can control."

Christ. Why couldn't Melanie have just married one of the Sanchez boys, or Cole?

Johnny sighed and settled deeper into the chair, but relaxing was out of the question. The slide of the razor over his skin was a disturbingly intimate caress in the close confines of the bathroom. Bing's fingers were dark against his cheek, the pink of her nails bright points of color as she pulled the skin taut and stroked, gentler than he was with himself.

He was suddenly, intensely aware of each individual point of contact, and the stir of her breath against his temple. Grasping at any distraction, he asked, "Do you have a real name?"

"Joan." She rinsed the razor, tapped it on the side of the sink, then squirted a dab of shaving cream onto her hand and stroked it onto his neck. Damn, that felt nice. "Wagner," she added.

"Joan Wagner." He couldn't make that incredibly ordinary name stick to the woman who leaned over him, smelling of chili, bread dough, and hot tropical beaches. "Why Bing?"

She tilted his chin up, carefully negotiating his Adam's apple. "When I was a toddler, every time someone tried to leave the house without me, I'd chase after them yelling, 'Bing! Bing! Bing!'"

"And it stuck all this time?"

"On the rez, nicknames are forever." She bent lower to inspect the underside of his chin, and in the mirror he watched her blouse gap, giving him an unobstructed view of the full, brown curves of her breasts and the cream-colored lace that fought to contain them.

His breath hitched and she glanced up, catching him dead to rights. Her eyebrows lifted. "Enjoying the view?"

"It's...stunning."

Her gaze drifted down to the open front of his shirt. "It's not bad from where I'm standing, either."

Much to his disappointment, she set down the razor to fasten another button on her blouse. But now every brush of her fingers and shift of her body sent tingles racing over his skin to settle in his groin. Shit. He could not look at her that way because...because...

He lost track as she laid her finger along his bottom lip to shave just below. It was all he could do not to suck that finger into his mouth. And oh crap. Did he just lick her?

This time, she did jerk away.

"Sorry. I didn't mean..." *To taste you?* Christ. He plastered the towel over his face, scrubbing away the shaving cream. "None of this would be happening if they'd had a decent father."

She paused for a deliberate beat, then said, "Or if their father had gotten the treatment he needed."

He dropped the towel to his lap. "Me? For what?"

Her gaze traveled from the trash can to the shaving cream and then back to him.

His face heated. "I get pissed sometimes. That's not the same."

"Are you sure?" She leaned against the vanity and folded her arms over breasts that were now directly at his eye level. *Dammit, Johnny. Focus.* "According to Hank, there were a lot of days when your temper was totally unreasonable. *Like a rattlesnake with a sunburn*, he said."

Johnny wadded the towel in his one good hand. "Yeah. I can be a real prick."

"Why?"

The blunt question made him blink. "Money, work, my wife, you name it. I'd swear this time I was gonna be patient with Hank, I wasn't gonna yell, and the next thing I knew…"

"What did it feel like?"

What? The sour bile that filled his gut when he heard the echoes of his angry voice? The way it made him even more furious at himself and everything else?

"When you get irritated, what do you feel?" she persisted. "Shortness of breath, pressure, heart palpitations?"

He stared at her. How had she guessed? "Tightness. A weird tingle in my chest. And so edgy that anything sets me off."

She nodded, looking awfully pleased about it. "Extreme irritability can be a manifestation of anxiety, and both are common in the aftermath of a catastrophic event." Her face softened along with her voice. "Think about it, Johnny. The fire took your home, your entire life history, plus there was the horror of all the livestock. You had to watch your career and your father's health go down the tubes, and then your marriage came apart. It would be a damn miracle if there wasn't something wrong with you."

He shook it off. "Everyone around here went through the same thing."

"So therefore everyone should just suck it up?"

Well, yeah. "Are you saying I have PTSD or something?"

"Possibly. Regardless, you are a textbook case for irritation anxiety."

His jaw sagged. "I'm pathologically cranky?"

She laughed. "Hey, at least you're not a true asshole. You just act like one sometimes."

"Gee, thanks."

"You're welcome."

Their gazes caught, and her amusement faded. She reached out a fingertip to scoop up a dab of shaving cream that had dropped into his chest hair.

"Damn fine scenery." She studied the foam for a moment before flicking it aside. "Just my luck, it has to be out of bounds."

She made her getaway while he tried to remember how to breathe. Then he closed his eyes and swore. Yeah. That was pretty much how his luck ran, too.

Chapter 38

GRACE STEPPED INTO THE ARENA ON SATURDAY morning and found Tori and Shawnee already horseback, settled in to wait for her with that *You have some explainin' to do* look on their faces.

And this is why you don't sleep with the friends of your friends. Or their brothers.

But if you did, you'd better be prepared to own up, which was why she'd texted Shawnee offering her a ride to the Brookman ranch after they finished roping. Grace flipped her rein around a fence rail, then stepped well out of Betsy's reach before facing them.

"Yes, we had sex," she said. "Yes, it will probably happen again. And yes, I am aware that it was too soon and it could put the rest of you in an awkward position."

Tori hitched a shoulder. "It's all relative, I suppose. I dragged Delon out of a New Year's Eve party and had my way with him two hours after we met."

"On a barstool," Shawnee added as Grace gaped at the offhand confession.

"I swear, you are obsessed with that barstool." Tori reached out and poked Shawnee's arm. "And you jumped a guy who is basically a brother to one of your best friends. Hell, that's still awkward."

"Only because I make a point of oversharing every chance I get," Shawnee said with a proud grin.

Grace gave her head a shake. Wasn't this where her

older, wiser friends were supposed to talk some sense into her? "So, um, there's no problem, then?"

"Oh, there's bound to be problems," Tori said. "Just not between us girls."

"Except Melanie," Shawnee clarified. "He *is* her baby brother, and she can be pretty damn vindictive."

Tori rolled her eyes heavenward. "Like after you threw her brand-new cowboy hat out the window of the pickup in the middle of rush-hour traffic?"

"Hey, I told her before she bought it that I wasn't travelin' with somebody wearing a hat that ugly. She didn't have to go fillin' every one of my pockets with baby powder."

Grace had to laugh, but she sobered immediately. What had made perfect sense when she was with Hank sounded like pure folly when she imagined confessing it to Melanie.

"I talked to her this morning," Shawnee said, suddenly all business. "She said to tell you that under the circumstances, it's best if she and Wyatt remain impartial."

In other words, *don't* call. Don't try to explain. Don't ask for advice from the one friend who knew all her circumstances. Just leave Melanie out of it, to avoid more strain on her relationship with Hank. Heat stung Grace's cheeks, even though this was what she should have expected—and no more than she would do if Jeremiah got involved with one of her friends.

And these were, first and foremost, Melanie's friends. A chill settled over Grace. Melanie had made her a part of this circle. Without her blessing—

"Goddammit, Shawnee. You weren't supposed to scare her." Tori gave an exasperated huff. "The point is, we're already a huge mess of in-laws and outlaws and everything in between. And *most* of us"—she aimed a pointed look at Shawnee—"are capable of acting like reasonable adults. Whatever happens between you and Hank, we'll deal with it. Nobody's getting kicked to the curb. Got it?"

"Got it," Grace said, going limp with relief.

Tori gave a clipped nod. "Good. Then let's rope."

It was almost straight up noon when Grace and Shawnee walked into Johnny's house to find the men lounging around the table, sipping Cokes from the can. Hank's smile looked relieved, as if he'd doubted she'd show up.

"Sorry," Grace said. "We should've quit before that last pen of calves."

Cole snorted. "That'll be the day."

"Practice makes the checks grow bigger," Shawnee said, flinging herself into the chair next to him.

Then Hank's dad stood, and Grace found herself staring up at Johnny Brookman. His hair was lighter than Hank's, his jaw squarer, and he was built like a former high school linebacker who hadn't let his body go at all.

He was also Maddie's grandfather.

"Hello, Grace. We've never officially met." His hand closed around hers, big, warm and calloused, but he didn't quite meet her eyes. Oh, yeah. Definitely awkward.

"Uh, hello, Mr. Brookman." Her voice squeaked, and she blushed.

"Call me Johnny." His smile was stiff but still packed a punch. The man had been divorced for how long? Why wasn't every single woman within three counties parked on his doorstep?

And how was that working, with him and Bing living in the same house and Johnny not exactly an invalid anymore?

Bing set a bowl of chopped green onions and another full of shredded lettuce in the middle of the table alongside grated cheese, sour cream, tomatoes, black olives, and salsa. The rich scents of chili and frying bread made Grace's nose twitch in anticipation as Bing returned to the stove to turn several palm-sized, oblong pieces of dough that were bubbling in hot oil.

Grace sniffed. "Is that yeast bread?"

"Yep. That's how we make it up north, not like the Navajos with their baking powder."

"I didn't realize there were different kinds."

Bing flashed a superior smile. "Ours is better."

Grace certainly wouldn't argue—even if she disagreed. Hank jumped up to pull out the chair next to his, and Grace sank into it, shoulders rigid, as she waited for him to sit down and mimic Cole, draping a lazily possessive arm over the back of her chair. He went to the kitchen instead, to help Bing carry a steaming pot of chili and the platter of golden, puffy fry bread to the table, and when he sat down again, he didn't have eyes for anything but the food.

Well. Good. They were just lunch buddies again, and that *was* what she'd told him she wanted.

They all grabbed pieces of bread to set on their plates, then ladled chili over top and piled on toppings. At the first bite of crispy bread and savory chili, Grace groaned in appreciation. "Oh man. That is the best."

Bing smiled archly. "Told you."

Everyone dug in, and for a few minutes, the

conversation was limited to "Please pass me the..." and various appreciative noises. Then Johnny asked, "When are you heading to Vegas for the Finals?"

"Tomorrow," Cole said. "Delon and Gil left this morning with the stock."

Hank dropped a big dollop of sour cream onto his taco. "How much are you taking?"

"Twelve horses and three bulls." Cole paused in the midst of plowing through his taco to flash a rare grin. "They posted the draw for the first round yesterday. Delon's got Blue Rose."

Hank's eyebrows shot up. "That colt out of Blue Duck and Riata Rose?"

"Yep. He's seven now and really coming on strong. I swear, instead of getting half of his genes from his mama and the other from his daddy, this colt got it all from both of them." It was more words than Grace had heard him string together in the past month, but when it came to his stock, Cole could go on for...well, minutes anyway. "If he has his best trip with Delon, it's gonna be good watchin'. And you could sorta call it a chance for some redemption."

For Grace's benefit, Hank said, "The stud, Blue Duck, is the horse Delon was riding when he wrecked his knee."

The crash that had nearly ended his career—until Tori came along and, with Gil's help, completely retooled his riding mechanics. With his new, laid-back, wide-open style, Delon had returned to win not one, but two world championships. This year, though, he was starting the National Finals with a fifty-thousand-dollar deficit, thanks to a record-breaking regular season by a young phenom out of Canada.

"Damn," Hank said. "I'll have to go down to the Watering Hole on Thursday night to watch. I don't have a TV in my apartment."

Shawnee quirked her eyebrows. "Or you could go to Grace's."

Grace froze with a chunk of taco stuck on her fork. "I'm horse-sitting at Tori's while they're gone."

"The trailer has satellite," Shawnee said, unfazed.

Grace tried to shoot her a quelling look without anyone else noticing, but those sharp, dark eyes of Bing's didn't miss a thing, and Shawnee was quell-proof. "You said you have JV-only wrestling on Thursday, so you'd be home by the time the rodeo starts at nine."

"I'll bring dinner," Hank chimed in. "Smoke Shack?"

Now they were all staring at her, and Grace couldn't help thinking how that big ol' couch in Tori's trailer was made for snuggling, and Hank was so good at it... among many other things. Her face heated. Shawnee smirked.

Grace gave her plate her undivided attention. "Throw in a Dr Pepper, and you've got a deal."

She refused to even glance toward the other end of the table. Let Hank deal with Bing's reaction. Grace flinched when a chair scraped abruptly on the floor, but Bing only said, "I'll get the rest of the fry bread out of the oven for dessert."

⌁⌁⌁

Hank slathered his fry bread with enough butter to melt and drip into pools on his plate and added a generous dose of honey. One thing about being half-starved for months, it seemed like his stomach had no bottom. But when he took the first bite, it wasn't the honey-butter heaven that made him smile.

He had a date with Grace. And an assist from Shawnee, which was huge. He'd seen how it was with Melanie and Violet all through their single years. A thumbs-up from the best friend could tip the balance in a guy's favor—and a thumbs-down could bury him. But five days was a long damn time to wait, and tomorrow was forecast to be sunny and calm, if a little chilly. He'd watched Grace light up as they rode along the river bottom last weekend. Maybe he could talk her into coming back—

A phone rang and everyone jumped, patting their pockets.

"Landline." Hank jabbed his fork at the bar behind where Bing sat. "Grab it, would you?"

The sound of her voice obviously caused confusion on the other end of the line. "No, you have the right number. Just a minute, you can talk to Hank."

Shit. Why hadn't she passed it off to his dad? Hank got up and took the receiver.

"Hey, Hank. I didn't realize you were back in the country. This is Bob Decker, from up at Gruver. We were driving by on our way home, and those stockers of yours are running down the highway."

Hank swore. "How many?"

"Couple dozen at least. They tore a pretty good hole in the fence, but we stopped the rest from followin'."

Crap. At the rate yearlings moved, the strays would be scattered for miles in no time. "I'm on my way."

"What's wrong?" his dad demanded as he hung up.

Hank strode toward the mudroom. "The calves busted out."

"Why?" Grace asked.

"Because they're calves, and they like to tear shit up," Hank said. Or they'd been spooked by coyotes, or a bobcat, or another damn pig. Who knew with stocker calves?

"You're gonna need help," Johnny said, but Shawnee and Cole were already pushing their chairs back.

Bing jumped to her feet. "I'll take the side-by-side and try to slow 'em down while you get saddled. You wanna come, Grace?"

Grace looked startled, then disappointed as she glanced at the clock. "I have to get to work, but you go on ahead. I'll clear the table before I go."

Damn. Hank had really wanted a few minutes alone with her. Now he would have to try to make his case for a Sunday trail ride over the phone.

"Thanks, Grace. I'll talk to you later." He grabbed a pair of leather gloves and headed out the door, hearing his dad ask, "What about me?"

"Help Grace do the dishes," Bing told him.

Hank had to grin at Johnny's response. Then he broke into a jog toward the barn. God, he hated cows.

Chapter 39

IN LESS THAN FIVE MINUTES HANK WAS TROTTING out of the yard on Ruby, with Shawnee on Tick and Cole on Ranger. When they reached the wheat field, he started toward the man and woman guarding the hole in the fence.

"You go on. We'll stay right here," the wife yelled.

Hank raised a hand in thanks and kicked his horse into a lope. Half a mile ahead, Bing had managed to get around the thirty or so calves that were making tracks down the highway. She parked in the middle of the road and beeped the horn. The herd parted and went around her, intent on going anywhere they didn't belong.

"Away to me!" Hank called to the dogs.

Mabel streaked down the barrow ditch and around the right side of the herd with Spider on her tail and the riders following at a safer pace.

"Cole, take Mabel and stay on that side. She can keep 'em off that crappy fence." Hank pointed at rusty barbed wire that sagged between wobbly posts. The cotton field beyond hadn't had livestock on it in years, and the farmer's fence was worse than nothing at all, barely slowing down a cow but preventing a horse from following—as Hank knew from aggravating experience.

Cole called the dog and moved out, yelling, "Hyah!" at a balky Hereford calf.

"Come on, Spider," Hank said and turned to Shawnee. "If you and Bing can hold the middle, I'll take the other side."

"No problem." She shook out the rope that had already been strapped to the saddle horn, Tick's steel shoes clattering on the asphalt as they turned the tide of cattle back the way it came.

Hank kicked his mare into a trot, cutting off a wayward steer. As they approached the wheat field, he saw the chore pickup angled onto the shoulder of the road with the flashers on to warn oncoming traffic. Johnny was obviously not doing the dishes. Hank hustled the mare up and around to get in front of the bunch. His dad was pacing back and forth, shouting at the calves inside the field, who pressed against the gate. This was always the trickiest part—getting the strays in without spilling the rest of the herd.

"Git 'em up!" he told Spider.

Hearing the command, Mabel zoomed over to help send them skittering off across the field. His dad had already climbed back in the pickup, and when Hank flung back the gate, he drove into the field. The main herd followed with greedy eyes fixed on the cake feeder. Johnny drove to the opposite side and dumped a few piles to keep them busy while Hank vaulted onto his horse to keep the strays from running on past the gate. As they reached him, the calves paused, snorted, and milled around in a nervous bunch. Shawnee and Bing had them contained on one side, Hank on the other, and Cole and the dogs were between them and the river. Their only option was the wide-open gate.

Or they could wheel, break, and scatter, the way

bone-headed asshole yearlings were prone to do. They dodged past Cole, kicking up their heels at Mabel and leaping over Spider. Wire screeched as they hit the decrepit fence and tore on through to thunder across the bare, tilled field in a cloud of dust.

Hank muttered a string of curses as the whole crew stared after them. Johnny pulled up beside him, and the window of the pickup slid down. Shit. Here it came. *What the hell happened? Do you know how long it's gonna take to gather them back up out of the breaks?*

Yeah, Hank knew. He could kiss any Sunday plans goodbye. And probably Monday and Tuesday, too.

Johnny propped his wrist on the steering wheel and said, almost casually, "You know, I've always hated cows."

What the… Hank glared at him. "You're just mentioning this now?"

"Bing told me to make a list of the shit that pisses me off." He squinted at the lingering haze of dust. "That right there would be number one."

———

Hank declined Cole's offer to stay and help him go after the calves. If they were pulling out for Vegas in the morning, Cole would want to check, double-check, and probably triple-check everything at his own place this afternoon. Cole proved him right by heading straight for his pickup after they'd unsaddled and turned the horses into the corral.

As they paused beside the four-door dually, Hank said, "Thanks for giving me a hand."

"Even if it was a massive fail," Shawnee grumbled.

"We did get the corral gate fixed." Hank shoved

his hands in his pockets and jerked his chin toward the house. "Thanks for giving Grace a nudge. I'm gonna need all the help I can get."

Instead of some wisecrack, Shawnee nodded. "You dug yourself a doozy of a hole there, but it's good to see you finally threw away the shovel."

"More like Bing yanked it out of my hands."

"So I've heard." Shawnee skewered him with pointed stare. "But don't forget who was there for you all those years before."

Miz Iris. And Hank hadn't forgotten anything. But there was only one way to get back in her good graces, and he had yet to find a way around, over, or through the wall of resentment between him and Wyatt—and Melanie.

He didn't bother to make excuses, just nodded and wished them good luck in Vegas. As he strolled toward the house, he could see his dad and Bing through the window, sitting at the bar. The way their bodies were angled toward each other made the back of his neck tighten. It was too…

Then Bing straightened and jabbed an angry finger in Hank's general direction. Johnny hitched his good shoulder in a *What do you expect me to do?* gesture. Bing threw up her hands and marched off into the kitchen.

The tension bled out of Hank's muscles. They were just arguing, as usual. He walked through the door…and smack into Bing's dark glare. He'd known she wouldn't be thrilled, but he tried to play dumb. "What?"

Her eyes narrowed dangerously. "Really, Hank? You and Grace? This isn't about some argument in a bar anymore. She had your *baby*, for Christ's sake."

"I know." He set his shoulders. "I realize we have a

lot to work through, but we can't do it by avoiding each other, and I can't be around her without wanting to *be* with her."

Bing hissed in frustration. "Can't you wait until everything settles down?"

"No," he said simply. "This isn't as crazy as you think. The mistake was not sticking around the first time."

Bing glared at his dad. "Don't you have anything to add?"

"Not that you want to hear." Johnny shifted on his stool, looking pained but stubborn. "Hank and Grace go way back. She's always been good for him, and who's gonna understand better about the whole instant fatherhood thing?"

Bing gritted her teeth. "Fine, but if you start throwing sex and romantic expectations into the mix, it's gonna get messy."

Hank considered telling her that his expectations already stretched out to forever, but she was in no mood to hear it. "Grace is important to me. When I'm with her, I feel…centered. Like I can handle anything."

"And it doesn't bother you that Wyatt is also her *friend*?"

Hank winced but held firm. "So maybe she can persuade me to stop wanting to strangle him."

Bing folded her arms and glared. Hank forced himself to hold her gaze. After a dozen angry breaths, she swore and kicked her heel against the front of the stove with a *bang!* "This is a bad idea."

"I don't think so." Hank walked over and squeezed her rigid shoulders. "But if I'm wrong, you are welcome to say you told me so."

She dropped her head against his collarbone with a *thunk*. "Don't think I won't."

"I have no doubt." He dropped a smacking kiss on the top of her head. "Love you too."

His dad made a gagging sound.

"You see how I turned out this way?" Hank turned to frown at Johnny. "And while we're talking about feelings—if you hate cows, and I hate cows, how come we've got a whole ranch full of 'em?"

Johnny shrugged. "It's what my dad did, and his dad...I figured that was what I was supposed to do too."

"Geezus. That's depressing."

"You're telling me." Johnny lifted his coffee cup toward Hank. "If you've got any better ideas how to keep this place afloat, I'm all ears."

He just might, based on a conversation he'd overheard at Miz Iris's house during Thanksgiving dinner. It would be an excellent way to rid themselves of their bovine affliction, but Hank would have to sell the idea to one of the most powerful men in Texas. And he would have to promise to stay right here, living and working on the ranch...with his father.

"I'll give it some thought," he said, and made his nightly escape to the apartment.

Chapter 40

IT HAD BEEN THE LONGEST WEEK OF GRACE'S LIFE... and it was only Thursday. *The* Thursday. The opening night of the National Finals, when she was finally going to see Hank again.

He had kept in touch. Two or three texts a day—mostly funny pictures of Spider and Mabel, or of the horses, or the sun streaming down on the river bottom with Wish you were here, maybe next Sunday? And he had called on Wednesday night, almost exactly when she walked in the door of her apartment, as if he'd been counting down the minutes to when he guessed she'd get home. Her heart had done an uncertain swoop and dive at the sight of his number. Was he calling to confirm their date, or call it off?

Or, it turned out, set some ground rules. After a few mindless minutes of conversation—her day, his day, and yeah, he'd finally tracked down the last of the calves—he had cleared his throat. "So, um, about tomorrow night."

Grace closed her eyes. *Damn. Here it comes.*

"I can't have sex with you," he blurted.

Her eyes popped open. "What?"

"I mean, I can't have sex with you there." He heaved an embattled sigh. "The last summer I worked for Jacobs Livestock, Shawnee borrowed Tori's trailer. She and Cole hooked up *in that trailer*. There is literally no place in, on, or up against where I could have sex with you and not imagine them there before us."

"Ah…okay. I see your point." And more than she'd ever wanted to about Shawnee and Cole. "We could go over to my apartment for a few hours."

"I know, but I've been thinking." He cleared his throat, sounding reluctant but determined. "We have both changed, Grace. I'd like to get to know you again, and the sex makes it hard for me to see straight. How 'bout we just hang out until the Finals is over and you're back in your own place?"

She dropped her bag on the floor. When she'd said she needed time, she didn't mean *ten days*. The hum that had been building inside her all week faded, a dying whine like a jet engine shutting down at the arrival gate.

"If that's what you want—" she began.

Before she could add the *but*, he jumped in. "Great. I'm glad we agree. Now I've gotta go. The damn cows busted the cake feeder today shoving each other around to get there first, and I have to weld it back together so I can feed in the morning. But I'll see you tomorrow night."

What could she do but agree?

And now Thursday was finally here, and it felt like there was a swarm of grasshoppers jumping around in Grace's stomach when she pulled into Tori's yard and saw Hank's old maroon-and-white Chevy parked beside the trailer. He met her at the door wearing black nylon sweats, looking dark and delicious, and looped his arms over her shoulders to draw her in for a long, lazy kiss that had her seeing stars.

He eased away to grin down at her. "Hi, honey. How was your day?"

Endless. "Fine. You?"

"There were cows. Other than that, it was great."

The trailer was usually chilly when she got home, but Hank had already cranked up the thermostat so it was toasty warm inside, and filled with the scent of barbecue wafting from the cartons on the counter.

Hank caught the direction of her gaze and gave her a little shove toward the closet. "I'll warm everything up while you get changed."

Following his lead, she grabbed sweats, a T-shirt, and a BLUEGRASS ATHLETICS sweatshirt. It was probably silly to be self-conscious at this point, but she went into the bathroom to undress. After a moment's hesitation, she shucked her bra, too. Might as well get really comfortable. She unclipped the barrette and let her hair spring free, then finger-combed the mess of curls.

When she came out, he had supper waiting on the small bar. Damn. His butt looked even better with a snug, black waffle-knit shirt accenting the long, graceful line from shoulders to hips as he reached into the cupboard and got her a plate. "Dish up. I'll turn on the TV."

While she forked up brisket, he swung the flat-screen around on the wall mount so it faced the couch and punched buttons on the remote that had given Grace fits. The distinctive voices of the NFR commentators filled the space, crackling with anticipation.

"You're more at home in here than I am," Grace said.

"When Shawnee and Cole didn't have the DO NOT DISTURB sign on the doorknob, I spent as much time as I could in here." His chest brushed hard and warm against her shoulder, and she inhaled the woodsy scent of his deodorant as he reached over her head for another plate. "She had satellite TV, the best food, and the best air conditioner."

A pang shot through Grace, imagining what it must be like to travel week after week, rodeo to rodeo, all across Texas and the adjoining states. "Don't you miss it?" she blurted.

His body went still for a heartbeat. Then he rested his hands on the counter, framing her between his arms as he said softly, "Every. Single. Day."

Grace let her silence ask the question. *Then...why?*

His chest rose and fell against her back as he sighed. "I choked, Grace. I didn't let that bull run me down in Toppenish. I just...froze."

"But at the Buck Out—"

"I didn't have time to think. Suiting up and walking out there with everyone counting on me?" His body moved restlessly. "I can't do that unless I'm sure."

And how could he be sure, short of actually putting himself and others in danger? She scooped macaroni salad onto her plate, then stared down at it. "What was wrong with you that day?"

"You mean, what was I on?" He gave a soft, mocking laugh. "Gummy bears."

"What?" She cranked her head around, expecting a joke, but he was anything but amused.

"Washington State has legalized pot, and after I saw Mariah that first night, I was wired pretty tight. One of the bull riders gave me a couple of pot gummy bears to help me chill." He tipped his head back to stare at the ceiling, as if still asking himself *Why?* "I wasn't planning to eat them, but then I couldn't sleep. The first one didn't do anything, so after about an hour I ate the second one. And then—*wham!* I was messed up, and so freaking paranoid I couldn't even sit still. I was so wiped out when I got to the rodeo that afternoon, I couldn't see straight. I should have called in sick."

Yeah, like that was something bullfighters did. And besides… "Who would have taken your place?"

"I don't know. Someone who wasn't semiconscious?"

"And at least three steps slower than you and even more likely to be out of position."

He breathed a laugh into her hair. "Have you been talking to Bing behind my back?"

"No. It's just logic."

He gave her waist a grateful squeeze. "I can't logic those pictures out of my head. And I can't take the chance that I'll snap in the middle of the arena again."

Grace wanted to argue, but there was nothing she could say that he hadn't already heard from Bing—and probably from Gil, too.

Hank turned her loose. "Grab your plate. The rodeo's starting."

And the bareback riding was just getting under way, always the opening event. There was Delon, the silver fringes of his chaps sparkling as he danced from foot to foot on the platform behind the bucking chutes. Grace slid into the banquette, and Hank bumped her over with his hip so he could sit beside her, instead of across. The brush of his arm against hers sent tingles racing through her body.

No, Gracie, this isn't high school anymore.

And then the camera zoomed in on Delon as he lowered himself into the bucking chute.

"Delon Sanchez couldn't start the Finals with a better draw," the commentator declared. "Blue Rose is even more spectacular than his mother, Riata Rose. If they get tapped off, this could be the ride of the night."

Grace felt the tension winding up in Hank's body, echoing her own as Delon worked his glove into the rigging. Steve leaned over the chute, lacing his fingers in the horse's mane, gently rocking him back and forth while Cole set the flank strap. Then Delon slid into position and nodded his head.

The first jump out of the chute, the horse leapt so high that he seemed to hang in the air, Delon square in the middle of his back. Again, and again, and again, Blue Rose launched his body into space as Delon's heels set high in the horse's neck and dragged clear to the rigging, his shoulders thrown back and chaps flying. By the time the clock ticked off eight seconds, the roar of the crowd drowned out the whistle.

The pickup man rode in and Delon flung an arm around his waist, swinging free of the bucking horse and landing on his feet, only to jump in the air and punch a fist above his head, once, twice, three times as the noise level in the building reached a thundering crescendo.

"Eighty-nine points!" the announcer shouted. "Delon Sanchez has thrown down the gauntlet with his first trip out of the chute. He's got a lot of ground to make up, but that young Canadian better not stub a toe, or Sanchez will be picking up his third gold buckle."

Unlike Delon, his rival looked tight and nervous. He made a decent ride, but at eighty-one was five points shy of placing. When it was all said and done, Delon had won the go 'round.

"Sweet!" Hank held up a palm for Grace to slap. "Twenty-six grand for first place. He just closed half the gap with one ride."

As she watched Cole and Steve pounding Delon's

back in congratulations, Grace had another pang. It was gonna be party time in Vegas tonight, at the ceremony where the round winner and the contractor who owned the horse were presented trophy buckles. Grace could picture them all: Delon and Violet with Beni grinning ear to ear between them, flanked by Tori and Joe, Steve and Iris, Cole and Shawnee, and Gil and Merle Sanchez. As family portraits went, it didn't get any better.

A commercial for Justin Boots began to play, and Hank stood to gather their plates, catching the yawn Grace tried to stifle. "Wanna crawl up above to watch the rest?" he asked.

"I'll doze off if I get too comfortable," she warned.

"And you'll already be in bed, with someone to turn off the lights and the television after you crash." He waited a beat, then added, "If you don't mind me staying."

"Um, no. That's fine." Somehow she would suffer through having Hank wrapped around her all night.

He paused the television while she brushed her teeth, then climbed the steps into the nose of the trailer and crawled into the waiting circle of his arms. He pulled her into another of those slow, easy kisses, just hot enough to get her blood humming again. Then he settled her head on his chest and her arm around his waist and aimed the remote at the television, where the first steer wrestler was frozen on the screen, about to nod for his steer.

Grace had a hard time focusing on the action, her senses too full of Hank: his scent, the hard muscle pressed along the length of her body, his fingers toying with her curls. He couldn't seem to get close enough, and it made her feel precious, but at the same time powerful. He *wanted* her. She flattened her palm down his side and along the lean curve of his hip, reveling in the freedom to touch him.

She was playing a dangerous game of chicken with her heart, though. Whatever this was on his part—a coping mechanism, a whim, some misguided attempt to make up for not being there before—it would pass, the way it always had.

How close could she let him get before it was too late to avoid a crash?

Chapter 41

IT WASN'T WHAT HANK WOULD CALL MORNING WHEN Grace wriggled out of his arms. He mumbled in protest, but she fended off his sleepy grab.

"I have to get up."

He cracked an eye to see it was pitch-dark outside. "Told you I'd do the chores so you could sleep in."

"I did," she said. "It's five thirty."

Hank swore.

She laughed. "Go back to sleep. I'll see you tonight?"

He sighed his agreement, buried his face in her pillow, and inhaled. *Mmmm. Cookies*. He didn't hear Grace leave. It was after eight when he arrived at the ranch to find Bing dressed as if she had someplace to go, with a bag by her feet. A jolt of panic shot through him. "What's with the clothes?"

"Good morning, Bing!" she said brightly. "You look great!"

"Sorry." He belatedly realized she only had her laptop bag, not a suitcase, and breathed a sigh of relief. She wasn't so pissed about Grace that she'd decided to abandon him.

Johnny shuffled out and glared at her through sleep-drugged eyes. "Why do you look like that?"

She gave him a wide, red-lipped smile. "Wow. The Brookman charm is in full force today."

He growled and slumped onto the stool across the bar,

hair standing on end and the stubble already thick on his jaw. Hank got a cup of the magic potion that would turn Johnny from bear to human and set it in front of him.

"I am going to work." Bing stood, picking up the computer bag at her feet. "My supervisor emailed and asked if I would do the mandatory chart review that's supposed to be finished by the end of the year, so I'm borrowing a desk and the high-speed Internet at the Sanchez office."

Johnny's head jerked up. "Are you gonna be gone all day?"

"You mean *Do you expect us to feed ourselves?* Yes." She put a hand on Hank's shoulder and turned him toward two tattered cardboard boxes on the living room floor. "That is the sum total of Christmas decorations I could find, and it's mostly junk. If you go into town today, take the grocery list and don't come home without a tree and all the trimmings."

Hank set his coffee down with a clunk. "I don't know anything about tinsel and crap."

"Figure it out. And no damn tinsel. It sticks to everything." She pulled on her coat, plucked the keys for Johnny's pickup from where they'd been tossed on the bar, and left.

His dad smirked. "Have fun with the shopping, honey."

"Bull*shit*," Hank said. "You're coming with me."

Johnny's brows snapped flat. "The hell I am."

"Your choice. I'm gonna head on over to Dumas when I'm done with chores." And at this rate, his old Chevy would be able to navigate the route on its own. "I'm having lunch over there, but you're welcome to stay here and rustle up something for yourself."

Johnny breathed out a curse. "I'll be ready."

—⁓—

Three hours later, they stared down the Christmas aisle at the Super Saver store. Johnny poked a nearby box. "There must be twenty kinds of lights. How do you know what to buy?"

"White." Hank scooped the closest four cartons into their cart. "That way, we don't have to worry about whether they match whatever else we get."

"*Match?* We used to just throw any old thing on there."

"I remember…which is why we're getting new stuff." He held out the smartphone he'd borrowed from his dad to browse for inspiration. "Nowadays, they're supposed to look like this."

Johnny recoiled. "I am *not* doing a pink Christmas tree."

"There are others. Just swipe." Hank demonstrated with what he felt was remarkable patience. "What's your favorite color?"

"Purple."

Of course. It couldn't be red or green or even blue. Hank flicked through more screens. "Here. What about this?"

Johnny studied it closely. "Looks pretty easy. We've got the white lights. Just gotta grab some purple ornaments and those silver things that wrap around."

"Garland," Hank read from a package he'd picked up farther down the aisle. Then he spotted some three-dimensional silver snowflakes and set one spinning slowly. "Cool."

"These look classy." Johnny held up a carton of clear glass balls with silver decorations.

"Nice." This wasn't so bad. Hank peered at a ceramic replica of an old-fashioned stone bridge over a frozen pond. When he turned the crank on the display model, tiny skaters began to circle to the tune of "I'll Be Home for Christmas." And for the first time in three years, he would be. Then one of the tiny figures caught his eye, and he grinned. Oh yeah. He had to have one of those.

When they were done, they had two full carts, including a fake tree. Hank had campaigned hard for a real one, but his dad whined about pine needles in the carpet.

"Besides, then we have to do this again next year," Johnny pointed out.

Next year. As if it was a given that they would be spending Christmas together from now on. A part of Hank still balked, sure the minute he relaxed his guard, the rug would get jerked out from under him. Something must have shown in his face, because his dad gave a pained sigh.

"I'm not saying you have to take up permanent residence, but I'm not gonna lay awake at night wondering where you are. And you can damn well come home for Christmas."

Before he could respond, a woman sideswiped their cart, then glared as if it was Hank's fault. Over the speakers, George Strait professed his undying love for Christmas cookies, and down the aisle, a toddler got hold of a set of sleigh bells and gave them an enthusiastic shake. Not exactly the best place for a heart-to-heart.

Hank cleared the lump from his throat. "Okay."

"Good." Johnny grabbed a set of cowboy-shaped cookie cutters and tossed them in the cart. "Now get on that phone again and look up what we need for cookies. This damn song is giving me a craving."

He plowed off through the shoppers while Hank searched for recipes, and returned with a potted plant.

"What's that for?" Hank asked.

"Bing."

Hank's gut did another of those weird clutches. "Because?"

"Can you bake?" Johnny scowled at him, then at the plant. "If we want cookies with sprinkles, we're gonna have to suck up to her."

"*You* have to suck up. She likes me." Hank gave the pot the side-eye. "And I'm not sure that's the statement you wanna make."

Johnny just grunted and stuck it in the basket of the cart. When they'd fought their way through checkout and piled the back seat full of bags and boxes, Hank steered the pickup north on Main Street, the opposite direction from the café.

Johnny frowned. "I thought we were going to eat."

"It's only eleven o'clock. You're not gonna starve if you have to wait an hour."

"I might. Shopping is hard on a man."

Hank angled into a parking space in front of a full-service barbershop. That morning, looking in the mirror, he'd realized the image staring back didn't suit him anymore. He wasn't the man-child who'd left the Panhandle—thank God—but he wasn't the fugitive from humanity who'd hidden out in the Montana woods, either. Forty minutes later, he emerged from the shop looking more like he felt—a man who was slowly but surely finding his place somewhere in between.

Plus the woman who'd cut it said he looked hot. He sure hoped Grace agreed, since he'd talked her into letting him come over again tonight.

Back at the ranch, they unloaded their booty. When they

got in from doing the evening chores, Bing was standing in the living room, contemplating the mountain of boxes and bags in the corner. "Let me guess. You weren't sure what to buy, so you grabbed one of everything."

Hank laughed. "Something like that."

She glanced over at him, and her eyes widened. "Wow. The house isn't the only thing getting spruced up."

"You like it?"

"Very nice." She took in his dad's clean-shaven face and short-clipped hair. "Looks like it was boys' day at the salon."

Johnny grunted and disappeared into his bedroom, then came out a moment later carrying the potted plant. He thrust it into her surprised hands. "Here. This is for you." When she just gaped at him, he scowled. "Consider it a thank-you for everything you've done around here. And I'm not just talking about the cooking."

For a rare instant, Bing was speechless. Then she tilted the pot, examining the scatter of delicate pink blooms among thousands of needle-sharp spines. "So you bought me a cactus?"

"If the plant fits…" Then he shrugged. "I figured you could take it home. Something to remember us by."

The two of them just stood there, staring each other down, and there was a syrupy kind of tension in the air that made Hank uncomfortable.

"He also wants cookies," he said.

"I should have known there was a catch." Bing broke away to set the cactus on the bar, then made a beeline for her room. "I have to change clothes."

The door *thunked* shut behind her. After a few beats, Hank asked, "Was that a yes or a no on the cookies?"

"Who the hell ever knows with that woman?" And Johnny stomped off to his own room.

Hank stared down the hall after them, that indefinable itch crawling under his skin. Then he shook it off and went to build a sandwich from the cold cuts they'd brought home. He had enough on his mind. Bing could deal with his father.

When all else failed, he knew he could trust Bing.

Chapter 42

SATURDAY MORNING, GRACE WOKE UP WRAPPED IN A warm, lean body and the distilled scent of sleepy male. She could get used to coming home to happy horses, good food, and a hot man.

She could, but she shouldn't.

Right this minute, though, it felt too delicious to let her doubts wriggle between them. Closing her eyes, she drifted for a while before peeling herself away from all that lovely heat. When she sat up, taking the comforter with her, Hank rolled onto his back and laced his fingers behind his head, his T-shirt hitching up to expose a few inches of flat stomach above the low-riding waistband of his sweats.

The next time she got him naked, she going to put her mouth *right there*.

And damn, she loved that haircut—long enough to fall over his forehead but not quite in his eyes, perfect for running her fingers through. Even though it was shorter, it somehow failed to make him look more like his former self, but his expression was as sulky as ten-year-old Hank's. "Why are you always in such a hurry to get out of bed?"

"It's after eight. In about five minutes, Betsy will be over here kicking down the door, wanting her grain." She tried to tame her bedhead with her fingers, but Hank didn't seem to notice one way or another. That was good, right?

He heaved an exaggerated sigh and kicked off the blankets. "Fine. I'll do the chores if you'll make breakfast."

"Deal." She slid down off the bed and started for the bathroom before temptation could drag her back into his arms.

———

When Hank came in from feeding the herd, Grace was at the stove, frying bacon with one eye on the television. She looked so soft and pink and edible that Hank could have gotten over his squeamishness about getting naked in the trailer if he hadn't gone and told Grace about his ten-day vow of abstinence.

The previous night, Delon had spurred his way to a third-place finish, gaining more ground on the season leader. Now Grace was watching the replay of a western talk show that was recorded live in Vegas every afternoon during the National Finals. While the host did his opening spiel, Hank washed up and brushed his teeth. The bathroom was still steamy from Grace's shower, and he breathed in her scent, picturing her naked and soapy. Better, the two of them together, his body slick and wet against hers, inside hers, and his hands following hers to all the places that would make them both come apart.

He splashed cold water on his face and adjusted his jeans. *Down, boy.* Tonight, at least, wouldn't be a problem. She'd invited her younger brothers to stay so they could watch the rodeo, and Hank hadn't been invited to the slumber party. That was going to be another hurdle—winning her brothers over. Especially Jeremiah. If the story had reached her father, Jeremiah must have also heard every detail of what Hank had said and done that night at the Lone Steer. Distracted, he walked out of the bathroom as the talk-show host said, "…my first guests, National Finals bullfighter Wyatt Darrington and his lovely wife, Melanie."

Hank froze as they strolled hand in hand onto the stage—Wyatt looking like he was sauntering down a red carpet, and Melanie…

God. Melanie looked incredible. She'd let her hair grow even longer, falling sleek and shiny to her waist, and her legs were endless in heeled boots and snug jeans, topped with a chocolate-colored turtleneck and a leather jacket the rich bronze of Texas bluegrass in the fall. As she settled in hip to hip with Wyatt on the big, black couch, she glowed in a way Hank had never seen before.

For the first time it really hit him, like a blast from Norma's shotgun. His sister was in love. Truly, deeply, happily-ever-after *in love*. With Wyatt. *Shit*.

Grace turned off the flame on the bacon and lurched for the remote. "I'll just—"

"No." The sound creaked out of him. "Leave it."

Staring at them was the equivalent of grabbing onto Bing's cactus, but despite a thousand needles of pain, he couldn't let go.

The host leaned in, his elbow on the armrest of his easy chair. "So, big changes on the horizon. You are in the process of becoming foster parents."

"Yes." Was that Hank's imagination, or did Wyatt's smile lack its usual high gloss, as if he'd put it on without polishing it first? "A sister and brother, fourteen and eleven."

"Wow. That's a lot to take on."

Wyatt rolled his shoulders. "It's terrifying."

Laughter rippled through the audience.

"*And* you've got ankle surgery scheduled as soon as you get home," the host added.

Melanie spoke up. "Actually, Wyatt has decided to postpone his arthroscopy until the kids are settled in."

The host's eyebrows rose. "Any idea when you'll be back in the arena?"

Wyatt cast a glance toward Melanie. Their gazes met and something in that look—uncertainty on his part, reassurance on hers—made Hank's gut twinge. What the hell? The great Wyatt Darrington didn't get nervous.

He cleared his throat, another very un-Wyatt-like hesitation. "I won't be coming back. When this National Finals is done, so am I."

Even over the airwaves, Hank could hear the surprised gasps of the live audience.

"Wow," the host said, taken aback. "I mean, you did turn forty last year, but this must have been a tough decision."

Wyatt shook his head. For once, there was no calculation in his expression, and his eyes were the clear, transparent blue of a morning sky. "I don't like to be on the road now that I finally have someone to stay home with."

Finally. The word rang with the relief of a weary traveler who'd almost given up on finding a safe place to lay his head. And it struck a familiar note in Hank's chest. One that sounded an awful lot like Grace made him feel.

A murmur rose from the audience, heads swiveled, and the camera swung around to show Joe Cassidy climbing the steps onto the stage. The host leapt to his feet and met him halfway, clasping his outstretched hand as they exchanged shoulder slaps. "Hey, Joe! Nice of you to drop in uninvited."

Joe grinned, unfazed, as he took the microphone a flustered assistant ran over to him. He plopped down beside Melanie, cocking one booted foot on the opposite knee.

"Obviously, you knew this was coming." The host shot his gaze from one man to the other. "Wyatt Darrington and Joe Cassidy have been the bullfighting dream team of professional rodeo for over a decade. What's it going to be like, working without him?"

"I have no idea," Joe said, his cheerful relaxation making Wyatt's tension more obvious by comparison. "Jacobs Livestock is growing by leaps and bounds—not to mention my kids—so Violet and I decided this was a good time for me to move behind the chutes."

The host gaped at him. "*You're* retiring too?"

"Yep." Joe grinned again, enjoying the shock waves that rippled through the crowd. "I have eight performances left, then I'm hanging up my cleats to focus on the business and my family."

"I'll be doing the same," Wyatt said. "I want to be involved in the day-to-day operation of our bar, the Bull Dancer, and give our foster kids as much of my time as they need."

"And continue his quest to be the world's worst team roper," Melanie drawled.

Wyatt gave a mock scowl and nudged her. She elbowed him back. For an instant they were so wrapped in their private joke that it made Hank's throat close.

The host seemed to be having similar difficulties. "I…wow. I'm speechless. We're going to a commercial break while I recover, but first, let's hear it for our future Hall of Famers!"

He waved Wyatt and Joe to their feet as the crowd

rose in a thundering, foot-stomping ovation, cut short by a commercial for cheap car insurance.

Hank looked at Grace, dazed. "What the hell was that?"

"History." Grace turned off the television as he sank down at the table. "Are you okay?"

"I'm…" Hank gazed down at his hands, spread on the table to anchor him. Since the Buck Out, the old dreams had been sneaking up on him at random moments. Visions of himself at a rodeo, facing the chutes, waiting for a cowboy to nod. In every one of them, he glanced over to see Joe, locked and loaded. Now it could never happen again.

Panic trickled like acid through his veins. He hadn't realized that his one ray of hope had been fueled by the assumption that Joe would be there to back him up. Now if Hank tried to make a comeback, he'd have to do it alone. There would be no Joe to smack him upside the head when he needed it or slap him on the back when he deserved it.

No Wyatt to blame if it all went to shit again.

"Can you believe he was going to let Melanie go?" Grace asked softly. "After they came to see you in Montana and Wyatt realized that we couldn't tell you about Maddie yet, he was going to let her leave him."

Hank scowled. "Why would he do that?"

"Because he couldn't keep lying to her, and he couldn't ask her to lie to you. If she hadn't found out by accident…" Grace shrugged.

That righteous bastard would've made himself and Melanie miserable in the name of doing *the right thing*, and made Hank the asshole in the process. Geezus. And people wondered why he wanted to knock out a couple of those pearly white teeth.

He fisted his hands and pressed them to his temples. "I never asked him for anything."

"No shit. If you were dangling over a cliff and Wyatt was holding the rope, you'd pull out your knife."

Ouch. So much for being in his corner. But Bing had warned him. Grace owed Wyatt a lot. "I guess we know whose side you're on."

"There are no sides!" The words exploded with frustration. "There's just a random line in the dirt that you drew because Wyatt makes you feel inadequate. Well, news flash! Wyatt makes *everyone* feel inadequate, other than Joe and your sister. It's what he hates most about himself, considering it's the reason he was damn near forty years old with nothing to show for it but two ex-wives and a cool car." She walked over, caught Hank's head between her hands, and squeezed as if she could force her point into his brain. "Wyatt is as much of a mess as everyone else. He just looks better doing it."

Hank stared at the bottom button of her polo shirt, that stubborn knot in his gut refusing to let go, no matter how he worked at it. But why was he fighting with Grace? None of this was her fault.

Sighing, he slid his arm around her waist and leaned in to rest his head on her chest. "But he does have a really cool car."

"Yes, he does," she agreed.

"And a plane. And the ex-wives are both really hot."

"Yes, they are." Her palm smoothed down the back of his head. "I don't think that made the divorces easier."

"Probably not." He sighed again and closed his eyes, nuzzling the soft inner curve of her breast as she stroked away the tension in his shoulders. God, that felt good.

He could stay like this for an hour, breathing in time to the quiet beat of her heart.

His Grace. His salvation. His love.

He lifted his head. "Come riding with me tomorrow, after you take your brothers home. We'll go down along the river and I'll show you one of my favorite places on earth."

She hesitated, but said, "It *is* supposed to be a gorgeous day."

"And you don't want to spend it stuck in town."

She sighed and ruffled his hair. She seemed to like doing that. He'd have to tip the barber extra when he got his next trim.

"What time?" she asked.

Joy and relief burst out in his smile. "Around two? Then you won't have to rush."

Plus it would be the warmest part of the day, and once he got her to the ranch, he might be able to persuade her to stay and help put up the tree, since Bing had designated Sunday evening for that purpose and had warned Hank not to make other plans.

If he couldn't go to Grace, he would bring her home for supper, decorating, and the original cartoon version of the Grinch—mandatory viewing, Bing said, since he was Johnny's kindred spirit.

Hank wanted to share all of it with Grace. And he intended to follow Cole's advice and keep showing up until she agreed to share her life with him.

Chapter 43

SATURDAY HAD BEEN THE BEST DAY SINCE JOHNNY'S wreck. The sun was shining, the wind was only moderately annoying, and he and Hank had spent the entire afternoon down in the river bottom replacing broken posts. Johnny had only driven the pickup—towing the hydraulic post pounder along the fence while Hank did all the real work—but he was still feeling a nice tingle of accomplishment until he walked in the house and saw Bing's suitcase by the door.

Johnny's stomach gave a nasty lurch, but he covered it with a glare. "You said you were staying."

"In Texas." She gave him one of those maddeningly cool smiles. "Not necessarily in this house."

"Where are you going?" Hank made no effort to hide his alarm, unlike whatever had kept him quiet and distracted all day. Johnny assumed he'd heard about the big retirement announcement, but he was happy to let Hank decide when he was ready to talk about it.

Bing turned that implacable gaze on Hank. "Now that your dad isn't staggering around like a one-armed zombie, he doesn't need a babysitter. Call me old-fashioned, but I don't like how the neighbors have been looking at us, so I'm taking your apartment."

Hank's jaw dropped. "What?"

"It's not like you're using it." Her mouth pinched

into a disapproving vee. "Analise said you haven't slept there since Wednesday."

His face reddened, but he didn't flinch. "Grace and I have been staying up late to watch the rodeo. It's easier to crash there."

"I'm sure it is, but in case that doesn't work out, I vacuumed your room and washed the bedding. And yes, Johnny, there's beef stew in the slow cooker." She grabbed her suitcase and computer bag and turned to Hank. "As long as you've got your coat on, you can drive me into town."

Hank tugged the suitcase away from her. "That'll leave you on foot."

"There's nowhere in Earnest that I can't walk in five minutes. If I need to go farther, Analise will give me a ride. But I will be here tomorrow night, so don't think you're weaseling out on the decorating." And she breezed out the door without so much as a backward glance.

She didn't even take her damn cactus.

Johnny peeled off his coat and jammed it onto a hook before stomping in to pour himself a cup of coffee. The carafe he snatched off the machine was empty. He banged through cupboards to find the makings for a fresh pot, a silent stream of curses looping in his head. Just when a man got used to having a woman in the house, *bam!* They were gone. And a woman like Bing left an impression—echoes of her laugh, the bright flash of her smile, her scent creeping out of the bedroom even when the door was closed.

She was right to put more space between them. They had been keeping as much distance as possible when they were both in the house, especially after Hank left in the evenings, but since that moment in Johnny's bathroom, there was no way to ignore the awareness that hummed between them. It might not have been so painful if he didn't know the attraction was mutual.

And that acting on it would destroy every wobbly bridge he and Hank had built. If there was any doubt, all Johnny had to do was look to Melanie for an example. *I chose Wyatt*, she'd said. Her life, her happiness over Hank's. Considering all she'd sacrificed, trying to be everything for her brother that his parents weren't, she'd earned the right to grab her own happiness.

Johnny hadn't earned jack shit. Hell, he was so far in the hole he might never see daylight, even if he got credit for turning his back on a woman who was unlike anyone he'd ever met or was likely to again. Tough, but vulnerable. Hard sometimes, but soft when you least expected it. Fearless when it came to defending what she had claimed as her own. And yes, beautiful. But even if he was free to reach out, what would she want with a beat-up old wreck of a heart like his?

While he waited for the coffee to brew, he peeked into the slow cooker. There was enough stew to last a couple of days. His gut clutched again. Would he see her at all now? Then he shook off his own foolishness. She cared too much about Hank to keep her nose out of his business. And Johnny…well, she cared too much about Hank to stop trying to fix his father.

He took his coffee into the living room, and his footsteps seemed to echo despite the carpet. What was that song? "Alone Again (Naturally)." Sighing, he set his mug down on the table beside his recliner, went to the door, and called the dogs to keep him company.

A sharp yip woke him from a fitful doze filled with the old nightmares of being at a rodeo and, when the announcer called his name, suddenly realizing that he didn't have his horse, or his rope, or—his least favorite—his jeans. After all these years you'd think he'd be over those dreams, but everyone had their own version. Melanie's was arriving at the rodeo only to discover she'd forgotten to load her horse in the trailer. Anxiety dreams, she'd told him. They came when things were changing too fast or you felt unprepared.

No shit.

As Johnny scrubbed his hands over bleary eyes, the dogs raced to meet Hank in the mudroom. He was carrying a scuffed duffel bag. Catching Johnny's gaze, he hitched a shoulder. "Looks like you're stuck with me."

Johnny's mood gave a hopeful bound, but he asked, "Don't you have a date with Grace?"

"Her brothers are with her tonight." Hank toed off his boots and padded toward his bedroom but hesitated at the door. "I suppose you already knew about the retirement."

"Melanie called yesterday morning."

Hank ran his thumb back and forth along the top of the doorknob, as if he wanted to say more but was having trouble spitting it out. The thump of Mabel's tail was the only sound as she waited for Hank to notice and scratch her. Spider rooted her head under Johnny's hand, and he automatically rubbed her ears.

"Seeing them together was…weird," Hank said. "Somehow I pictured her as just one more of his things, you know? But it's the other way around. She *owns* him."

"As far as I can tell," Johnny agreed, a fact that both amused and amazed him.

Hank gave a soft *huh*. "Guess I'll see for myself at Christmas."

"If they come." The words popped out before Johnny could stop them.

Hank's gaze went sharp. "I know they've got the whole foster-kid thing going on, but I assumed they'd fly down for a couple of days."

Johnny knew he should just tell him the truth, flat out. *Your sister doesn't want to upset you.* But it didn't feel like it was his place to say what Melanie was thinking, and he didn't want to go blundering in and make it all worse.

Dammit, Bing. Where are you when I need you? "They've, um, got stuff. At the bar. A big Christmas dinner."

Hank's face had gone still and hard, bringing to mind that first night they'd run into each other at the Smoke Shack and sending a chill down Johnny's spine. In an instant, it felt as though a chasm had reopened between them. Then Mabel nudged Hank's hand and he blinked, and just like that he was back, his face softening as he scratched the dog. "I'm gonna unpack."

He pushed into his room, waited for Mabel to follow, then shut the door behind them. Spider rested her chin on Johnny's thigh and whined softly.

"I know," he said. "I suck at this."

Spider licked his hand. Johnny sighed and gave her another rub. Lucky for him, after all the times he'd cursed her, loudly and at length, the damn dog wasn't smart enough to hold a grudge.

<center>~~~~~</center>

Hank dropped his duffel on the floor and walked over to plop onto the edge of the bed, hands dangling between his knees.

Well, shit. Now he really felt like a jerk. Mentally, he'd kept avoiding the issue of Christmas the same way he'd figured he could avoid Wyatt and Melanie. If he didn't feel up to happy family time, he'd just go off somewhere with Bing until they left. But that damn interview this morning had dragged them front and center in his brain, where they had remained planted all day. He couldn't stop seeing Melanie—but not the sister who had constantly nagged him and scolded him, bailed him out, and yes, cheered him on.

Instead he'd seen a beautiful, confident woman who had her husband twisted around her little finger. In some bizarre way, watching them together made Hank feel as proud as when he'd watched Melanie win the college national championship. The mighty Wyatt had fallen, and Hank's big sis had been the one to bring him down. And now Hank had the power to make or break their Christmas.

Mabel parked herself between his feet, gazing up at him expectantly. He cradled her head in his hands and scratched both ears. She moaned in pleasure. Hank laughed softly, then gave her a final pat.

"Looks like it's time I finished growing up, Mabel." He stood and made a slow circle, taking in the cluttered walls. Like his hair, they didn't fit with who he was now. These were a kid's dreams, and like everything else, he needed to clear out the clutter so he could start fresh.

Unlike too much of what had come before, he took care not to damage anything as he peeled ancient, curling tape and pulled stick pins, adding each poster and photo to the stack on the bed. Last of all, he took down the autographed picture of Joe that had started it all. Then he stepped back and studied the bare walls. The paint had faded unevenly so that the shapes of things were still visible, and there were holes from the pins and sticky yellow residue from tape. As always, the past had left its marks.

But Hank had stopped expecting perfection, from himself or anyone else. Even someone who seemed as flawless as Wyatt had scars. Regrets. And a huge Melanie-shaped soft spot.

Hank smiled as he dragged an old Justin Boots box down from the shelf in the closet. It reminded him of Grace's shoebox—he still hadn't gone through those pictures—but this one held the life and times of Hank Brookman, from a strip of wallet-sized school photos to a rodeo program from Cuero, Texas, with him listed as one of the bullfighters. He sank down to sit cross-legged on the floor, Mabel beside him, while he picked through his memories and found the ones he treasured most.

Chapter 44

SUNDAY WAS EVEN WARMER THAN PREDICTED, pushing into the seventies, with barely a whisper of a breeze to stir the summer-soft air as the horses ambled down the trail to the river with Hank in the lead on Ruby and Grace following on Tick. The dogs bounded in and out of the tall grass, as if they knew that today was about pleasure, not business. When they spooked up a flock of quail, Hank let them go streaking off in hot but pointless pursuit.

Grace turned her face up to the sun as the dogs came trotting back with huge grins and lolling tongues. She knew exactly how they felt. If Hank hadn't been watching, she might have thrown herself down to roll in the grass just like Spider.

The night before, she and the boys had had their own NFR viewing party, with Cokes and pizza, and ice cream pie from Dairy Queen for dessert. The bareback riders had faced the eliminator pen—the rankest, hardest-to-ride horses in the world. Over half of them had hit the ground. The young Canadian had struggled to make the eight-second whistle and scored only seventy points.

But Delon had not only covered his horse, he'd dominated. Eighty-seven points, another first place, another twenty-six-thousand-dollar check, and an early lead in the ten-round aggregate, which would pay an additional sixty-seven thousand when all was said and done. Grace hadn't gotten to bed until after midnight, but she'd slept until eight this morning, leaving her happy and rested. Then Hank had greeted her with one of those smiles that made her feel like he'd been starving for the sight of her, and a kiss that promised he was going to prove it the next chance he got.

Instead of crossing the river, he turned to ride along the wide strip of packed silt exposed by low water. "Ready?" he asked.

"For what?"

She barely got the words out before he clucked his tongue, kicked his horse, and was off. With a leap of her heart, Grace followed suit, pulse pounding as they thundered down nature's version of a racetrack. Her horse wasn't nearly as enthusiastic as Hank's, so he'd already reined to a walk when she caught up a couple hundred yards later.

He tossed her an exuberant grin, so much like the boy that it made her breath catch. "I can never resist… but only after I've checked that there aren't any washes or holes from the last rain, so don't try it on your own."

Something in his voice, the unstated assumption that she would spend enough time at the ranch to ride here alone, caused an uneasy prickle in her gut. Not that she wouldn't love to gallop through this paradise every chance she got, but—

"This way." He made a sharp left, up a steep bank, and ducked to avoid a branch as they rode between two huge cottonwoods and emerged into a tiny slice of heaven.

"Oh." It came out on a sigh as Grace took in velvety, emerald-green grass circled by a ring of trees and clumps of tall grass, as perfectly landscaped as if it had been planted and lovingly tended by woodland nymphs. "Who put this here?"

"Mother Nature." Hank swung off his horse and crouched to brush a hand over what looked like a groomed lawn. "In places where there's shade and water, the buffalo grass stays green, and the cows keep it grazed off short."

Grace climbed down to join him. "It's beautiful. Like one of those secret glades from children's books."

"That's what Melanie said. We used to bring sandwiches down here and have a picnic." He shrugged off the backpack he'd had ready when Grace arrived at the ranch. "I was dead set on building myself a cabin here. Then I realized that would spoil it."

He took her horse, and Grace wandered the perimeter, lifting her hand to ruffle the brilliant red leaves of a stand of head-high grass as she walked. On the far side, she found a blackened fire ring sunk into the ground from years of use. "Did you make this?"

"My dad did, when he was a kid." Hank had looped their bridle reins around a sturdy, low-hanging branch, and now he pressed his hand to the trunk of the tree. "Cottonwoods have thick bark, and the fire blew through here so fast it barely touched these guys. This is one of the only things from my dad's childhood that was still here when I came along. Otherwise—" He shrugged. "The school has some pictures from when he played basketball and football, and Miz Iris had scads of Melanie and Violet growing up, but I've never even seen my parents' wedding pictures."

Grace started to ask why they hadn't replaced them, but she suspected the answer might be that neither of them had cared enough to bother.

She wandered over to observe as Hank opened his pack and pulled out a lightweight blanket, a pair of Butterfinger bars, and two insulated aluminum bottles… and his cell phone? He spread the blanket in the middle of the clearing, where the sun was the warmest, and gestured for her to get comfortable while he sat down and keyed in a number.

Then he caught her eye…and her hand. His palm was damp, his grip tight. "I have to make a call, and I need all the moral support I can get."

—~~~—

Hank's heart slapped harder against his ribs with every ring. *One. Two. Three.* When it went to voicemail, he swore and punched the end button. So much for his dramatic moment. Maybe if he waited a few minutes—

He gave an embarrassing yelp when his phone rang in his hand. The number on the screen was the same he'd just dialed. He drew a long, bracing breath and answered.

There was a roar of voices in the background, then, "You called me?"

He struggled for some vestige of cool. "Hey, Sis. It's Hank."

Beside him, Grace sucked in a breath. In his ear, there was another pause before Melanie stammered, "I… excuse me, it's really loud here. Did you say…Hank?"

"Yeah."

"Oh. Um…wow. Give me a second." It was more like twenty, each tick like a hammer strike on Hank's sternum. He pulled the phone away from his ear and switched it to speaker mode so Grace could hear. Voices came and went, snatches of conversation in passing, then there was a thump and silence. When she spoke, Melanie was breathless, as if she'd either been running or was as flustered as Hank. "Sorry. Violet and I are in the middle of our annual Cowboy Christmas shopping expedition."

That explained the noise. The trade show that accompanied the National Finals drew thousands of people to booths that filled the entire Las Vegas Convention Center, offering everything from original artwork to herbal health products to horse trailers. Hank was amazed that Melanie had managed to find a quiet corner.

"Is something wrong?" she asked, her voice sharpening. "Is Daddy okay?"

"Fine. I just…I saw you on TV. You looked great. Wyatt was a wreck."

She gave a surprised laugh. "It was kinda a big deal. Then Joe told him if he got choked up, he had to work the last round of the Finals in full face paint and old-school baggies. And Joe got to pick his shirt."

Grace suppressed a snort, and Hank shot her a grin at the image of Mister All-Class-All-the-Time in grease-paint, suspenders, and humongous Wranglers. Joe would've have turned Las Vegas upside down to find the loudest, ugliest shirt on the strip.

"Joe seems pretty chill about the whole thing," Hank said.

"Why not? He's just moving on to the second half of his rodeo career. For Wyatt, this is the end. He won't really be a part of it ever again."

Shit. Hank knew how that felt, but he still had a hard time putting himself and Wyatt in the same zip code, let alone the same boat. Speaking of which…

"Dad's pretty bummed about not seeing you at Christmas." Another deep breath, and he added, "Me too."

There was another beat of stunned silence, and her voice actually squeaked when she said, "Really?"

"Would I kid about this?"

She gave a choked laugh. "I wouldn't put it past you."

Okay, he'd earned that with all his stupid pranks. "I'm serious, Mel. And yeah, you can bring Wyatt."

"That would..." The words choked off, and she had to clear her throat. "We'd like that."

Hank had to work to keep his voice light. "Bing took my apartment, so your old bedroom is open. Just remember, I'll be right across the hall so you're gonna have to keep it down."

She made a gagging noise. "Now I'm gonna be too paranoid to sleep in case I roll over and the bed squeaks. We might have to stay with Cole and Shawnee."

"Not Violet?"

"Last time they visited here, Rosie flushed a three-hundred-dollar pair of cuff links and drew crayon happy faces on a hand-pieced wooden coffee table—and we were only in charge of her for two hours."

"Who the hell wears cuff links?" While she sputtered a laugh, Hank took yet another deep breath. At this rate he was gonna hyperventilate. "Stay wherever you're comfortable, as long as you come home. We have a lot of catching up to do."

"Yeah. We do." Her voice trembled when she added, "I've missed you."

"Me too." Geezus. He was croaking like a toad.

She sniffed loudly. "I've got to go. I'm at a Dodge truck booth, and the salesmen look like they're about to call security on the crazy lady who's dripping all over the steering wheel of their display model."

Hank barked a laugh at the image. Leave it to Melanie to commandeer a brand-new pickup as an impromptu phone booth. They should count themselves lucky she hadn't needed to get across town in a hurry.

"Make a run for it while you still can. And stay in touch."

"Isn't that my line?" she asked.

"Not anymore."

He'd barely hung up when Grace threw herself at him. He wrapped her up tight in his arms and buried his face in her hair.

Grace drew back and gave him a wobbly smile. "I'm proud of you."

And I love you. A fierce joy bloomed in his chest, pushing the words dangerously close to the surface.

He couldn't say it yet. But judging by the way she dragged him down onto the sun-warmed blanket and kissed him senseless, he was getting closer.

Grace burrowed her hands under his untucked flannel shirt, her hands cool on his hot skin. "We're not in the trailer anymore."

He groaned as she punctuated the statement with a rock of her hips. Yeah. This was why he had resisted the urge to shove a few condoms into his pack. With Grace warm and willing underneath him, his self-control would have crumbled in three seconds flat.

"But the Finals isn't over yet. That was the deal." When her mouth pushed into a pout, he nipped at her bottom lip. "Today we're pretending that I finally snuck you away while your daddy wasn't looking and brought you here to make out." He moved to nibble along her jaw to her neck. "If I'm lucky, maybe I'll get to first base."

She gave him a shove when his teeth grazed her neck. "Give me one of those famous Hank hickies, and I'm gonna call a technical foul."

He laughed. "You're mixing your sports. And if I give you a hickey..." He slid his body down hers until his mouth found the vee of her shirt and licked a circle on the subtle curve of her breast. "It'll be in a place no one else will see."

Then he rolled off to stretch out on his back. The stripped-down branches of the cottonwoods sketched lines across the deep blue of the sky, and the grass was springy and soft. He laced his fingers through Grace's, and despite the hungry ache in his groin, contentment settled over him like the blanket of warm sunshine. Here, inside his secret glade, he had everything his heart desired.

And for the first time, he let himself seriously consider a future on this ranch.

Chapter 45

As the sun set on Sunday evening, Johnny prowled the house, one eye on the barn. Shouldn't Hank and Grace be back by now? They'd been gone almost three hours, and he was simultaneously trying not to think about what they might be doing and wondering if he should have started worrying sooner. He gave the curtain an impatient shove. Ten more minutes, then he was taking the side-by-side out to look for them.

Then he saw the flicker of movement at the edge of the bluff and realized it was the flash of Ruby's white blaze and stockings coming up the trail. Great. They were safe. And he had nowhere to go and nothing to do.

That was the problem with feeling better when he still couldn't do crap. His neck and arm ached from being strapped down, so he peeled the sling off and tossed it on his bed. *Ah. Better*. He cautiously worked his arm through the limited motion the doctor had allowed. He was scheduled to start weekly therapy sessions in Dumas on Wednesday, and even though he *could* drive just fine, he hadn't been given official clearance yet, so Hank would talk Bing into taking him.

Bing.

The thought sent him stalking out into the kitchen to find her bending over to slide a foil-wrapped loaf of garlic bread into the oven. His gaze tracked straight to her butt, which irritated him even more, so instead of keeping his distance, he purposely got into her space, grabbing a mug from the sink and reaching for the coffeepot on the counter beside her.

When she straightened, no more than two feet separated them. Johnny poured his coffee and leaned back against the counter to take a sip. "Nice move. Are you happy now?"

"That depends. What am I taking credit for?"

"Trying to keep Hank away from Grace."

Her eyebrows sketched graceful arcs. "I'm doing a pretty lousy job of it, considering they're out in the south forty doing who knows what."

"They just got back. But he's not going over there tonight because he thinks I shouldn't be here alone yet. Funny how you had a sudden urge to move out when you realized they were hooking up."

Bing gave a sharp laugh. "That's really what you think?"

"What else?"

She rolled her eyes heavenward. "Honest to God. Are all of the Brookman men this clueless, or is it just the two of you?"

Before he could think of a decent comeback, she removed the coffee mug from his hands to set it on the counter. Then she curled her fingers into the front of his shirt, yanked him forward…and kissed him.

He made a startled sound as his hands reflexively went to her waist, sending a quick zing of pain through his collarbone. Then he lost track of everything except her taste—coffee, sugar, and dark, forbidden places—and the lush curves of her body against his, under his hands.

He angled his head and took charge, pushing the kiss beyond what she had intended, judging by her gasp. For a delirious moment he was lost in the heat and the rush. Then she shoved away from him, color running high under her coppery skin.

"*That's* why I moved out," she said. "I don't trust us alone here. Satisfied?"

Not even close, but any minute now Hank and Grace were going to walk through the door. Johnny swore and stumbled away to wash the incriminating lipstick off his face.

Damn that woman.

If the bang of pans and cupboard doors behind him was any indication, he wasn't the only one cursing.

—⁓—

Grace had to fight the temptation to hide behind Hank, intensely aware of what his dad and Bing would assume they'd been doing, and of her body grumbling about what they hadn't. She had tried to beg off, but Hank had insisted Bing was expecting her for supper. He hadn't gone so far as to claim that Bing would be thrilled to see her—and Grace could hardly blame her. Alone with Hank, it all felt so natural and easy, but the instant they faced any kind of scrutiny, Grace felt something shrivel inside her, like the bright-yellow blooms of her mother's evening primrose in the blinding glare of the morning sun.

Friends, family, coworkers—faces lined up in her imagination, grim as jurors, with Bing leading the cross-examination. *Can you explain to us, Miss McKenna, how you came to take up with the daddy of the baby you didn't want? A man you didn't see fit to even tell about his child?*

Then Hank would kiss her, or smile at her, and those specters faded, banished to the dark closets of her mind.

The flesh-and-blood version of Bing glanced over from where she was draining a pot of pasta in the sink, and if there was judgment in her eyes, it was hidden by the steam. "Right on time. Go wash up and we'll be ready to eat."

As Grace started toward the guest bathroom, Hank's dad stepped into the hallway, also looking freshly scrubbed. "Ah, Grace. Hello."

"Hi." They stalled there for a moment before she gestured at the bathroom. "I'm just gonna…"

He didn't seem to have anything to add, so she dove through the door to escape. Now that was the definition of *awkward*. She pressed a hand to her jittering stomach. How was she supposed to choke down food while seated across from that man and Hank's über-protective foster mother?

But they'd barely settled into their chairs when Hank said, "I talked to Melanie about Christmas."

His dad fumbled the basket he'd just picked up and cursed as slices of garlic bread bounced and rolled across the table.

Bing set the salad bowl down with a heavy clunk. "What do you mean by *talked to*?"

"I told her we had a vacancy if they need a place to stay while they're home." Hank scooped spaghetti onto his plate, elaborately casual. "She said they'd think about it." Everyone waited for him to go on. Hank drowned his spaghetti in meat sauce and handed the serving bowl to Grace. "You want Parmesan? I picked some up when we bought groceries."

"They're thinking about coming home?" his dad asked.

Hank grabbed the can of sprinkle cheese and shook a thick layer over his pasta. "No. Just about staying here instead of at Cole's house, where they have their own bathroom to clutter up with all their makeup and fancy aftershave and shit."

"But they are coming home," Bing said.

"Yep." Hank twirled his fork in the spaghetti. "Grace convinced me to suck it up and be reasonable."

Grace started, scattering cheese across her place mat. "I what?"

Johnny bent over his plate, but she distinctly heard him mutter, "Told you."

"Well…that's great." Bing snatched up the bread basket and began tossing the spilled pieces into it with slightly more force than necessary. "I'm thrilled that you finally worked it out."

Hank leaned over to whisper in Grace's ear, "She's really bad at being wrong."

"I heard that." Bing glared at him.

Hank gave her a sunny smile. "Do I lie?"

She held her scowl for a long moment, then huffed out a breath and shoved the bread basket in Johnny's direction. "I am *very* happy that Grace has been able to help you patch up your relationship with your sister."

Grace felt like she'd wandered into an argument already in progress and might get skewered by one of the unspoken points they were flinging around, so she concentrated on eating her spaghetti without dripping sauce down the front of her shirt.

Oddly enough, the exchange seemed to clear the air. Hank's dad asked what Grace thought Dumas's chances were in the next round of the football playoffs, since she'd seen them up close when they played Bluegrass, and they all debated the merits of a high-flying offense versus a stingy defense. Even Bing jumped in, being a rabid Denver Broncos fan and, Hank teased, never lacking in opinions.

Hank and his dad cleared the table and loaded the dishwasher while Bing bundled the leftovers into the fridge and Grace found a channel on her phone's browser that streamed nonstop carols. Then Bing ordered them to sort out the decorations while she mixed up a batch of gingerbread from a box, filling the air with the scent of molasses and spice, and made peppermint hot chocolate.

Hank and Grace unpacked and assembled the tree, moving an end table and shoving the recliner over to make space while Johnny hauled the dusty boxes to the kitchen table and sorted through the old decorations.

Bing strung out lights in the hallway and then stood, hands on hips. "These are all outdoor lights."

"What?" Hank leapt up from adjusting a snowy-white tree skirt to go see.

She hoisted a string between her outstretched arms to show rows of short strands intended to dangle from the eaves of a house. "This doesn't go on a tree."

"They're gonna have to," Johnny said as he shoveled everything into the box except half a dozen handmade ornaments. "They're all we've got, and I am not going back to that place."

"I'll make 'em work." Hank took the lights and began fiddling around the tree, testing different ways of draping them.

Working her way through the new garlands and

ornaments, Grace paused when she realized there was a definite theme. "Wow. Purple. That's…interesting. What made you decide to color coordinate?"

Johnny's eyes narrowed, as if he suspected someone might have pulled a practical joke on him. "Hank showed me pictures from some website."

Oh Lord. Grace imagined the two of them stumbling onto a page where people pinned elaborate, designer-style trees and had to stifle a grin. Hank's dad didn't look like he'd be amused to hear that they had gone *way* overboard.

"This will be beautiful," she assured him.

And it was. Hank arranged the lights to look like icicles dripping from the branches, reflecting off the silver and crystal ornaments and a dazzling array of purples, from deep royal to pale lavender.

"You outdid yourselves," Bing admitted with a grudging smile.

Grace wandered over to examine the ornaments Johnny had left on the table. She lifted the first one and realized she owned a mate to it. Fourth-grade art class—a wreath made of green-painted jigsaw puzzle pieces with Hank's gap-toothed, grinning face in the middle. Lord. He looked so much like Maddie.

And fifth grade—that was a birdhouse made of Popsicle sticks, garnished with petrified gummies and red-and-white-striped peppermint candies. Hank wrapped his arms around her from behind and rested his chin on her head. "Yours was a lot cooler."

"I didn't eat most of the decorations."

"But you shared yours so I'd have enough to cover my roof."

Grace sighed, sinking into the bottomless pool

of memories they shared. Christmas pageants and construction-paper Mother's Day cards with pipe-cleaner flowers glued on the front, sticking out green-stained tongues at each other after licking the frosting off St. Patrick's Day cupcakes, and exchanging cheap, cartoon-themed Valentines with all her classmates, but taking extra special care to pick out the one she gave Hank.

The candy conversation heart he'd given her that said *My cutie*, still tucked in her jewelry box.

Then Grace frowned, realizing what wasn't on the table. Unlike Hank's creations, which dated all the way back to handprint turkeys from preschool, there were only three for Melanie—third, fourth, and fifth grade. No anniversary or wedding ornaments. None of the cherished, old-fashioned glass bulbs Grace's mother had inherited.

"There's so much missing," she said.

"Yeah. The only thing Granddad saved from the house was a cedar box of my grandmother's, full of letters and pictures and stuff from when they were dating."

"She was Madeline," Grace said.

"Yeah, how—" Then he gave a surprised laugh. "Maddie?"

"Purely a coincidence, unless you believe in divine inspiration." Grace touched the jigsaw puzzle ornament. "It's nice to know there are pictures of her namesake, though. She'll want to see them someday."

"And me."

"Yes." She laid her hand on top of his at her waist and squeezed. "Her parents would like both of us to be a regular part of her life, so it all seems natural rather than going through a big adjustment when she's older."

Hank angled his head to check her expression. "How do you feel about that?"

Uncomfortable. Anxious. Deficient in some basic, female sense for being able to walk away from every encounter without a pang—except for the guilt. "It's okay," she said.

But when she glanced over and caught Bing watching them, there was a dark kind of understanding in the woman's eyes that made Grace feel transparent. She jerked her gaze back to the ornaments. "Can we hang these on the tree, or will that ruin the whole effect?"

Hank hung the handmade ornaments along the curtain rod so they didn't interfere with the glorious purpleness of the tree. Bing cut everyone slices of warm gingerbread with heaps of whipped cream while Hank refilled their hot chocolate, and they settled in to watch the *How the Grinch Stole Christmas* and then, much to Hank's delight, *A Charlie Brown Christmas*.

As the closing credits rolled, he jumped up and went into his room to fetch a box that had previously held cattle wormer. Candy canes and stars had been doodled all over it with, she assumed, the same black marker that was still visible on his arm.

"This made me think of you." He set it carefully in her lap and plunked down beside her on the couch. "I took it out of its box to set it up, so that was the best I could do for wrapping paper."

She opened the flaps and breathed out an *aww!* when she saw the little skating pond. Lifting it out carefully to avoid toppling any of the tiny skaters, she admired the snow-crusted stone bridge and miniature Christmas trees. Hank moved the box out of the way so she could set it on her knee and turn the crank. The music played and the skaters began to twirl, and she was about to ask why it had made him think of her when she saw it.

One of the skaters was a red-haired girl in a plaid skirt. As the little figure did a jerky pirouette, Grace's heart stumbled and spun with her.

God, she loved this man. Deeper, wider, more honestly than she had been capable of loving the boy. If it could only be just the two of them, in their private glade, with the rest of the world far, far away...

The song wound down, the skaters stuttered to a stop, and Grace leaned over to give Hank a quick kiss. "Thank you. It's awesome."

She cradled his lovely, thoughtful gift in her hands and tried to still the anxious twitch of her gut. Everything really was awesome—the day, the evening, Hank.

So why did she feel like she needed to hide from Bing's sharp eyes?

Chapter 46

SIX DAYS LATER, HANK PUSHED END ON THE CALL he'd just made, then set his phone on top of the nearest fence post and stared at it as if he expected his message to be returned immediately. Not likely, when it was the final Saturday of the National Finals Rodeo and the recipient was in Las Vegas.

A sensible man would've waited until next week, but now that he'd decided he wanted to stay on the ranch, the urge to set his scheme in motion was irresistible. His plan didn't hinge entirely on the result of that phone call, but if he could get his—actually *their*—foot in that golden door, it would make everything a damn sight easier.

All he could do was wait, which was the other reason he'd made the call today, the final day of his moratorium on getting naked with Grace. It had been worth the pain—he hoped. There were times when she looked at him a certain way and his heart swelled, but there were others when she seemed to be deliberately fighting what he thought he saw in her eyes.

Just keep showing up. And Sunday he didn't intend to leave her apartment unless the place caught fire.

Tonight, though, they would cheer Delon toward what would hopefully be another world championship, and the hardest fought of the three. He and the Canadian kid had slugged it out all week, trading one jaw-dropping ride for another, and leaving the rest of the field in their dust.

Delon's only setback had come in the eighth round, when his horse didn't buck hard enough to score more than the seventy-nine points Delon had eked out, while his rival won second place and closed the gap both in the world standings and in the aggregate score.

So it had come down to the tenth and final ride. If Delon maintained his top position in the aggregate, he would collect thirteen thousand dollars more than his pursuer, meaning the kid would have to win no less than third place in tonight's go 'round to overtake him.

But Delon could not get bucked off, and he had drawn what might be the rankest bronc Hank had ever seen.

Hank could only imagine how Delon felt, waiting out those excruciating hours before he climbed down into the chute, nodded for the gate, and let the final battle rage.

Until then…Hank dug a pencil out of his pocket and started walking the arena, stopping to wiggle each post, tallying the rotten ones on the back of an envelope. He'd worked his way clear to the other end of the three-hundred-foot-long fence when his phone rang.

He spun around and sprinted clear back to the other end to snatch the phone off the post, then saw the number and tamped his heart back down into his chest. He let it go two more rings while he caught his breath, then punched the green button.

"Hey, Korby. What's up?"

⁓

The noise in the gym was approaching jet-engine decibels.

With only eighteen seconds left in the heavyweight match against Canyon, the Bluegrass wrestler got an escape to break a 3–3 tie. The screams rose to a fever pitch, Grace straining forward with the rest of the crowd as both sides exhorted their man with "Shoot! Shoot!" "Takedown!" and "Move your feet!"

Just as the Canyon wrestler went low and got hold of an ankle, the towel came flying in to end the match. The Bluegrass team and fans roared, while Canyon groaned. As the boys met in the middle of the mat and the referee held up her wrestler's hand in victory, Grace's phone buzzed.

Her heart bumped when she saw the text from Hank. Change of plans for tonight. Call me when you have a chance.

There was a fifteen-minute break between matches, and the lighter-weight wrestlers spilled onto the mats to roll each other around or jump rope in the corners, prepping for the beginning of the second round. The bigger boys refueled with water and energy drinks and grazed from lunch coolers packed with bananas, oranges, and the old standby for quick energy—peanut butter sandwiches.

Grace meandered from one group to another, checking to see if anyone needed anything from her before retreating to the back hallway to call Hank.

"Hey, sunshine," he said. "How's it going?"

"We won the dual against Canyon. Amarillo will be another matter."

"Isn't it always?"

"Pretty much." As one of the biggest schools in their division, Amarillo High tended to dominate the smaller towns like Bluegrass. She fought to sound totally cool when she asked, "What's up with our plans for tonight?"

"Korby called to nag me about coming to the big tenth-round viewing party at the Lone Steer. I've barely seen him since I've been back, and I hate to blow him off again. Wanna go?"

Grace cringed. The bar would be packed, much of the crowd the schoolmates who'd been Hank's friends…but not hers. The thought of walking into the Lone Steer with Hank made her shrivel right down to the roots.

"I know," he said quietly. "It'll be mostly the same people who were there the last time, but that's the point. Let them all see me trailing after you like a whipped pup. You can kick me in the balls and stomp out if you want. Lord knows you've got a free shot coming."

Was that why he wanted her there? Another line item ticked off his list of wrongs to be set right? "It's been a really long week…"

"You'll be home in time for a nap. And if Delon wins, it'll be a hell of a party. Come with me, Grace. It'll be fun."

For him, maybe. Everyone Grace wanted to party with was in Las Vegas. Without Shawnee, Tori, and Violet, who would she even talk to?

"I'll be there at eight thirty," Hank said. "We'll watch the bareback riding, then leave if you want."

But in the meantime, all those hundreds of pairs of eyes would see them, and all those mouths would be talking. Putting together the pieces? *Oh my God, he's with Grace. Do you remember when he said…and how she took off…*

What could she say, though? *I'm too paranoid to be with you in public?* She heaved a resigned sigh. An hour, maybe two. She could manage that much, couldn't she? "Okay. I'll be ready."

He gave a happy whoop and promised she wouldn't regret it.

Yeah. She'd heard that before. As she made her way back out to the wrestling mats, she realized that her high school fantasy had finally come true. Hank Brookman was taking her to the cool kids' party.

And she was dreading every minute of it.

———

It had occurred to Hank that his dad would probably also like to go watch the rodeo, and that it would be rude to leave Bing sitting at the apartment, so when he went in for lunch, he eyed Johnny over plates of green-bean casserole.

"You've been driving around here just fine. I don't suppose you could sneak down, pick Bing up, and bring her to the Lone Steer tonight? You could hit the prime rib special."

Johnny's mouth went mulish. "I'm not calling to ask her."

Hank rolled his eyes. "I'll do it. And if she can't stand to be in the same pickup with you for the five minutes it takes to drive out to the Lone Steer, that's her choice."

"What about you?"

"I'm taking Grace."

Johnny's brows shot up. "That'll set the town buzzing."

"I know."

And that *was* exactly the point. Like the decades of graffiti on the ramshackle barn just outside Earnest, he wanted to paint over his old, ugly words with something bright and shiny. And he'd keep adding layer after layer until, even in Grace's mind, there was nothing left of that night but a faint memory.

Chapter 47

IT FIGURED THAT THE ONLY OPEN TABLE AT THE
Lone Steer would be stuck off in the far corner of the
massive honky-tonk. As they wove through the maze of
tables, many of the occupants called out greetings to Bing,
and she returned them with a wave or a friendly word.

"What the hell?" Johnny asked as he held her chair.

She tilted an amused look up at him. "Did you think
I'd been sitting in the apartment all week?"

Honestly? He'd spent more time thinking about
where she wasn't — across the breakfast bar from him
sipping her morning coffee, breezing in from helping
Hank, curled on the end of the couch, painting her nails.

In his kitchen, kissing him senseless.

She asked the waitress for water with a lemon slice before
turning back to Johnny. "I have breakfast every morning at
the café, and I've been going to yoga class with Analise."

"Oh." Johnny ordered a beer, then thought twice. "Do
you mind?"

"I accepted an invitation to a bar, so obviously not."
Her hair had grown, and she'd feathered the ends around
her face instead of spiking it on top. The result was
softer, but her gaze was no less direct. "I don't have a
drinking problem, but booze has contributed to most of
the worst days of my life, so other than special occasions, I prefer to keep it nonalcoholic."

As always, her bluntness was disconcerting. Johnny

had played—and lost—the *guess what I'm thinking* game with his wife for so long that he couldn't get used to simple honesty. Not that there was anything simple about Bing.

In the muted light of the dusty wagon-wheel chandelier, her golden-bronze skin glowed against her newly turquoise nails as she propped her chin on her hand to study the crowd. What was it about those fingernails that drove him to distraction? His wife had had hers done at the salon every other week, and all he'd ever noticed was the cost.

Now he couldn't stop seeing Bing's nails gliding over his skin as she'd shaved him. Digging into his back as he…

She cocked her head, eyes quizzical. "What are you thinking?"

"Things I shouldn't be."

"Ah. That." She sounded as if she could relate.

The waitress arrived with their drinks, and when they'd both ordered the prime rib special, he slouched back in the chrome and red vinyl chair, shifting his focus to something other than Bing. The tables were packed with folks like them who'd opted for a late supper. Korby was bellied up to the bar that stretched the length of one wall, testing his charm on a well-stacked brunette who appeared to be keeping her options open, but Hank wasn't anywhere in the three-deep crowd around them.

At a table near the door, enterprising 4-H club members were selling replicas of Delon's National Finals back number—the traditional red-and-white shield with D. SANCHEZ above a black 23. And as a nod to the season, red and green twinkle lights had been tacked up here and there, and the moth-eaten deer heads wore Santa Claus hats. Instead of his usual cigar and sombrero, the stuffed armadillo next to the cash register had a glittery party horn and a miniature top hat.

And of course sprigs of mistletoe hung from every light fixture. Johnny tilted his head back to give the one over their table the stink eye. "Did you know that mistletoe is a parasite? It eventually sucks the life out of the trees it grows on."

Bing's brows rose. "Is that a metaphor, or your idea of romance?"

He hitched his good shoulder. "Hearts and flowers have never been my strong point."

"No. You're more of a cactus kind of guy." But she smiled to soften the jab. "What about your kids?"

He frowned, not following her.

"They both have a lot of heart," she said. "I'd say they came by it honestly."

She…what? "I didn't think you liked me."

And he sounded as if he was in middle school, still waiting for his balls to drop.

Her mouth curved into the kind of smile that did crazy things to his pulse. "I thought I'd made it obvious."

"That's different." At her cocked eyebrow, his face heated a few more degrees. "I mean, you can like someone that way without actually *liking* them…can't you? I mean, don't women…" Oh, geezus. Could he cram his foot any farther down his throat?

"I like you." A wicked gleam came into her eyes to match that smile. "And I *like* you."

He gave a strangled growl. "You're killing me. You know that, right?"

"I'm sorry." She poked at the lemon slice in her water with one blue-tipped finger. "It won't be much longer."

His gaze jerked up to her face. "I thought you were staying until New Year's."

"Plans change. I thought Hank would have to make his peace in spite of his father, not because of you. The two of you don't need me."

"Bullshit." Damn. He needed to be able to reach across this dinky table and grab her hand. Force her to listen. He leaned in as far as he dared. "And I think you need us, too. I know you have to go home, but give Hank a few months to settle in, and he might actually be happy if I could persuade you to come back for good."

She pressed her lips together. "That's the problem. It's like I got dropped into the middle of a fairy tale— hunky cowboy, my son by another mother, the ranch— everything my heart could desire."

Hunky? "Why is that bad?"

"Because I learned a long time ago that I'm no Cinderella." There was something far darker than regret in her eyes, and it twisted up his gut. "You can only bust that glass slipper so many times before it can't be glued together again, and I won't bet what I have with Hank on my ability to make a relationship work."

Dammit. All the battles she'd survived, and she picked now to give up without a fight? There had to be a way to convince her—

A flurry of shouts caught his attention, and he glanced over to see that Hank had arrived with Grace in tow. Johnny watched a shock wave of turning heads and dropping mouths ripple across the room. Who could blame them? All they knew of Hank and Grace was what they'd seen on that awful night three years ago.

And Grace looked…wow. She'd done something with her hair that made it into little ringlets that practically sparkled under the lights. She was wearing more makeup and a cropped denim jacket over a peacock-blue shirt that she'd left untucked but cinched with a wide belt low around her hips. Her jeans were snug clear to her ankles, tucked into short high-heeled boots that brought her almost to Hank's shoulder.

"Hot damn," Bing said. "Little Gracie turned it up a few notches."

Hank caught Johnny's eye and waved before Korby dragged them into the middle of a huddle of twentysomethings—rodeo friends from across the Panhandle, schoolmates, and at least two former girlfriends.

But he'd never treated them the way he did Grace. This was no casual hand propped on a shoulder, his date half-forgotten while he bumped fists and exchanged insults with his buddies. The arm that tucked Grace close to Hank's side was protective and blatantly possessive, and the way he looked at her…

"*That* is terrifying," Bing said.

Johnny agreed, but he still shook his head. "He couldn't do better than Grace."

"Probably not, under other circumstances."

"Meaning the—" He caught himself before saying *baby* as their server arrived with massive slabs of prime rib swimming in au jus. Crap. He had to watch his tongue.

When the girl was gone, Bing reached over and slid his plate to where she could cut up his meat. The couple at the next table smirked. Johnny ignored them. "You said he was handling it really well."

"He is." She pushed the plate back to him and tackled her own. "Hank isn't the one I'm worried about."

Johnny paused in the act of dipping a chunk of meat in the little plastic cup of horseradish. "Grace? But she's had all kinds of time."

Bing shot him a pitying look. "Three years is a snap of the fingers. Even if she is one hundred percent comfortable with her choices—and my gut says she's not—I'm betting the last thing she expected was for Hank to turn *to* her instead of away. Look at her."

Johnny looked. Grace was smiling at something Korby said, her cheeks pink and her eyes bright. "She seems happy."

"Look closer."

He did, and noticed that the fingers hooked through Hank's belt loop were clenched tight, and Grace's gaze kept darting here and there as if plotting escape routes. "I'd be self-conscious too, considering," he argued.

"I'm sure that's part of it." Bing took a bite of prime rib. "*Mmm.* Very nice."

"But?" Johnny prompted.

She chewed, swallowed, and sipped water, maddeningly slow to answer. "Watching her, I see a classic deer in the headlights...except she knows the crash is coming and still can't make herself step aside."

"How can you be so sure?"

Bing sighed. "What she went through can really do a number on a woman. And being raised in a family like hers..."

"Have you explained that to Hank?"

"You heard him. He's convinced she's what he needs, and if I push it, I risk alienating him." She shrugged, resigned. "There's nothing I can do. We just have to be ready to pick up the pieces."

Talk about positive thinking. But before Johnny could say so, a cowbell clanged as the bar manager stepped onto the bandstand and shouted, "It's nine o'clock! Who's ready to rodeo?"

Cheers rose above a fluttering sea of SANCHEZ back numbers. Then the noise settled back to a nervous chatter as the unmistakable arena came into view on all five flat-screens. Whoops sounded when the camera zoomed in on Delon, relaxed and smiling with his protective vest unzipped as he exchanged *go get 'em* shoulder slaps with the only man who could snatch the gold buckle out of his hands.

Tonight, with all the chips on the table, they would be the last of the fifteen cowboys to nod their heads. As each of the rides before them was completed, the tension in the bar ratcheted up another notch, reaching a nearly unbearable pitch before the event wound down to the final two. Delon had clawed his way to a slim lead in world standings, so he had the advantage of riding last and knowing exactly what he had to do to come away the winner.

A hush fell over the bar as the youngster climbed down into the chute, flipping the legs of his chaps clear of his feet as he settled onto the horse's back.

"Well, folks, the moment has arrived," the commentator said. "Will a Canadian be the world champion bareback rider for the first time since 1933, or will Delon Sanchez cement his spot in the Hall of Fame with his third title?"

"The other cowboys aren't making it easy," his partner chimed in. "Remember, if Sanchez has a qualified ride tonight, this young man needs to place third or better in this go 'round to have a chance at winning the title. And with all the great rides we've seen, he'll have to score at least eighty-six points."

As the Canadian worked his gloved hand into the rigging, the camera panned to Delon, jaw set and eyes intense as he rocked side to side and rolled his shoulders, his focus entirely on the horse in the chute below him. Johnny realized his own fists were clenched and forced them to relax.

With a nod of his head, the Canadian burst from the chute, his heels set solidly in the horse's neck. One jump…two…three…every stroke was perfectly timed as they crossed the arena. If he kept it up, this was gonna be… But six seconds into the ride the horse reached the fence and hesitated, breaking the cowboy's rhythm. He missed a single stroke when the bronc rolled left, then finished strong.

One mistake. Was it enough?

"Oh man," the commentator groaned. "Eighty-four points! That leaves him just short of taking the title outright. Now all he can do is sit and watch while the pressure shifts to Delon Sanchez. He only needs seventy-four points to maintain his lead in the aggregate and take home the gold buckle, but this big mare is unbelievably strong, and she'll do everything but pull a knife to get a cowboy off her back."

Once again, the camera zoomed in on Delon. As in every other round, Steve Jacobs stood on his right, ready to haul Delon to safety if the horse acted up, but the hand that clapped his shoulder as he scooted his hips up snug to the rigging didn't belong to Cole. Tonight, Violet had his back.

Johnny's lungs were so tight he could barely draw a breath as Delon leaned back and cocked his free hand. Then he nodded, the gate swung open, and all hell broke loose.

The mare's front end shot straight in the air and she hung there, nearly vertical, for what seemed like forever. Somehow, Delon set his feet and held them solid in her neck through the rear, the descent, and the slam of her forefeet into the dirt.

And then the fight was on. The horse's grunts were audible as she threw her body to the right, then left, then right again. Unlike his previous rides—shoulders thrown back and spurs raking clear to the rigging— Delon stayed compact, his upper body tight and his knees tucked in closer to the midline, stealing the power from the horse's lunges. Muscles bulged in his forearm and his teeth flashed in his dark face, gritted against the torque of eleven hundred pounds of horseflesh doing her damnedest to rip his hand out of the rigging.

Five… six… seven… eight…

The instant the whistle blew, Delon's grip broke and the mare sent him flying head over heels to crash face-down in the dirt. Inside the bar and on the television screen, spectators sucked in a collective breath.

Then he pushed onto his knees and thrust a triumphant arm into the air, and the Lone Steer Saloon exploded. Johnny leapt to his feet along with everyone else, nearly tearing his sling in half when he forgot and tried to clap. He had to settle for pounding his fist on the wood-paneled wall.

As a grinning, sweating Delon strode back to the chutes, the commentators shouted over the din. "Eighty-one points! Ladies and gentlemen, there is your world champion! What a veteran move by Delon Sanchez, dusting off his old riding style to be sure he got to the whistle and took this title back to Texas!"

The cameras swung up into the crowd, where Tori and her dad were hugging it out while Shawnee howled and pounded her chest and Gil did a complicated hand jive with Beni. Up at the bar, Hank had hoisted Grace off her feet and was kissing her as though they were the only two people in the room.

Johnny caught Bing's eye and tipped his head toward his son. "I think you'd better stick around as long as you can."

Worry dug a crease between her brows. "I think you're right."

Johnny heaved an invisible sigh of relief.

He was tired of settling for whatever life decided to hand him. And he had seen enough of Hank since he'd been back to believe that, after the initial shock, he would give Johnny his blessing if he promised to do everything in his power to keep Bing happy—and in Texas.

Johnny just had to convince her that this cranky, unromantic Prince Charming wouldn't turn into a toad.

Chapter 48

THE MINUTE THE COMMOTION OVER DELON'S RIDE died down, Hank was ready to leave.

He'd been so busy worrying about Grace that he hadn't considered how uncomfortable he would feel, and not only from the stares, or the bitter taste of the single beer he'd allowed Korby to buy him, mingled with the hazy memories of his last visit to the Lone Steer.

Falling back into his relationship with Grace had seemed so natural that he had sorely underestimated how much he'd changed. He was so accustomed to solitude that he caught himself retreating from the hubbub into silences that unnerved people who only knew the guy who'd chattered nonstop and would go to any lengths to avoid his own company.

Yeah, it was good to see old friends, but all he really wanted was to be somewhere quiet with Grace. As the team roping ended, he leaned close to her ear. "Wanna go?"

She was headed for the door before he finished asking, and they barely paused to wave to his dad, who was deep in a bullshit session with a couple of other ropers his age, and Bing, who was helping Analise supervise the cash box for the 4-H kids. Outside, the cool night air was a relief after the mind-numbing din and suffocating closeness of the bar. As they walked hand in hand to the far reaches of the parking lot, distorted reflections of the huge, steer-shaped neon sign flickered in every windshield.

"Not feeling as sociable as you thought?" Grace guessed.

He screwed up his face, but his disgust was with the younger Hank who had constantly chased the noise and the crowd. "I think Cole might've rubbed off on me."

"Last I heard, autism isn't contagious." She ducked under a rearview mirror as they wove through rows of four-wheel drives, duallys, and flatbeds, a sure sign that the cowboys had come to town. "Maybe you're just getting old."

"Feels like it."

She swung around to face him as they reached her pickup. "That's not the only reason you wanted to leave."

It figured Grace would see through him. He tucked her hands between his. "Tonight is the last time Joe and Wyatt will fight bulls together. I assume they'll make a big fuss at the end, and you know how us Brookmans hate for people to see us cry."

He said it like a joke, but her eyes were solemn when she freed a hand to lay it against his cheek. She understood that for Hank, this moment was deeply personal. Joe had been his hero, his mentor, and his occasional partner in the arena. To know all of that was coming to an end made Hank's breastbone feel like it was going to crack.

"I won't tell." Grace kissed the corner of his mouth. "Take me home, cowboy."

By the time the bull riding started, they were settled into the trailer's massive leather couch in Hank's favorite TV-viewing position—with Grace propped between his thighs, her head on his shoulder and his arms around her. He hadn't watched the bull riders in any of the previous nine performances. Tonight, he drank in every jump, every spin, and especially every dodge and feint of the bullfighters. From Joe's shaggy hair to the gravity-defying spring in his steps, he looked exactly as he had when he'd come bounding into the arena where Hank had first had the unimaginable thrill of working with him. And Wyatt…

Wyatt was ice to Joe's fire—cool and smooth, always sliding into just the right spot. For the space of those fifteen rides, Hank let himself be swept up in the exhilaration of watching two masters show the world how it was done.

And then it was over. The last whistle blew, the last rider jogged safely away, and the last bull trotted out the catch-pen gate.

The arena went dark. "Ladies and gentlemen," the announcer intoned. "Tonight marks the end of not one, but two of the greatest careers in bullfighting. It is impossible for me to put into words what these men have meant to the sport of rodeo, so our video crew has put together a highlight reel. If you'll turn your attention to the big screen…"

The video began to play. God, look at that baby face. Joe at nineteen, nothing but raw talent and grit. And Wyatt, making his debut at the ripe old age of twenty-five.

Shit. Hank was the same age now as Wyatt had been when he worked his first professional show.

Ride after ride, rodeo after rodeo, year after year, they danced and leapt and sometimes limped across the massive screen, until it ended with one final image. Two dusty, sweating men standing face-to-face, exchanging weary but triumphant smiles—warriors congratulating each other on a battle well fought with hands clasped in a high five.

A single spotlight snapped on. Joe and Wyatt met in the middle of the circle for a quick, back-thumping hug, then looped arms over each other's shoulders to take a bow, and the crowd rose in a thundering ovation. And as the cheers went on, and on, and on, gruff, tough Joe Cassidy tilted his head back to gaze up at the image on the screen with tears creeping down his face.

Johnny had been annoyed when Bing insisted on driving from Sanchez Trucking to the Lone Steer, grumbling that he'd made it in from the ranch just fine. But she had pointed out that there were likely to be cops loitering around the honky-tonk tonight, and he didn't need to go getting a ticket for driving while his license was temporarily suspended.

As she parked the pickup beside the Sanchez shop, though, he realized that it played right into his hands. She got out. He got out. They both walked around and met in front of the pickup.

"Well. Thank you for a lovely evening," she said with only a touch of sarcasm.

Johnny stepped closer, catching his fingers in the pocket of her coat to keep her from backing away. "It's after midnight, and your coach hasn't turned into a pumpkin yet."

"Give it time." But he caught the flare of her pupils in the orange glow of the security lights.

"That's all I'm asking from you." He leaned in and

laid his mouth over hers, an easy *getting to know you* kind of kiss. Her lips parted, but he didn't accept the invitation, just took one small taste before straightening. "Give it time. And a chance. Cowboy boots suit you a lot better than some flimsy glass slipper anyway."

And then he let her go, climbing in his pickup and driving away before she could think up a way to ruin this nice, warm glow he had going on.

Grace yanked out a couple more tissues to snuffle into. Hank had gone into the bathroom to splash cold water on his red-rimmed eyes, while she sank into the couch, momentarily drained.

So much drama had been packed into one night, starting with the bittersweet vindication of walking into the Lone Steer so totally, emphatically with Hank. At first, she'd assumed he was playing it up for her benefit, but as people had lobbed questions at him—*where've you been, what are you doing with yourself these days*—she'd gradually realized that he was reverting to wolf-boy mode, his eyes going dark and cautious and his words clipped.

In this one way, he could no longer go home. Hank wasn't the life of that party anymore.

She had been more than happy to get out of that bar, but the sheer rush of Delon's victory compounded by that heart-twisting tribute to Joe and Wyatt had left her vibrating with pent-up emotions. Luckily, she knew the perfect way to blow off some steam.

When Hank came out of the bathroom, she strolled over to him, laced her arms around his neck, and pulled him into a kiss hot enough to curl *his* hair. When she finally let him take a breath, he smiled down at her through a haze of lust. "Did I mention that you look incredibly hot tonight?"

"You did." And the blaze of appreciation in his eyes had given her the boost of courage she needed to face the mob at the Lone Steer. Now, she drew a finger down his throat and into the vee of his shirt, pressing the tip against the thud of his heart. "But if you think this outfit looks good on me, you should see it on my bedroom floor."

He went still for a few accelerated heartbeats. Then he said, "I'll meet you there."

They drove separately and collided at her front door, mouths, hands, bodies slamming together with a hunger built of a two-week fast. She jabbed the key blindly at the lock, her vision gone red with lust. Finally she had to give it her full attention, or as much as she could muster while Hank pulled her butt tight against him and let her feel what she did to him.

What he intended to do to her.

They were shedding clothes before she got the door shut. Jackets dropped to the floor, boots were kicked off to thud against the entryway walls. There was a satisfying *pop, pop, pop* of pearl snaps as she ripped his shirt open. A brief, maddening break in contact as she yanked her shirt over her head and sent it flying, followed by her bra.

They groaned in mutual appreciation as his hands closed over her breasts and they performed a disjointed, circling dance toward the bedroom, pushing denim, cotton, and lace down over hips, digging fingers into bare flesh for balance as they wriggled out of jeans and toed off socks.

They were naked when they sprawled onto the bed, his erection hot and heavy against her thigh. She clutched at him, drawing tight as a bowstring as the need pounded inside her. *Now, now, NOW*.

He pulled away to reach for her nightstand drawer. When she tried to roll with him, he barred an arm across her chest to hold her off. "Easy, there. I wanna take this one a little slower."

He tore open the condom with his teeth, centered it, and rolled it down by thrusting into his fist, eyelids lowering in unapologetic enjoyment of his own touch. "I used to imagine being with you when I did this."

Everything inside her clutched. Dear Lord. No wonder he got turned on when she touched herself. She pushed aside his restraining arm to feather her fingertips down his taut belly, toying with dark, coarse hair while he squeezed and stroked.

His hand flattened over hers, fingers gliding between fingers and slipping their joined hands between her thighs. "Show me what you like best," he whispered.

Heat flashed over her skin as she guided his finger-tips. *There. Just…there. And like this.* Sensation built and coiled, tightening, tightening, so close but not… quite…her hips shifted restlessly, seeking the exact touch that would make her come unwound.

She hissed in protest when he pulled away instead, and then sucked her breath back in as he pressed her onto her stomach, his words hot as steam in her ear. "I remember what you like, Grace."

He moved over her, pushing her legs apart and wedging his hips between her thighs until his erection nudged against her. "Okay?"

"Ah...*oh!*" He pushed into her just enough to make her gasp. Her back arched to give him better access, and her fists clenched in the comforter when he took the hint, filling and stretching her to the limit.

He pried her right hand free and once again guided it between her legs, moving their fingers in slow, tortuous circles, then guiding her back to cup and squeeze him as he gave a guttural groan. "Oh, geezus, yes. Just like that."

His fingers found her again as he began to move— short, hard strokes that hit all the right places inside her without pulling him out of her reach. Her body clenched around him as he stroked her, and she caressed him until the intensity of all those combined sensations blanked her mind and sheer, animal need took over. Her hips moved in rhythm with his fingers, and she took him deeper, faster.

Oh God. Oh sweet heaven, she was so...so...

She bucked under him, a long, feline moan torn from her throat as her free hand clawed at the comforter, fighting to get a grip as the world dissolved into wave after wave of searing light and heat.

Hank's breath was harsh against the nape of her neck as she floated back to the surface, his body pressed hot and slick against hers, inside and out. "Doing okay?"

She did some combination of a gurgle and a groan, unable to manufacture words.

He laughed, triumphant, and reared onto his knees, lifting her with him to drive into her again, again, and again, until he made a rough sound, his body going rigid as his climax pulsed inside her.

Then they collapsed onto their sides, boneless and spent. After a few moments, he eased away, taking great care with the condom, she noted with hazy approval.

She sprawled on the bed, beyond caring that she was utterly exposed. All her circuits were blown, and she had no desire to bring reality back online.

After a moment, his shadow cut through the light from the door. When she opened an eye, he stood with one elbow braced on the jamb above his head, the other hand propped on a lean hip, gloriously naked and smug as all get-out.

"Did I do permanent damage?" he asked.

"Unhh." She flopped a *leave me be* hand at him.

His grin widened, and he strolled over to smack her lightly on the butt. "Crawl under the covers, sweet cheeks. We've got most of the day tomorrow, and I've saved up a whole list of things I've been wanting to do to you again."

Grace let him gather her close, smiling. She'd always loved a man with a plan.

Chapter 49

HANK SLEPT IN SUNDAY MORNING—BIG SHOCK—BUT when he called to say he was on his way while scrambling for his clothes, Johnny informed him that the chores were done. And when Hank staggered home Sunday night, his dad declared that he didn't need a damn babysitter, either.

So Hank spent Monday night at Grace's. And Wednesday. But Tuesday and Thursday she had games, and after she'd put in a fifteen-hour day, he felt guilty keeping her up half the night, no matter how much they were enjoying it.

It was probably good to pace themselves anyway, so they didn't burn out like a Roman candle. Well, more like the whole damn fireworks show, actually. And to be truthful, he enjoyed the time with his dad, watching college basketball and arguing over coaching decisions.

Even with Grace commandeering every other thought, Hank's silent phone weighed heavy in his pocket. By Friday, he had decided that either Tori hadn't passed along his message to her father, or the esteemed former U.S. Senator Richard Patterson hadn't thought it was worth returning the call.

Hank was taking his frustration out on the barn floor, ripping up a broken board, when his cell phone rang. His heart slammed square into his rib cage at the sight of the Canyon-area number on the screen, and he willed his voice not to crack like an overexcited seventh grader. "Hank Brookman speaking."

"Hello, Hank." The smooth baritone was unmistakable, having been the voice of Texas politics for over two decades. "Sorry I'm so slow getting back to you. I went straight from Vegas to meetings in Houston and just got home last night. Tori tells me that you and your dad are interested in training some horses."

"Yes, sir." Hank's palm had gone clammy against the phone. "I heard your trainer is leaving. Would you consider sending some colts out?"

"Hmm. We never have before, since we've got all the facilities we need here at the ranch."

Was that a yes, a no, or a career politician's nonanswer? Hank waited to be enlightened.

"What about your father's injury?" Richard asked.

"It's coming along. Doc says eight weeks before he can ride." Hank paused to take a breath and slow down. *Cool. Confident.* "It's his left arm, so he can already swing a rope just fine."

"Mm-hmm. Well...I can't fault Johnny Brookman's credentials. What's your part in this?"

Hank had to remind himself that the senator wasn't questioning his general worth, just his experience with horses. "I learned from the best, and I have references from a couple of ranchers in Montana who had me break colts for them."

"I see. Are you free on Sunday?"

Hank gripped the phone so hard it nearly squirted out of his sweaty hand. "We can be."

"Excellent. Two o'clock at my place? I'll give you a

tour, we'll look over the horses, and the three of us can dig into the details of your proposal."

"That sounds good." Great. Un-freaking-believable. "Thank you."

When the call was disconnected, Hank whooped and did a touchdown dance with two yipping, leaping dogs as partners. Then he went to tell his dad what he might have gotten them into.

––––––––

"Richard Patterson," Johnny repeated, dumbfounded. "You just called up the richest man in the Panhandle and said, *Hey, how 'bout we train some horses for you?*" Another thought struck and he shuddered. "Geezus. Do you realize some of them are worth more than this whole ranch?"

Hank poured himself a cup of coffee, irritatingly calm. "He won't send those here. What would we do with a highfalutin reining horse?"

"Probably ruin it."

"There's the attitude that's gotten you everything you never wanted," Bing said dryly. She'd rolled in an hour earlier bearing food—beef enchiladas *and* corn bread—driving an old four-door of Delon's that Gil had lent her for the rest of her stay.

Hank snorted at her smart-ass remark, and the clink of his spoon as he stirred his coffee made Johnny's toes curl. The familiar tension knotted inside his chest, irritation buzzing at his nerve endings. Pushing his mug away, he focused on the breathing trick Bing had taught him, letting the air ball up at the back of his throat as he inhaled, then imagining his stress huffing out with it.

So far he'd just made himself light-headed, but he supposed that was better than mad.

"Ever since Tori moved back to the Panhandle, the senator has been getting more and more into roping… and rope horses," Hank continued, sliding onto a barstool. "He's not gonna find anyone who can do better by 'em than you."

Good to know at least one person in the room thought he still had the touch. The picture Hank painted hovered in front of Johnny, bright and shining, but a part of him refused to believe it wouldn't pop like a soap bubble if he reached for it. "Who's gonna take care of the calving?"

"We'll hire someone."

"What's the point if we're putting money in one pocket just to take it out of the other?"

"We don't spend every day doing something we hate?" Hank shot back.

Bing sliced a hand through the air between them. "Time-out. And you." She showed Johnny her teeth, making it clear she *would* bite. "Try opening your mind a teeny, tiny crack and looking for doors instead of walls."

He didn't need help building that particular castle in the sky. In the early years of his marriage, he'd rambled on about it for hours as they'd driven from Oregon to Alberta, Arizona to Kansas, chasing the championships that would make him a name in rodeo households. Johnny Brookman, the cowboy who brought the best horses to the game. Once his reputation was built, all he had to do was throw open the doors and wait for the customers to roll in.

But he hadn't made it past *go*, and it had been so long since he'd set foot in a rodeo arena, no one outside of

Earnest, Texas, remembered that he'd been pretty good back in the day. Now these two wanted him to drag those old dreams out and shake off the protective layers of dust he'd let build up, year after year.

Reluctantly, he began to sketch out the blueprint. "We'd have to find someone to run the cows on shares. They do all the work, and we split the profit on a percentage basis."

"They'd have to live close by," Hank said, frowning into his mug.

"Brandy Gilman's husband is being discharged from the Army at the end of January." The words kept coming, sneaky and seductive. "He'd really like to get into the cow business—God knows why."

Hank's head came up. "They're right down the road. Hell, he'd be as close to our calving pasture as we are here."

"*If* we could feed ourselves on what's left over after he takes his cut."

Hank shrugged that one off. "I can live on pretty much nothing."

"But horses can't." Johnny plowed on. "And this place needs a shit ton of work."

Hank dug in his pocket and pulled out an envelope with a bunch of scribbles on the back. "I walked the arena. We'd have to replace about twenty posts and buy ten new steel panels for where the damn cows have torn 'em up. The corrals are fine. Oilfield pipe might be butt ugly, but it never rots. And I figured up how much lumber we need to repair the floor and the stalls in the barn. All totaled, it'll cost us about two grand and a lot of sweat."

Damn. Hank had put serious thought into this. "What about cattle?" Johnny asked. "You'd need at least twenty roping calves."

"Based on this week's market, two-hundred-pounders would run us around five hundred dollars a head." Hank grabbed a pen and adjusted a line item on his list. "That's another ten thousand, but you'd get some return on that money by selling them once they get too big to rope."

"Don't count on it," Johnny said morosely.

Bing punched his arm.

Hank ignored both of them as he worked at his calculations. "Add six hundred dollars a month for feed—horses and calves—which is probably on the high side, but best to be safe. That's thirty-six hundred a year, plus the calves, plus repairs…" He scribbled the total with a flourish. "Rounded up, I'd say we need to plan on putting seventeen grand into it in the first twelve months."

Johnny shook his head. "That's a pretty damn big hole to start off in."

"Not necessarily. If we make a deal with Richard Patterson, we'd have a guaranteed income. And Gil asked if I'd be willing to be on standby and take a load for them now and then if they're in a crunch, so that'll help buy the groceries."

Bing grimaced. "Not if the collections agency garnishes it."

"Actually, that's not a problem." Hank focused on his hand as he smoothed the envelope, creased from being jammed in his pocket. "The people who adopted Maddie have some serious cash. They paid off my medical bills… and they put twenty grand into an account for me."

Coffee sloshed over the rim of Johnny's cup. "Twenty thousand *dollars*?"

"Yeah. I feel weird about it, but they did it anonymously so there's no way to give it back." Hank doodled a series of dollar signs on the paper. "Grace says it's meant to make me feel beholden to them, so I'm less likely to raise a stink about my parental rights, but I had already decided that she made the right choice before I found out about the money. I don't have anything to offer a kid right now. If we invest that money in building ourselves a business, though, by the time she's old enough to want to come around, I might be someone she'd like to know." He lifted his eyes to meet Johnny's. "You too, Grandpa."

Grandpa. Geezus. But if Hank had that kind of money to invest, and they did swing the deal with the senator...

"Are you sure you want to dump that much cash into something that's gonna tie you to this ranch?" Johnny asked.

Hank jerked a shoulder, his gaze fixed on his scribbles. "I've got no place better to be, if you don't mind me sticking around."

Johnny's voice was embarrassingly gruff when he said, "Mind, hell. You've fixed my gates, my pickup, and my dog. And you do know your way around a horse."

The corners of Hank's mouth twitched like he didn't want to let himself grin, but he couldn't hide the shine in his eyes. "Then I guess we're in business."

Johnny's heart began to beat faster and his lungs felt tight, but not from anxiety. This was good old-fashioned excitement—and as scary as it was, it had been too damn long since he'd allowed himself the thrill of chasing a wild-ass dream.

Grace could *not* get her head in the game.

The stands were packed on Friday night as her boys' varsity basketball team battled it out with Plainview. She should have been on the edge of her seat—the last chair at the end of the home bench—but as usual, all she could think about was Hank.

She had floated through most of the week in a perpetual cloud of lust. If she wasn't stumbling around rubber-kneed from postcoital bliss, she was either wandering off into fantasies about what they'd already done or imagining what Hank might come up with next. She crossed her legs tightly and folded her arms over nipples that had perked up in anticipation, despite the mob of parents shouting insults at the referees from the bleachers at her back.

Honestly, anyone who'd uttered the phrase *just get it out of our systems* must not've been having this much fun. It was the French onion dip and ripple chips of sex—the more she had, the more she craved, and they rarely stopped at just one.

And speaking of snacks, Bing was in the throes of holiday stress baking. One of her coping mechanisms, Hank had explained, along with the text messages that had scared the crap out of Grace the first couple of times his phone went off in the wee hours. Listening to his steady, reassuring murmur when he called her back, Grace had had to reexamine her assumption that Bing was another of Hank's crutches. Obviously, the leaning was mutual.

Meanwhile, the woman was cranking out so many calories that Hank had started working them off in the weight room tucked into a corner of Sanchez Trucking, taking his dad along to pedal off some of his excess energy on their elliptical bike. Grace could swear the results were already starting to show. Hank's butt had looked good before, but now—

"Watch it!" A hand shot out and deflected a wayward basketball an instant before it smacked her in the face. Grace blinked as the nearest benchwarmer shook his head at her. "You gotta pay better attention, Miz Mac."

She nodded a sheepish thank-you and made an effort to concentrate on the action on the court, instead of what she'd been getting on the side. Then she glanced over and there he was, lounging against the wall near the lobby door, looking lean and unbelievably hot in well-worn jeans and his black Sanchez jacket, with that hair falling almost in his eyes.

And awfully pleased with himself...or so she assumed, since no one else was smirking at the crappy call the ref had just made. His presence was like a magnet, drawing her blood to the surface and setting it simmering. Grace had always had a healthy sex drive, but this was ridiculous. All the man had to do was walk into a crowded building, and she was practically panting.

A buzzer sounded, whistles screeched, and her team exploded from the bench, pumping fists and slapping hands. Grace blinked at the scoreboard. Huh. The game was over, and somewhere along the line, the Bluegrass boys had gone up by fifteen points.

Hank headed her direction, cutting across the floor so he didn't have to wade upstream through the departing spectators. When he got close, he started to reach for her, but she dodged his grasp.

"Not in front of the players! I'll never hear the end of it." And if he kissed her, she was likely to forget herself and give the entire crowd something to talk about.

He tucked his hands in his front pockets and grinned. "Yes, Miz Mac. Can I help you carry some of this stuff?"

"Grab the water bottles. The student manager left early for Christmas break." She dodged the coach's preschoolers, turned loose to play tag on the gym floor while they waited for Daddy to wrap up his postgame speech, and led the way back to the training room. It was empty, the team still in the locker room. Grace dumped her bag in its usual spot beside her desk while Hank set the racks of water bottles in the oversized sink. "What's got you looking like you're about to bust at the seams?"

He crossed his arms over his chest, so full of pride and excitement he could barely hold it in. "Dad and I are going to start training horses."

"What?" Grace had heard each of the individual words, but together they made no sense. "You…and your dad." The man who'd once practically run him out of town on a rail. "You didn't speak to him for three years, and now you're going to be business partners?"

"We've sorted a lot of things out with Bing's help." He ducked his head and slanted her a look from under his lashes. "And it means I'll be staying in the Panhandle."

Right here within easy reach. She should be thrilled, but that creeping sense of dread coiled around her gut again. It would have been so much simpler if he'd just packed up and disappeared again. Painful, yes, but every athletic trainer knew a clean break healed faster. The damn stress fractures were what lingered forever, the result of a thousand tiny impacts that inflicted microscopic damage, adding up and up until a body could no longer function.

He was looking at her like he expected something so she blurted, "You aren't even a roper."

"Wrong." He jabbed a thumb into his chest. "Panhandle Junior Rodeo nine-and-under boys' break-away champion, right here."

Figured. It was bred into him after all. "Why did you quit?"

"Same old crap. Once Melanie left for college it was just me and Dad, and we couldn't get along. We both stopped roping…and that sucks because he has a gift and it's going to waste."

He's not the only one. But that was an argument for another day.

"So will you come with us?" he asked.

She blinked at him. "Where?"

"The Patterson ranch on Sunday. We're going to talk to the man about his horses." He hit her with one of those *Please, Grace* smiles she'd never been able to resist. "I could use some moral support."

Uh-huh. Just like always. But what happened when he got this new venture rolling, and everything was just peachy with his dad, and he and Melanie had made up. What would he need from Grace then?

The door banged open, and the room filled with loud, sweaty boys in search of the tape cutter, or an ice bag, or Grace's opinion on whether they needed to put some-thing on that floor burn on their elbow, all the while shooting Hank curious glances. Her cheeks glowed, but she refused to acknowledge their curiosity.

Nothing to see here, boys. Just an old friend pop-ping in for a visit. She wasn't comfortable having her personal life invade her professional space, especially when said person had a track record of wandering off, both geographically and metaphorically.

She went to her desk to scribble names and dates on her paper treatment log for later transfer into her electronic records. The minute the door swung shut behind the last player, Hank's hands closed warm over her shoulders and he nibbled at her ear, sending tingles racing down her spine. "If you come along, I promise to make it worth your while."

Her eyes fluttered shut, and she sighed. Dammit. This was what it came down to: no matter what it cost her—Hank had always been worth it. She turned in his embrace, slid her arms around his neck, and pulled him into a kiss that went from zero to ninety in the blink of an eye.

"I'm taking that as a yes," he said when she let him come up for air.

"Mmm. And I expect payment in advance." But she pulled away at the sound of voices in the adjacent locker room. Crap. The coaches were still here. She made a shooing motion at Hank. "Give me a couple of minutes to lock up, and I'll meet you outside."

Grace loitered until she was sure she'd be the last one out of the gym and the parking lot. She was *not* ashamed to be seen with Hank. Lord, who would be? She was just…discreet. It was going to be hard enough when they parted ways without having to explain his absence to everyone at her school.

Especially now that he wasn't actually going anywhere.

Chapter 50

THE PATTERSON RANCH WAS SPRAWLED OVER thousands of acres of prime native grassland south of Amarillo, adjacent to Palo Duro Canyon, but Hank was surprised at how ordinary the main house looked. With three large gables and a wide wraparound porch, it wasn't more than twice the size of Miz Iris's house and had an equally lived-in aura. Every rail was decorated with pine garlands, but instead of Christmas wreaths, each post held an antique horse collar, the heavy leather polished and mounted with red bows and silver jingle bells that sparkled in the sunlight.

As they stepped out of his dad's pickup in the circular drive, the front door opened and Richard Patterson strode down the wooden steps in a denim shirt, faded jeans, and a King Ropes cap. Hank suddenly felt overdressed in his version of Sunday best, all starched to a crisp—along with his nerves.

"Grace!" Richard flashed a delighted grin. "I didn't know you were coming."

She emerged from his hug flushed and smiling. "Tori has been nagging me to come see her new pet project. Have you met Hank and Mr. Brookman?"

"Johnny." Hank's dad stepped forward to offer a hand.

"And please, call me Richard." He shook Johnny's hand, then Hank's, then offered a smile to Bing. "And you need no introduction."

"I hope that's a good thing," she said.

"The best. Let's head on down to the barn."

He gestured to the crew-sized utility vehicle. Johnny took the front seat, while Hank, Grace, and Bing wedged into the back, which gave Hank an excuse to loop his arm around Grace's shoulders. She put her hand on his knee and squeezed in silent support.

Then they rounded the tree belt that screened the house from the outbuildings, and Hank sucked in a breath, no longer underwhelmed. It was a horse owner's fantasyland. Acres of emerald-green pasture surrounded a massive steel building, flanked on one side by a long, low barn. The foundations and corner pillars of both buildings were set with native stone, and Richard stopped beneath the covered portico supported by matching columns. Everything in sight was groomed to perfection.

Hank's stomach lurched. Jesus Christ. What had he been thinking? Any horse raised in this place would refuse to set a hoof in the Brookmans' shabby little pole barn.

Richard gave Bing a hand out of the UTV and escorted her through plate-glass doors into a tiled lobby, complete with a reception desk on one side. Veering toward the hallway beyond, he said, "The new physical therapy facilities are down here. We can take a look on the way to the arena."

The hall led into a rubber-floored room full of state-of-the-art equipment—weight machines, stationary bikes, a treadmill, and a whole lot of other stuff Hank couldn't identify.

"We have two full-time therapists who work with the patients both in here and with the horses," Richard said, lapsing into a practiced spiel. "And cost isn't an issue for participants, since the program is funded entirely by donations to our charitable foundation."

Grace wandered over to peek inside a door marked HYDROTHERAPY and another marked EXAM 1. "This is amazing."

He smiled. "I thought you'd like it."

Another short hallway opened onto a mezzanine raised a few feet above the arena floor, which could be reached by way of a ramp or a wheelchair lift. Padded chairs were lined up along the railing.

Their host waved a hand. "This is the friends and family viewing area. Go ahead, have a seat. Anyone want a drink?"

Was a shot of tequila an option? Holy crap. The arena was so big Hank could barely see the rider working a horse in precise circles at the far end. He slid a glance toward his dad, who was so stiff Hank doubted he could swallow his own spit.

"I'll have sweet tea," Grace said.

Bing held up a hand. "Mountain Dew, if you have it."

Richard passed around the drinks, then settled into a chair and tipped his bottle of water toward the stunning palomino, whose flaxen mane and tail rippled like silk with every butter-smooth stride. "That is Dinero. He was a reserve world champion as a futurity colt. This year our newest trainer will be showing him in the non-pro division."

Hank tried not to fidget as the cowboy rode the palomino to the center of the arena. He hadn't come to see a reining exhibition, but maybe Richard was trying to make a point. The pair in the arena launched into one of the standard patterns—a large, fast circle to the right, a small, slow circle, then switching leads for two identical circles to the left.

Then, with a barely visible flick of the reins, the cowboy sent the horse flying down the middle of the arena. A slight lift of his hand set the horse into a spectacular sliding stop, dirt spraying from beneath his hooves. After a moment's pause, he flicked the reins again, and the horse spun into a trio of dizzyingly fast pirouettes, a blur of flying mane and tail.

They came to a precise stop, facing straight toward where their impromptu audience sat. Grace and Bing broke into spontaneous applause, and despite his nerves, Hank smiled at the pure power and beauty of it. Lord, that must be some kind of rush. The rider flicked his reins again and, breaking the pattern, raced the horse straight toward them and slid to another stop, peppering the concrete wall at Hank's feet with dirt.

Richard stood, clapping enthusiastically. "Wonderful! I expect to see a placing at the Fort Worth Stock Show."

"We'll do our best." The cowboy leaned back to pat the horse's rump, and Hank saw with a jolt that he was held in the saddle by straps around his hips and thighs. He'd barely had time to absorb what that meant when the rider lifted his head...and the earth shuddered.

Dakota Red Elk gave him a crooked smile. "Hey, Hank. Fancy meeting you here."

—◦◦◦—

Bing made a noise that dragged Grace's attention away from the stunning horse ridden by an equally breathtaking man—dark skin, black hair, and a face that was chiseled perfection. At Bing's reaction, Grace glanced over, saw Hank's stunned expression, and jumped out of her chair. By the time she'd reached him, the name had registered.

Dakota. Shit. This was the bull rider who'd been injured at Hank's last rodeo. Grace clamped a hand on Hank's shoulder as if she could forcibly hold him together. She felt the fine tremor of shock in his muscles, and the deep breath he took to fight it off. Then he reached up, laced his fingers through hers, and stood, one hand braced on the railing, the other squeezing hers nearly to the point of pain.

But his voice was remarkably steady when he said, "Wow. Dakota. That was a great ride."

Grace had never admired or loved him more than she did at that exact moment. She leaned into his arm, silently offering whatever support he needed.

Dakota ran a hand down the horse's long, silky mane. "Thanks. Dinero always turns it up a notch when he has an audience."

"I didn't realize you were in this part of the country." Hank almost made it sound like it hadn't come as a complete shock.

"Same here," Dakota said. "I knew you were from Texas, but I didn't realize you were tight with the Pattersons until Richard told me this morning that you were coming down."

"How did you end up here?" Bing asked, suspicion layered under the curiosity. Who else among Hank's friends or family had been keeping secrets?

"Hey, Bing!" Dakota's smile made it obvious he was a member of her fan club. "After I got hurt, my cousin searched the whole country for the best equine therapy program. This is it."

Hank relaxed a few more degrees, his grip on Grace's hand loosening, and she felt her own muscles unwind in response. The moment of potential crisis had passed. Like his mountain, Hank had tapped into his solid core and was drawing on the coping skills Bing had taught him to face this latest challenge.

He gestured toward the skid marks in the arena. "Looks like you've been here a while."

"A year and a half," Richard said. "Dakota started as . a patient, but it was immediately obvious that he was a gifted horseman. I've never seen anyone with such a natural feel for reining. He was barely here a month before we offered him a position."

Hank started. "Position? You're not…"

"Still a charity case?" Dakota's smile flashed again, sharp at the edges. "Nope. I'm an apprentice trainer."

With the shock fading, Grace took a better look. He was older than she'd thought, and good Lord, he was *gorgeous*. And built, with the upper body of a gymnast—compact, powerful, and shown off nicely in a snug gray T-shirt. His gaze caught Grace's from under thick, black lashes, and his eyes took on a knowing gleam.

Busted. Grace blushed fiery red, and his smile widened. "Who are you?" he asked.

"Uh, Grace. McKenna." And *he* was way too aware that he could make a woman stutter, even when she was holding her…um…friend's hand.

Beside her, she could feel Hank quietly breathing his way through the aftershocks. Grace could only imagine what was going on inside his head—the assumptions he'd made, images he'd constructed of what Dakota's life must be like since the injury, smashed into a million pieces by this vibrant, borderline cocky man.

"I'm surprised I hadn't heard you were here," Bing said.

Dakota shrugged those impressive shoulders. "I've been too busy to stay in touch with my rodeo buddies… and it was hard for them to stay in touch with me."

Uncomfortable, he meant. They didn't know what to say, or how to act. For some, he would be a too-vivid reminder of the danger of the sport they'd chosen. And from his perspective…

Grace took in the understated elegance of the arena, the stunning palomino whose golden coat and flowing mane, tail, and forelock were groomed to salon perfection. The man lounging against the railing who, despite his clothes, radiated the power and privilege of someone who had once mingled regularly with heads of state. It was a world away from the rough and tumble of the rodeo circuit, and this Sioux cowboy from one of the poorest reservations in the country sat at ease in the middle of it all.

"I don't suppose you have much in common with your old friends these days," Grace said.

"My brother says I think I'm too good for them now." His smile thinned into an ironic twist. The horse snuffled and blew, and Dakota picked up on the reins. "I'd better go put this guy away."

"Can we tag along?" Hank asked.

Dakota shrugged again. "Sure."

"The rest of us will wait here," Richard said with a subtle bite of authority that had Bing sinking back into her chair.

When Grace made to do the same, Hank hooked his arm through hers and dragged her with him, down the ramp to what looked like a veterinarian's examination stock—an open stall wide enough for one horse with a single pipe down each side at belly level and a bar across the front, allowing ease of access. This one had a narrow ladder set out from the side, anchored top and bottom, leaving just enough space to park the armless, sport-style wheelchair.

The palomino stepped into the stock and stood motionless while Dakota leaned out to grab one of the rungs of the ladder and, with his other hand on the saddle horn, swing himself off and into the waiting chair.

He gave Grace another of those *I see what you're looking at* smiles as he flexed his arms, making his biceps pop. "I can get on by myself, too."

Dakota wheeled the chair backward, and the horse obediently followed as they pivoted toward an open door in the corner. He led them across to the barn, where he looped the reins around a hitching post and tugged the horse's head down to swap the bridle for a halter, then loosened the cinches, pulled off the saddle and wheeled into the spacious tack room to hoist it onto a rack. Every movement was practiced and efficient, squelching any urge Grace might have had to offer to help.

Hank tore his gaze off Dakota and let it run the length of the barn, along rows of polished hardwood stalls with black iron bars, the spotless floor made of rubberized bricks to mimic the original stone. "This is some place."

"No shit. I been in houses that weren't half this clean." Dakota started off again, and they had to hustle to keep up. When they reached the block of sunlight streaming through the back door, he stopped and pointed to a handful of cabins scattered along the bank of a large man-made pond, shaded by oak and pecan trees. "That's where all the crew lives. It's pretty damn amazing to wake up every morning, go out on my porch, and stare at our own private lake. Makes me wonder sometimes how I got so lucky."

Hank made an involuntary noise, and Dakota angled him a perceptive glance. "I know, it sounds like a load of crap, but horses have always been my thing. I only rode bulls because a glove and a rope were all I could afford. From the time they packed me out of the arena in Toppenish, I was trying to figure out how I would get horseback again." He reached up to rub behind one of Dinero's ears. "I been pretty wrapped up in my own shit. I didn't know you were taking it so hard or I woulda got in touch sooner, let you know I was doin' good."

"Thanks. I appreciate that." Hank lifted a hand toward Dinero's neck, then let it drop as if the horse was a work of art that he wasn't sure he was allowed to touch. "Fort Worth is a big show. You think you've got a shot at placing?"

"Screw placing. We're gonna win that bastard." The horse nuzzled his shoulder, and Dakota pivoted to slide his hands up the palomino's cheeks and cradle its head, the two of them nose to nose. "If I hadn't got hurt, I never woulda touched a horse like this. Never woulda guessed I had this talent. If I could go back to that day and decide not to get down on that bull...I don't know what I would do. Giving up all this..." He shook his head. "I might not be able to walk, but me and this guy, we can *fly*."

They were exquisite—man and horse—so close together they were breathing each other's air. Grace turned away to swipe at a tear, and she heard Hank swallow once, then again. His voice was a little hoarse when he said, "I've always wanted to try it, just to see how it feels."

"Yeah?" Dakota pushed Dinero away to look at Hank. "Come down sometime. I'll give you a lesson on one of the beginner horses. You can pay me in beer." Dakota glanced around to be sure they were alone and then lowered his voice. "I wouldn't mind hanging out with some regular cowboys, you know? These show-horse people are a whole different breed."

"So I've heard." Hank stuck out a hand. "I'm glad things are working out for you. If I'm gonna be down this way, I'll give you a call."

"Sounds good." As Dakota pumped Hank's hand, the horse lipped at the brim of his hat. He gave a low laugh and shoved it away. "Spoiled brat. I've gotta walk this guy out and rub him down, but I'll probably see you when you come to pick up the colts."

Hank's chin snapped up. "The what?"

"Richard's got a couple of five-year-olds picked out to send to you." Dakota laughed at Hank's astonishment. "Don't let him kid you. He's so excited to have Johnny Brookman trainin' his horses he can't hardly stand it. Happy early Christmas!" He flashed another of those sinful smiles. "And it was real nice to meet *you*, Grace."

"Excuse me?" Hank cut in. "In case you hadn't noticed, she's with me."

Grace started to open her mouth to…argue? Clarify? *No, really, we're just…what?*

But Dakota only laughed, and with a wave of his

hand, he rolled off to get on with his day, the palomino's glossy tail swishing as he ambled alongside.

———∿∿∿———

Hank gave Bing the keys for the drive home. With everything that was spinning inside his head, he was the definition of a distracted driver.

There was joy—they'd gotten the job! Shock, to be sure. A dizzying sense of relief. But also shame, that he'd been so certain a life that didn't include the unhindered use of every part of his body wasn't worth living. All those nights he'd fought the darkness. The miles and miles he'd hiked through the brush, over the hills, into the mountains, cursing himself for every step he took that Dakota couldn't.

Meanwhile, Dakota had been too busy building a bigger, better life to give Hank a second thought. But if Hank was honest with himself, he'd been sliding toward the edge for a long time. If Dakota's injury hadn't pushed him over, something else would have.

And where would Hank be now if Bing hadn't been there when he crashed?

Dakota wasn't the only one who felt lucky. And now they were going to be friends. Hank had felt it in the certainty of that handshake. They were bonded not only by a single, irreversible instant, but all the fear, pain, and raw determination it had taken to drag themselves back to a place full of sunshine, green grass, and spectacular horses.

Johnny settled into the front seat, rolled his injured shoulder, then let out his breath in a whoosh. "The next time I whine, go ahead and kick my ass."

"Ditto," Bing said.

Grace slid across to sit next to Hank in the back seat, her hand on his knee in a silent *You okay?* He wrapped his arm around her shoulders and buried his face in her curls to kiss her ear. In response she leaned into him, solid and warm, the anchor that had reeled him back in when he'd felt like he'd been shot into space. He could have survived this day without her, but like everything else, it had been one hell of a lot better with her there.

Grace stifled a yawn. Hank had been too nervous to sleep the night before, so she hadn't gotten much rest either—not that she'd seemed to mind. He curved his hand around her head and tucked it against his shoulder, a feeble attempt to return some of the comfort she gave him. She yawned again, sighed, and within minutes had dozed off.

Her breath tickled inside the vee of his shirt, little puffs of heat across his skin like a featherlight caress. And when he closed his eyes, there were no demons waiting to taunt him. Instead, he saw Dakota and Dinero flying across the arena...and his heart soared with them.

Chapter 51

THE LAST WEEK OF SCHOOL BEFORE CHRISTMAS break was damn near a complete waste. The kids had no interest in developing a healthy eating plan for the holidays, and Grace constantly had to prod them back on task, irritating students and teacher to no end. By the time she locked up the training room on Wednesday evening, all she wanted was to go home and crawl into a pair of sweats and Hank's waiting arms.

Except Hank's arms weren't waiting because she had to go to a stupid birthday party.

Scratch that. The party wasn't stupid. Matthew was turning thirteen, and her mother rightly insisted that they make a fuss so the occasion didn't get swallowed up by holiday hubbub with only three days until Christmas. Besides, Grace hadn't seen Jeremiah since he'd gotten home the night before.

But when she staggered up the walk and through the front door, clutching her coat against the buffeting wind, she was greeted by her father's glare instead. He was in his easy chair, Bible in his lap, marking passages for the sermon they would have to endure before Matthew was allowed to blow out the candles and rip into his gifts.

As Grace tried to finger comb her hair into some kind of order, he tipped his reading glasses down to glower at her. "You haven't shamed yourself and this family enough? Now I hear you've been parading around with that Brookman boy again."

And good evening to you too, Papa. Grace was tempted to turn around and walk right back out, but she refused to wither in the face of his disapproval. Or tolerate the way he said *Brookman boy*, as if Hank was a piece of trash she'd scavenged from underneath the bleachers.

She set Matthew's present on an end table and peeled off her coat, fighting to keep the temper out of her voice. "Hank is a man, not a boy, and he has truly repented for his actions toward me and others." She gave the Bible a pointed look. "I forgave him."

Her father puffed up, indignant. "Forgiveness is one thing. But throwing yourself—"

"Grace! You're finally here." Jeremiah bounded in, whirled her into a hug, and hauled her toward the kitchen. "Come and help me put the candles on the cake."

As he deposited her safely out of range, she whispered, "Thank you."

"You're welcome," he whispered back, then narrowed his eyes. "Is it true? You and Hank?"

She stuck up a hand between them. "Not now. Please."

"Fine. But you are gonna have to explain yourself."

Yeah. That was what she was afraid of. As she was drawn into the noisy bustle of getting dinner on the table, jostling and laughing with her brothers, she tried to imagine Hank here, in her mother's kitchen. She came up with a blank, as if her mind either couldn't or wouldn't go there.

Thankfully, her father had decided this wasn't the time to lecture her on her lack of morals, so dinner passed as peacefully as you could expect with three teenaged boys at the table. Then they all bowed their heads and Grace tried to keep a straight face as Jeremiah nudged her during the most ponderous segments of a sermon on the obligations of a man toward family, church, and God.

"Thirteen years old," their father declared, *finally* closing his Bible. "You're not a boy anymore, Matthew. We'll expect you to take more responsibility for yourself from now on."

Like choosing what he wears, what he eats, and what he reads?

Grace wasn't sure why she'd been the first child to rebel. Too much Internet? Or was it the move to Earnest and stopping by the Corral Café after school to sip a Coke and twirl on one of the vinyl-topped stools at the counter while B.J. and Carl, the openly gay couple who owned the place, exchanged jokes and gossip with crusty old ranchers. They seemed awfully nice for people condemned to burn in hell.

She'd made the mistake of broaching the subject with her father, hoping for an explanation of why that kind of love was wrong, and had been banned from the café instead. That was the beginning of her understanding that her father was not only unwilling but incapable of considering alternative points of view. His existence was built on a framework of rigid doctrine, and to question any piece of it was to risk bringing the whole works tumbling down.

Mama brought out the cake, Jeremiah lit the candles, and everyone but her father belted out "Happy Birthday" as Matthew leaned in to make a wish, his eyes shining in the reflection of the flames as he blew them out.

After wolfing down his cake, he ripped open his presents, including a bundle of athletic socks from Grace. When he came around the table to give her a thank-you hug, he whispered, "What did you really get me?"

"Socks," she said.

"C'mon, Grace!" he wheedled.

"Inside the middle pair of socks," she whispered back. "I downloaded the next three books in the Wings of Fire series onto my iPod."

"Sweet!"

Grace elbowed him, but too late.

"What's going on?" her father demanded, his gaze suspicious under his heavy gray brows.

"Matthew, you have one more gift to open." Mama set a large, flat package on the table.

Matthew sighed. It would no doubt hold the usual button-downs with corduroys or khakis, their version of Grace's dresses.

But when Matthew picked it up, his eyes widened. "It's heavy."

Their mother folded her hands and waited as he made short work of the paper, gasping as the logo on the box was revealed. "Is it really…?"

"Yes." Mama's shoulders squared as their father snapped to immediate, irate attention. "I've read that having Internet access and a computer at home greatly increases a student's odds of success in school. But you will have to share with your brother."

They all jolted as Papa's fist slammed onto the table. "You bought him this thing without consulting me?"

Their mother's expression remained placid, but Grace could see the pulse fluttering in her throat. "It's called a laptop. And I have always taken the responsibility for our children's education."

Checking their homework, helping them build dioramas for earth science, attending every teacher conference, not—

"That does not include dragging filth into our house!" Papa thundered. "This so-called Web is nothing but the Devil's trap, full of pornography and—"

"Knowledge," their mother cut in, the first time Grace could recall her interrupting him. "My coworkers in the chiropractic office rely on it to help treat patients more effectively, and when I checked it out, I found the whole world of history, science, and classic literature right at my fingertips. Even the scriptures," she added pointedly.

Their father snorted like an enraged bull. "Boys this age will not be reading *Moby Dick*."

"As you said, Matthew is almost a man now. He and Lucas have to learn to make good choices on their own, rather than us doing it for them." She lifted her chin, meeting his anger with dignified defiance. "And Jeremiah can get the parental controls set up to filter out the worst."

Jeremiah started. "What? Why me? I suck at computers."

"Another reason your brothers should have one. Do you remember Mrs. Jeppson from church?" When Jeremiah's expression went sour, she nodded. "Of course you do. She pulled me aside after Bible study last week and let me know that her son has seen you on campus with a new girlfriend." Jeremiah went stiff as a poker as their mother continued in the same mild tone. "I understand that she's majoring in some kind of computer programming. And she's Japanese?"

"She's *what*?" their father demanded.

"Korean," Jeremiah corrected tightly. "There's a huge difference."

"I'm sorry." Mama's gaze fell to her hands. "I'm embarrassed at how little I know about the world. Maybe I can borrow Matthew's laptop to catch up."

Matthew had extracted it from the box and had it clutched to his chest. "I get to keep it?"

Somehow, their mother's firm "Yes" drowned out their father's shouted "No!"

"You are going to ruin our children." He shoved to his feet, one fist planted on the table as he jabbed a finger at Grace. "Do you want them to turn out like her?"

Before she could muster a response, her mother said, "You mean thoughtful, intelligent, and self-sufficient? Yes. I would like that very much."

They faced off down the length of the table, an angry, embattled man and a pale but resolute woman, separated by the very children they'd created together. And then he wheeled around and stomped out. A few moments later, the front door slammed behind him, the sharp bang puncturing the bubble of tension that enveloped the kitchen table.

Their mother let out a long breath and raised an unsteady hand to her temple. Grace put a hand on her arm. "Are you okay, Mama?"

"I'll be fine." She gave herself a shake and forced the smile back onto her face. "I'm sorry to upset your party, Matthew, but I assume you and Lucas would rather go test-drive that new computer, so you're excused."

They didn't wait to be told twice, scrambling for their room before she could change her mind. Mama patted

Grace's hand where it rested on her shoulder. "And you can have your tablet back now if you need it."

Grace flinched. Dammit. Lucas had promised to keep it hidden. "You know about that?"

"This is my house, and you are my children. I know everything." Her mother settled a meaningful look on Jeremiah, then transferred it to Grace. "It's especially hard for a girl to hide secrets from her mama."

Oh. Dear. God. Grace's heart felt like it had dropped through the floor, taking several other vital organs with it.

Mama bowed her head, suddenly small and defeated. "It was a terrible thing to realize my daughter couldn't turn to me in her time of need. That my silence was the best I could do for her. I had let your papa dictate every word and thought for so long that I couldn't see any other way."

"But you do now?" Grace asked carefully.

"Yes. I've watched you stand up to him, and teach your brothers to do the same. I told one of my work friends I wished I was that brave." Her mouth folded into a rueful line. "She practically sang 'Hallelujah.' They arranged for me to see a counselor...during work hours so your papa wouldn't suspect." She gave a soft, humorless laugh. "He would have insisted that I see someone at our church."

"Talk about drinking from the poisoned well," Jeremiah muttered.

"It didn't used to be so bad, but these past few years..." Mama pushed a hand through her faded curls, which had once been truly red. "The message has changed. Good people have left, and those who've taken their place are, well, more like your papa. They feed each other's anger and fear, validate each other's intolerance, and become more angry, fearful, and intolerant." At Grace's raised eyebrows, she smiled faintly. "That's what the counselor told me. Long story short—I was planning to ask your father to move out after New Year's."

The quiet declaration was like an ax, cleaving Grace's world into *before* and *after*. From here forward, her family would be equally divided. The big three would side with Papa, of course, while she and Jeremiah and the boys stuck with Mama.

"Why do this now?" Jeremiah asked, gesturing at the scattered remains of the birthday party.

"The things that Jeppson woman said about your girlfriend... And she expected me to agree." Mama's face tightened in revulsion. "Your papa would have heard soon enough, and he was already on a tear about Grace's friend Hank. Since he was going to make the holidays miserable anyway, I decided to launch a...what do you call it?"

"Preemptive strike?" Grace guessed, surprised she could find the words in her scrambled brain. *Divorce.* Her parents. Sweet Jesus.

"Yes. That. So..." Mama drew a deep breath and squared her shoulders. "We are going to get through Christmas the best we can. Then the day after, I'll gather everyone together to break the news."

The cake and ice cream in Grace's stomach rolled into a queasy lump. It would get ugly. There was no way around it. They would try to badger and shame Mama into submission, and when she failed to crumble, blame would be thrown around like flaming spears.

Grace expected plenty would be lobbed in her direction—and they didn't even know the worst.

"I'm sorry," Mama said when neither of them spoke. "If I could find another way—"

"No!" Jeremiah said.

"No," Grace agreed more quietly. How many times had she been forced to concede an argument to Papa out of pure futility? The only way to survive was to disengage. "You have to do this, for yourself and for the boys. Jeremiah and I will back you up any way we can."

"Thank you." Tears trembled on their mother's lashes as she reached out one hand to Grace, the other to Jeremiah, as if they were preparing to bless their meal. "I'm not sure I could do this alone."

"I'll be right here, Mama, for as long as you need me," Jeremiah vowed.

Grace squeezed her mother's trembling hand. "Me too, Mama."

She squeezed back. "After the way he treated you tonight, I understand if you have someplace better to spend Christmas."

Grace snatched her hand away. "It's not like that with Hank."

"How is it?" Jeremiah asked, eyes narrowing.

"Friendly," Grace said, acutely aware of her mother listening to every word.

Mama let go of their hands and stood, pressing her fingers to her temple again. "I'm going to find an aspirin. Grace, you go on home now and try to get some rest. I'm sure you've got a long day tomorrow."

Grace could only nod obediently. "Yes, Mama."

When she was gone, Grace slumped into her chair and met Jeremiah's equally dazed eyes. "She knows."

"Uh-huh."

"And she's never said a word, or let on in any way."

"Nope. About any of this."

Grace breathed a curse and closed her eyes.

"You can say that again." Jeremiah's face hardened. "About Hank—"

She held up the stop sign again. "You heard what I told Papa. We are putting the past behind us."

"How is that possible when it's out there walking around?" Jeremiah demanded, his voice low and furious.

I don't know. And she sure as hell couldn't figure it out tonight. She pushed to her feet, locking knees that wanted to wobble in the aftermath of the emotional storm. "It's better for her if we're friends."

"Uh-huh. But is that best for you, Grace?"

She turned away, refusing to engage. She'd had a lot of practice at that in this house.

Outside, the wind was so strong it nearly ripped the pickup door out of her hands. The weather suited the typhoon inside her head, thoughts flying everywhere, but one kept slapping her in the face.

Mama knew. She *knew*. And she felt so guilty about not being able to help her daughter that it had driven her to break away from her husband.

So in essence, Grace's pregnancy had destroyed her parents' marriage. It was going to take a while to sort out how she felt about that.

Chapter 52

DRIVING TOWARD THE DUMAS AIRSTRIP LATE ON Friday afternoon, Hank wished desperately that Grace was with him, but they had agreed her presence would complicate an already touchy reunion. Besides, she had been in a strange mood since her brother's birthday party. Or rather, moods. One minute she was broody and distant, the next she ravaged Hank with a fierceness that was almost disturbing.

Lord knew, finding out that her mother planned to leave her father was reason enough to be upset. Even though Hank had been there and done most of that, when he tried to talk to Grace about it, she shook him off and said it was family business. Considering that he wanted to *be* her family, that didn't sit real well, but he'd decided he should hold off pushing until she'd survived the confrontation with the whole mob of McKennas. So he'd held his tongue—and held Grace as often as she would let him.

And speaking of family...he had his own to deal with. As he pulled into the visitor parking near the squat brick terminal building, he saw Wyatt's Piper Cherokee already parked and tied down with Melanie and a pile of luggage beside it. Hank's heart thumped at the sight of her, tall and leggy with her hair rippling in the breeze like she'd stepped out of a shampoo commercial.

"You good?" his dad asked.

"Yeah." Hank jumped out and strode to the narrow pass gate that led through the chain-link fence and onto the tarmac. As he approached, Wyatt dropped out of the open door of the plane and froze. He looked damn near grubby in a baseball cap, plain old Wrangler jeans, and a nylon pullover with a BMCC Timberwolves logo, the deep-navy color making his eyes glow an unearthly blue in contrast. He stood rigid as Hank gave him a deliberate once-over, then turned to tell Melanie, "Your husband isn't nearly as cool as I thought."

"Hank!" his dad protested.

A cautious smile curved across Wyatt's face, and Melanie grinned. "Don't worry, Daddy. He meant it as a compliment."

Three hours later, they had navigated dinner without any major incidents, but Hank had to retreat to his room to just breathe for a while. He and Wyatt had talked around each other—horses, roping, the foster kids, the new house—but not directly to each other. To be honest, Hank couldn't find anything to say. All the questions he might have asked Wyatt had already been answered by either Grace or Gil, and the apologies due from both sides canceled each other out. What did that leave?

A soft knock sounded on the door, and when he called out, "Come in!" Melanie stuck her head inside. "I'm working out our schedule for tomorrow. What time do you want to do Christmas Eve supper?"

"Six o'clock?" That would give him plenty of time afterward with Grace, who intended to make the briefest possible appearance at the McKenna family gathering.

"That works." Melanie pushed the door open wider and stepped in, her gaze running over the bare, scarred walls. "Love what you've done with the place."

He shrugged. "My designer is working out the new color scheme."

"Mmm." She moved over to the dresser, where he'd stood the only three pictures left in the room. Picking up the first, she touched the glass. "I'd forgotten this one. Wow. We do look like Dad, don't we?"

The way he'd looked at thirty-one, leaner, younger, and smiling, with one arm around his wife, the other cradling his newborn son and Melanie standing in front, skinny as a willow switch.

She skipped past the second picture—one he'd brought from Montana of Bing and Hank with the majestic bulk of Chief Mountain in the background— and rested her fingertips on the wooden frame of the third. "I've never seen this."

"That's when we won the regional championship." In the photo, Hank's hair was dripping with sweat, his eye black was smeared down his cheeks, and his football uniform was streaked with grass stains and dirt, but his smile was wider than Texas as he hoisted a laughing Grace into the air in triumph. "Miz Iris gave me a bunch of pictures she took at the game. All the time we've been friends, and that's the only one I have of just me and Grace."

Melanie's expression went somber as she continued to study the photo. "We brought the paperwork with us for you to sign. Laura and Julianne are over the moon."

"I'm glad."

And really, what more was there to say? Hank waited for her to comment on his relationship with Grace, but she turned and came over to plunk down beside him instead, mimicking his forearms-dangling-between-knees slouch. "I swore I wasn't gonna play the know-it-all big sister anymore, but I have to ask—why haven't you been to see Miz Iris?"

"I went." He scowled down at his hands. "The first day I was back. She acted like she didn't know what to do with me."

"You did pop up out of the blue, and you weren't exactly yourself." She reached up to give his hair a flick. "I like this a lot better, by the way."

"Me too. You think now that I got it cut, she might invite me in, instead of chasing me over to Cole's?"

Melanie sighed. "It wasn't all about you. Violet says Miz Iris is having a hard time since she went on this diet. Food has always been her way of connecting with people, and now that she doesn't have a plate of cookies to offer, sometimes she isn't sure what to do."

"Seriously?" Hank shook his head in disbelief. "Talking has never been a challenge for Miz Iris."

"It never used to be for you, either." Melanie's gaze fixed on a lighter square where a poster from the San Antonio rodeo used to hang. "You know, she always thought of you as hers. She feels really bad that you didn't come to her for help when you needed it most."

Guilt shafted through Hank's chest, but he set his jaw against the pang. "Well, they did fire me, so that made it kinda awkward. And I'm here now, but she's still being unsociable."

Melanie lifted her brows. "Unlike you?"

"I haven't…"

The words died as he replayed the three times he'd

been in Miz Iris's company. He could give himself a pass on that first visit to the ranch, but at Thanksgiving he'd barely thanked her for dinner before running off, and he hadn't even stayed for a glass of sweet tea after the Buck Out. Hell, he'd gone out of his way to avoid speaking to her that whole day, for fear of what she might have to say to him. And then he'd pouted because *she* wasn't friendly?

He dropped his head into his hands and groaned. "Every time I think I'm getting smarter."

"Don't feel bad." Melanie patted his back. "Hell, it took Wyatt five years to figure out that I was in love with him, and he graduated from Yale."

They sat for a few minutes, comfortable with the silence and with each other. Finally, Hank said, "You're really not gonna say anything about me and Grace?"

She shook her head. "I'm too tangled up in all of this. Grace and I got to be good friends while she was in Oregon. And on top of everything else, Wyatt is Maddie's godfather."

A bubble of the old anger tried to well up, then deflated in the cold light of reason. Feeling the way Wyatt did about Melanie, there was no way he would have done any of this if Gil hadn't trapped him. "So does that make you the fairy godmother?" he joked.

"I'd have to meet her first."

Hank snapped upright. "You've never seen her?"

"I couldn't." She twisted her fingers together between her knees. "Not until you do."

"But Wyatt... Has he been avoiding her too, since you got married?"

"No. He adores her, and I'm sure she feels the same. I

couldn't ask him to drop out of her life. We just...work around it."

Geezus. Who did that, parking a massive neon elephant in the middle of their lives out of loyalty to a brother who'd all but flipped her the bird when she'd told him she was marrying Wyatt? He angled her an exasperated look. "You're nuts, you know that?"

She leaned sideways to nudge him with her shoulder. "Runs in the family."

He snorted. "No kidding. Mom goes without saying, and talk to Bing about Dad sometime."

"I'm glad the two of you are working things out." Her sigh was half nostalgia, half regret. "He was so different before the fire. Fun and kinda silly. Happy, I guess. I always felt bad that you never got to know him then."

Hank angled her a glance. "So you spent the next twenty years trying to make it up to me?"

"I suppose. It's complicated. If I was pissed, it wasn't at you. I mean, yeah, I was mad at you a lot, but you usually earned it, brat." She put an affectionate hand on his knee, then squeezed in the way that never failed to make him yelp. He jerked away, and she laughed. "I can't believe you're still falling for that."

He scowled at her, rubbing what felt like an exposed nerve. "I can't believe you're still picking on me. And they say I need to grow up."

"Past tense." He flinched when she reached out again, but this time she just gave his arm a gentle punch. "Mission accomplished, job well done."

He ducked his head, overwhelmed by the emotions crashing through him. "Thanks."

"You're welcome." But her expression had gone pensive.

"Wyatt makes you happy," he said quietly. "That's enough for me. And besides, I always thought he was some sort of Superman, so it's a kick in the ass to see that my sister is his kryptonite."

She gave a husky laugh. "I just wish…"

"I know." He shook his head, stymied. "It's not that I don't want to talk to him. I just don't know how."

"That makes two of you."

"Really?" Damn. He'd figured Wyatt always knew what to say and what to do. "Well, we'll figure it out eventually. Right now, I'm gonna head over to Dumas before the highway turns into a skating rink." He pushed to his feet, walked over to the dresser, and fished a small box out of the top drawer, wrapped in crinkled paper and about half a roll of tape. "I want to give Grace this tonight, since it's not technically her Christmas present."

When he turned, Melanie's eyes were wide and fixed on the package. "Is that—"

He grinned. "Nah. Just something I found while I was cleaning out my room that I should have given her back when that picture was taken." He balanced the box on his palm and met his sister's gaze over it. "But I am going to marry her, whenever I can persuade her to have me."

Melanie's brows pinched in concern. "It could take a while."

"I know." He looked at those three pictures that were the signposts of his life—birth, rebirth, and his hope for the future—then back at her. "I'm not going anywhere."

"Oh, I think you are…when you're ready." She stood and hugged him so hard his ribs creaked. "Just don't forget to come home again."

Chapter 53

Wisps of fog fingered across the highway as Grace drove home from the last practice on Friday evening. She was officially on vacation—two whole days before the supposedly optional post-Christmas practices started up.

Optional for the kids, not for Grace.

But at least this cold, wet air mass would have moved along by then. The air was so damp she could feel invisible droplets hitting her face as she walked from her pickup to her front door, and the temperature was falling fast.

Even the weather had decided to be miserable this Christmas.

The chill crept down Grace's neck as she tried to wrestle the door open without dropping any of her bags. She had only just finished her Christmas shopping tonight after work. With so many in the family, the adults drew names, but she always bought gifts for Jeremiah and the boys, plus something small for each of the half dozen nieces and nephews who were still young enough to be more interested in the wrapping paper than the picture book inside.

Her failure to be an enraptured aunt should have been her first clue that she lacked whatever it was that made other women stand in line to cuddle babies.

God. There would be three of them this year under the age of two. Her brain whimpered at the thought of being crammed into her parents' house with all that nonstop squawling and squabbling—and that was just the adults.

She hadn't heard a word from Hank since his sister and Wyatt had arrived. Hopefully no news was good news. She should be worrying about how Hank and Wyatt were getting along. Instead, selfishly, all she could think was that Melanie was home, but she and Grace wouldn't be getting together for lunch, or for a girls' night with what Violet had dubbed the Earnest Ladies Club. Melanie had respectfully removed herself from their friendship, pending the outcome of Grace's relationship with her brother.

And Grace had lost the one person other than Hank that she'd been able to talk to without reservations.

She dumped her armloads of bags onto the couch and sank down beside them with a weary sigh. She hadn't even started wrapping gifts, and she'd promised her mother that she'd make a batch of butterhorns for Christmas Eve, her annual and much-anticipated contribution to the holiday feast. Now exhausted tears balled up in her throat at the prospect of all that kneading and rising followed by rolling, buttering, rising, and rolling again, four times over, to make them flaky and light. And then there was still the icing.

Maybe she could just toss them in the front door and run before she had to speak to her older siblings. Or, more to the point, before any of the big three had a chance to speak to her. She'd heard more than enough of Suzannah's opinion three years ago, when they'd brought the horde home for Presidents' Day weekend.

I told Mama and Papa they shouldn't let you spend

so much time with that Brookman kid. Everyone said he was just using you.

At the time, Grace had been in state of mute panic, almost three months pregnant and convinced that everyone could tell at a glance, even though she'd actually lost weight from the stress and thankfully mild queasiness. Every ounce of her energy was devoted to seeming normal and happy until she could escape to Oregon. She'd had nothing left to defend herself, and no reason to defend Hank.

Now? All she could do was repeat what she'd told Papa. *He repented. I forgave. The Bible told me so.* Not that she would try to argue scripture with them. It was the equivalent of engaging in a debate with a machine gun. They had scoured the good book for psalms and verses that supported their beliefs and kept them lined up like bullets in a magazine, ready to fire in rapid succession.

Poor Mama. But at least *she* had Jeremiah to defend her.

He wasn't exactly mad at Grace, but he wasn't happy with her, either, and his disapproval ate at her. He had accepted her decision to give up her baby without hesitation—until he found out she'd taken up with Hank again. Not that he'd said so, but she saw the question in his eyes.

How could you, Grace?

And Mama. Her acceptance should have made Grace feel better. Instead, she found herself replaying conversation after conversation, weighing every word, every glance, the tiniest inflection in her mother's voice or her slightest frown, in search of deeply buried disapproval.

In other words, Grace was making herself crazy, and telling herself so didn't do a damn bit of good.

She pushed at curls gone wild from the humidity and tried to work up the ambition to take off her coat. She would never be so happy to have the holidays over, and that included the year she'd spent Boxing Day curled up in the fetal position, shaking with dread but pretending to have cramps from the period that had failed to make an appearance.

Her doorbell rang. She checked the clock and groaned. It was already seven o'clock? Rather than hoisting herself out of the couch, she waited, and after a few moments a key scraped in the lock. She'd given Hank her spare purely for the sake of convenience, since she never knew exactly what time she would get home from work.

But he always rang first so he didn't sneak up her— one of a hundred little ways that he continued to respect her space.

Tonight he walked in, took one look at her, and said, "Whoa. Bad day?"

"Not really. It's just…" She made a vague circle toward the heap of bags. "Christmas is the day after tomorrow, and there's just so *much*."

He crossed over, caught her limp wrists, and pulled her forward so he could push the coat off her arms. Then he gave her a soft, warm kiss and rested his forehead against hers. "I'll help—if you don't mind your gifts looking like they were wrapped by a monkey with five thumbs."

Her laugh was too high and too brittle. "How are you at making butterhorns?"

"Not worth a damn, but I give a killer back rub."

She moaned softly. "Oh God, that would be wonderful, but then I'd be really worthless for the rest of the night." She watched him from under drooping lids as he cleared a spot next to her. "You seem pretty chipper. I take it everything went okay?"

"Not a drop of blood spilled or an f-bomb tossed. You would have been proud."

She was already proud. He had come so far in the short time he'd been home. Been torn down to almost nothing and had somehow kept the parts she'd always loved best in the process of rebuilding. Maybe he and Bing could tell her how to do the same for what was going to be left of her family.

He settled in beside her but didn't immediately tuck her into his arms like usual. And he was still wearing his coat. He angled to face her, their knees touching. "Before I start mutilating your wrapping paper, there's something I want to give you."

He pulled his hand from his pocket and held out a small package. He wasn't kidding about his gift-wrapping skills. It was basically a wad of paper plastered with tape. But the size. And the shape.

Her heart launched into an unsteady *ker-thump, KER-thump, ker-THUMP*. Surely that couldn't be…

"I know. It's a mess. Here." He hiked up a hip to pull the knife out of his back pocket. "I'll cut the tape for you."

He sliced most of the way around the box and peeled off the top half of the wrapping like a clamshell. Grace's breath came out in a *whoosh* when she saw that it wasn't a jeweler's box inside.

Too impatient to wait for her to do it herself, Hank lifted off the lid and set the box in her lap. "You said you were never my girl, but you should have been. And there's never been anyone else I wanted to give this to."

Stupefied, Grace stared down at his high school class ring, strung on a gold chain. He was…he wanted…

No. Instead of reaching for the box, she jerked her hands back. "I can't take that."

He smiled reassuringly. "It's okay. I'm not afraid you'll lose it or anything."

"No." She said it out loud this time, shrinking back into the couch cushions. "I can't do that."

His smile faded, replaced by concern and the beginnings of apprehension. "What do you mean by *that*?"

"You. Me. *That*." She made a jerky motion toward the box as her heart pounded harder and her lungs started to flail. "I can't *be* with you."

His face softened, and he picked up one of her clammy hands. "I know I've let you down too many times to count. This is just one of the ways I intend to prove that I love you, and I don't ever want to hurt you again."

I love you.

The words rang inside her like a warning gong, reverberating through her chest and into her guts. *Damn* him. Now, when it was far too late, he finally gave her what she'd wanted so desperately for so long? She yanked her hand free. "You can't."

"Love you? Yes, Grace, I can. I do." He tried to reach for her again, but she pulled her hands away. He blew out of breath full of remorse and hard-fought patience. "I know…it took me way too long to figure it out, and I don't blame you for not just taking my word for it. But can you at least trust me enough to let me keep showing you how I feel until you can believe it's real?"

Trust? It had nothing to do with trust. She made a

shaky fist that she pressed to her mouth. "You don't understand. We can't do this to Maddie."

"Maddie?" His brows drew together in confusion. "What does this have to do with her?"

"*Everything!*" Grace leapt from the couch, sending the ring flying, suddenly frantic to create space between them. She backed away until she came up against the wall, then dug her fingernails into the plaster in a pathetic attempt to steady herself. "How can I be with you after I gave her away? What am I supposed to say to her? *Yes, honey, I've loved your daddy since we were nine years old. I just didn't want you?*" Her voice was shrill, on the verge of hysterical. "What do I say to my mama, or to Jeremiah, who think I only gave the baby away because I couldn't go it alone?"

Hank's jaw had gone slack. "That you love me, and I love you, and someday I want you to be my wife."

"*Wife?*" The word came out on a harsh laugh, and she started shaking her head—left, right, left, right— mechanical as a demented doll. "No. I'm not getting married."

He still looked more confused than hurt. "I'm not asking you to run off to Vegas next week. But in a year, or two…however long it takes."

She kept shaking her head. "Never. I'm not ever getting married. I gave that up."

"You…what?" He gaped at her, dumbfounded. "Are you trying to say that you can't have a family because it might make Maddie feel bad?"

The words were like stones, thumping into her chest. "You. Don't. Know." Her breath was coming in choked gulps. "You weren't there, and you don't know *anything*. You haven't even looked at the damn pictures."

That arrow hit its mark. His eyes went dark, his face shuttered, but he made no move to leave. "You're right. I wasn't there. But I'm here now, and I told you before, I won't run out on you again. As for the pictures…" He jumped up and strode into her bedroom, yanking open the top drawer of her dresser to grab the shoebox. He settled it on his knees as he sat down again. "You're right. Come and sit down. You can tell me all about them."

And rip out her heartstrings one by one in the process. *Here's the reason I can't have you on her first birthday. And look! Here she is dressed like a unicorn for her first Halloween.*

"Take them with you," Grace said, her voice so raw it was barely recognizable.

His head jerked up. "What?"

"I just…I can't do this. Please go."

Alarm flared in his eyes, along with the beginnings of hurt, but he didn't budge. "I'm not leaving you alone when you're upset."

"I wouldn't *be* upset if you hadn't come and said things and brought that." She made a jerky motion at the ring glinting under the coffee table.

He stood slowly, as if even his body refused to listen to her. "Grace, you don't mean—"

"Don't tell me what I feel! You obviously have no fucking idea." He flinched at the profanity. Good. Maybe she'd finally gotten his attention. She closed her eyes. "It's too late, Hank. I don't want this. I don't want *you*."

The silence was interminable, but she refused to open her eyes and see what the words had done. Then she heard the rustle of his jacket, and the jagged echoes of her pain in his voice when he said, "I can't leave you like this."

"Please." It was a whisper. A plea for mercy. The last fragile thread of her composure slipping through her fingers.

Finally, he said, "If that's what you need me to do."

The quiet click of the door echoed around the silent apartment. Grace squeezed her eyes even tighter and slowly slid down the wall to huddle on the floor, arms clutched around her knees, her body racked by sobs so powerful they felt as if they were being ripped from the very bottom of her soul.

Chapter 54

JOHNNY WATCHED THE TAILLIGHTS DISAPPEAR INTO the thickening fog as Melanie and Wyatt drove away, then rolled his shoulders as if shedding a massive weight. Tonight he'd had everyone who mattered most to him gathered around the table, and even if it wasn't perfect, it had been a damn sight closer than they'd been in a long, long time. Maybe ever. His kids had patched things up, and they were all paired up and happy.

Now it was his turn—he hoped. A noise caught his attention, and he turned to see Bing reaching for the coat she'd draped over the back of one of the barstools. He walked over and laid his hand on her arm, stopping her.

"Stay for a while. Keep me company."

"I shouldn't." She pressed her lips together, as if that would stop him from wanting to kiss her…and her from wanting to kiss him back.

He tugged at her wrist, turning her to face him. "Everyone else gets to have someone tonight. Why not us? If I don't tell, and you don't tell, who's it going to hurt?"

"Johnny…"

"Please. It's cold out there, and without you, it's cold in here too. Stay and keep us both warm."

She closed her eyes, took a deep breath, and nodded. "Just for a while."

"Thank you." He turned on the old boom-box-style radio tucked into a corner of the counter, and it filled the dimly lit kitchen with the sounds of "White Christmas." Just two days earlier, the doctor had released him from the sling, so he could put a hand on either side of her waist and pull her close. "Dance with me."

She only resisted a moment before melting into his arms. They began to move, slow and easy, as she looped her arms around his neck and swayed closer. He closed his eyes and drew a deep breath, her night-flower scent going straight to his head as his hands shaped her waist, her hips, then up the curve of her back. It wasn't enough.

He cupped the side of her face and tipped her chin up to capture her mouth and lose himself in her taste, her heat, the silken slide of her tongue against his and the hot press of body to body. God, he wanted her. In his arms. His bed. His future. The music changed to something up-tempo, but they kept up the same timeless rhythm. Man. Woman. Two hearts beating as one and all that romantic crap. He could do this—just this—for hours. Hold her. Kiss her.

Love her.

If she would just let him, he knew he could get it right this time. With this woman.

Her hand splayed across his chest, and her fingers hooked in the top button of his shirt. She popped it free, then the next, then slid her palm inside to press it over a heart that was thudding dangerously hard. There was a muffled roaring sound, and for a confused moment he thought he might have actually busted a vein from the intense pleasure of her touch.

Then the door banged open...and they froze.

Hank stood in the mudroom, his face drawn tight with pain and his eyes black pools in the shadows—a wounded animal in search of a place to go to ground. He stared at them for a long, awful eternity. "What the *fuck*?"

Bing jerked away, taking a step toward Hank with her hand outstretched. "Wait, Hank. Just let me—"

The box under his arm fell to the floor, spilling pictures and pieces of paper. He started to crouch, then with another curse, he spun on his heel and was gone, leaving the door hanging open and the dogs staring from one human to another in wide-eyed confusion. Bing ran out, Johnny on her heels, but the old Chevy roared to life, lurching in a backward arc before the tires spun, flinging gravel as it shot out of the driveway.

"Shit. *Shit!*" Bing pressed shaking hands to her face. "What happened? What the hell happened to make him come back here, looking like that? And he saw us…"

"You can't chase him down. Not in this fog. Geezus. You can barely see across the yard." He toed the sidewalk, coated with a thin layer of ice. Goddammit. This was no night to be driving, even in a decent state of mind. Johnny scraped a hand over his head. "We have to think. Where will he go? The shop? Maybe Korby's place?"

Bing spun around and barreled in to snatch the phone off the bar and shove the receiver into his hand. "Call them."

"Who?"

"Everyone. Anyone who might see him or know where he'd go. We can't leave him alone, especially driving around in this weather." Her face was pasty, her breath coming short, as if she was on the verge of an anxiety attack. She pressed her hands together in prayer. "Please, God, don't let anything happen to him."

—◦◦◦—

The first number Johnny tried was Hank's cell. Not surprisingly, there was no answer. He called Cole's house next, and within minutes, the alarm had gone up across the Jacobs network, while Johnny hung on the line with Melanie. Meanwhile, Bing was trying to reach Gil on her cell. His phone rang but went to voicemail. She dialed again. And again. And again.

"Tori and Delon are watching the highway into Dumas, in case he went that way," Melanie said into Johnny's ear. "Shawnee called the Watering Hole and the Lone Steer so they'll let us know if he shows up, and Violet got ahold of Korby. He was gonna check Sanchez Trucking, then head toward the ranch in case Hank slid off into the ditch along the way. The road was black ice damn near all the way down here."

Not what Johnny needed to hear. His head filled with images of Hank's old pickup upside down, or wrapped around a telephone pole, or—

"It's about goddamn time!" Bing said into her phone.

"We've got Gil," Johnny said to Melanie.

Bing gave a rapid-fire account of what had happened, made a *Yeah, it was stupid* face as she listened, then said, "You can do that?"

"Hang on," Johnny said into the phone. "It sounds like he's got an idea."

Bing jerked a nod. "Hank's cell is one of the Sanchez Trucking phones, and to quote Gil, those sons-a-bitches lose 'em faster than he can buy 'em, so he puts tracking software on all of them."

Johnny relayed the information, then ground his

teeth through a long, tense silence as Gil logged into his system and entered the phone number. Then Bing's shoulders sagged in relief. "Okay. Great. Thank you."

"What?" Johnny demanded.

"He just pulled into Miz Iris's driveway."

Thank God. Johnny collapsed onto a barstool, barely able to string words together to tell Melanie the good news.

Gil said something else, and Bing's mouth twisted into a semblance of a smile. "You're probably right, but I'm betting you've already got your car keys in your hand."

"What did he say?" Johnny asked when they'd both hung up.

"That Hank seems to be the only one who didn't overreact."

"He's going to talk to him, though?"

She nodded. "Gil's his sponsor. That's what you do when someone might be in a crisis."

He and Bing stared at the floor for several minutes, letting the fear and adrenaline drain away. Then she got up and walked heavily into the mudroom to gather up Hank's box and the scattered contents.

"What is it?" Johnny asked.

"Pictures of Maddie." She swore softly, then lifted her head. "Will you go with me to Dumas?"

"Now? Why?"

She waved a hand over the box. "Whatever happened, it obviously has something to do with this, and judging by that look on Hank's face before he saw us, I doubt Grace is doing so great, either."

Johnny frowned. "*You* hardly know her. And Tori could be there in five minutes."

"But she doesn't know about the baby." Bing stood

and put some of the steel back into her spine. "And if this is what I think, Grace needs a mother."

―⁓―

If all else fails, go back to the beginning.

Bing had told him that. *Bing.* And his dad. Geezus. But what did he expect? She was a beautiful woman, Johnny was a good-looking guy, and Hank had practically shoved the two of them together, once again oblivious to anything but his own feelings.

Were there feelings? Or was it just—

He cut that thought dead along with his headlights. Whatever it was, he would have to figure out how he felt about it later. Right now, he had exceeded his coping capacity, leaving him no choice but to hit the reset button. *Go back to the beginning.*

Hank felt as if he'd been doing nothing else for so long, he'd lost count of all the beginnings and endings. He was literally wandering in the fog...but his old pickup had remembered the way, even if he'd forgotten.

He started to get out of the pickup, then paused to type in a two-word text and hit Send. Still breathing.

He didn't wait for a response, just tossed the phone on the seat and picked his way across crunchy, ice-crusted grass to the kitchen door. It flew open as he put his foot on the first step, and Miz Iris stood silhouetted in the light, clutching a robe over flannel pajamas. "Hank?"

"Yes, ma'am."

Her face registered profound relief. "Cole called. They were worried about you."

"I'm fine."

"I don't think so." Miz Iris peered at him under the

porch light. "If you were fine, you wouldn't be out driving around on a night like this."

"I'm sorry. I shouldn't have come so late. It's just..." His voice choked off, and once more, he had to start over. "Can I come in? Please? You don't even have to give me a cookie."

"Oh, Hank." Tears welled in her eyes as she held out a hand. "You've always been welcome here, no matter what. I'm so sorry that we let you think otherwise."

He took one step, then another, reaching out and letting her draw him into the light and the warmth. "I didn't make it easy for you."

"*Pfft!* What's easy got to do with family?"

His laugh was embarrassingly soggy. "Not a damn thing as far as I can tell."

Then he stepped inside and into the arms of the woman who'd patched up more scrapes and bruises and cuts than he could count. As he hugged her tight, he prayed she could work her magic one more time because the worst stomping he'd ever taken in the arena hadn't hurt half this bad.

Hank had just wrapped his hands around a mug of hot chocolate with extra marshmallows when another, unmistakable set of headlights ghosted out of the fog as Gil's Charger rolled to a stop beside his pickup. Gil rapped once on the door and let himself in.

"Geezus," Hank said. "Is there anyone they didn't call?"

"Within a fifty-mile radius? Probably not." Gil gave Miz Iris a one-armed hug and accepted the mug she had begun to fill when she saw his car. "Thank you. It's a nasty bitch out there."

And yet, here was Gil, willing to come out in the ice and the fog to be sure Hank was okay. "So...anything we need to have a private man talk about?" he asked Hank.

Code for: *Anything about the baby?*

Yes. And no. If Grace had absolutely ruled him out because of Maddie, there wasn't a damn thing he could do. But if this somehow did come around to a matter of trust, and redemption, then he still had a sliver of hope. Between them, these two people had helped him through some of the hardest and best times of his life. Maybe they could guide him now.

So he said, "I need to figure out how to make Grace love me again."

Gil slouched back in his chair and hiked a foot onto his opposite knee. "And here I thought it was gonna be something difficult."

Chapter 55

GRACE HAD DRAGGED HERSELF FROM THE LIVING room floor to the shower and stood under the spray until the water ran cold. As she pulled on sweatpants and her warmest sweatshirt, she realized she should have called or texted or something to let Gil or Bing know that Hank needed them.

She would text Gil. He'd make sure Hank had arrived in one piece.

Her head and chest and stomach all ached from her crying jag, and she felt…emptied out. As if something inside her had dissolved and been washed away with her tears. Possibly her heart. She shuffled into the kitchen to find the bottle of ibuprofen she kept there and was just tipping the tablets into her palm when the doorbell rang. She jerked, and pills scattered and rolled, dropping into the sink and onto the floor to disappear under the stove.

Had Hank come back? She peered out the narrow kitchen window and gulped when she saw the fog was so thick she could barely make out the car on the far side of her parking lot, other than the red gleam of taillights.

Oh no. *Hank*. She'd sent him out into *that*.

The doorbell chimed again, longer and more insistent, as if someone was leaning on the button. "Grace?" The voice was muffled but familiar through the door. "I know you're home, and I'm not going away."

Grace rushed over and yanked the door open to find

Bing, thumb on the doorbell and shoulders hunched against the cold. The sidewalk, the curb, the trees—everything glistened with a coat of ice. Grace's breath caught. "Oh my God. Did Hank…is something wrong?"

"He's safe." Bing stepped inside and caught Grace by both shoulders, taking in her swollen eyes and blotched face. "What did he do?"

Grace dipped her chin, hiding from eyes that saw too much. "He, um, tried to give me his class ring."

"Ah. I see why that would be a problem."

Grace jerked away. "If you came to make fun of me, you can go now."

"That wasn't sarcasm." The door *thunked* shut behind Bing, and she followed Grace into the living room.

Grace could barely work up the energy to sigh as she dropped onto the love seat. "Shouldn't you be with Hank?"

"Miz Iris has him. And I came to tell you a story."

"I'm really not in the mood…"

"I'll keep it short." Bing sat down and caught one of Grace's hands between hers. Grace wanted to pull away, but the contact was oddly comforting. "You probably know that I had a baby when I was fifteen. The father had already knocked up at least two other girls, so he wasn't even a consideration, and I was too scared to get an abortion. Adoption barely crossed my mind. So I kept her, but I didn't raise her. I dumped her on my mother and my grandmother while I went on partying my way through high school and college, and my daughter followed right in my footsteps, except she had her baby when she was fourteen."

"If you're trying to tell me that I made the right choice—"

"Shhh." Bing rubbed Grace's cold hand as if to restore the circulation. "So, now my daughter is forty years old. She's been with at least two men who hit her, and she has a five-year-old daughter that I've never seen. My grandson has been dead for two years."

"I'm sorry," Grace said, her voice barely audible.

"Me too." Bing leaned in to meet her gaze more directly. "I wonder, where would we all be if I'd been brave enough to admit that I didn't want to be a mother? If I'd given her to someone who did? Would she be happier? Have a career she loves, instead of a job at the casino that gets her from one month to the next? Would she still have to put flowers on her son's grave? But I didn't think of those things then. I just knew that everyone expected me to keep my baby, so I did."

Grace swallowed. "You were very young."

"Yes, I was. And I didn't have people like Gil and Wyatt to swoop me up and carry me off so my baby could be a secret." She tilted her head, those dark eyes amazingly warm with sympathy. "But not forever. You made the adoption open so she wouldn't have to wonder about her birth parents. And because of that choice, you never get to stop fighting the expectations. There will always be people who believe you're less of a woman than me because you gave up your baby and I kept mine. And yet, your daughter has a wonderful home, wonderful parents, and will probably go to an Ivy League school and cure cancer or something. And mine…" She shrugged. "It's backward, and it's unfair, and there's not a damn thing you can do about what they think."

Grace dragged in a shuddering breath. "Wow. With

pep talks like that, I can't imagine why Hank ever wanted to leave Montana."

Bing laughed, then gave her hand a squeeze. "The point is, Grace, are you going to keep being one of those people?"

Her gentle question packed the emotional wallop of a slap in the face, and Grace's head actually jerked at the impact. *One of those people*. Like her father. Sweet Jesus. She'd almost let him win. How had she not recognized that the insidious whisper in her ear was his?

No one else had condemned her. Not Hank. Not her mother. Not Jeremiah. Certainly not Bing or Wyatt or Melanie. Gil had been nothing but supportive in his acidic way. But somehow Grace had let Papa creep into her subconscious, offering none of the compassion she would have readily given anyone else in her situation, and damning her to years of loneliness for not conforming to his suffocating standards.

Stuffing her heart into an airless box that her father and his kind had built and labeled *A Real Woman*.

"Grace?" Bing asked softly.

"It's just me," she said faintly. "*I* have to decide." Again. Or maybe it was finally. After all this time, she had to not only accept the choices she'd made, but the reasons behind them. Her reasons. Her life. *Hers,* dammit.

But also Maddie's. "How would our daughter feel if she saw the two of us living happily ever after without her?"

Happily. Ever. After. With Hank. Grace's heart flailed helplessly as all her daydreams and fantasies flooded her at once. But she had to focus on Maddie.

Bing let go of her hand and leaned back, expression

thoughtful. "Have you considered the alternative? Let's say you both marry someone else. Maybe have kids. How will they feel about the daughter you had with another lover? If they don't want your past to come visiting, Maddie loses."

"That sounds like a convenient way to justify doing what we want."

Bing folded her arms. "What's convenient about choosing a relationship that will expose both of you to a lifetime of disapproval?"

Put that way, Grace had no idea. This was the conversation she'd wished she could have with her own mother. One she could imagine having with Melanie. But Bing? "Why are you here?" she asked.

"Because Hank *was* right. He is the best version of himself when he's with you. And after all you've been through, you deserve a man who loves you like no one else ever will."

"*Thinks* he loves me," Grace argued, but her voice had lost all conviction.

"Uh-uh. It's for real." Bing's smile was almost wistful. "I've known almost since I met him, just from the way he talked about you. And if you didn't feel the same, you wouldn't be so scared."

"I'm not..." But she couldn't force out the lie. She was terrified. Without the guilt to hide behind, there was nothing to stop her from falling. He had hurt her *so much* even when she'd known it was coming and tried to hold back. If she let him love her, gave him everything in return, and then he changed his mind, there would be nothing left of her.

But Bing was sure, and she knew Hank better than

anyone. If she was convinced that he loved Grace, shouldn't Grace be able to believe it too?

"He didn't want to leave me." Not tonight. Not three years ago. He'd told her so.

"No. He has always wanted to be with you."

Grace drew a shuddering breath, recalling her harsh words. "I hurt him tonight. A lot."

"But he will let you fix it." Bing lifted an eyebrow in a not-so-subtle suggestion.

Yes, he would. He'd already proven that he could forgive her almost anything, then turn around and hand over his heart the way he'd offered her his class ring. She lifted her hands to indicate the mess she'd made of the night and herself. "How can I be sure this isn't going to happen again?"

"We keep talking and being honest. All of us. Together." Bing cocked her head, questioning. "So… are you staying here, or do you want Johnny and me to take you to him?"

A simple choice. Be alone, or be with Hank. Cling to her fear and her guilt, or reach for happiness.

Grace lifted her chin and squared her shoulders. Now, when it mattered most, she refused to be her father's daughter.

"Can you wait while I fix myself up a little?" she asked.

Chapter 56

HANK HADN'T JUST POURED HIS HEART OUT. HE'D extracted it from his chest, set it in the middle of the table, and let Gil and Miz Iris peer into every nook and cranny. Everything except the baby. He'd promised Grace, and he couldn't go back on his word.

While Hank talked, Gil got up and made himself more hot chocolate. Miz Iris sipped unenthusiastically from her own cup—sugar free, no marshmallows. There was a lot to process when you started all the way back at the first day of fourth grade and didn't end until, "And then I walked in and found Dad and Bing kissing."

Miz Iris's eyebrows shot up. "That must have been… awkward."

"No shit." Gil fished a half-melted marshmallow out with his spoon and popped it in his mouth. "Did you stomp out because you're pissed, or because 'Ew, my dad is kissing my best friend'?"

Hank thought about it, then shrugged. "Some of the first. Mostly the second. If I hadn't already been upset, I might not have completely lost my shit."

"But you're cool now?" Gil asked.

Hank made himself replay the scene he'd witnessed. His dad. Bing. Other than a juvenile instinct to cringe… "I needed to talk to her, and she was with him. So I was pissed."

Gil sucked the marshmallow goo off the tip of his spoon. "Think you can get used to sharing?"

"I guess. If that's what they want..." Hank trailed off and scrubbed a hand across the wire-tight muscles of his neck. "My own love life just went belly up. Theirs is gonna have to get in line."

Gil hitched a lazy shoulder. "If it's no big deal for you...then it's no big deal, period. Gotta say though, I'll be disappointed if I don't have anyone left to check up on in Montana. I was starting to enjoy the scenery, if you know what I mean."

Miz Iris's gaze sharpened. "Why can't you go visit the scenery?"

"Then she'd think I came all that way just to see her, and that's a surefire way to spoil the view." Gil smiled blandly at Miz Iris's aggravated scowl. "Don't bother. I'm not interested in being fixed, so let's worry about Hank."

"Yeah, well, worrying is about all I can do." Hank thumped a fist on the table in sheer frustration. "It's like I'm stuck in a rotating door. She won't let me get too close because she's sure it won't work, and I can't prove it *will* work if I can't get close to her."

"It is a very big leap of faith for her," Miz Iris said. "Especially if her family isn't supportive."

Hank ground his teeth. "Again...how can I win them over if she won't let me near them?"

He could see it now—the pattern he'd so stubbornly overlooked. How she'd excluded him from anything to do with her brothers. The way she'd avoided being seen with him in public and practically squirmed when she couldn't. She'd been hedging her bets from day one.

"I don't think this is the best time to meet the in-laws," Gil said. "That's gonna be an ugly divorce."

"I want to be there for Grace. Wherever and however she needs me." *The way I wasn't before*, he added with a speaking glance.

Gil inclined his head. Message received.

"Are you *sure* about how she feels?" Miz Iris asked.

"She said she'd been in love with me since she was nine years old." In the same breath that she'd insisted they could never be more than whatever the hell it was they'd been doing.

"Well, that's pretty clear." Miz Iris took another sip, shoved her cup away, and reached across to swipe the one Hank had barely touched, heaving a blissful sigh at the first taste. "That's more like it. What about the brother? Jeremiah, isn't it? You could wait until he's back at school and go have a talk with him, man to man. If you could get him on your side—"

"We've got more company," Steve announced from the living room, where he'd taken refuge from all the feelings flying around his kitchen. "Looks like that old car of Delon's."

Shit. His dad. And Bing. He was gonna have to deal with them whether he wanted to or not. He kept his gaze fixed on the sticky marshmallow ring his mug had left on the table while Miz Iris went to the door, but his head jerked up at the note of surprise in her voice. "I wasn't expecting quite so many visitors, or I would have changed out of my pajamas."

They shuffled in from the entry—Miz Iris, then Bing, then Johnny. Then Hank's heart lurched as Grace stepped from behind his dad, face pale, eyes pink-rimmed, fingers twining nervously together as she gave him a tremulous smile. "I guess I was the one who needed some moral support this time."

Hank had to blink, not sure his eyes weren't playing tricks. But she was really here. Despite the fog and the ice and everything else that had tried to keep them apart, Bing—God bless her—somehow Bing had brought Grace around, both literally and figuratively. Hank shot to his feet, his chair teetering dangerously before it thumped back to the floor, a counterpoint to his pounding heart. He closed the gap to catch both of Grace's hands, but his gaze was locked with Bing's. "Thank you."

She nodded, her eyes solemn. "I'm sorry about earlier. I should have told you about, um, things."

Not, he noticed, *I shouldn't have been making out with your father.* So it was like that, then. "Well, now I know." He transferred his gaze to his dad, who was rigid as a fence post. "Feel free to keep sneaking around, though. The less I actually see, the better."

Johnny's shoulders sagged in relief. "I'm good with that."

"What are you…" Then Grace's eyes went wide as they ricocheted from Johnny to Bing. "Oh."

"Yeah," Hank said. "Like 'I Saw Mommy Kissing Santa Claus,' but with the Grinch."

"Hey!" Johnny protested.

Bing punched his arm to shut him up.

Hank shoved out of his chair and reached for Grace. Just the feel of her hand in his was enough to make his heart settle back into that strong, sure beat. It was as if his love for her was the bass line of his emotions and all the other notes—high and low—wove in and around the steady thump. He drew her toward him, another layer of tension peeling away when she didn't resist. "We need to talk," he said. "Privately."

She nodded.

"You can use Cole's old room," Miz Iris said.

"Thanks." As he started up the stairs, tugging her along, he glanced back at the small crowd. "Don't wait up. I'm not letting her go again tonight."

Or ever.

—~~~—

"I'm sorry," Grace blurted the instant the bedroom door closed behind them. When he swung around to say no, it was him who should apologize, she pressed her fingers to his lips to silence him. "I underestimated you so badly. Every time I imagined telling you about Maddie, it ended with you walking away. And when you didn't…" She gave a helpless shrug. "It dredged up issues that I had been avoiding. Instead of acknowledging them and being honest with you, I persuaded myself that this was just an extended repeat of what happened before, and it was only a matter of time before you lost interest."

His mouth twisted at the reminder of the pain he'd caused her. "That's my fault."

"And mine." Her fingers traced the line of his jaw to his neck, then settled on his shoulder, sending warmth radiating through his body. "For two people who've always tried to take care of each other, we've managed to do a lot of damage, mostly because we were afraid to admit how we really felt, even to ourselves. I'm tired of fighting it, Hank. I want to just let us *be*."

His breath caught, but he reined in the leap of hope. "What about Maddie?"

"It wasn't about her. Not really." She smoothed her hand over his chest, drawing his blood to the surface like iron to a magnet. "I was all tied up in worrying what people will think. How they'll look at us. But everyone whose opinion matters will understand, or they wouldn't be the people we care about."

"There will be talk," Hank felt obligated to say. "And some of it won't be very nice."

"Probably not, but compared to what Maddie's mothers or any other queer or mixed-race couple have to deal with? A few gossips are nothing." She caught both of his hands and clasped them between her breasts. "But you have to understand, Hank. I didn't just give Maddie up because I was afraid of raising her alone. I didn't want a child at all."

"I know."

She blinked. "You do?"

"Gil told me, while I was trying to punch him."

"Oh." Her eyes searched his face. "And you understand that's probably not going to change?"

"Yes." He lifted their joined hands to kiss her knuckles. "I am the product of two people who really, truly should have used better birth control—although I'm obviously glad they didn't. And I have so much shit of my own to get straight, I can't even imagine being a parent. So if you don't *want* babies, I'm fine with that. But if you don't think you *deserve* another baby…well, that's something different."

"I'm pretty sure it's the first."

He pressed another kiss to her knuckles. "We can work

it out together. I happen to know a mental-health professional, and it looks like she might want to stick around."

Grace drew back to give him a wary look. "Are you sure you're okay with that?"

"I will be, once I get past the *oh yuck* stage."

Grace choked on a laugh. "It could have been much worse."

"Don't even say that." He shuddered dramatically, then dropped his hands to her hips to pull her up snug against him. "I do love you. You know that, right?"

"And you know I've basically never *not* loved you." Her smile was almost bashful as she reached into her coat pocket and held out the ring he'd left where it had fallen. "If you still want me to have this, I would be proud to accept it."

Joy washed through him, a rush of emotion that left him shaken, so his fingers fumbled the chain and she had to help him untangle it before he could carefully ease it over her curls. She closed her hand around the heavy gold ring and centered it between her breasts. "I'll wear it right here, until we're ready for something with a little more sparkle."

Hank's vision blurred, clouded by hot tears. She was finally, completely his girl. His world. His saving Grace. He tipped her up onto her toes, filling his kiss with every ounce of love and longing that he'd stockpiled over all those years. She responded in kind, the kiss going so wild and hungry that he had to pull back, tucking her head under his chin and her cheek against his stampeding heart. As he looked around the room at shelves cluttered with school trophies and Cole's face staring out at him from a dozen different photos, he groaned.

"What?" Grace asked.

"I'm not taking you out on those roads tonight, which means we're stuck in another damn place where I can't get you naked."

She laughed softly, reaching up to feather her fingers through his hair. "But think how much fun we'll have making up for it tomorrow."

"Promise?"

"With sugar and sprinkles on top." Then she kissed him again, and they tumbled onto the bed to whisper and laugh and remind themselves that yes, this time it was really real, until they finally fell asleep wrapped up in a handmade quilt and each other.

Chapter 57

WHEN THE FOG LIFTED, IT LEFT A GLITTERING wonderland behind. Every post and branch and strand of barbed wire was coated in hoarfrost, the Panhandle serving up a unique version of a white Christmas.

Melanie and Wyatt had offered to help Johnny with the chores, so Hank had brought Grace home to wrap gifts and make butterhorns. Her mother had told her the baking wasn't necessary since Grace was only stopping in for a few minutes, but they were Jeremiah's favorite so she insisted.

She taught Hank how to knead bread, and while it was rising, they slipped into the shower and found all kinds of creative uses for her favorite vanilla-scented soap. Then she had to roll out the dough, butter it, fold it in thirds, and set it to chill for another hour, so he brought in the shoebox that Bing had left in his pickup, and they looked at the pictures together.

Halfway through, Grace hesitated but reminded herself they weren't holding back anymore. "Do you want to meet her?"

"Now?"

"Whenever. It's up to you."

He ran his thumb along the edge of a photo of Maddie and both moms laughing on a merry-go-round. "Yeah. I do, but I'd like to wait until you're out of school and we can go spend a week or so in Pendleton. See Mel's house, meet the foster kids, check out the famous Bull Dancer Saloon."

"That sounds wonderful." She settled into the hard curve of his shoulder, smiling dreamily. "Can we drive? I have this fantasy of taking a road trip with you."

He nuzzled her neck. "It'll take an extra week with all the pit stops along the way."

"Mmm. That's why it's a fantasy."

At the bottom of the stack, he found the picture of himself that he'd given her what seemed like a lifetime ago. She let him study it for a moment, then plucked it out of his hand. "I was saving that for Maddie, but I changed my mind."

He made a face. "To remind me of what an ass I was that day?"

"No. Look." She ran her finger over the inscription. "It was the first time you told me that you loved me."

"I should have listened to me sooner."

Then he kissed her, and they spent the rest of the hour in her bed and were sprawled, naked and deliciously spent, when the kitchen timer went off, signaling that the dough was ready to be rolled again.

"How many times do you have to do this?" Hank asked.

"Four total."

"Huh." He tugged on one of her curls with a lazy grin. "I think butterhorns just became my new favorite."

But he pulled on his clothes and kissed her *see you later* at the door, surrounded by the yeasty aroma that meant Christmas to Grace. From this day forward, Hank would be as inextricably tangled in that scent as he was every other part of her life.

"Six o'clock," he said with one last, quick kiss. "Drive careful, and don't be late. I have plans."

———

Hank swung by the Super Saver on the way out of Dumas and made one more trip down the decimated Christmas aisle. Luckily, they'd just restocked the shelf with the lights that he wanted. He grabbed three boxes, then added a fourth just to be sure.

The temperature was still below freezing, but the dark asphalt had warmed enough in the hazy sunlight to melt the glaze of ice, so he made good time going home. Stepping out of his pickup, he followed the sound of voices to the vicinity of the barn. He found his dad and Wyatt in the round pen, with a wooden sawhorse tied against the fence so one end stuck up to mimic the hind legs of a steer.

Hank watched without comment as Wyatt roped the dummy, catching both legs several times in a row despite being bundled up against the cold.

"I don't know why I can't do that in the arena," Wyatt said, coiling the rope in disgusted jerks. "I'm lucky to catch half the time at the ropings."

Johnny's gaze slid over to the gate. "Ask Hank. He's better at heeling than any of us."

Well, damn. It *was* a brave new world if Wyatt was looking to Hank for advice. "I assume you've been to a roping clinic," Hank said.

"Two. Mike Beers and the Minor brothers."

Hank nodded. There was no shortage of world-class team ropers in the Pacific Northwest. "And you've watched all the videos, read all the articles, and picked every brain you could get your hands on at the rodeos."

"Pretty much."

Yep. That would be Wyatt. Give him a problem and he would plan it, dissect it, and train it to death. "Then there's only one thing left...switch to heading."

Wyatt bristled. "Just give up?"

"More like accepting reality." Hank leaned his shoulder against the gatepost and crossed his arms. "Heeling steers is like dancing, or painting, or music. Hard work will only get you so far. After that, it's all feel and instinct, and you've either got it or you don't. Besides, heading is more your style. They're the ones who have to analyze the shit out of everything. The heeler mostly just reacts."

"But Melanie's a header," Wyatt argued. "If I don't heel, we can't rope together."

"And what's more romantic than a long drive home with the most competitive woman in the world...after she's headed a steer to win first and you missed the heels," Hank drawled.

"She never complains," Wyatt said defensively.

"Ugh. Pity. That's even worse." Hank allowed himself a sly grin. "Imagine how much more fun it would be to rope *against* her. Especially if you win."

Wyatt started to open his mouth, then stopped as the wheels began to spin behind those baby blues.

"Give it some thought," Hank said, as if Wyatt was capable of doing anything else. "Meanwhile I have an idea, but I'm gonna need both of you to help me pull it off."

When he was done explaining, his dad left to get the side-by-side and gather up old fence posts for firewood, but Hank held up a hand to stop Wyatt from setting out on his own errands.

"About Grace." Wyatt tensed, and Hank paused a little longer than necessary just to mess with him. Then he extended that same hand. "Thank you for taking care of her when I wasn't there to do it myself."

Wyatt shifted the rope to his left hand and they shook, short but firm. "I did my best."

Hank shoved his fists in his pockets, watching his words turn to puffs of vapor in the frigid air. "Like Bing keeps telling me, if you can say that at the end of every day, you've got nothin' to be ashamed of."

"Then I guess we're doing okay," Wyatt said carefully.

Hank smiled. "Yeah. I guess we are."

Something was up.

All through dinner, the three men had been squirming like kids itching to be excused from the table, and Grace had caught Hank and Wyatt exchanging a suspiciously conspiratorial smile. Hank had barely scraped up the last of his pecan pie before he jumped up.

"I'm going to check the horses."

He was out the door in a flash. Melanie frowned after him. "They're in the barn. We fed them an hour ago."

Wyatt and Johnny exchanged a quickly smothered grin. Johnny made leisurely work of a second piece of pie, then pushed back from the table. "Leave the dishes. We've got something to show you."

Hank had told Grace to bring warm clothes in case they went out for a ride on Christmas day, so she bundled up along with everyone else and they trooped out to the barn, frost crunching under their feet.

The horses were saddled, but Ranger was missing.

"You and Wyatt can ride the horses," Johnny told Melanie. "I'll drive Grace and Bing in the side-by-side."

The route he took down off the bluff and along the river bottom was different than when Grace had gone with Hank, so they were almost to his secret glade before she realized where they were going. She squinted, seeing a flicker of what looked like firelight and hearing a quiet hum and…music?

Hank met them at the edge of the trees and waited for Melanie and Wyatt to dismount before taking their horses. "Go on in."

Frost showered onto their heads and shoulders as they ducked under branches—and stepped into pure magic.

The hum she'd heard was a compact, nearly silent generator that powered an array of laser lights, scattering pinpoints of sparkling red and green over the circle of sugarcoated trees as if they'd been decorated by magical elves. Camp chairs were situated in pairs around a fire that blazed in the stone ring, and "Carol of the Bells" played from somewhere, the notes rising on the cold, clear air along with the sparks. As they all took in the surreal beauty of the scene, a breeze stirred the treetops, whisking ice crystals from the frosty branches and sending them swirling into the night sky to be set alight by the lasers as they drifted down into the clearing.

Grace's breath caught in awe. "It's snowing fairy dust."

"Just for you." Hank looped an arm around her from behind and pulled her close. "Merry Christmas, Grace."

Her heart was so full at the moment that it felt like it might burst right out of her chest. She turned to catch his face between her mittened hands and kiss him. Then she turned him loose with a grin. "And a Happy New Year?"

He groaned. "I'm gonna be making up for that for the rest of my life."

"Count on it," she said, and kissed him again.

Then they all gathered around the fire to laugh and talk, sip hot chocolate from thermoses, and occasionally pause to gaze in silent wonder at this place they had filled with joy and light and love.

Epilogue

Easter Sunday—three months later

As the voices of the congregation rose in the final bars of "Old Rugged Cross," Grace linked one hand with her mother and the other with Hank and let her heart float with the music. Her family filled the entire pew—Jeremiah and the boys on Mama's right, Johnny and Bing on Hank's left, with Melanie and Wyatt on the end. Having failed to convince their new daughter that Wyatt's plane wasn't, as she put it, a beer can with wings, their kids had stayed in Oregon under the eagle eye of their older brother and would be helping serve the complimentary Easter dinner at the Bull Dancer.

Wyatt might be on uneasy terms with organized religion in general, but he was willing to smile and bear it—unlike Grace's father, who had quit his job and gone to live with her sister rather than stay in Earnest and face the daily humiliation of having lost control of his family. Thanks to an ace attorney from the Patterson firm, the divorce had been final for almost a month—record speed in Texas.

But there had been very little to divide up except the family.

The hymn ended, the minister gave the final blessing, and they exchanged hugs and handshakes all around as they filed out into a warm but blustery spring day. The wind whipped Grace's bright-yellow sundress around her legs and made her tuck the cardigan more securely around her shoulders. On the front steps, the older Jacobs sister, Lily, stood beside her husband greeting the faithful, the picture of the small-town minister's wife if it hadn't been for the irreverent "See you at Christmas!" and "So that's why my lightning detector went off!" comments that she tossed out along with her smiles.

The Jacobs-Sanchez-Brookman contingent milled around on the lawn as the rest of the crowd scattered. Gil was the only one absent, gone to Oklahoma City to hear Quint sing at mass. The fact that his son was an actual choirboy was a source of much amusement back in Earnest.

Lily's baby had started to fuss, and Miz Iris passed him to his mother before moving off to greet friends she hadn't seen in ages, judging by their exclamations.

"I have to go help Tim divvy up all those pots of Easter lilies." Lily patted the baby's back, casting an eye around. "Can someone take him?"

Violet shook her head, engaged in a tug-of-war with Ruby. "I've got my hands full keeping mine from running out to play in traffic."

Grace sidled behind Hank, so that Lily's gaze fell on Shawnee and Tori. They both threw up their hands and backed away.

"Wow, I'd love to, but we've got to go do..." Shawnee trailed off, but Tori jumped in.

"That thing. With the Easter eggs. Sorry."

"And I have to help them," Melanie said, hot on their heels as they escaped to the parking lot.

"Honest to Pete." Lily rolled her eyes heavenward.

"Where are the women who are supposed to be elbowing each other out of the way to cuddle a baby?"

"You're hanging with the wrong crowd," Hank said dryly.

"Here, let me." Grace's mother gathered up the little one and cradled him against her shoulder, pressing her cheek to his downy head. "I've been missing my grandbabies. Which doesn't mean any of you need to go out and make me more," she added, with a stern look at her three boys.

Grace could laugh along with everyone else because they had talked about her lack of interest in motherhood, to which Mama had replied, "Whatever makes you happy, sweetie. Children are supposed to be a blessing, not a requirement."

As her mother rocked and cooed, Steve's deep voice boomed out over the hubbub. "Dinner will be on the table at noon!"

In less than a minute, the parking lot was empty.

When the dinner plates had been cleared, Johnny strolled out onto the covered back deck of Miz Iris's house, freshly poured coffee in hand. Normally he would have migrated toward where most of the men were gathered, debating Delon's chances at a huge winner-take-all rodeo that had become the sport's version of the U.S. Open, pitting weekend warriors against world champions for a chance at a million dollars.

If Johnny had been fifteen years younger, he might've given it a shot.

But the slight pang was swept away by the sight of Bing laughing with Melanie as they leaned against the railing, more vibrant than the beds of flowers in their bright spring dresses. He ambled over to join them, perching close enough to Bing that his shoulder brushed hers and earning himself an *I know what you're up to* smile. After dealing with her house and waiting for Indian Health Service to find her replacement, she'd only been back in Texas for ten days and he could hardly stand to let her out of his reach.

She'd laughed the first time he asked her to marry him, but he wasn't too concerned. He could wait a few months, while she settled into her new job at the mental health clinic in Dumas. Lord knew he and Hank could find a way to pass the time, between the three Patterson horses that had just been delivered and the half dozen others that had been arriving for the past month. As of last Tuesday, Johnny had full clearance from the doctor, and he couldn't remember a time when he'd ended his days sweatier, dustier, and more happily exhausted.

And they were just getting started.

"So that's the new buckle," he said to Wyatt, who was showing off his prize to Grace.

"Yeah." Wyatt hooked his thumbs in his belt with a grin that reminded Johnny of a mutton buster who'd been handed his first trophy, forget the stack he'd collected for being pro rodeo's Bullfighter of the Year. It turned out he was as good at heading steers as he hadn't been at heeling, and judging by that gleam in his eyes, he was well and truly hooked.

Johnny eyed him—dressed in jeans, boots, and a button-down shirt instead of the slacks and loafers he'd sported on Easter Sunday last year—and shook his head at his daughter. "Way to go. You married a fine, upstanding citizen and managed to turn him into a team roping bum."

"Who spends the rest of his time running a bar." She gave a mock sigh, then looped her arm through Wyatt's and smirked. "Ain't it grand?"

Amid the laughter, Wyatt said, "Don't forget Grace. She kicked some serious butt at the rodeo last weekend."

Grace blushed, but her smile was fierce. "I'm hoping to make a habit of it."

"Me too." Wyatt held a hand up, and they exchanged a high five. "Here's to the latecomers."

Johnny laid his hand over Bing's on the railing, sliding his fingers between hers so he could still see her nails, each one poppy red with a tiny cactus in the center, her *Honey, I'm home* present to him. Lord, he loved her hands, especially when they were on him and all she was wearing was her nail polish. Hank had finally stopped coming in the house without texting a ten-minute warning, swearing they were gonna warp his already fragile mind.

Make that formerly fragile. Johnny continued to be amazed at his son's determination and resilience, rolled up inside such a cheerful, easygoing package. Love, career, family—Hank had watched them all go up in flames, then dragged himself out of the ashes to rebuild everything he'd lost and more.

Given his history, Johnny supposed it was fitting that Hank would choose Easter Sunday for his final resurrection.

———

Late that afternoon, Hank stopped in the open gate of the Jacobs arena to watch the breeze send miniature dust devils spinning across the plowed dirt. He and Joe could have done this any time since Christmas, but he'd thrown himself into the repairs and upgrades at the ranch instead. If all went well, Hank would eventually be hitting the road again, but not full time, and not until the business was well established. Plus he didn't want to be away from Grace more than a couple of weeks at a time.

Since he was in no big rush, he'd decided to wait until the gang was all here. Now butterflies danced above the wildflowers along the arena fence and in his stomach as he did a couple of squats, accustoming his body to the familiar bulk of braces and pads, feeling his cleats dig into the ground.

"You coming or what?" Joe called out. He was standing out in front of the chutes in a pair of bleach-stained gray sweatpants with frayed soccer shorts pulled over the top and a neon-orange bandanna folded and tied headband-style to keep his hair out of his face.

A few yards away, Wyatt was adjusting the ankle strap on his Aircast. His color-coordinated shorts and jersey had designer logos and were worn over the high-tech, moisture-wicking compression tights favored by professional football players.

"We're all set," Cole declared, one hand on the middle chute gate.

As if in agreement, the bull inside banged his horns on the wooden planks.

"Us too!" Shawnee yelled from down the arena, where she and Violet sat horseback with ropes at the ready. An unnecessary precaution, but Shawnee had declared that she preferred the view from inside the fences.

The whole crowd had straggled down to watch, strung out along the fence in lawn chairs or lounging in the sparse grass, their Sunday best swapped for jeans. Hank glanced over to where Grace and Melanie sat on upended buckets, elbows on knees and chins on fists, settled in for the show.

Grace smiled at him. "Go get 'em!"

Hank hauled in a huge lungful of air, then let it stream out as he strode into the arena to take his position—starting at the beginning one more time. He looked at Joe on his left, then Wyatt on his right, and then at Cole.

"I'm ready," he said. "Turn him loose."

*He's the one you've
been waiting for...*

GIL SANCHEZ IS BACK, AND READY
TO TAKE THE WORLD OF TEXAS RODEO
BY STORM. BUCKLE UP: IT'S GOING
TO BE ONE HELL OF A RIDE.

COMING
SUMMER 2019

Acknowledgments

For everyone in my life who tolerated being shushed, ignored, forgotten, unfed, and unlaundered during the five months that I did almost nothing but try to pound this book out: it shall forever be known as the Christmas book that ruined Christmas. And Thanksgiving. And New Year's. And Valentine's Day. And my husband's birthday. And my personality in general. Thank you all for sticking around anyway.

To Lee Haygood at Indian Mound Ranch in Canadian, Texas, for answering a random email and agreeing to chat about all the ways that ranching is different in Texas than up here in the frozen tundra, and for telling me about your cake feeder so my husband could go out and get one just like it. Our cows thank you.

To Jerri Hill, thanks for being an extra set of eyes to help me be sure no one got lost in the cast of thousands.

To my agent, Holly Root, who was called upon more often than usual to be the voice of reason when I lost all track of mine.

To the staff at Sourcebooks—from the executive office to editorial, sales, marketing, and production— who shuffled and scrambled and put in extra time and effort to accommodate my battle to finish this book, the beer's on me next time I'm in Chicago.

A big thanks to my cousin, Chad Johnson, for the loan of his Canadian Finals Rodeo contestant jacket for the cover, and Dawn and the rest of the art department for making it gorgeous, as always.

To Deb O'Brien, for once again letting me tap into her years of experience as a mental health practitioner.

To Amberly Snyder, for providing both inspiration for the character of Dakota Red Elk and a wealth of information about the day-to-day life of a disabled horseperson.

To the original Bing, a.k.a. Mrs. Hugo Johnson. All other aspects of this character are fictional except the part where no one knows her by any other name.

To Max and Spike the cowdogs, who are almost exactly as Mabel and Spider are portrayed in these pages. Yes, I am finally going to start paying more attention to you.

To the great Chief Mountain, for always being right there outside my living room window to provide inspiration—or at least something awesome to stare at when the words won't come.

And finally to you, the readers. If you've reached this point, you have slogged through a crapload of pages and you deserve a prize. Stop by KariLynnDell.com and drop me a line. I'll send you a personal thank-you for hanging in there.

About the Author

Kari Lynn Dell brings a lifetime of personal experience to writing western romance. She is a third-generation rancher and rodeo competitor whose family ranch in northern Montana is located on the Blackfeet Nation, within spitting distance of the Canadian border and on the doorstep of Glacier National Park. She exists in a perpetual state of rodeo-induced poverty with her husband, son, Max and Spike the cowdogs, a few hundred cows, and too many horses (as if there is such a thing). Between graduating from Montana State University and moving back to live with her parents, she spent twenty years wandering from Texas to South Dakota to eastern Oregon, working mostly as a high school athletic trainer like Grace McKenna, the heroine of *Mistletoe in Texas*.

Also by Kari Lynn Dell

TEXAS RODEO

Reckless in Texas

Tangled in Texas

Tougher in Texas

Fearless in Texas

ROCKY MOUNTAIN COWBOY CHRISTMAS

Beloved author Katie Ruggle's new series brings pulse-pounding romantic suspense to a cowboy's Colorado Christmas

When single dad Steve Springfield moved his family to a Colorado Christmas tree ranch, he meant it to be a safe haven. He quickly finds himself fascinated by local folk artist Camille Brandt—it's too bad trouble is on her trail.

It's not long before Camille is falling for the enigmatic cowboy and his rambunctious children—he always seems to be coming to her rescue. As attraction blooms and danger intensifies, this Christmas romance may just prove itself to be worth fighting for.

For more Katie Ruggle, visit:

sourcebooks.com